T0248090

NEXT OF KIN

Also by Samantha Jayne Allen

Pay Dirt Road
Hard Rain

NEXT OF KIN

A Novel

Samantha Jayne Allen

MINOTAUR BOOKS
NEW YORK

First published in the United States by Minotaur Books, an imprint of St. Martin's Publishing Group

www.minotaurbooks.com

Library of Congress Cataloging-in-Publication Data

Names: Allen, Samantha Jayne, author.
Title: Next of kin : a novel / Samantha Jayne Allen.
Description: First edition. | New York : Minotaur Books, 2024. |
    Series: Annie McIntyre mysteries ; 3
Identifiers: LCCN 2023056128 | ISBN 9781250863836 (hardcover) |
    ISBN 9781250863843 (ebook)
Subjects: LCGFT: Detective and mystery fiction. | Novels.
Classification: LCC PS3601.L4355 N49 2024 | DDC 813/.6—dc23/
    eng/20231206
LC record available at https://lccn.loc.gov/2023056128

Our books may be purchased in bulk for promotional, educational, or business use. Please contact your local bookseller or the Macmillan Corporate and Premium Sales Department at 1-800-221-7945, extension 5442, or by email at MacmillanSpecialMarkets@macmillan.com.

First Edition: 2024

10 9 8 7 6 5 4 3 2 1

For my dad

NEXT OF KIN

Chapter One

I settled in behind the wheel and took a deep, rib cage–opening breath. Wyatt buckled his seat belt and I turned the ignition. We were running late to my cousin's party after our cat, Tate, refused to let me catch him and put him up for the night. Wasn't about to let the devil stay out past dark and end up a coyote's supper, but he'd tried me.

Our house, a limestone seventies ranch we rented out in the country, shrank in the rearview as I pulled away. "Did you turn the hose off?" I asked.

"Yeah."

"You're sure?"

He reached over, gently cupped the back of my head in his hand. He liked to touch my hair when I wore it down. "You're stalling. Quit trying to get out of this."

I laughed—he was right and he wasn't. I wanted to celebrate my cousin Nikki and her fiancé, Sonny, but always found it hard to leave that little house behind. That slice of time between sunset and nightfall when we watered the tomato plants and peppers, talked—that was what I'd be missing. Wyatt cranked the AC and I turned down the farm-to-market road toward town. Life is long. Hard to see a shape or any kind of arc while you're living it. I never thought I'd be living this life—a good life, but one of a million possible options. Decent options. I could've stayed gone after college and never come home to Garnett, and who knew what would've happened then. But, also, being with Wyatt felt like a cascading row of dominoes. Click after satisfying click. He was someone I felt my truest self around.

Clint, Sonny's brother and also his best man, had offered to host a get-together for the wedding party at his place. The address was on a nice, sycamore-lined street in the older part of town. I parked in a line of cars that stretched from the driveway down the block. Smoke hazed the air, tinting the blue dusk bluer. The smell wafted over me as I got out and I straightened my neck. No crispness to the breeze, no hint of fall. This smell was an alarm sounding in the animal part of my brain. Like when our neighbors burned trash in the pasture and the wind changed course—stinging, sour. I looked at Wyatt. "Where's that coming from?"

Wyatt stretched, swept his eyes over a sky ribbed with pink and dark purple. "Another wildfire west of town, I'll bet."

We'd had a long, dry summer after a wet and volatile spring. The land as it was now reminded me of the chaparral in old westerns, with its cacti, mesquite, and gnarled live oaks punctuating an endless brown. A tumbleweed had even rolled down Main Street the other day. Nights like this when it would stay a hundred out, I felt a slow-building panic, a sense of waltzing into the impending apocalypse. But that was August in Garnett every year: hot as hell and quite literally on fire. I grabbed a six-pack of Shiner from the backseat of the bullet—I drove a used Pontiac I'd dubbed the silver bullet on account of my superstitious nature and its color. Dinged up and not much to look at now, but it got me where I was going.

We cut across the grass toward the white bungalow. Wyatt's fingers grazed mine, but it was too hot to hold hands, and neither of us were really hand-holders anyway. I moved mine to his waist, my thumb through his belt loop. The wide front porch had string lights tacked onto the railing, which a couple of old bikes leaned up against. It was crowded with cardboard cases of crushed beer cans. The front door was open, laughter spilling out. Nikki, bride-to-be, saw us coming and met us in the hall, wrapping me in a sweaty hug. She wore a white eyelet sundress that flattered her, her mess of blond curls bouncing around her shoulders. I spied her other bridesmaids not far behind, another cousin of mine using her car keys to shotgun a beer.

"What's up?" Nikki said, a bite in her voice.

"You look great. That's a cute dress," I said, figuring she was nervous. "Sorry we're late."

A pretty woman with long, balayage'd hair met us in the hall. She twisted her hands, letting out a deep breath as though she'd been eagerly awaiting us. Tall, thin, and angular, she looked like a model. Sharp, contoured cheekbones a contrast to pillowy lips, a soft smile. She managed to pull off one of those prairie dresses that look dowdy on anyone but models. "Annie, right? Nikki's said so much about you. I'm with Clint," she said, leading us into the kitchen. "I'm Amanda."

"Hey, nice to finally meet you," I said, wiping my hand on my shorts—denim, a fashion nonchoice I now regretted—before offering it. "This is my boyfriend, Wyatt."

They exchanged pleasantries as I looked over Wyatt's shoulder. Clint had come in from the backyard. He sauntered through the living room with an acoustic guitar in one hand, a beer in the other. I normally would find the guitar red-flag behavior, but Clint Marshall was a real-deal musician. He'd opened for some big country acts on his last tour, and had a single on Spotify that was rumored to hit the Americana charts any day now. He looked the part of lead singer with his square jaw and handsome smile. His sandy, dirty-looking hair was loosely knotted into a bun, a strand left hanging into dark eyes. He adorned himself with turquoise rings and leather bracelets, with ink on his arms, black vines that traced his collarbone. He'd grown up around here, was around my age, our mothers had even been acquaintances, and yet I hadn't known him before Sonny introduced us.

He laid the guitar on a stained, worn-out couch that looked like many a guy had passed out on it still wearing their shoes. The whole place had that vibe—like a house where fraternity brothers lived, or, I supposed, a band. I was pretty sure Clint had moved here alone, though, to be closer to his family. Nikki had said this was his and Sonny's late father's house, and it was a nice house despite the mess, with high ceilings, crown moldings, wooden built-ins. Like with the right décor it might've been on some HGTV special. Clint smiled and shrugged at me in the way of hello, and I nodded back.

Amanda clapped her hands together, turning her gaze on me. "Everyone like Patrón?"

"Girl, you've already done too much! That's expensive, stop," Nikki said, edging out Wyatt to stand between Amanda and me. Limes were sliced and in a neat pile on the cutting board, a dish of flaky salt beside them. There were cocktail napkins, homemade guacamole, three types of salsas, warm chips, veggie platters—all of this was on real plates, too. Despite Nikki's protests, Amanda took a tray of shot glasses she'd been icing from the freezer and handed me the bottle of tequila. The whole presentation was a little at odds with the beer cans piling up and the lone box of Tombstone on the freezer shelf.

"We're going to toast to you and Sonny," Amanda said, mock stern. "In fact, Wyatt, how about you and Clint round up the others?"

Wyatt looked relieved to be given a task, and Clint clapped him on the back as they walked outside. He knew Sonny, of course, but none of the groomsmen, who were all Sonny's friends from high school or his army buddies. Wyatt was always fun and laid-back at parties, but I knew part of his chillness was actually a preference to draw inward, be the one listening instead of doing the talking. He was curious—a quality I liked about him—though he sometimes came off as aloof or shy. There was an exuberance specific to weddings and wedding-adjacent events that tired him—tired me, too, for that matter.

I placed a lime on the rim of each glass, trying to pinpoint why I felt sheepish—because Amanda was being a good hostess, I realized. I needed to up my maid of honor game. When Nikki and Sonny got engaged last spring, I'd been openly skeptical. I knew they were in love, but worried they'd break each other's hearts. They'd gotten engaged after only six months of dating, during which they'd split up twice. Besides that, Nikki was twenty-five, only a year and change older than me. Too young. Nikki liked to say she and Sonny kept each other on their toes, that if you fought you got to make up. Me and Wyatt, not our style. We'd been together since high school. Well, in high school, and later, after college when our paths detoured back to Garnett. The restlessness I felt about the future wasn't him, though—I'd never wanted a relationship I had to guess at. No, my problem was like loving the wind but being afraid of flying. I'd always had a hard time being present, whether I wanted something different or was worried about losing what I had.

The rest of the wedding party trailed in behind Wyatt. Sonny took a tequila shot off the tray as I walked past him, whooped, and beat his chest. That was Sonny, happy to be here and proud to tell it. He grinned at me, giving me a quick sideways hug. I liked Sonny, I did. Even if at first I'd thought his keep-the-party-going persona made him shallow. I now saw his nature for what it was, that he was infected with a strong desire to please. He cared too much, and damn it if I didn't know what that felt like.

"Here's to the happy couple," Amanda said, raising her glass.

Nikki sipped the shot. One of her false eyelashes was coming unglued and she blinked furiously, making her smile look forced. Sonny downed his and replaced it with a Marlboro, listing as he hooked his muscled arm around her. The ex-football player to Nikki's ex-varsity cheerleader, he was also blond and tanned. Nikki had been on him to quit smoking—indoors, at least—and I braced myself for one of their play fights, likely to evolve into a real one if the tequila kept flowing.

Amanda cut her eyes between me and Sonny, giving me a knowing look. "So, Annie," she said, raising her voice so that everyone could hear. "Sonny was telling us you're a private detective. You must have some insane stories, yeah?"

"A few," I said tightly. Didn't mind talking about my work, but hated making light of the hard parts. Requests to tell crazy stories delivered in a bemused, slightly condescending tone often came to me at bars and at parties. And I got defensive, not because I was embarrassed, but because it mattered. Being a detective wasn't a job to me; it was me. What started as a shaky-at-best situation—working for my ex-sheriff grand-father until I figured out what to do with my life—had become my life. Me, the straight-A student that always wanted a career-identity. I told myself it was ambition, this intensity, but my desires weren't so much about competition or comparison anymore. I felt like my heart was flint in want of a whetstone. Maybe that was what people saw, what they also wanted—to glimpse the dark, to touch the sharp edges. Like a podcast come to life, they wanted me to lecture on the criminal mind in a deep, seductive voice, to give them a scare. Mostly, they wanted me to dish on other people's secrets.

"Have you found killers and stuff like that?"

"It's not usually like *that*," I said, meeting Amanda's wide-eyed gaze. "But yeah, I have."

"Like, who's the evilest criminal you've investigated?"

"I don't think people are evil, only that our actions are good, or bad, or a bit of both," I said. "Or yeah, evil."

"So, you think it's nurture then?" Clint leaned over Amanda, his face slack but intense in the way drunk people can really focus. His hair dangled in front of one eye and he moved it behind his ear all seriously. "You think criminals are made, not born?"

"Well—"

"Here we go with the nature and nurture bit," Amanda said, shooting me another knowing glance, a quick eye roll and half smile. Like I hadn't only met her. "Did you know Clint was adopted? Speaking of that, did you get the results back, babe?"

Clint blinked hard and shook his head.

"I ordered him a DNA kit," Amanda said to me. "It's just so fascinating, right?"

Sonny slung his other arm around Clint's shoulder, spilling

beer onto both Nikki's dress and down his expensive-looking western shirt. "Man, it's weird how I always forget."

"Yeah, man, it's 'cause it doesn't matter," Clint said quickly, fooling with a guitar pick left on the counter. "Not to me. My parents are my parents. Sonny's my brother. They're who raised me."

"And that's the truth," Sonny said. "Hell, we ought to drink to that."

Nikki lifted Sonny's arm, freeing herself from where she'd been pinned against his wide chest. Amanda was measuring out more shots, but I excused myself and followed Nikki down the hallway, finding her in the guest room where all of our purses had been deposited onto a daybed, the rest of the room a catchall for moving boxes and junk.

"Hey, you," she said.

"Something the matter?"

She shrugged. "No, these wedding get-togethers just make me self-conscious. Feels like I'm watching all of it on home video in my mind. Does that make any sense?"

"I know what you mean," I said, leaning beside her. "There's a lot of pressure for it to be perfect. Moments to treasure that you'll tell your grandkids about. You know that Aunt Jewel's going to start asking how long until the baby comes the minute y'all get back from the honeymoon—"

She laughed, palming her forehead.

"Just relax," I said, squeezing her shoulder. Easier said than done. I knew that level of anxiety, I felt it all the time, and I hated that my outgoing, free-spirited cousin felt it, too.

"What do you think of Amanda?"

"She's really nice," I said. "Maybe trying a little too hard, but can't say I blame her. Think she just wants for y'all to be friends."

Nikki lowered her voice. "Clint told Sonny that he's thinking of proposing. She worked for a music promoter or something, that's how they met. This guy, her old boss, he's a kiss-his-ring-to-get-airtime kind of guy and they're still close."

"That's convenient. But she seems like a catch regardless of who she knows."

Nikki smirked. "Yeah, she is. She's in nursing school, too. Sonny says Clint's crazy about her. But I mention it to say I think she has him wrapped around her little finger. He's good, you know."

I'd listened to Clint's single. The lyrics were forgettable—not quite catchy, either—but his voice more than made up for his songwriting skills. And of course, he had the look. "He's talented," I said. "So, wait, what did she do? Why don't you like her?"

"I do like her. I'm just in a mood."

"Go in the bathroom and splash your face with cold water. I'll get you a fresh beer when you come out."

I watched her go into the bathroom, then walked down the hallway. The living room and kitchen were now empty, the group had moved out into the backyard, and I relaxed, realizing I was alone. There was a record player on one of the bookshelves, next to it a massive stack of vinyl. I pulled a couple out, mostly sixties country records, some folk albums. Townes Van Zandt, Dylan. I flipped over an old Marty Robbins record, startling when I heard footsteps.

Clint held a trash bag out. "Grabbing up empties."

"Oh, here you go," I said, handing him an abandoned White Claw. "If you're worried that I'm snooping, I definitely was."

He smiled, flashed perfect teeth. "*Gunfighter Ballads*. One of my grandpa's favorites."

"My granddad loves this one too," I said. "And me. I like old songs."

"I've been working on some new old stuff. You're giving me hope someone'd actually listen to it," he said, looking at his feet in what felt a little like false modesty.

I eyed a Red Raiders pennant behind the shelf. "You go to Tech?"

"Got a business degree I've put to exactly no use. My real major was playing around Lubbock."

"Bunch of musicians from there."

"Nothing to do but join a band or go to church. I'm butchering someone else's quote, but you know what I mean."

"Has to be more exciting than Garnett."

"It is. I kind of don't recognize myself down here anymore. Don't know what I'm doing if I'm not working—not playing, I mean—like I've got too much time to think. Too much time with the *old* Clint," he said, looking at me for a moment with tension in his brow. Despite the contemplative singer-songwriter cues, moodiness wasn't a natural look for a face like his. He also wasn't as drunk as the others, I realized. He looked over my shoulder at the sound of the toilet flushing through the wall. "Nikki feeling okay? I probably should've put the burgers on *before* the tequila came out."

"She's fine," I said. "Think she'll be out in a minute."

"When I was here at Christmas and got introduced to Nikki it was 'Annie and me this, me and Annie that,' all day. It was like that with me and Sonny, too. We drifted apart when we got older, but we're solid like y'all are. Always have been. Which reminds me, you never answered my question earlier."

"About what?"

"Nature or nurture?"

"Probably both, I guess. Why do you care so much what I think?"

"Because I think I can trust you," he said, leaning on the shelf next to me, his elbow propped next to my head. Heat radiated from his arms, and his chest looked flushed through his open collar. His skin was smooth, and a warm cologne, like sun and pine needles, lifted off him.

"Maybe," I said, laughing a little.

"No, I'm serious," he said. His lips were slightly parted, tongue pressing against his teeth. He wasn't talking about the question anymore—what, exactly, I didn't know, but something inside me lit up. Sharpening, coming into focus. I wanted him to know that he was right, that trusting me was in fact like betting on a winning horse.

"Annie?"

Wyatt stood in the open screen door.

I ducked under Clint's arm. "Hey!"

Wyatt narrowed his eyes in Clint's direction, then opened the door wider. "Come see the fire," he said, and I followed him into the backyard. The wind was like a hair dryer on my neck. The others stood in a half circle or were seated in folding chairs, passing a bowl. It smelled like sour smoke— not the weed, not Sonny's Marlboros. I looked west to where the low hills were ridged with gold, the flats painted orange. Didn't see any wildfires.

I looked back at Wyatt, the wind lifting brown curls off his forehead. "I don't see—"

"No," he said, turning my shoulder. "Behind you."

There. A thick column of smoke billowing in the wind, and closer, red lights flashing on the sky. I couldn't see the fire or the trucks, but their lights weren't far off. Had to be a house fire. I craned my neck, trying to get a better look, trying to get at what I knew was there but couldn't quite see. I really could've used a second set of eyes back then.

Chapter Two

I liked Mondays. At least getting past Sunday, which I associated with hangovers, the *60 Minutes* clock on TV and weak
lamplight in the living room, and chores and goodbyes. I often
worked weekends and odd hours, but the feeling of having
a clean slate made me eager for Mondays. I had the radio
on as I drove. The AM station run by a teacher at the high
school was mostly Steers football coverage, but also the police
blotter, the weather, and occasional local stories reported on
by him or his students. *The Garnett Signal* had folded years
ago, so besides checking Nextdoor and Facebook—or the an-
alog version, hitting up the café—there was no other place
to get local-local news. My breath caught when I heard that
a man died as a result of the house fire Saturday night; he'd
succumbed to injuries while being airlifted to San Antonio.
I nosed into a parking spot near the office, then checked the
sheriff's department page on my phone. No names. Smoke
in the air had been part of the sticky feeling I'd carried with
me all of Sunday, a lingering sense all was not right. I turned
the radio off and got out of the bullet, holding tight to the

clean slate feel, though that animal part of my brain was lit up again, telling me *run*.

McIntyre Investigations was on the second story of a red-brick building right on the square. Garnett is the county seat, and its square—statue of a vaquero on horseback, trim lawn, a century-old courthouse built of limestone quarried in the Hill Country—was at the center of town, a place that after living in Garnett nearly all my life still impressed upon me a feeling of stateliness and order. Sudden beauty, even. Our office was as old as the courthouse, but was in sad need of a paint job among other repairs. The warped door was stuck and I jiggled the handle back and forth a few times before it swung open, morning light from the leaded glass windows splashing into the hallway.

The coffeepot was broken. Mary-Pat, my boss—or senior partner, as she liked to say—shot me down when I suggested buying a new one, said she'd fix it herself. I cussed under my breath, knowing I didn't have time to run across the street to the café. Had an appointment at nine, a repeat customer—a woman who hired me every few months to follow her sister, whom she hadn't spoken with in over thirty years. The sister was healthy, married, living in a pricey suburb of Houston. I didn't know the reason for their falling out, only that the results of my investigation never changed and that my client never attempted contact. One thing I'd learned is that it's almost impossible for people to accept the past as static. She wanted the truth to change, though only her relationship to it might—I couldn't control what she did with the information I provided her; I couldn't make her heal the relationship or move on. Didn't feel great taking her money time after time, but that's another thing I'd come to know: being in a client's confidence often felt like more than it was, which was business. I'd only just sat down when I heard a knock.

When the door opened, Clint Marshall stood in its frame.

He smiled nervously. "Hey, Annie, I wanted to talk to you about a job. Thought it'd be better to talk in person."

"Oh, sure, it's just I have an appointment who'll be here any minute," I said. Uncanny, like seeing a person you've had a dream about the night before. I'd had a feeling he'd come find me—hoped he would. I wanted to know what he wanted from me. We hadn't talked since the party, not alone. I motioned for him to sit. "We can discuss it until she gets here, though."

He took the hardback chair opposite my desk. "I wanted to ask you about finding my birth parents."

"Yes, I can do that," I said, watching as the tension in his jaw relaxed. A hard question for him to ask, though a fairly simple request for me, in this line of work. "How about I draw up a contract, and then we can talk specifics."

"You sound pretty certain. I like that." His gaze drifted over my shoulder. "That must be your granddad?"

"The one and only," I said. He was looking at the framed *Texas Monthly* article. A story that came out after Leroy and his former deputy in the Garnett County Sheriff's Department, Mary-Pat, solved a cold case that brought them notoriety across the state, and nationally after an episode aired on *Dateline*. That notoriety allowed him to open McIntyre Investigations, and even though the case had left many people's minds, Leroy and Mary-Pat maintained a solid—if not storied—reputation. Though I'd been working for the firm a year, had been made partner, a lot of the work I took on was work they'd assigned. I'd built connections of my own, but it was hard; I'd never been in law enforcement and I was young. My last name often sparked recognition, often inspired confidence—though, occasionally, wariness. Clint nodded as he scanned the article, clearly impressed, and I felt a rush of pride. "Listen, Clint, I can't one hundred percent say I'll find both your parents, or guarantee a reunion. But I can promise my best work, and honestly, my best is better than most."

"No one knows I'm here," he said, looking back at me.

"It can stay between us."

"Good. I don't want to hurt my mom's or Sonny's feelings. Plus, it'd distract from his big day. Our dad's dead, and he and my mom separated before that—long story I don't need to get into—but, anyway, it's mostly her I worry about. She's very protective," he said. "And sensitive."

"I understand. So, she and your dad didn't tell you much about the adoption? When did you find out?"

"I always knew, but only very little. This hush-hush thing. When I was a kid, I used to imagine I was, like, royalty or something, and my real parents, the king and queen, might come for me any day now."

"Well, I used to play that game, too."

He laughed a little. "No, like, I really believed it. Not the royalty part, but that something was missing. Just *off*. Sounds like a cliché, but it's the truth. Sure enough, on my eighteenth birthday, Mom sat me down and told me the whole story. That she had complications after Sonny and it had just about broken her that she couldn't have more kids. Adoption wasn't an easy route, either, but they kept praying and I was the answer to those prayers. She asked me if I knew how much she loved me with these big tears in her eyes—I can't stop thinking about the look on her face. She was scared of losing me,

I think, or of me betraying her. It's stopped me from ever trying anything like this."

"Do you know your birth mother's name?"

"No."

"Was it a closed adoption?" I hadn't worked an adoption case before, but I knew from all the filing I did of Mary-Pat's cases that closed adoptions were less and less common these days. For someone Clint's age, still a bit unusual. In Texas, if an adoption was closed, it would be impossible to obtain original paperwork without a court order. And then, good luck with that.

"My birth certificate has my adoptive parents' names on it. Don't really know where else I should be looking—kind of screwed up this isn't easier, right?"

"I can think of a few reasons a mother giving up a baby might want to retain her privacy," I said, wincing as Clint's face drew down. This wasn't a hypothetical scenario for him, I reminded myself. It was his life. "But I also think you deserve the truth. What made you change your mind and decide to search now, if you don't mind me asking?"

"Guess I tried not caring. Told myself it didn't matter, but it's been building. Random thoughts will bug me. Like, I'll wonder if my old man is into music."

I nodded, stole a quick glance at my phone. My client was late if she was still coming, and part of me hoped she wasn't.

He frowned, looking over my shoulder again for a moment. "It must be nice, having this special connection with your granddad?"

"Being a lawman runs in the blood, or so he claims. But I've never been a cop, and my parents never nudged me in this direction. It was complicated," I said, stopping short of the full truth. That at times, I really did believe in talent, but at other times, a needling, middle-of-the-night voice kept me awake. I didn't tell him that Leroy had hired me less as a protégée and more to get back at my dad, himself a former cop who wanted no part of the business. Or, probably because I was one of a few people who still put up with him. "I chose this," I said, and my shoulders relaxed, speaking it out loud—that particular truth canceled out the rest.

"Yeah, I hear that," he said, but his eyes had wandered. He'd already moved on. "I'm at this point in my life where I just need to make a change. I'm twenty-six, which is kind of like getting up there in my industry. I need to give it a go in Nashville, like now or never."

"Sounds like a big move," I said. My phone lit up. An email from the client asking to reschedule. "Hey, my appointment's not coming now. Why don't you let me get you a coffee across the street?"

Clint smiled. "Do all clients get this personal touch? Or am I special?"

"Office coffeepot's busted, but sure," I said, standing. "Might even buy you breakfast. I haven't eaten."

"I was planning to pick something up for Amanda and me both on the way back, but I guess she's probably already eaten at this point. She thinks I'm at my mom's now."

"Up to you," I said, walking toward the door when he nodded. I wasn't sure what to make of his white lie. Hiring a P.I. wasn't something you broadcasted, private by definition, but Amanda had bought him the DNA kit, for one, and two, Nikki had said they were about to be engaged. "If you go to Nashville," I said, keeping my voice light, "will Amanda go with you?"

"Maybe," he said, and took the stairs down while I locked

up the office. He paused on the sidewalk, holding the outer door open. "I need to figure some things out about myself before I can move forward with anything. Heal this primal, psychic wound I have. Maybe that's a little woo-woo"—he laughed—"but it's like there's gum stuck to the bottom of my shoe with this whole being adopted thing. That's a terrible metaphor, but do you know what I mean?"

"I do," I said, sun hitting my face as I walked into the open air. I'd spent all this time trying to explain me to me—so much time on invisible ghosts. Whether this dwelling on the past was a byproduct of coming home or the reason I'd come in the first place, I didn't know. "Amanda had mentioned a DNA kit on Saturday. That could be really useful here," I added.

"I lied the other night. I did actually get the results back. Turns out I have a distant cousin."

"Oh, well—that's great," I said. The sun was still in my eyes, now shining off a speck of metal in my periphery. A truck drove toward us on Clint's side. There was a stop sign at the intersection and a blinking red light, so I didn't think twice before I entered the crosswalk, and before I could finish my thought on his DNA kit, Clint yanked me backward.

Not two seconds later the truck blew the stop sign.

"Jesus, what an asshole," I said.

He let go of my arm as we reached the opposite curb. "Weirdest part was they totally saw us. Like at first, they slowed down. Not like they weren't paying attention and just rolled the stop sign, but like they deliberately tried to hit us. Or scare us. They accelerated only after they saw you step off."

"I wasn't even looking at them—did you see who?"

"Just a black truck with tinted windows is all I saw," he said. "Lift-kit tires. Probably a dumb kid."

I nodded, shivering as we walked into the café. I slid into a booth by the window, the only open table. The café was busiest in the morning and late nights after home games. School was starting back next week, the home opener Friday. The picture window had GO STEERS with all the players' numbers painted on it, purple and gold streamers strung across the pane. Retired ranchers sat at their post—up at the counter, there since dawn with black coffee and greasy platters of steak and eggs—and carried on about the new quarterback, only a freshman. The waitress took our orders, filled our mugs and water glasses, and Clint watched the old men at the counter for a moment.

"I never got into football, much to the disappointment of my dad," he said. "Sonny probably could've been a walk-on if he'd gone to college instead of the service. He was this hot shot in high school—he'd invite the girls to parties after the game, then I'd swoop in with my bad poetry."

"How'd that work out for you?"

He flashed me a grin, staring for a little too long—his comment earlier about the personal touch had embarrassed me, I realized. "So, this cousin of yours," I said, and pulled out a legal pad from my bag. "You found them on Ancestry.com?"

"Her name is Kimberly Soto."

"Give me your log-in, if you don't mind," I said, sliding the paper over. Not the most distinctive name, but not a needle-in-a-haystack name, either. "Why haven't you messaged her on the site?"

"Because I don't want to go in blind. See, I was adopted out of foster care when I was four, not even a baby, so something bad must've happened to my parents, or they're dead, or they were unfit, or . . ." He paused, running his finger around the rim of his coffee mug. "Or shit, what if it was me?"

"I guarantee it was about the adults in the situation, not

you, but yeah, I think you're right to have waited," I said, watching him closely again. "So, I get why you haven't told your mom and Sonny about your search, but why keep this from Amanda?" I felt weird asking so much about his girl-friend. Clint was good-looking, a shameless flirt—I felt an implication there even if I stared a little long. But I also sensed something unsaid. Like walking into a tidied-up room and just knowing that if you opened the closet, all this shit would come tumbling out. Leroy always told me, even on an intake meeting, to let your intuition drive.

He lowered his head. "Feel bad I haven't told her, but she'd be on my case to message this woman every five minutes. We're just a little different in the way we think. She was adopted herself, from Romania, and like four of her siblings are also adopted. Her parents are those types of Christians. Real con-servative. Amanda kind of rebelled against them when she moved out for college, started partying, started hanging with the music promoters—that whole crowd. I've only met her family once. Also, her being open, quote unquote, about her adoption and trying to get in touch with her heritage is a whole thing. Guess that was part of what drew me to her."

"Makes sense," I said. He didn't want being adopted to be his whole personality, and Amanda was part of that reckon-ing. I'd seen it, felt it before myself. You drive away the person that mirrors you. Push and pull. "But back up—you weren't adopted until you were four. Do you have any memories of the time? Any detail might help."

He closed his eyes. "Very hazy ones. Images mostly. I re-member a dog, and me and another kid, a boy, in the backseat of a car. Like one of those grandma cars with the bench seats and maroon fabric? A Buick or a Lincoln. It was hot and I was mad the dog tried to lick my foot. Then—this is a different day, I think—I remember being at a ranch, with alpacas and ponies. I remember being held over the fence to pet the animals and being really happy."

"A petting zoo, or you lived there?"

"I don't remember. But I know it was from before, because I said something to my mom about her taking me there, and she swore she'd never seen an alpaca in her life. Thought I imagined it."

"That's it?"

"How much do you remember from when you were that age?"

"Not a lot," I said, recalling the texture of my world. My earliest memory was being down at the creek behind my old house. Three, I think. Momma was running, swinging me out in front of her, yelling for my dad after I'd stepped in a big fire ant mound. Only scared because they were. I also remembered things I had no way of remembering—things that had happened to my parents—because I'd seen them on home movies, had the story told to me enough times so the memory became mine. I often felt that sort of déjà vu sitting here in the café. I'd waitressed here for about eight months after I came home from college. Mornings here were like every morning— people ran their lines, had memorized the blocking. Orders, the same. The ranchers knew to leave their seats at the counter in time for the coffee klatch ladies, the school kids after that, and always, the cops sat in the cop booth, the only place in the café where no one had their backs to the door.

The owner approached our table as if on cue. "Hey, y'all, how about a top-off?"

"Thanks," I said, holding out my mug. "Marlene, this is Clint Marshall. He's Sonny's brother."

She smiled. "Small world. Sonny and my boy were in basic

training together. Travis is overseas again, else I'm sure he'd be at the wedding."

"Good to meet you, Marlene. And thank you for the coffee, but I've got to get," Clint said, flashing her one of his handsome, toothy smiles. "Sonny's spoken real highly of Travis, and I'm sorry I won't meet him. I'm grateful for his service."

Marlene's round cheeks pinkened. "Thank you, sweetheart. Y'all need anything, just holler," she said, and rushed off to pick up a ticket, then turned up the radio when she got back behind the counter. Marty Robbins barreled through the speakers, and again, that uncanny feeling I'd had when Clint stepped into my office washed over me. Foretelling in the note, that lilting, tumbling forward rhythm.

"El Paso." Clint drummed his fingers on the table. "Asked for a guitar when I was thirteen," he said, smiling again at Marlene when she brought our check. "I loved listening and loved when I could make the same sounds. Maybe I should try Austin before I move all the way to Tennessee, but I've already got it in my mind. Go big or go home."

"Never know until you try," I said. We weren't so unlike, me and Clint. I didn't tell him I'd left Texas, too—maybe I would've if he'd asked, but this wasn't about me. It wasn't so personal. I waved him off when he fished his wallet from his back pocket. "I was serious about the coffee. Wait till you see my invoice."

"Thanks," he said. "So, I have a show at that old honky-tonk in town tomorrow. You should come out and bring Wyatt. I'll comp you. Sonny and Nikki are coming."

"Maybe we will," I said. "And I'll be in touch about what I find."

"Thanks, Annie."

He touched my shoulder as he passed by, then walked out of

the café. I pushed my eggs around my plate, watching through the window as he came to where he'd parked his truck in front of our building. Held my breath a bit as he cut across the intersection. Scaring pedestrians with your truck was not something that happened here often, but also totally something boys around might do—boys and jacked-up trucks, bored and feeling mean. When he reached the courthouse lawn, Clint tipped his head back as though to admire the building and all the light spilling through the oaks like liquid gold. It could be beautiful here—he saw that, too, didn't he?

Marlene slapped my debit card on the table. "What're you smiling about?"

"Nothing," I said. "Was thinking about tying on an apron. You're busier than usual today."

"Did you hear the awful news flying around about that trailer park fire?"

"About the man who died? Awful."

"Gets worse," she said. Lowering her voice, she looked over at the cop booth. "Turns out it was arson."

Chapter Three

Headed to Leroy's house, I drove the back roads that hugged the river. The sun was high and bright. I couldn't see the water through the grasses and cypress, only flashes of silver when I passed a cleared-out section of pasture. I rolled my windows down and a hint of smoke still mingled with the water's algal smell. I cut through the neighborhood where the crime had occurred. Police tape hung across a gateless fence, cordoning off the long driveway that led into the trailer park. All I could make out were a few singed-black trees, but pictured a metal husk with ash collecting underneath, imagined a blurry figure running toward the thick brush over the fence. Who, though? And why? Even if the arsonist didn't know a man was inside, there were likely other trailers within spitting distance, kids' tricycles and plastic toys littering the dirt between them. A sheriff's cruiser came around the bend in the road and I sped up, not wanting to get caught rubbernecking. Leroy lived on the west side of town, not far away, and I pulled into his driveway with a white-knuckled grip on the wheel.

I needed to talk to him about Clint's case. It had only taken several hours' worth of research to identify his biological father. Sometimes it really was that simple. The distant cousin he'd matched with on Ancestry.com had passed away, but before then she'd created a family tree which I paid to get access to, and then checked her work against public records. For this woman and Clint to be second cousins, they'd have shared a great-grandparent—but on which side? A lucky break was that she'd only been able to have second cousins on her mother's side, her father not having had any first cousins, himself an only child as well. From there, I'd narrowed it down to two men—all of her mother's first cousins were male—one of whom had been killed in a car wreck three years before Clint was born.

That left one candidate. A man named Ronald Mott, Jr.

Clint Mott. I tried the name out loud as I ran a simple search of Ronald Mott, and as the results loaded, my stomach dropped. Ronald Mott was an inmate at the federal prison camp at Bingley, currently serving a thirty-year sentence for his involvement in an armed bank robbery back in the nineties. Here, right in Garnett County. Leroy had been sheriff at the time, and he—alongside his deputy, Mary-Pat Zimmerman—had ended a hostage situation at First Bank Garnett–Parr City, stopping the robbers from escaping with over two hundred grand, which would've made it the largest robbery in Texas history. A man had held up a teller and the branch manager, who'd been shot but had lived, so the charge was elevated to attempted homicide. Ronnie Mott—I'm surprised I hadn't recognized his name at first—had been the getaway driver, and a good one. He'd hidden himself well. Had evaded capture for months, and it was never known exactly who'd helped him or where he'd been hiding. He was eventu-

ally arrested, but only after being pulled over for a traffic viola-
tion nearly a year after the robbery. A cocky grin had played at
the corner of his mouth in all the media photos taken at trial,
even in his roughed-up mugshot. Sandy hair worn a little long,
a sloping brow and a square jaw, a small man built like a banty
rooster.

It was like looking at Clint.

Unlike Clint, whose eyes were a little sleepy-looking, Ronnie's gaze was forceful, if not slightly disturbed. He was skinny
in these photos, rangier than Clint. Penetrating is the word
that came to mind while staring into those eyes—barbed, a
mean look. I shut the laptop, surprised by the swift, physical
revulsion I felt. A tight, uneven sensation had been building
in my chest already, trying to remember what it was I'd forgotten. After breaking for a glass of water and a pace about
the office, I kept reading. My heart landed in my throat. That
was it. One of the bank tellers who'd been held up that day
was a young woman named Diedre Marshall.

Marshall—as in Sonny and Clint's mom, Dee.

How would Clint feel about this? One, that his father was
a criminal, and two, that the man had played a role in one of
the scariest days of his adoptive family's lives? I didn't think
my job was to provide emotional context to him, if that was
even possible, but I hadn't been able to shake my sense that
there was more to Clint's ask than lineage. Did he know without knowing? His primal, psychic-wound talk had made me
think he wanted to break free from a part of himself he didn't
quite know how to name. Clint also seemed to want external
permission for this excising—for one thing, he could've found
out the information himself if he'd halfway tried. Why he'd
chosen me to deliver this permission I didn't know, but I felt

set up for a test I wasn't sure how to pass. I turned to stare out the window, at the live oaks bending in the wind. The past was a shadow, I might tell him. Not the structure, not the light.

I believed that, didn't I?

The next thing to do would've been to write Ronnie Mott, but before I did that—and before I located the rest of the puzzle, the identity of his mother—I gave in to my heart over my head. Clint wasn't the only one who craved assurance. I had to see Leroy.

"Little darlin'," he said. Saluted me from the porch as I stepped out of the bullet. "Mighty fine of you to come by, but what's the occasion?"

"Sorry to barge in—tried calling first," I said. Leroy was officially retired, about to turn eighty-five. Not to say he was out of touch, only that he didn't have the same anxieties I felt about being unreachable for long stretches of time. His voice-mails were full, he didn't like to text, and he only checked email on his desktop once a week. Despite this, he always acted surprised when I showed up in person. Or worse, bothered. "I have a new case I wanted to talk to you about. This guy hired me for an adoption search."

He waved his hand out. "Never ends well."

"Why not?"

"Mind, darlin'? I'm a might parched," he said, eyes drifting toward the beer fridge. "Why? Because what you find out is not what they expected—or worse, it is what they expected, only they were *hoping* for something different. Say the birth parents don't want nothing to do with them. The client won't understand."

"But is it really my place to tell him how to react? He's an adult capable of making his own decisions," I said, handing him a Budweiser.

"No, no, that's not what I'm saying, darlin'. I'm not even saying don't take the work, only to brace him and yourself."

"For what it's worth, I think after he's had time to process it, he'll be better off not wondering anymore," I said, and paused, butterflies in my stomach now that I knew he had such a wary stance on the matter. I felt scolded. "So, the real reason I'm here is because I already found his dad. Turns out you know him. I'm pretty sure it's Ronnie Mott."

Leroy gripped the arm of the porch swing and planted his feet. "Don't go getting involved with a Mott."

"I wasn't looking for permission," I said, face hot. "I wanted to see if you had any information about that family. Information I could use or pass along to the client."

"Warning you," he said, pausing for a swig of beer. "The man's a sociopath. Kind of terminology gets thrown about all willy-nilly when it comes to criminals, but he truly is, that one. Cold-blooded. You're gonna introduce a whole lotta heartbreak—maybe even danger—into your client's life if you get him tied up with Ronnie Mott."

"What do you think Ronnie's going to do? He's in federal prison."

Leroy shrugged. He wasn't wearing his usual Stetson, and his hair, still dark and mostly full, looked wilted to his head and in need of a trim. His appearance was otherwise tidy: cotton pearl-snap shirt only a little tight around the belly, starchy Wranglers, his good boots. He sighed again heavily in way of response, cradling his chin in his hand, and I walked to the other end of the porch. A hummingbird dove its beak into one of the cavernous flowers on the tangled trumpet vine. I was put out, frustrated by this listlessness. Worried, even. Leroy had had a difficult year and was recently back to being mobile with only the occasional use of a cane. Then, last week, he'd found out his driver's license wouldn't be renewed on account of his vision. He'd seemed to take the news in stride—had long been relying on Mary-Pat and me for transportation—but knowing the situation wasn't temporary must hit differently.

"I don't want to lie to the man," I said.

"Well, then, trust your instincts," Leroy said, tapping the center of his chest. "Trust the tuning fork in there."

"Okay," I said, still a little deflated. I'd worked this job for a year now. He and I spoke about cases like colleagues, most times, but at the end of the day, he was still my grandfather. He was still the hero of this story, all stories I'd known. I respected him—no, revered him—and hated how he had me feeling like a dumb kid begging to stay out past curfew. His dark eyes met mine, watering a bit, and I crossed the porch to him. The other half of the swing was full of the kind of stuff he'd always gathered—a shoebox of rusted door hinges and glass knobs, reused plastic shopping bags filled with petrified wood and river rocks. "Your birthday's coming up," I said, leaning on the column. "Want me to get you one of those DNA kits like he used? Might be interesting."

"We're mutts," he said. "Think it was your momma or dad said they'd done one awhile back, hadn't they?"

"First I'm hearing about it. Have you talked to Dad lately?"

"Nope." He opened his mouth like he might say more but instead took a pull of beer. He and my dad didn't get along—never had, not really—but especially since both had left the police force, back when I was a baby. Dad had been a rookie, Leroy the sheriff when a bad car wreck ended both their careers. Leroy took early retirement and Dad took disability. Dad's injury never quite healed, but he'd been doing better lately. Was three months sober. Sobriety felt fragile, and not just because his self-imposed terms included setting boundaries with people who were unlikely to change—people mostly meaning Leroy. I kept thinking about this speech Nikki had given Sonny when she was on him about cigarettes. She'd read somewhere that quitting successfully was like flipping a coin, same odds no matter the number of flips. Didn't matter if it was your first time quitting or your fiftieth, you weren't more or less likely to have it stick. I could see it both ways, but she'd meant it as a positive. It meant that people changed all the time.

"I might do a kit."

"Suit yourself," he said, and was quiet a moment, reaching to pat my shoulder. "Will say, I suppose it'd be interesting to learn more about my granny. Been thinking about her lately. Her face—I can't quite see it anymore. It's more associations now when I recall her. A whiff of pipe tobacco. The cedar brake on the hill. Rain in the cistern."

I nodded, remembering then what Clint had said about the old lady car smell, the dog's sloppy tongue, feeling happy—why was it that happy memories tended to fuzz and blur, leaving only sensation? Distance had that effect on all memory, but for me, anyway, it was the troubling moments that came into sharpest relief. Leroy's grandmother, Sarah Anne, had also been sheriff in our county. She'd been a Pinkerton detective, had met a local lawman—Leroy's grandfather—on a case, and then settled on a parcel across the river. A hundred acres of scrubby, unused ranchland split by a dry creek and a small hill with a view of the escarpment to the northwest. There was a photograph of my great-great grandmother I often thought of, one of her in middle age wearing a cowboy hat and a man's shirt, silver star pinned to the pocket. Maybe I could find it, frame it for Leroy as a birthday present.

31

"Ronnie Mott," Leroy said after a moment, his voice now almost a whisper. "That's a face I can't forget."

After Leroy and I ate a bite—bologna on white bread, typical slim pickings from the inside fridge—I drove back to the office. Mary-Pat and I had just missed each other; she'd surprised me by buying a new coffeepot, the box left on my desk and a receipt from Walmart for me to file. She and I came and went throughout the day, making sure at least one of us was here during business hours to answer the phone, to greet the very occasional walk-in. After I'd gotten the new coffeemaker set up and had brewed a fresh pot, I sat down at my desk.

Ronald Mott, Jr., I had written in a notepad left open beside the laptop. Admittedly superstitious—and a skittery feeling left under my skin after Leroy's warning—I pressed my hand to my chest and opened the desk drawer. The desk had been Leroy's—massive, solid oak, darkened with age—and he'd never bothered to clean it out. I'd even found his old sheriff's badge in the clutter. He probably shouldn't have kept it, should've turned it in when he retired—not entirely his idea—but here it was. I touched the cold metal for bravery and said my good luck mantra, then put it back in the drawer where it stayed hidden underneath yellowed papers and a fifth of his Wild Turkey. I drummed my fingers on the laptop. Who was Clint's mother, then? I ran another search on Ronnie, and found that he had an ex-wife, Lorena Mott. They'd been together at the time of the trial, a photo taken of her leaving the courthouse after he'd been convicted. Midstride, her head down, all I could tell was that she was tall, slender, and blond. Her last known address was one county over, in Price.

Before I got too deep into my research, I needed to hit the post office. Ms. Alma would be locking up in thirty minutes. In her late seventies now, she'd been Garnett's postmaster for nearly fifty years. Nice enough lady, but everyone around here knew that if you rushed her, it'd only make her go slower. Approach her counter with a poorly taped packaged and she'd send you to the back of the line. I pulled up Word to hammer out a letter to Ronnie. He'd need to call out if we were to talk on the phone. I wasn't sure what to write—God, what if he didn't know about Clint at all? What if Clint's mother had not been his ex, but an affair? I decided to throw out a line and see what happened.

> Dear Mr. Mott,
> I'm a licensed private investigator who has been hired
> to seek out my client's birth parents. I'm writing to
> confirm that you have a twenty-six-year-old son who
> was adopted in Texas in 2001. If this is in fact the
> case, and you might be his father, perhaps you and
> I could speak before I present this information to
> him. Please see my enclosed contact information, and
> thank you for your time.
> Sincerely,
> Annie McIntyre

I chose not to obscure my last name, deciding that if Ronnie connected the dots to former-sheriff Leroy, he connected the dots. If this was about unsealing the truth, maybe I ought to be as forthright. There were so many odd points of connection in this case, so much hiding in plain sight that I had to wonder, was this all an open secret and Clint was the only one in the dark? Did his adoptive parents in fact know he was kin to the wanted man? For now, I printed the letter. Stole a stamp from Mary-Pat's desk, then hurried out the door to drop it off before the evening mail pickup.

Chapter Four

I got to the post office right as the sign flipped to CLOSED, but Ms. Alma took mercy on me. Cracked the door with her foot, and snatched the letter from my hands. I thanked her and paced outside the building for a minute. There was something about the momentum of things going easily so far—like being on a winning streak and kind of knowing you should stop. I considered getting takeout for me and Wyatt, thinking I'd drop it by the house—the café special on Mondays was chicken fried steak—but knew I'd get sucked into another conversation with Marlene about the arson, and at some point, all that conjecture turns to gossip. I decided to drive out to the Mott place instead, to see if I might talk to Ronnie's ex-wife Lorena.

Price County was to the west of ours, and my hour-long drive was a pretty one. I cruised down the empty farm-to-market roads instead of the interstate, turning onto a two-lane highway as the land pitched upward then flattened. Price was dry, liquor stores and a few hole-in-the-walls smattered along the county line, a stretch of road people called the "beer-way."

Farther in, Branch Creek was a town of two churches, a gas station, and an elementary school. Historic-looking houses sat along the main drag, but most of the homes here were tiny and square, sun-faded and dull. Yards with clotheslines and cars on cinder blocks that looked like beetle shells in the dead grass. The Mott house was of the latter kind, with white limestone siding, a tin roof, and blue trim that reminded me of painter's tape. The house was on a corner lot with a big live oak throwing good shade. Maybe a double lot. There was space in the driveway, but I parked on the street, a packed dirt lane at the intersection of an alleyway.

A black Corolla was parked under the carport. Wiping my palms on my jeans, I took the steps quickly before I could lose my nerve, ringing the doorbell. No one answered and I stepped off the porch a bit relieved. I couldn't think of a delicate way to launch into this conversation, and my plan had been to simply be blunt, for better or worse. The backyard was enclosed by a chain-link fence, a scary-looking toolshed off to the side of the house. Two of the neighboring properties looked abandoned, but the house catty-corner was probably an older person's home—metal washbasins turned into tomato planters, pinwheels stabbed in the dirt, numerous bird feeders. I crossed the street and knocked. A sturdy-looking woman wearing a scrub T-shirt over jeans waved me inside. "You can drop your purse wherever, but the bedroom's to the right. Now, she's got to eat with her meds—"

"Oh, I'm not here for that," I said, eyes adjusting to the dimness. "Do you live here?"

"I'm Mrs. Flores's nurse." She crossed her arms as an older Mexican lady came into the room wheeling an oxygen tank. Younger than Leroy upon closer inspection, but aged by poor health.

"You're not the new overnight girl."

"No, ma'am," I said, and sidestepped the nurse, who seemed intent on me leaving now that she knew I wasn't here to relieve her. I addressed Mrs. Flores instead. "I'm wondering if you could tell me a bit about the house across the street. I'm looking for someone who might've lived there around twenty-six, twenty-seven years ago named Ronnie Mott, or his wife, Lorena?"

She shuffled across the room in terry cloth house shoes, the sleeveless cotton dress she wore gaping at the neck when she lowered herself into a chair. She motioned for me to take the couch. Her nurse let out a series of huffs and retreated to the kitchen. Heat seeped into me like I was on a rotating plate in the microwave. The thermostat had to be set at like ninety. Mrs. Flores didn't seem to mind, going so far as to shiver and rub her arms. "Been in this house almost fifty years," she said, a cough rattling her whole body. "Whole time I wished the trash across the street would move. That was Ronnie's grandmother's house, then she died, I don't know, maybe in the late nineties. After that was when Ronnie's wife and their little kids took the house. Lorena. I always got a sense Ronnie—and his brother for that matter—were into some bad stuff, but I wasn't about to stick my nose in it. Turns out I was right."

"How many children did Ronnie and Lorena have?"

"Three. Little girl who was a sweetheart despite it all. Then there were the two boys. One was just a little thing when social services came and, well, that was sad. Ronnie was in prison—still is, I believe. Lorena got her act together eventually and moved back into the house. To her credit she's really cleaned up the place. I've seen one of the boys—grown man, now—come around pretty regular, but I don't exactly know the situation. Cody is his name. Don't remember the littlest boy or know what happened to him or the girl."

So, there had been two boys, and one was Clint's age—Lorena might be his mother after all. "Social services came? Do you know what had happened to the kids?"

"I don't know," she said, nodding at the far wall, at the coffee table. "I had my own family to mind."

There was an entertainment center built around a television, the shelves filled with many framed photos of the same young woman, a pretty girl in braids and braces, then a striking older teenager on prom night, with dark, smiling eyes, and honey-brown hair that had been permed and coiffed. There were stacks of photo albums on the table covering its entire surface, snapshots of her spilling out of the plastic sleeves. I got the sense that Mrs. Flores wanted me to look at them. "Oh, how many children do you have?" I asked politely.

"Two. My son lives in Dallas, and there's my daughter," she said, pointing to the shelf. "My beautiful Faye."

"Does she live around here?"

"She's dead, honey."

The heat was now making my skin pulsate. I couldn't have known she was dead, and somehow, I had—the shelf and all the albums were clearly a shrine. "I'm so sorry for your loss."

"Thank you," she said. Her cheeks had flushed, her skin dewy with perspiration. "Am I crazy or did you not tell me your name?"

"No, I'm sorry," I said again, though it was she who had invited me to sit straight away, had seemed so eager to dish. "It's Annie McIntyre."

Her head turned sharply. "McIntyre. You grow up around here?"

"Yes, ma'am. In Garnett."

"Why're you here?"

"I'm a private investigator and—"

"No, I shouldn't be running my mouth—I really didn't mean anything so bad about those people."

"I don't work for the Motts and I won't share that you've spoken with me, if that makes you feel better."

"Well, it doesn't," she said, standing shakily. "I've got to eat and take my medicine. Carla?"

The woman was done with me and I didn't see a point in pushing her. It would be better to talk to Lorena directly anyhow. I helped Mrs. Flores into the kitchen where the nurse was shelling peas over the sink, then let myself out the front feeling whiplashed. Was Mrs. Flores that afraid of the Motts? Or was it me and my name that had set her off? Speaking about her daughter had touched a nerve—her voice had been distant, polite, but her face looked raw. Pinched, as if she'd bitten into something sour.

I rang the bell at the Mott house and again no one answered. I backed off, and was about to drive away, when a second car pulled up. A tall woman, maybe five ten and rail skinny, got out of a Lincoln and hefted a sack of dog food over her shoulder. She had the kind of burnished-looking skin that comes from years of hitting the tanning bed, and long, white-blond hair that looked equally fried. The Town Car—in a distinctive shade of burgundy—made me wonder if this was the same one Clint had remembered riding in as a little boy. After she'd gotten to the front door and unlocked the house, I stepped out of the bullet and quickly crossed the street, the tall, dry weeds sprouting through the cracked driveway tickling my ankles.

"Lorena Mott?"

She dropped the bag of dog food, reached inside her purse,

and pulled out a can of mace. She wasn't aiming, but her eyes said *try me*. Eyes that were a watery shade of blue, lined with thick black pencil. She tilted her chin, daring me to come closer.

I put my hands up. "Not trying to bother you, ma'am, I just—"

"Then git," she said. She dropped the mace in her purse, and walked inside. A dog came running from around the back and hurled itself at the chain-link, a pit mix with chewed-up ears and a droopy, mean mouth.

A man came out of the toolshed around back and whistled.

Had he been here in the yard the whole time? Shit, what if he'd seen me across the street talking to Mrs. Flores? He wore a limp white T-shirt that looked to be collecting several days' worth of wear, baggy jeans, and work boots that had cracks in the dry leather upper. He looked older than me, maybe thirty, and I could see a resemblance to Clint immediately. The shape of his eyes and nose and mouth were replicas of Clint's, but set closer together. He had a blond buzz cut, a long, narrow face, and his eyes were a faded blue much like the woman's. He was paler than her, with colorless lashes and eyebrows, and looked a little sunburned. The combination made it look like someone had taken a hard pink eraser to him.

"Hey, it's okay," he said, putting his hands on his hips. "Bark's worse than her bite. What can I do for you?"

I wasn't sure if he meant the dog or the woman. "I didn't mean to offend her," I said. "Is that Lorena?"

"Yeah, don't take it personal," he said, glancing back at the door she'd disappeared behind. "But we're not much for solicitors."

"I'm not here to sell y'all anything," I said, extending my hand over the fence now that the dog had settled at his feet.

"Annie McIntyre. I'm a private investigator. I'm here on behalf of a possible biological relative of hers."

He studied me for a second, his eyes darting back and forth before he took my hand. "No shit?"

"Are you Lorena and Ronnie Mott's son?"

"Cody, yeah. Cody Mott. This about my little brother?"

"Yes, if you have a brother, or half-brother, who was adopted in—"

"Clint? Is that still his name?"

I nodded.

"Clint's my full brother, yeah. Wow, this is fuckin' insane—" His face reddened. "Sorry, I don't know what to say."

"No, I'm sorry to drop such a bomb on you, but wasn't sure how else to say it. I honestly wasn't one hundred percent sure of it until I saw you."

"I thought I'd never see him again," he said, and his pale eyes welled with tears that he quickly brushed away. "I don't know how Lorena will take this. Probably better if I talk to her first. In fact, why don't we get out of here."

I looked at the house. Yellowed curtains moved in the window, so slightly that I wasn't sure if I'd imagined a bony finger pull them aside. "I can't just explain the situation to her?"

"Trust me on this one," Cody said, and motioned me toward the black, scraped-up sedan I'd noticed earlier. "Come on. I need a drink."

Chapter Five

I drove myself. Followed him onto the interstate for one exit, then turned off the feeder road onto a side street that petered out to gravel, dead-ending at a dirt parking lot. Cowboys Pool Hall, the sign read. Black metal grates covered the windows, neon beer signs glowing through the small holes. A handful of other cars were scattered around the lot, but it was mostly motorcycles. As I stepped out of the bullet, a little voice in my head told me *no*. Told me this wasn't a dive in the way Mixer's was, or even the VFW bar that turned into a honky-tonk when there was a band. There's a difference between old and unfussy and downright seedy, and this was not the type of place you stumbled into, not as a woman alone. Still, I was curious, and felt it my duty to vet out the family dynamics as much as possible for my client.

Cody took a seat at the bar, ordering a Budweiser and two shots of Jameson. I also ordered a Budweiser, and he thanked me for the drinks. I decided not to rock the boat and remind him that he'd invited me, not the other way around. "Tell me about your family," I said.

He raised his index finger, taking the shots in quick succession. "Mostly it boils down to we're a fucked-up bunch."

"Clint might want to know more about you and how you were separated."

"I take it you know who our dad is."

I nodded, sipping my beer. The bartender seemed to be listening to us while pretending not to, taking a sour rag to a nonexistent spill by my elbow, and I made a point of turning my shoulder toward Cody. The pool hall was small and airless, dark despite the early hour, damp despite floors partially covered in sawdust. The walls that weren't built of gray cinder block were slats of unfinished plywood, marred with notes and crude pictures etched in marker. License plates and a couple of Texas flags had been pinned higher up toward the back. The pool tables took up most of the single room, and something about them lined up like that reminded me of coffins in a funeral parlor display—the frames were mahogany and brass, polished to a shine, the felt smooth and tight, low-lit by green glass lamps hung from the raftered ceiling. There was a reverence to the way people approached the tables, no wet-bottomed glasses set anywhere close. Cody looked forlornly between me and his beer bottle for a moment, like maybe he'd regretted the invite. His head turned when a couple of loudmouthed guys came in and started racking the balls, setting wagers.

"Our dad went to prison when Clint was a baby, and not long after that, our mom went downhill fast," Cody said finally, tensing his jaw. "Broke her heart. You can guess the rest. Started seeing some asshole, fell off the wagon, just totally checked out on us. My older sister took care of us mostly. One day us kids are walking home from the store and some neighbor or other calls CPS, tells them Lorena had been gone for days. We'd walked out the store with fistfuls of candy and a jar of peanut butter. Me, I was like six at this point, so Clint must've been about three? We all got separated in the system, which sucked. Was years before Lorena got her shit together and we were back living under one roof. But Clint, he just, like, disappeared. No one talked about him—and I mean no one. Like forbidden. Lorena would flip her shit or pretend she didn't know what we were talking about."

"But you knew he'd been adopted?"

"Yeah," he said, sucking down the rest of his beer. "Yeah, I don't really remember how or when I learned about that, but I knew some other family had taken him in permanent."

"This must be painful to talk about."

"Yeah, well, what are you going to do?" He bit his lip, a black dot visible where he had a piercing but no ring. Hard enough it looked welted. "I want to talk to him," he said. "Give me his number."

I waffled for a second. "How would your mother feel about it? I think Clint's interested in meeting at some point, too, but I don't want to cause any more heartbreak—"

Cody's face tensed up. "It's not up to her. She won't want to see him, besides. If she did, she would've tried to find him years ago. Hell, I don't know how she agreed to give him up like that in the first fuckin' place. A real piece of work, my mother—I had to move back in with her after I got out and we nearly killed each other. I'm the only one she has who still gives a crap," he said, and maybe seeing my eyes widen, added, "Juvenile, long time ago. Got popped for possession with intent to sell when I was sixteen. Set me back a good bit, all that and some other stuff. I'm finally keeping my nose clean."

I thought for a moment, nervously peeling the damp label

of my beer bottle. Clint and Cody were only three or so years apart, but Cody seemed like he'd lived a whole life. Clint had an edge about him, too, I supposed, but more like a fizziness—the way he flirted, or the way he was constantly biting back a smile, a bright surety that he was some next big thing. Cody looked like he was on the edge of falling. Even in the soft, forgiving light of the bar, he had worry around his eyes, wrinkles creasing his forehead etched too deep. I couldn't imagine giving up a kid, but maybe Lorena's thinking had been as simple as this, right here: future Clint versus future Cody. Maybe she'd known, somehow, Clint would have a better shot. I worried what it would be like when Cody realized this—when he saw good-looking, college-educated Clint with his vintage guitar, his nice truck. A guy who had the kind of confidence that was material and spiritual—the means to try and make it as an artist, of all things.

"What's Clint's last name now?"

"Marshall," I said, though still a little uneasy. Clint should probably be forewarned, but the ship had pretty much sailed. Cody knew Clint was out there now, could just as easily find him himself if he really wanted to. "Let me talk to him first before you look him up," I added quickly. "How about you give me your number and I'll share it with him."

"Oh, right," he said coolly. Took my unlocked phone and punched in his number, letting out a long sigh when he handed it back. "I mean, I get it. I know it'll be weird, but I think I need to talk to him. Hear his voice, if nothing else."

"I understand," I said. The beer had grown warm in my hand, and I pushed the bottle aside. "You ever talk to your dad?"

"No," Cody said, motioning to the bartender. "Man, get me another of these and a Jameson. Annie, you want another?"

I shook my head. Damn, I was going to have to pick him up off the floor if he kept going like this. He'd already started to slur his words. "No, not ever? Your dad, I mean?"

"The man, the myth, the legend? No as in *nev-er.*" He took his shot and chased it with half the beer. His words had sounded overloud—I realized that the guys at the other end of the bar had quieted. That's when out of the corner of my eye I saw the tall, dark-haired man that stood in the outer door. The man wasn't exactly good-looking, but he had a bullish, provocative energy and broad shoulders. Stop and stare type. A prominent chin and slight underbite that made it hard to tell if he was grimacing or it was just his face. A red ball cap obscured his eyes, but when he turned in profile I knew where I recognized him. Why the hairs had lifted on my arms. The door closed, darkening the room, but I knew it was Eli Wallace, a local drug dealer who I'd had a run-in with a few months ago. Violent, nasty temper. He knew I'd once tipped off the cops to the location of his stash house—that I was the rat.

Cody inched his fingers toward my beer bottle, tapping my hand. "You okay?"

"Sorry, but I have to leave," I said, and reached into my purse for my wallet. I felt dizzy, my ears ringing and hot. There was no way Eli wasn't going to notice me—there were maybe fifteen people in this bar, and I was one of like three women. I stole another glance over my shoulder, saw Eli had his back to me and was talking to the guys at the pool table. I pulled out a wad of cash and handed it to Cody, not wanting to raise my voice flagging the bartender. "I'll be in touch."

"Wait," Cody said, standing at the same time as me. He caught his toe on the barstool and stumbled into the guy sitting next to us. Cody's face turned into a snarl and he stuck out his chest. "Move it, asshole!"

Said asshole slapped him across the mouth.

I didn't think the slap was that hard, but Cody was drunk enough that he fell on the floor. I reached down and he swatted away my hand. Swiveled his torso around to grab the man by the leg and punch his thigh. It felt like my fault—I'd been the one who'd gotten him twisted up, the one who'd wrung the pain from deep inside. I should've ordered food or gotten him water when he started slurring. I also knew that once the fists started flying, I'd better move fast—and shit, where was Eli? I bent low, crawling backward to stay hidden under the barstools. The bikers who'd been posted at the end of the bar formed a circle around them wrestling. I angled toward the emergency exit. Stole a glance behind me, saw Eli cut across the room and disappear behind a door in the back. I ran out. The light was disorienting—what time even was it?—and I dug around for my keys, fingers slipping against the metal. Shadows stretched over the parking lot, the malty smell of crushed beer cans in the dirt filling my nose as I kicked up dust.

"Hey, wait," called a man's voice from behind. "Can you get him out of here? He's cut off. I'm keeping his car keys."

Heart thudding, I turned to see the bartender had hoisted Cody up under his armpits. The bartender shoved Cody off and he staggered forward, limping toward me. I could tell he'd have a shiner tomorrow. His jaw was swollen, his lip split. He shifted his gaze between me and the black Corolla, nearly tipping over in the process. A shadow moved in front of the metal window grate, blocking out the neon. Everyone inside was watching us. Without a second thought I pulled him with me to the bullet.

"Thanks for the ride," he mumbled. He tried to click the seat belt and gave up.

"You didn't give me much choice," I said, reversing out. Gravel met pavement at the county road. Truckers must've used this as a cut-through to the interstate—the asphalt cracked around some nasty potholes, and I drove as fast as I could. Cody had his head leaned against the window, and I nudged him to open his eyes. "Where am I taking you?"

"Take me home. Get off at 226 and turn right," he said with effort, like maybe he'd lost teeth. "Then my place's real close— those apartments over there behind the strip mall." Bent into a C shape, his knees nearly touched his chin. He was tall, much taller than Clint, and must chronically slouch for me not to have noticed that fact for this long. He clearly favored Lorena while Clint favored Ronnie. He caught me stealing looks and I turned my eyes back to the road.

"So, you know Eli," he said.

"Who?"

"Come on," he said, rolling down the window to spit. "Don't lie. I saw your face when he walked in. Looked like you'd seen a ghost. Shit, I kinda feel like that when I see him, too."

"How do you know him?"

"Everybody knows everybody."

True enough, but I didn't know Cody from Adam. For all I knew he and Eli were buddies. Sweat pricked my underarms— God, what had I done, giving this guy a ride? I unlocked my phone and placed it in my lap. The sooner he was out of my car, the better.

"'Specially in Cowboys," Cody added, drawing in a sharp breath. "Everybody owes somebody money over a bad game. Man, that fat bastard kicked me in the ribs! Good thing I distracted Eli for you, sounds like. Sounds like you ought to be thanking me."

"You did that on purpose?"

His laugh was pained, a hiss between clenched teeth. "Yeah. Seeing as how I was a hero back there, maybe you'd let me take you out sometime."

"No," I said, hands damp on the steering wheel.

"Are you at least going to tell me what's up with you two?"

I shook my head, could see the strip mall, a sliver of red roof shingles behind it and across the overpass. Two minutes, tops, and he'd be gone.

"Understandable," Cody said, his voice slurred again. "Well, I've had my share of run-ins with Eli Wallace and let me tell you, you don't want to fuck with that guy."

"What type of run-ins are we talking?" I asked, glancing over as I rolled to a stop at the intersection. He was staring at me now, too, his eyes glassy and red.

"Before I got my job at the garden center, things were bad. I was broke, staying at Lorena's, and then it was like one thing after another—thought I might sling product again," he said quietly, clearing his throat. "Make some fast cash. Didn't work out is all I'll say. I'm acting right now, so don't look at me like that."

"Like what? None of this is my business," I said. But it was my business. When nothing had come of Eli Wallace's threats a few months ago, he became a specter to me, ghostlike. I was scared now, but weirdly relieved—validated to know the shadow I'd sensed was not me being paranoid. I turned into a small, two-building apartment complex named Shady Grove Place. The complex looked like it had been built in the seventies or eighties, the pale limestone structure chalky and drab. I knew the insides would have shaggy beige carpets, beige linoleum in the kitchen and bathroom, itchy-looking popcorn ceilings threaded with silver. The place was also about as far from a shady grove as you could get, the parking lot completely treeless.

"Just promise me you'll keep this private"—I motioned between us—"you know, us talking about your brother or that you know me."

"Fine, fine," Cody said, pointing to the building on the right. "Last unit on the end. Park right there, by the stairs. Can't walk too far." He opened the passenger door and unfurled his long body, wincing as he stood. Before he closed the door, he leaned in, close enough that I could smell the alcohol he was sweating out. His lip looked like raw meat. "Thank you," he said. "I mean it."

"Of course," I said, a pinch in my chest—I don't know why, maybe because of all our earlier conversation about his family, or how I knew he must be hurting, but I pictured him suddenly as a little boy. The boy in the backseat of the burgundy old-lady car, petting a dog. Happy. Something so plainly vulnerable about the way he looked at me now, I had to cut my eyes away.

"I'll talk to Clint," I said to the windshield. Cody nodded and closed the door, hobbling toward his apartment.

Chapter Six

I had a feeling Clint was avoiding me. Maybe it was just that, a feeling, but I'd texted him to tell him I had a major update in his case and he didn't reply until the next afternoon. He could have been busy—his show at the VFW was that evening—or he was nervous about what I might tell him. There'd been years of buildup, a whole lifetime of wondering. It was a little anticlimactic that it had taken me less than a day to find his family. I kept thinking about Lorena and the infamous Ronnie, or Cody all glassy-eyed and sad, that asshole Eli Wallace sauntering inside the pool hall—all of it impossible to scrub from my head. This was the kind of talk that you had in person, so I'd asked Clint to come by my office. He was nearly an hour late when I called him.

"Are you still coming?"

"Hey, Annie," he said. "Totally forgot we were meeting. Can we just talk here before the show?" High-pitched and overly enthusiastic, like how you'd answer a call from someone you'd been shit-talking. *Totally forgot?* It annoyed me he acted like this important conversation was an item he'd forgotten to check off his list—had I totally misread the situation, projected onto him this tortured ambivalence?

"If you're sure," I said, reaching for my keys.

The VFW bar turned into a honky-tonk on the nights that they had live music. The longtime owner of the bar, Jimmy Ryland, would push the tables to the walls and the old wooden boards became a dance floor, scuffed smooth. Tonight, because there was a larger turnout than normal, he had the doors propped with speakers and old picnic tables moved outside for overflow. I'd known Clint and his band had a following, but kind of thought it was relegated to the college town where he'd been living. The bartender looked to be suffering the most, a line twenty deep forming. The VFW was only beer, wine, and set-ups, but you could bring your own liquor—countless tequila bottles and flasks passed between the tables as I shuffled through the crowd. Wyatt, Nikki, and Sonny were supposed to meet me here tonight but I didn't see them yet. I also wasn't really looking, angling as I was to get backstage.

Clint and his bandmates startled like I had caught them in the act—of what, I didn't know—and again, this impatience bubbled up. I'd stuck my neck out for Clint last night. Maybe it was me knowing so much about him, or maybe it was his eyes on me—good-looking, lead singer Clint—that made my face flush. I stood there for a full thirty seconds before he set his beer down and came over to greet me. His hands were in his leather pants pockets, his head lowered and cocked to the side. "Lay it on me," he said. "Am I royalty?"

My laugh came out fake-sounding.

"Guys, I'll be a minute," he said, walking with me to the side exit, his hand grazing my back. There was an alcove behind the stage, a utility area with mops and buckets, old sound equipment, and the scoreboard for when Jimmy called bingo. Clint's hand was hot through the thin fabric of my cotton dress, and I stopped to face him.

"I did find out who your parents are. Neither could speak with me, so I'm not one hundred percent certain, but probably ninety-nine. I don't want to mess up your set by going over this now, though. We can wait till tomorrow—or whenever—if now's not a good time."

"No, it's okay," he said, and his face softened. "Sorry I've been putting you off. Guess I panicked a bit. I do want you to tell me, though. I don't want to wait."

"Ronnie and Lorena Mott," I said, handing him the notes I'd typed up and bound, followed by a summary of my hours to-date. "They lived just fifty miles from here, about an hour west, over in Price County. That's where you're from. They had some hard times after you were born. You and your siblings went into the foster system and—"

"Wait, my parents were together? I have, like, full siblings? I assumed I was born to a single teen mom who couldn't take care of me or something. Or shit, that they were dead."

"I'm sorry. This is a lot to take in."

"But who adopted my siblings? Did you find them, too?" He opened the report, his eyes roving the first page, and I looked away to give him some privacy. "Ah, okay. I see," he said. "My dad's in prison."

"I'll attempt contact again, with him and your mother both. I wanted to give you an update, like I said I would. I'll let you know when and what I hear from them."

"No need," he said, clearing the choking sound from his voice. "Think I've learned enough. I can get you a check to-morrow. Is there anything else?"

"No," I said, his sharp tone catching me off guard. He crossed his arms over his chest, folding the report up under his armpit. "This is in my notes, but I also thought I'd tell you that your biological brother, Cody, is willing to meet if you are. I wrote down his number in there. And that's fine about the check. I'll email you the invoice total."

"Dude, you back here? We better get going!"

Clint spun around.

"Hey," I said to his back. "I should've argued harder against us meeting here. I can tell you're upset."

"I'm fine," he said, facing me. "Just a lot to think about."

"Understood," I said, and walked with him toward the stage where we split off. His girlfriend, Amanda, was sitting at the round top closest to the stage, perched on the edge of her chair like an exotic bird. She gave me a quick wave, smiled, but there was tension in her eyebrows. She had a friend with her and made a point of turning back to their conversation after the little gesture of politeness. I spotted Wyatt in line at the bar, so I squeezed my way through the crowd and hooked my arm through his, relief washing over me when he looked down, hazel eyes crinkling. He was wearing his good going-out jeans and the boots I'd saved up for months to buy him last Christmas.

"Nikki and Sonny are here, too, but we don't think we can get a table," he said and handed me a beer.

"Fine by me," I said, spotting them at the far corner of the room. They appeared to be arguing, and my stomach tightened again.

I tapped her on the shoulder and she spun around like I'd thrown water on her. "Hey, girl!"

"What's going on?" I asked, leaning in close to her while Sonny was saying hey to Wyatt.

"I just said something stupid. It doesn't matter."

She was right. Sonny was unperturbed—or so I thought—wrapping me in a hug then whooping along with the crowd as Clint and his band walked onstage. He looked back at us. "Clint's always been really talented," he said, cupping his mouth to be heard over the crowd. Staring straight at Nikki, he added, "And he's always been full of shit!"

Wyatt laughed a little too hard. He wasn't the type to get easily riled up, and he trusted me to not play games, but something had bothered him about seeing me and Clint talking that night at the party. I'd broken my promise to Clint and told Wyatt—and only Wyatt—that he'd hired me, partly to stop him from being weird. Sometimes I took our ease with each other for granted. Forgot that he couldn't actually read my mind, even though at times I felt like I'd laid my whole heart at his feet.

"I'll always love him," Sonny said. "He'll always be my little bro."

God, would Clint ever tell Sonny what I'd found? I hadn't gone over all the specifics of what Ronnie Mott had been imprisoned for in my report. That he'd been a getaway driver for the man who held up a bank teller, the same woman who would later adopt him. The information was out there if Clint chose to pursue this further, I knew, but I ought to have provided more context. I should have warned him, advised him to keep it close until he had time to think it over carefully—I'd call him tomorrow. One of the first times I'd hung out with Sonny was here at the VFW, I remembered. I'd been with Leroy, and when Sonny met him, his whole face had lit up—he'd thanked Leroy for saving their mother's life that day of the holdup. Said he was a legend in their house.

Nikki rolled her eyes. "Clint's the one who ought to be

practicing for a toast, not you. Save it for when you're the best man."

"Did y'all say hey to Amanda?" I asked, seeing her in line at the bar now.

Sonny barreled past me. "Here's what I've tried telling Clint, though, and I'm curious what y'all think. He thinks that to be an artist you have to like, live the life. Be all sad and shit, live on pennies and get in your hard knocks. In other words, cook up drama for himself. He acts like he's not on the family phone plan and it's ridiculous, you know? He needs to get over himself."

Now it was my turn to laugh a little. It was unlike Sonny to be this harsh unless he was drunk. When he drank too much, he was often his most incisive—always a shock coming from good-time Sonny. Maybe being around family stoked a little meanness in him. I knew what he meant, though, and the thought had struck me, too, not necessarily in relation to Clint, but with creative-types I'd known in college. Rich kids who acted ashamed about having money, which was somehow snottier than being showy with it.

"Yeah, I don't know why struggling is a prerequisite to being an artist," I said. Art was about winnowing out the truth, wasn't it? Maybe that was the real hurt, trying to get your heart to beat outside of your body. To make people really see you, all the while fearing they wouldn't understand. Or maybe it was searching for something to say in the first place. My beer was ice-cold, and I took a long pull of it. A knot inside me loosened as the band warmed up. Leroy was a fan of two-stepping and the slow, sad waltzes played here. I loved this place, too. Loved the candy-colored light, the disco ball, the sound of a steel guitar both winsome and blue. A bit of a wallflower, I'd fallen in love with the idea of the dances more than dancing, it seemed.

Clint sang, and the sound of it was, in fact, like he'd opened his throat and a heart had come tumbling out. The whole crowd—honestly, nearly everyone—stopped talking, gasping because he was that good, that he was even better live. He'd chosen a fast-tempo drinking song to start the set. Someone brushed my shoulder roughly from behind—my eyes scanned the room, worried I'd turn around and Eli Wallace would be standing there. Since I'd seen him at the pool hall, I'd even started to wonder about that truck in the intersection at the café—was that far-fetched? I craned my neck, trying to see who this person was who'd shoved me.

Wyatt put his arm around my waist. "Are you okay?"

"Fine," I said, shifting to stand in front of him so I could see the stage better. Clint and the band played the Spotify single next, the forgettable song that everyone somehow knew and cheered loudly over. But midway into the first verse, Clint's face scrunched up and he stopped singing. The band started over, and again he got flustered. "Sorry, y'all, but we're gonna change it up. Try a song my dad used to play for me," he said, pausing. "This one's for Annie. Y'all just follow along."

Nikki pinched my arm to get my attention, but I swatted her away. Clint played acoustic, the notes sharp and tinny without the smoothing accompaniment of the bass fiddle and drum. A haunted-sounding ballad, and one I knew.

"To the town of Agua Fria rode a stranger one fine day," he sang, voice deepening, rounding the notes. It was "Big Iron," a Marty Robbins number about a fateful showdown between a ranger and an outlaw, a song from *Gunfighter Ballads and Trail Songs.*

"We—Clint and I—we talked about this the other day," I said, turning to face Nikki, Sonny, and Wyatt. "This album, I mean. Hey, anyone else want another beer?"

"Sure," Wyatt said tightly, handing me his empty. Both Sonny and Nikki shrugged and said no. I headed toward the bar, stuffy and self-conscious—as if anyone else here knew that Annie was me. On a whim, I surrendered my spot in line and headed through the open doors to my left. Groups had gathered on the dirt and patchy grass in front of the speakers, more stood smoking by the picnic benches. Still hot out, but cooler here than inside. I fanned myself. Looked out over the row of cars and trucks parked in the field and my heartbeat kicked up when I saw that the bullet was trapped in by an F-150 with Lift-kit tires who'd double parked. Clint's voice echoed through the speakers. He strummed the guitar hard and fast. I wished I could make the truth somehow easier on him, but that wasn't my job. He'd asked me to find out, and I'd found out. This song, the shout-out—why, then, did I feel like the stranger come to town with an iron on my hip, there to put the outlaw down?

A sedan reversed out of the line of cars. Maybe I should move onto the shoulder of the highway while there was an opening. I walked toward the bullet, and was about to fish my keys from my purse when I saw a shiny piece of foil tucked under my wiper blade. A matchbook. Red, and in silver cursive script on the front was *Yesterday Once More*, along with the VFW's address in smaller type below. I recognized it from the fishbowl by the door where the guy took your cover. A single match had been torn out and an *x* written on the inner flap. The foil in my palm glinted. Closer, the truck that had blocked me in looked familiar. Was that the same one that nearly plowed into me and Clint outside the café? I tucked the matchbook in my pocket, swiveling my head around. No one was watching me. The matchbook was probably just a weird thing some drunk person had done, but my skin felt tight and prickly, like maybe blocking the bullet had been a setup. I hurried back toward the bar to get Wyatt, feeling a sudden, strong desire to leave.

More people were milling about outside, and somewhere in the thick of it, I caught sight of a familiar figure. It was Cody Mott, standing next to a pack of guys. At first glance, you might think they were all together, but Cody wasn't part of their conversation. He watched the show through the open doors, face red, eyes locked on his brother, Clint. His mouth parted and his eyes narrowed to slits. Like a jealous lover, an expression that alternated between raw pain and longing.

I was maybe twenty feet away, and decided to talk to him. "Hey," I called out, pushing forward through the crowd, and louder, "Hey, Cody!"

He appeared to not see or hear, or was simply ignoring me. Spun on his heels when I waved, like he was in a hurry. He took one last look over his shoulder, back toward the stage, leaving as quietly as he came.

Chapter Seven

For the next two weeks, I did my best to banish Clint's psychic wound from my mind. And failed. I couldn't have articulated it then, but his story was too tangled with mine. There was Leroy the sheriff and Ronnie the getaway driver, legends both. The stories Leroy told had always felt to me like gospel—and him, he was so much bigger than any other person in the room. I felt both drawn to and snuffed out by this bigness, wanted to be part of his bright, buzzing light, but I also was afraid of the full story, of questioning too hard the narrative for what it might reveal. That was the other part that tangled me and Clint—fear. Resenting the sticky feeling under our heels, both obsessed and repulsed by the need to keep dwelling. Clint had mailed me a check, as promised, but hadn't texted or called me back. I never did tell him about his mother's loose connection to Ronnie Mott, and wondered how he felt, or if he knew.

I had another case to keep me busy, though. Nothing too complicated, but a paperwork-heavy job running background checks for a recruiting firm up in Austin. And of course, Nikki's wedding. Sleepovers and a bachelorette party that ended in tears, vomit, and our cousin Candice being permanently banned from two establishments. Afternoons were spent at my aunt's house assembling favors, handwriting place cards, arranging tea lights in votives Momma had found on sale at Walmart. I've always had the willpower to compartmentalize my anxieties, and besides, I really was happy for Nikki. But then all the tensions within our families that had been on simmer—my aunt's insistence on corsages the size of dinner plates, and Sonny's uncle appointing himself videographer and demanding payment, for example—came to a boil Friday at the rehearsal dinner.

We were all done setting up at the venue—the county's rodeo fairgrounds—and the rehearsal was supposed to have started twenty minutes ago. I'd gotten tired of sitting on the hot metal bleachers, so I headed toward the shade of the pavilion, adjusting the pink sundress I wore. The clingy, synthetic fabric continued to ride up my thighs as I clomped through the grass in heels. A jagged edge to Nikki's voice made me stop and look up.

"Where the hell is he, then?"

"That's what I've been trying to tell you," Sonny said, waving his hands over his head in frustration, sweat darkening the arms of his blue dress shirt. "I've called him like fifty fucking times!"

"What's wrong?" I asked, lifting my hair off my neck. Another casualty of the bachelorette party: my nearly waist-length hair. We were drinking and getting ready at the salon where Nikki worked, and she'd talked me into going shorter. I'd even let her talk me into layers, which backfired—my hair was too uneven now to pull up.

Nikki glared at me. "Clint's MIA and not answering his

phone. But Sonny hasn't even talked to him since his bachelor party last weekend!"

"Did y'all have a fight or something?" A bead of sweat rolled down my back. I wanted to ask if he'd said anything about his birth family, but stopped myself—not my place, certainly not the time.

Sonny let out a long sigh, and I couldn't quite read his expression. "Clint just does this shit sometimes. Lots of times. Hell, we didn't speak for like two years while he was on tour. Maybe I should go find him—"

"No, you ought to be enjoying yourselves," I said, inserting myself between him and Nikki. "If someone's leaving, let me go. Worst case, I know what to do tomorrow and all he has to do is follow my lead."

Nikki frowned. "What, do you know where he is?"

"No, but the groom can't leave. Sonny, has your mom tried him?"

"Mom's not here yet, either," he said, staring down at the stiff, pointed toes of his loafers. He looked like a kid playing dress-up. "She's on her way, at least. Said she was driving fast as she could, and no, he wasn't with her, then hung up on me."

"I'll also try and get ahold of Amanda," I said, remembering I'd added her to the text thread for Nikki's bachelorette. "She was supposed to come down today."

Nikki fiddled with her ring, giving me a look like *can you believe this crap*. "Just promise you'll hurry back," she said, and pulled me in for a hug. Her arms were taut as a springboard. The makeup she'd spent so much time on was starting to melt, her sweat mixed with a lilac-heavy perfume. She'd been taking out her pre-wedding jitters on me, on Sonny, on anyone who dared come close. I thought her anger now was less about his family, more that he was a convenient place to direct her frustration. I knew how well telling her to calm down would go, so I did what I'd been doing all week, which was to keep us on schedule. Part of me really worried about Clint—what kind of a best man, the groom's brother, at that, flakes on the rehearsal dinner?

"Thanks, Annie," Sonny said as I looked in my bag for keys. "Sorry."

By the time I'd driven to Clint's house it was after six. The way the shadows fell across the little white bungalow made it look dirty, sad, and without any of the charming quality that a quirky old house had in the clear light of morning or lit up with string lights at night. No illusion of it being a place one reminisced about, recalling the years when he sat strumming on the porch as a young, struggling artist destined for greatness. His truck was gone out of the short driveway. Blinds closed, no light emitted from within. I didn't even put the bullet in park, just turned left, headed toward his mother's place in Parr City. Maybe he'd driven by sometime after Sonny had talked to her? But I found a similarly empty house, no cars in the driveway. Calling Amanda had been as fruitless. I tried Clint a third time, and now his phone went straight to voice-mail. Worried that he might've been in an accident, I called the hospital—my mind couldn't help but rush to worst-case scenario—and found that no one by his name had been admitted. Dread gnawed at my insides, thinking of the various kinds of trouble he might've gotten himself into.

I thought of Cody slinking through the crowd at the VFW. The look of both desire and disgust as he gazed upon his brother. Eyes narrowing as he took in Clint's voice like it were a ray of white-hot sun. I got on the interstate, headed to

Price County. Clint said he didn't want me as intermediary, but another part of me knew I'd let my fear of how he'd react get in the way, not pressing. The unsettled feeling I'd had since delivering my report was tinged with guilt the closer that I looked. Sharing his full name with Cody, for one. I'd spent only a couple hours with the man and I'd had a run-in with a dealer and gotten swung at in a fistfight. Seeing him at Clint's show didn't exactly warrant an interrogation, but I didn't know what else to do now. I couldn't go back to the rehearsal without Clint. And even if Clint didn't want anything more than to know his family's name, it wasn't entirely up to him. Cody's life was changed now, too. I hadn't asked Lorena or Ronnie if they consented to me sharing *their* names, either—exactly why you'd hire someone like me instead of going through the courts, I knew, but I didn't feel good about what I'd done. Cody handily confirmed all my theories, sure, but I didn't have the full picture. I still had his number, and nearly threw the phone out the window when he didn't pick up.

The parking lot at Shady Grove Place was dimly lit. Sunset haze mixed with the greenish hue of a single lamppost by the stairwell, and I parked as close to the light as I could. Moths had gotten trapped in the bulb, snapping against the glass as they expired, and more flitted around my head as I approached Cody's door. I couldn't hear anyone, but the blue glow of a television screen bled through the poorly-fitted blinds. I squinted through them and saw it was a video game that had been paused. I knocked, waited, knocked harder, and that's when I realized the latch wasn't quite clicked into place. I turned the janky, burnished knob slightly and it swung open.

"Cody? Anyone home?"

Standing at the threshold, I peered into the shadowy living

room. I was somewhat surprised to see it was spartan in appearance, only one black Ikea bookshelf and matching coffee table, and a dismal, brown velour couch. He was a young, single guy, of course, but speaking with him the other night—maybe because he said he'd stuck around Lorena despite their dysfunction—I'd taken him for the sentimental type. Like he might hold onto birthday cards and ticket stubs, keep knickknacks on his shelf. There was some junk on the coffee table: game controllers, a bottle of Coke, cigarettes, and a shopping bag. A bedroom pillow and a faded, handsewn quilt were draped over the couch cushion like he'd been napping there, which touched me for whatever reason. I had a sudden, strong urge to leave, that this was getting too personal, but felt rooted to the spot. I called out for him again. My pulse quickened and I looked behind me, scanning the parking lot for a black Corolla. I didn't see his car, and before I could think better of it, stepped inside his apartment and closed the door behind me.

Seconds later, the air now sealed, I smelled it—the iron-rich scent of blood. A gamey, animal scent. Acid rose in my throat as I walked toward a postage stamp–size kitchen, a cell sectioned off from the living room by a half-wall cutout. I flipped the wall switch and a fluorescent bulb hummed overhead, casting a greenish, store-like glow that flooded the entire room. The beige linoleum was recently mopped, still damp, and the chipped counters smelled faintly of Clorox. Only a highball glass in the sink, no food left out that might cause the other smell. Nothing was obviously amiss, but the lid of the kitchen trash can had been left on the floor. The can was empty, the bag not yet replaced. Legs shaking, I turned down the hallway—I didn't know what I was doing here anymore, but didn't stop. What if Cody had hurt himself, I worried, had been dropped off drunk again and had banged his head, or was wounded in another barfight? As I walked down the hallway, the smell grew stronger, more bodily. A whiff of smoke and something more metallic hung in the air, like gunpowder. The bathroom to my left was dark. A bedroom door across the hall was cracked, lamplight glowing from within. A ceiling fan clicked, circulating the dank air outward.

"Cody?"

Pushing the door, I was met with resistance. Dull weight with a little give. I stopped and stuck my head around, peering down to examine the blockage. Blood spattered wildly and had pooled, settling into the carpet like a bucket of paint that had tipped.

"No—God, please, no," I begged, though Cody couldn't hear me now.

Chapter Eight

An officer tied yellow tape to the staircase railing, cordoning off the apartment. I turned my back when the stretcher came into view. I'd seen enough. The image of Cody curled on his side, blood and pieces of him on the carpet, the wall—that was burned into my brain forever. I didn't need to see him taken away to make it real. And yet, the whole time I'd been here—alternating between pacing the sidewalk and sitting on the crumbling asphalt ledge—waiting forever for the Price County sheriff to arrive, I'd had the surreal, underwater sensation of being trapped in a lucid dream.

"Ma'am?" A woman wearing dark slacks and a white button-down strode toward me. She was small but sturdy, hair in a tight bun, mouth set in a frown. As she drew nearer, I could see she was maybe in her mid-fifties, with a single white skunk streak in her jet-black hair. "Sheriff Kate Krause. Let's you and me go over what happened."

"Annie McIntyre," I said, heart thumping. Finally, I'd get to talk and get all that I'd been storing up—rehearsing the how, the why of it—off my chest. "You might know my grandfather,

Leroy McIntyre," I said, shaking her hand. "He was law enforcement in Garnett County for many years."

"Old Leroy is your grandfather?" Her eyes drew down, betraying her polite smile. She led me toward the second stairwell on the opposite side of the complex, away from the small group of onlookers who'd gathered after the sirens came pealing and whining, carrying over the din of the interstate. "Need water? Might could scrounge up a coffee—"

"No, thank you," I said, stuck on her reaction to Leroy's name. He'd retired decades ago, but they'd likely worked together at some point if she'd risen in the ranks locally. My chest pinched, instinct telling me I might need to be careful. Whatever had actually happened, breaking into the apartment of a man who'd been shot dead didn't look great. I'd interacted with several criminal defense lawyers over the past year, and their advice to never speak to cops without representation clanged like a bell in my ears. "I only mentioned my grandfather because I thought it might come up," I said quickly. "See, I work for his private investigation firm over in Garnett, and a case of mine is how I know—knew—Cody Mott. I had spoken to him about a biological relative that had wanted to make contact and I was following up, seeing if they'd spoken."

"I see." She had her legs in a wide stance and rocked on her boot heels. A good two or three inches shorter than me, even in the boots, yet I felt like she was looking down at me such was her intensity. "So, I hear you told the dispatcher he was dead when you found him. Why'd you go into the apartment if he didn't come to the door when you knocked?" My eyes must have gotten big, because she interjected before I could answer, "You're not in trouble, Annie," and softer, "I know this must be really upsetting for you."

My eyes welled unexpectedly. The façade cracking with that tiniest note of tenderness. All that I'd seen—the brutality of it—kept hitting. This man that I'd spoken with, so alive just the other day now stiffening, cold. It wasn't his face—or lack of a face, only mangled remnants—that I kept picturing, but his hands. Fingers curled, his skin waxy and pale, dirty, purpling at the cuticles. Those same fingers I'd seen twist around a beer bottle, drum the bar top. Words in sun-faded ink snaking around his wrist. A pistol had been lying on the carpet beside him. I swallowed hard, shaking the image from my head. "I don't have a good answer," I said. "Other than I was curious and eager to talk to him. The front door was open and I just went for it. I walked inside and something felt off, and then I found him on the floor in the bedroom. I called 911 right away."

The sheriff studied me for a moment. Maybe she did find my being in the apartment questionable but didn't want me spooked. She looked off, toward the crime scene worker on the opposite staircase. "To take one's life is terribly sad, isn't it? Had you known him well?"

My mouth went dry. "Oh, you're sure it was suicide?"

"Well, we found a note. The medical examiner will make the final determination, but yep, looks that way," she said. "'Course, that's not the only reason why I think it was suicide," she added, crudely miming putting a gun in her mouth.

"How long had he been there do you think?"

"Probably not long before you said you arrived."

My mind was racing. I couldn't articulate a solid reason why suicide didn't sit right—hell, I barely knew Cody. Maybe I just didn't want to believe it. *You never really know what someone's going through,* people always said when this kind of thing happened. Yet that didn't settle my unease. "Why was the door open?" I asked. "You don't think it's possible there'd been a robbery or—"

"I suppose I don't know one thousand percent," she said, and huffed as though saying so made her look bad. My shoulders tensed; an inability to sit with ignorance for a moment, to not rush to be the first one with an answer, had always bothered me in a person. Not all, but a lot of the cops I'd encountered around here had acted like this. "But robbery? No. Nothing big missing, his wallet and television were still there, and I simply don't see any signs of a break-in. No signs of a struggle, either. Gun was right there next to him, and this is not always the case, but I could visibly see residue on his right hand. Could see signs he'd been intoxicated. Now, you said the door was wide open?"

I shook my head. "Just unlocked. And, I don't know, but isn't it weird the place was all cleaned up?"

"He wanted someone to find him before long, I'd bet."

"Maybe, but—"

"It's impossible to know what all was running through a person's mind," she said. "What I'm trying to explain to you is there are calculations and preparations they make that from the outside in might not make the most sense."

I nodded, batting back more tears.

"Okay, well, I think I've gotten what I need from you," she said, her hand on my shoulder. "No judgment, but do you always work a case this dressed up?"

I looked down at my red, swollen toes, numb and still pinched into high-heeled sandals, at my pink clingy dress. "I was at my cousin's rehearsal dinner. She's getting married tomorrow, and the best man is my client, the biological relative I told you about. It was a long shot, thinking he'd be here."

"Well, tell you what. Try and enjoy your cousin's wedding

if you can, and I can talk to you again on Monday, get a formal statement. You're free to leave now. Should my deputy give you a ride? Know you must be shaken up."

My heart pounded in my ears. "No, ma'am."

She patted me on the shoulder again and I turned to leave. My feet were aching from standing around in these stupid shoes, so tensed up, and I didn't bother to blink my tears back now that no one could see my face. I pulled my keys out and saw my phone glowing at the bottom of my bag. No fewer than twenty missed calls and a dozen texts from Nikki. Another string of voicemails, texts, and missed calls from Wyatt. I unlocked the bullet, collapsing into the driver's seat. When I closed the door, the hot air warming every exposed inch of skin, I felt encapsulated, secure.

I'm sorry, I texted to both Wyatt and Nikki. I knew I should call one or both back, but couldn't bring myself to talk to them, reassure them, not yet. *Will fill you in later, but there was*—I paused, my thumb hovering over the screen—*an incident with the cops. But I'm OK. Will head home soon. Nik, see you first thing a.m.*

I hit send, then remembered why I'd been here in the first place.

I never did find Clint, I added. *Have y'all heard from him?*

My heart thumped in my neck as I waited for a reply. Maybe he and Cody never made contact. Maybe—

I looked in my rearview at the sheriff. She stood talking to a male deputy, the one who'd come inside the apartment, first to arrive after I'd called 911. Both of their gazes shifted toward me and the bullet, like they were waiting to see what I'd do next. I remembered her offer to have someone escort me home if I was too upset to drive, and not wanting that, I dropped my phone in my lap and turned the ignition. Put the bullet in gear and looked over the steering wheel for the first time.

There was the lifted F-150 I'd seen at the VFW bar, two spaces ahead. I squinted my eyes, and as I did, a pale shape flashed in the truck's passenger side window. When I flipped my headlights on, I saw I'd been mistaken. No one appeared to be inside the cab. I felt mirrored in both this figment and this blankness—felt so strongly that I needed to blink and rub away the strange sensation I'd been sleepwalking. That I needed to wake myself from a bad, bad dream.

Chapter Nine

The café was open 24/7, and when I'd waitressed here I'd come to know and love its late-night rhythms. Maybe "love" isn't the best word. I felt a heightened awareness. In the quiet, there was an element of anticipation—or fear, rather, when I worked alone—that anything might happen whenever the bell chimed over the door. There weren't regulars at night. The people who wandered in out of the darkness—barflies, shift workers, long-haul truckers—were strangers to me. And yet being alone with a person at 2 a.m. feels intimate, even if you don't speak, even if they barely look up at you with their strung-out eyes that seem to say *I know I should be elsewhere.*

It was well after midnight now, and I sat at the counter next to Mary-Pat who was intent on working out a piece of gristle from her ham and eggs. I took a bite of the cherry pie I'd ordered, the sugar perking me up. I'd been on the feeder road after leaving Shady Grove Place, about to merge onto the interstate and drive home, when a text pinged on my phone from Wyatt: *Still haven't heard from Clint.* I'd veered off into a Valero station to call Mary-Pat, and told her everything.

She'd been at the office, both an early riser and a night owl. I hadn't yet figured out when exactly she slept. Leroy used to joke and call her Creeper, a hangover from her time as a deputy when she preferred the overnight shift. She, too, liked to see what stirred at night.

She looked at my plate. "How's the pie?"

"Don't want to share, if that's what you're hinting at," I said, a laugh at the back of my throat. Sometimes when I'm bone tired, I get giddy—the night was still tinged with that nightmare-like unreality. How had I gone from Nikki's rehearsal dinner to seeing Cody—like that? I took a sip of coffee that left a sour taste in my mouth, his pale, purpled hands flashing through my mind. "So, you agree it's weird no one's heard from Clint?"

"I think you think there's a direct line between the two because you were after Clint when you came across the deceased."

"What if Cody was triggered by meeting his brother? Or just about me bringing up all this stuff with his family?" I said, remembering the hangdog look he'd shot me that afternoon at the pool hall, eyes shining wetly in the neon.

Mary-Pat wasn't the type to offer false comforts, but she sighed, squeezed my hand then. Her hands were strong, but when she touched mine, her skin felt loose and papery. Mary-Pat was in fact an old woman, though the thought rarely occurred to me. Her hands were bonier than I'd realized, thinner, ribbed with bulging veins. It wasn't unusual for her to not wear makeup, but her face tonight looked washed clean—maybe it was the concentration of her blue eyes on me that felt so naked. "I don't know all of what was going on," she said. "But Jesus H., Annie, I do know that this is not your fault. Had Cody and Clint been in contact?"

"Not sure," I said. "But I saw Cody at his show at the VFW.

And, of course, both parties were curious, at some point likely to connect. I feel bad I didn't follow back up with Clint."

"He paid you and you went on your way. I could've warned you how messy these adoption cases can get. He's an acquaintance of yours, to boot. You know what they say—"

"Shitting where you eat. Lovely sentiment."

She looked down at her mug. "What did you think of the sheriff over in Price County, Kate Krause?"

"She acted a little weird when I said I was Leroy's granddaughter," I said, noticing her arms had gone rigid as she waited for my reply. "Why? What do you think of her?"

"That she's an idiot."

"Tell me how you really feel."

Her smile was more of a grimace. "She and I used to see each other."

"Like, you dated?" Mary-Pat was fiercely private, even around people she knew well. She and I weren't exactly peers, but she'd known me since I was born and still rarely let me glimpse her personal life, especially when it came to relationships. Growing up gay in a place like Garnett back then was not a widely accepted thing. She'd explained to me once that her family politely ignored what they called "her lifestyle," and they had an expectation that she never drew attention to herself. What the whole town had expected, it seemed. It was in her nature to keep people on a need-to-know basis.

"Briefly," she said. "Kate started out as a rookie here in Garnett. Ended badly between us so I'm probably biased. But that's not what caused Leroy to get her transferred elsewhere. She mishandled evidence—just once, out of sheer stupidity, else he would've fired her. But there was something off about the whole thing and her attitude that made it uncomfortable to be around her. A rumor went around that it was no accident, and justly or not, it became hard to trust her. I suppose it was that she had no real remorse. Arrogant enough to think she was the smartest one in the room."

"And yet, she became sheriff over in Price County."

"Of course, that's all ancient history now. People deserve second chances, as your grandfather said. Maybe she's changed, maybe not. I've heard people sing her praises, but also that she bulldozes anyone standing in her path. 'Course, there weren't many people to bulldoze—you know there's more cows than people in Price County."

"There was something weird about the way she'd handled what happened tonight. And I thought that before you said anything about her."

Mary-Pat bit her lower lip, staring into space for a second. "It strikes me as odd that she spoke to you so candidly."

"Maybe because she knew that I work for you and my granddad?"

"Sure, maybe," she said, and sighed. "The death of this young man, his suicide, I suppose it seems clear enough—I wasn't there—but I think they ought to do an autopsy, an investigation at the least. I'm surprised and I'm not. This stinks like her old bullshit, honestly."

The hair stood up on the back of my neck, and thinking I'd heard someone, I whipped around on my stool. No one but the overnight waitress, Dot, sitting in a booth on the other side of the restaurant rolling silverware. My fear that someone had been watching me from that truck at the complex was like a phantom limb, still tingling. "Cody ran with some rough people, at least in the past. Eli Wallace, for one."

Mary-Pat turned her head sharply. "Have you had any more sightings of him?"

"Not since the pool hall, no," I said. "But at Clint's show I found a matchbook on my windshield. It was from the VFW, so maybe it was nothing, just trash caught in the wind, but it seemed left there intentionally. This truck was blocking me in, too—the same truck I saw tonight, I'm almost certain. I don't actually know that it means anything, if I'm losing my mind, but"—I pulled out my phone—"I took a picture of the license plate. If I text it to you, can you convince someone in the department to check who it's registered to?"

"'Course I can," she said, her voice hard. "When you go in to give your statement, let her know about Cody's relationship to the Wallace crew."

I nodded, gripping the counter.

"Are you ready for tomorrow?" she asked, flagging down Dot for the check.

"Tomorrow?"

"Your cousin's wedding," she said, and nodded at Dot as she slid the ticket over the counter. Dot looked at me with one eyebrow raised, what passed for a conciliatory gesture on her part. She didn't like me when we'd worked together, but I didn't really like her, either. "I keep up with these things, even if you think I don't," Mary-Pat said, softer. "I think you ought to get some rest."

I felt badly I hadn't thought at all about the wedding, but how could I have? What I'd witnessed in that apartment to-night would be a cold black shadow over all my days. I wanted to stop and hit rewind. As if I hadn't come along, he'd still be alive in some kind of alternate suspension. Alive in his apart-ment, a soft old quilt around his shoulders while he just sat on the couch and relaxed, just playing his video games, *just, just, just.*

"Go home," Mary-Pat said, and squeezed my shoulder. "Focus on your people. These kinds of nights, they remind you that you can't take your people for granted now, can you?"

She left the change and walked out the door, the bell chime pinging. That was the other thing about that sound the door made when I was waitressing—it made me blue when whoever had come in was now leaving. When I was left alone on the other side of it.

Chapter Ten

When I got up the next morning, woken from a black, dreamless sleep by our cat, Tate, biting my toe through the covers, Wyatt was already in the kitchen making smoothies. More like breakfast milkshakes: vanilla yogurt, frozen bananas and strawberries, a splash of orange juice. We had an awareness that blending spinach into this sugary concoction didn't yield it magic healing properties, but pretended otherwise. More virtuous than a swing past the taco place behind Texaco at least.

"Thanks," I said, letting him pull me close, kissing his unshaven cheek. "Sorry I scared you last night."

"Don't be."

I let out a deep breath. I'd gotten home last night and gone straight into the shower. He'd heard me crying through the door, got out of bed, and sat on the edge of the sink while I told him about Cody. He and I had an understanding that I didn't always want to talk about work, but last night I couldn't tame this restless feeling on my own. I felt like I was at the center of a big lake, scared and unsure how I'd swum so far from shore. Cutting, stroking, not treading lest I tire out and drown. What I needed from him was solid ground. This old, seventies, flat-roofed ranch house, Wyatt in the green-tiled kitchen, Tate hunting crickets in the yard—all this was more solid than anyplace I'd known.

"Nikki was pretty upset," he said carefully. Wyatt knew not to get between me and my cousin—that never went well for him—but I knew he must've had to defend me last night. Nikki preferred to lash out at me when she was stressed rather than someone who'd take actual offense and not see it for what it was—blowing off steam—but I was at my threshold, even if today was her wedding day. "I said I figured you'd gotten caught up with work, but she and Sonny both acted mad," he said.

"All I did was try and find his best man. And it's not my fault I walked in on . . ." I trailed off, somehow unable to say it. My face felt hot and tight, and I pressed the cold glass to my cheek. Shit—the best man. In the morning light, even though I hadn't slept very much or very well, I could see the situation more clearly. There was no concrete reason to think Clint was in any trouble himself. He'd probably flaked out last night for whatever stupid reason he and Sonny had argued, or no reason at all. But if nothing else, he deserved to hear the news about his brother from me first.

"What time do you have to go over to the salon?"

"Noon." I liked having my hair and makeup done by my aunt—she and Nikki were co-owners of the Beauty Shoppe—but there were few things worse than sitting in a salon chair and forcing the chipper mood I knew was expected of me, while these thoughts ran through my head. "I've got to run a few errands and help out a bit before then, pick up my dress," I said, wincing at the half truth. I didn't want to lie to Wyatt, but I also didn't want him to try and talk me out of going to find Clint.

"Won't see you till you're walking down the aisle, then."

I knew what he meant, of course, but there was a lag, my mind stuck on *me* being the bride. The closer we got to Nikki's wedding, the more these thoughts popped into my head. Things had started getting serious since we'd moved out of our shitty last apartment. The ranch house was a rental, too, but it was ours in a way that place never was, and we had a good-sized yard that was a little wild. Full of prickly pear and mesquite and a pretty little cluster of live oaks webbed with Spanish moss. The owner didn't care if Wyatt tilled the corner of the lot and put in a vegetable bed—not like much had survived the heat and the bugs, but again, they were ours. We'd started grocery shopping and meal planning together, referring to ourselves in the third person as Tate's parents. If I closed my eyes, if I let my mind go there, being married gave me butterflies, and not in a bad way. "You could ride with my dad or Leroy," I said.

"That's okay," he said, watching me chug the rest of the smoothie and grope around the living room for my keys. "Be careful, okay? You had a long night."

"I know. Love you," I said, voice wobbling dangerously as I walked to the door. I did my best to keep going, to look straight ahead. Closed the door sharply, quickly so Tate wouldn't run out, and hurried to the bullet. I dialed Clint and he didn't answer, drove again to his house and didn't see his truck. Idling at a railroad crossing, waiting for the arm to go back up, I watched the birds gather and bounce on the telephone wires. Cowbirds like bits of black lint, like the intruding images sticking to my thoughts the minute I let my guard down. Things that scared me, like losing someone. Like specks of blood on the wall. An empty whiskey bottle on its side. A patchwork quilt draped over the couch. The scuffed soles of his boots. One of his boots was loose, I remembered, halfway off his foot.

I made a U-turn. Headed west, toward the county line and Branch Creek.

When I pulled up in front of Lorena Mott's house, I realized I had no clue what I would say to her. That I didn't quite believe her son had killed himself? I wanted to tell her how sorry I was about Cody. But also, I wanted to escape this unreality. This sense that no one cared about him dying. The sheriff ruling his death a suicide just didn't sit right—why was his boot halfway off like that? Why was the front door open? How was I here in the bullet, driving, just going on about my life—how else would the sky be blue and ordinary if this wasn't actually a nightmare? My desire to see Lorena was partly selfish, then: a weird mix of me chasing the high of last night and a need to feel seen in my distress. When I saw her sitting on the front porch steps, I felt a pull and snap, metal meeting magnet.

I raised my hand in greeting, remembering how she'd shooed me with a can of mace last time. She lifted her chin again, daring me, her gaze drifting over my shoulder. I turned and saw the old woman I'd spoken to from across the street out on her porch, desperately trying to get Lorena's attention. Her arms flapped over her head as she yelled, "Lorena, you alright!"

Lorena cupped her hands around her mouth and hollered it was okay. Mrs. Flores had lost a child, too, I remembered. Her pretty daughter, Faye. Unable to hear Lorena, maybe, she hollered again, her voice wheezy and indecipherable, and I realized she was now pointing at me. The look on her face was one of pure contempt; she beamed me for a good long moment. I must've really set her off the other day—she'd either been stewing this long or was still that worried I'd tell Lorena she'd been running her mouth.

"Who are you and what do you want?" Lorena said. She had a mug on the concrete next to her, a cigarette with a lazy stream of smoke curling around her hand.

"To talk about your son Cody," I said. "May I please come up there?"

She gripped the metal railing on the porch and heaved herself up to standing. Still in her nightclothes, a man's undershirt and boxer shorts billowed around her in a sudden gust of wind. Her thin legs shook, and her swollen, tearstained face tightened to a grimace. "I asked who you are. I remember you come around here the other day."

"Annie," I said. "I'm a private investigator, and I was originally here on behalf of your other son, Clint—"

"Girl, are you kidding me? Get out of here."

"I'm sorry, I—"

"Listen, now, because I'll only tell you once. I can't change the past," she said, her voice cracking on the last syllable. She put her arm out to stop me from coming any closer, and sobbed, drawing in a hiss of air. "If I could change anything, anything at all, it would be to bring my Cody back."

"I'm really, really sorry for your loss," I said, inching closer to the porch. "I actually met Cody the other day. And last night, I was there on the scene—I'm the one who found him."

Her head snapped up. "What the hell do you mean 'on the scene'? I could tell Cody wasn't acting right, not acting himself these past couple weeks. Maybe ever since you came bringing up things that shouldn't be . . ." She trailed off, hitting another crying jag. "The cops aren't going to do a fucking thing to find out what really happened, but *I* will."

"What did the cops tell you?" I said, my heart thumping.

"That he killed himself," she said, her chin quivering. "But I don't believe it."

I stared at her a moment, sweat starting to bead on my hairline. I was afraid to push her too hard, afraid she'd shut down—

"That note they gave me, it's bull crap," she said, shaking as she pulled it from her waistband. The paper looked torn off from a yellow legal pad, wrinkled and limp from being held tight. Lorena balled it in her fist, reading aloud from memory. *"Dear Mom*—first off, he ain't called me mom. Ever. When he was a little thing he called me momma, but never mom. He called me Lorena, so judge me or whatever, but he's never called me mom. Hell, I might've believed he killed himself if he *hadn't* written me a note. He'd have never planned a thing this far out—maybe if he was high again or so far out of his right mind, but like this? With this lame-ass note and his place all tidied up? Never."

"You said he wasn't acting himself—"

"Yeah, so? He was off, but he wasn't off like that!"

"What do you think happened?"

"That someone shot him and fooled with his body! Fuck, I don't know how or who'd have done that, though," she said, and her face hardened like Quikrete, like an overdone imitation of a grieving woman's face. So stiff and wildly contorted with rage I had to take a step back. She paused, wagging a bony finger at me. "But I think if I find out *you* had something to do with this, girl, I'll kill you myself."

"I didn't hurt Cody, my God," I said, raising my voice. "Why would I be here now if that were the case?"

"I wouldn't trust you as far as I could throw you," she said, wiping her nose with the arm of her shirt. "Just leave me be, damn it."

The sun filtered through the trees, shimmering like hot metal. "Fine," I said, and walked off, shoulders tightening at the sound of her continuing to cuss me out. Nearly back to the bullet, I looked to my right, around the corner of the yard. Parked in an alley was the burgundy Lincoln—it reminded me Cody's car hadn't been at the complex last night. I spun around to ask Lorena if the Corolla was what he always drove, but she'd gone inside the house, releasing the pit bull from wherever she'd had it penned. The dog pawed the screen and bared its teeth. The sun beat down on me and yet a cold shiver shot up my spine. I hadn't even spoken with Lorena about Clint. The multitude of losses she'd suffered hit me. How she must push it all down, compartmentalize—memories, hard thoughts, and questions—all of it, away. Not so unlike the way she could shut me out now, unwilling to set aside her anger and suspicion and listen to what I had to say. To let me tell her that I believed her.

Chapter Eleven

Ginning up the courage to try Lorena again, I startled when my phone rang. It was Clint's girlfriend, Amanda.

"Hey, thank God," I said, sliding down in the driver's seat. "Sorry to keep calling you, but we were worried when Clint missed the rehearsal. Are you with him? Know what's going on?"

"I haven't seen or talked to him since yesterday afternoon," she said, her voice wobbling. "We broke up."

"Oh, no." I felt bad for her, for him, too, but at the same time relieved. Clint had probably just gone off to sulk last night, not feeling all the happy-wedding stuff, or maybe embarrassed and not wanting to make the evening about him—though, ironically that's exactly what he'd done. "I'm sorry to hear that, Amanda."

"No, I'm sorry. I should've called you back last night, but I just couldn't," she said, sniffing. "Like, hey y'all, here I am at this crappy hotel feeling sorry for myself. Speaking of which, I need to check out—probably goes without saying I'm not coming to the wedding."

"I understand. So, you don't know where Clint might be now?"

She let out a long sigh.

"Are you at La Quinta?" I asked, though that had to be it, if she was in Garnett. It was the only hotel in town, right off the interstate. Well, there was the Palomino Motel next to the Palomino RV and trailer park on the south side, but I couldn't see a girl like Amanda setting foot in there. "I'm not far from you. Go ahead and get packed up, or whatever you need to do, and I'll be in the lobby," I said, and hung up before she could protest. Branch Creek was actually about thirty minutes from the Garnett La Quinta, but I wanted to speak with her in person. Needed to be sure that Clint was okay and get a bead on him before noon. I crossed the county line, dark thoughts gathering like thunderclouds. The neon haloing Cody's long face. Lorena's, contorted with grief, hot with rage. If Cody had been murdered, Clint had better steer clear from his family and the crowds he ran with, at least until I knew more. And I would know more—Lorena was right about the police, even if she was wrong about me. Me, I wasn't going to let a person walk. Not a person who'd been so cold as to shoot a man then forge a note to his damn mother.

Amanda's car was in the side lot. I recognized the VW beetle from the night of the party. It was the aughts-version with the daisy on the dash—bright green, the color of a tart apple. Wearing a sundress and a straw hat, she sat under the awning in front of the valet area—not like there was a valet attendant at the Garnett La Quinta—and watched a group of girls, maybe ten-or eleven-year-olds, in cheer uniforms, walk off a charter bus with duffel bags, glitter spackled on their faces. I parked and joined her on the concrete bench. Despite a patch of shade thrown from the awning, the bench was shockingly hot against my skin. I shifted uncomfortably, pulling down my shorts. Amanda looked at me with a pitiful smile. Close up, I could see through the lenses of her big sunglasses that her eyes were swollen. She took a drag of a cigarette and blew the smoke out in a huff, coughing a little, and stubbing it out when the girls marched in our direction. Unlike Lorena, she struck me as the type who under normal circumstances only smoked a cigarette while drunk and only if it was offered to her. The girls bustled past us, giggling, fiddling with high ponytails.

"My mom used to clip those same big-ass bows right in the center of my head," I said, feeling the sore spot where the barrette used to press against my scalp.

"Least someone was doing your hair," Amanda said drily. "Clint broke up with me, if that's what you were wondering."

"I'm not here to get gossip, honestly. I am trying to keep things in motion for the wedding tonight, though—Clint is Sonny's best man, so it's pretty important he be there today," I said, stopping short of mentioning Cody. I wasn't sure if Clint had ever told Amanda about his birth family search, and didn't feel like it was my place to now.

She cleared her throat. "There's this guy, a friend of ours who's a concert promoter, he has a lake house. Clint went there for a writing retreat a few months ago. It's nice. This guy, he's one of those types who lets everyone play with his toys then immediately calls in a favor"—she raised her eyebrows—"but honestly, that's the only place I can think of that Clint might be if he's not at home. His bandmates are his main group of friends," she said, reaching for her phone in the bag at her feet. "I can ask the guy, hold on."

"Thank you," I said, watching her type out the text, her pale pink acrylics clicking against the screen. "You know, you're still welcome to come to the wedding if you don't feel up to driving eight hours. You could stay at my place."

"Oh, yeah, that wouldn't be weird at all," she said, then seeing in my face that I was serious, smiled weakly. "Thanks, Annie. That's sweet of you. I'm sad, of course, but I'm also furious about how inconsiderate his timing was. I drove all the way down here from Lubbock for the weekend with my bags, had got my nails done, you know? I felt like an idiot. Just couldn't make myself turn right around again. But Jesus, being here all alone was rough. I felt like I was going to die. I'm going to my parents' up home tonight."

I touched my hand to her back and she jerked against me, a sob rocking her whole body. Sweat dripped from the crook of her elbow and had darkened the armholes of her blue cotton dress. I'd had the impression Clint was laying it on thick with the charm, but not this—not so two-faced as to let his girlfriend drive all the way down here thinking they'd have a romantic, celebratory weekend. I didn't see him as this self-involved and quite frankly, as this much of an asshole. "It's going to be okay, Amanda," I said, and reached into my bag for a Kleenex and the frozen water bottle I'd grabbed on my way out that morning, slushy now.

"Thanks," she said, blotting the corner of her eye. Taking the cold plastic bottle to her neck, she looked up at me. "You know I know about you two—that he hired you to find his family. He told me yesterday. I don't know why he didn't say so in the first place."

I bit the inside of my cheek. "It didn't seem like my place to ask."

"Well, it is true that I would've been 'extra' about it from the get-go if he'd told me."

"He didn't say that," I said, looking at my feet to deliver the lie. "Most people who hire me hope to get some kind of control back in their lives. Finding out the truth—whether that's finding out their birth mom or whether or not their spouse is cheating—can be this empowering moment, or it can be even more confusing for a person."

She was a few inches taller than me, and she tilted her head down to study me a moment, her sunglasses sliding and revealing her wet, puffy eyes. "You're a nice girl, Annie. I'm sorry I made you uncomfortable the other night. It wasn't on purpose."

"What do you mean?"

"At the party when I asked you about work. I could see it on your face that I'd put you on the spot," she said, a laugh escaping. "I watch a lot of crime shows. Got too excited."

"No, I get it," I said honestly. Deep down, I think part of me liked to be asked for stories. My cases were stories in my head already—how I made sense of a nonsense world. What scared me was that I might not do the telling right. That no one would understand me or what these cases meant. What if no one cared? Or worse, what if I was understood perfectly—if I tossed out my heart and no one caught it? It was better to keep some things sealed. I smiled at Amanda, lightly touching her arm. "Maybe Clint just needs to figure out what all this family stuff means. Sounds like it's him, not you."

"I thought us both being adopted was this thing we had connected over, but whatever. I'm not mad about that. I'm more, like, surprised. He told me who his dad is, the bank robber? That's crazy."

"That had to be a big shock for him."

"Yeah. It's why he broke up with me. I mean, that's not all of it—we'd also been having growing pains being long-distance. I wanted him to move back to Lubbock and he wasn't ready to make a decision. I think he wanted to stay in his dad's house and fix it up."

He hadn't told her about Nashville, then.

"At some point you feel like you can't make someone enjoy your company," she said, her face reddening. She cracked open the water bottle. "Anyway, I got down here and he told me everything about his birth family search. After we argued about him keeping me in the dark for this long, he cuts me off"—she made air quotes—"and says he needs to take time to reexamine who he is now, alone. As if *I* would just wait around? I told him to take all the time he wanted. Left out the door and slammed it in his face."

"Wow."

Her lip quivered. "Guess you've figured out by now he didn't come after me."

I let her words hang in the air a moment. If I was her, I would've said and done the same thing—or liked to imagine that I would have—and yet, I detected a false note. Couldn't see her walking out the door as she'd described. She had pride, I got that. But there was something about the way she sat here tensed, how her movements were so tight. She'd had this same look about her the night of the show—she, just like Cody, had had this intensity as she gazed upon him, a flare in her eyes. Desire and disgust. Amanda was jealous of Clint, and I thought she likely had been for some time.

"The nicer part of me understands and wants to give him space. Let him come back to me," she said, fanning her neck. "But I don't know."

I nodded along, not sharing my growing sense that this split might be good for both of them. You could get over being a jealous lover, probably. Could salvage the relationship with trust and with time. Jealousy was close kin to envy, though, and how far was that from bitterness, spite? But I didn't know what I didn't know—I'd only just met Amanda, and Clint, too, for that matter. I did know that I needed to talk to him. Get him to be straight with me. Not about the breakup, but about our case and what he'd taken away from it. About Cody. I felt suddenly like every nerve ending was firing right under my skin. "Amanda, did Clint tell you if he'd actually spoken with any of his biological relatives?"

"Yeah, he did," she said, then shook her head sadly. "Didn't go well at all. He found his mother and went to her house. She told him that he was a mistake."

"Oh, God—"

"I know. I don't know what he was expecting, forcing a confrontation with the woman like that, but she should've been nicer to him. He apparently has full siblings—oh, but you already knew that—uh, but no, he's not met them. Don't think he's tried talking to his father in prison, either."

"His brother Cody died. You're sure that Clint hadn't had anything to do with him recently?"

Amanda's mouth hung open. "Seriously? What happened?"

"It's unclear," I said, waffling for a second. "But he was found dead in his apartment."

"That's awful. I don't know for sure I guess, but I really think Clint would've said if he'd ever met the guy, since he told me about his birth mom and all. When he hears about this, he'll be heartbroken," she said, a tear trailing down from under her sunglasses again. "That's so sad. And, like, what if Clint had found out about his family even just a month earlier? He might've reconnected with him. You have to wonder."

"It's a shame," I said.

Her phone pinged. "Oh, maybe that's him—Clint's friend, I mean," she said, pulling it from her bag. "I bet you anything he's at that stupid lake house." She wiped her face, holding out her phone so we could read the text at the same time.

Nope, haven't seen him was all it said.

Chapter Twelve

"You have got to sit still," my aunt said, aiming the curling iron at me.

"You're slinging that dang mimosa around," I said, touching my finger to the burn mark on my neck.

Sherrilyn laughed, reaching for the plastic champagne flute. "Lord, it does go to my head. Anything with bubbles," she said, and after a healthy swig, she wound another section of my bone-straight hair around the iron. Whatever flowery product she'd massaged through it was starting to smell like hot glue sticks. My mother plopped into the chair next to mine and patted my knee, but I was watching Nikki. She and the other bridesmaids held court at the back of the salon, their conversation drowned out by a nineties country playlist, a burst of laughter cutting through Shania on blast. By the time I'd left the hotel, I was already late—when I'd hurried through the bubblegum-pink doors of the Beauty Shoppe, Nikki had shot me a mean look and said, "Girl, get your butt in that chair. We're on a schedule and I don't want to argue."

I'd swallowed my pride. Nikki and I hadn't even talked

about Clint. Maybe she cared less than I thought, or hell, maybe she really was this mad at me. Momma reached for a roller brush and proceeded to fluff the hair on her crown. There's a stereotype about Texas women and big hair, which, at least for the women in my family, rang true. Few worse insults you could lob at a person than to say her hair was thin or that it looked stuck to her head. Momma stared into the mirror until she caught my eye. "Remember how you and me argued something awful that summer before you started college?"

"Sure, I was a bit of brat," I said. I'd blown up at her at Mervyn's of all places. Packing to head off to the private college I'd gotten into on scholarship, and she'd wanted to take me back-to-school shopping one last time. We'd never really *fought* fought before, and she'd looked so shocked when I argued with her over this pair of dumb, name-brand, full-price jeans. She couldn't afford them, but I didn't care; those jeans were going to fix everything that was ever wrong with me, make me a newer, hotter, all-around better person, armored and ready for whatever was coming that fall. She'd relented, and later, horrified with myself, I hardly ever wore them.

Momma laughed. "You were more than a bit of one. But I'm talking about you and your cousin! Sweet pea, she's acting out at you to make it easier on you both when she's married."

Sherrilyn pointed the iron at me again. "That's right, it's psychological. She wants to ease the separation. She loves you is all."

"Whatever. She's getting married, not moving away," I said, and sighed, feeling my shoulders loosen a little. At least I wasn't just imagining Nikki's attitude toward me had changed. But something smaller, harder had lodged itself inside me—I really was afraid of losing her and the thought made my throat close up.

Momma clicked her tongue. "Sonny and his brother—now, I don't know about *that* relationship."

My great-aunt Jewel, who'd said she was "just resting her eyes" while she sat under the dryer, suddenly perked up. The woman loved a good bitch sesh. "I tell you what, it's plain disrespectful," she said. "Not that I minded doing the catering, I didn't, but that boy wasted my dime last night. Whole plate of good food. Rude is what it is. Poor Sonny. That's all I have to say to have a brother who treats him like that."

My lips parted. They knew I'd gone searching for Clint last night, but not what else had happened. Despite my chosen profession I wasn't a natural liar, especially when it came to my mother, my aunts, or Nikki.

Sherrilyn saw my lip twitch, had started to say something, but trailed off as her eyes drifted to the shop window. "Speak of the devil, there's Dee now. I told her and the grandmother to come get ready with us girls. Lord knows Dee needs the help. I've been dying to fix her foundation, it's like two shades off. She looks like a little ghost."

Sherrilyn didn't dislike Sonny and Clint's mother, but she acted like it was us versus them when it came to the idea of Nikki having in-laws. Talk about armchair psychology. My family has always been loyal and clannish. Nikki and Sonny's whirlwind engagement—I wasn't the only one in my family who'd given her crap about it—didn't seem to bother Sonny's people, which struck us all as suspicious. Also, Nikki apparently had already starting calling Dee "Mom," which really set Sherrilyn off.

"Hey there!" Dee said as the bell above the door tinkled, and Nikki hopped up to give her and Sonny and Clint's grandma a big hug, pulling the women over to hang with the brides-maids. But pale, ghostlike Dee lingered at the door. Tiny and round, her hair was a nest of springy curls cut chin-length, her highlights to cover up grays now taking up most of the real estate. Momma perched on the counter and offered the salon chair to her.

"Tina, Sherrilyn, good to see y'all," Dee said.

Momma smiled. "Hey, hon, good to see you, too."

Dee turned to me. "Annie, my gosh, with your hair done up like that you and your cousin could be twins," she said with a little shrug of the shoulders. She wore a stretchy, baby-blue top and matching, floral-printed capri pants with tassels on the hems. Pink pudgy feet crammed into white kitten heels. She looked like an adult-sized Shirley Temple.

"Thanks," I said. "Can't believe it's the big day." Seeing Sonny and Clint's mother right now felt like meeting the friend of a friend you've stalked on Instagram. Like having to pretend you've no idea what their dog's name is or that they just came back from vacation. Despite knowing Clint was adopted, I could see something of him in her. Their smiles, maybe. How she tilted her chin and raised her eyebrows. Like how long-married couples seem to look alike, maybe the same was true of adoptive families. I wasn't sure if Clint had told her about his birth family. Fairly certain it was no, given how adamant he was that I leave her out of my research.

"I know! I can't believe these kids—no offense, Annie," Dee said, laughing. "That these actual children are getting married, y'all! I certainly don't feel that old."

Aunt Jewel and Momma laughed, and Sherrilyn poured her a mimosa. "Girl, you're telling me. Now, what do you want me to do with your hair and makeup? I'm almost done with Annie's."

"Oh, I'm already ready!"

Momma and Sherrilyn locked eyes in the mirror and smiled at the same time. "Oh, of course," Sherrilyn said. "You look great. Very relaxed."

Either oblivious or choosing to ignore the slight, Dee again did that little shoulder shrug, which I was beginning to think was a tic. "Well, I already apologized to Nikki, but I should apologize to you all, too. I'm sorry about Clint not coming last night. I still haven't been able to reach him today. I did talk with him yesterday, though. He was upset because he'd been having problems with his girlfriend. Think he was going to rip the Band-Aid off and break up with her. They'd been together for over a year."

Sherrilyn frowned. "We were only worried about him. Is that like him to not answer his phone? I mean, Nikki's glued to hers."

"Honestly, yes," Dee said, and her face crumpled a bit. "It scares me when he does it, but he kind of goes silent when he hits a snag. Bless his heart, Clint's struggled with depression and anxiety ever since he was a teenager."

Momma and Sherrilyn made sympathetic noises, but Aunt Jewel pitched forward from under the dryer. "What? Depressed? What's he got to be down about?" she said, and my face reddened. I couldn't stand to look at Jewel when she acted this obtuse, which was fairly often.

"It's a complicated disease, ma'am, and it got worse after my ex-husband passed," Dee said stoically, glancing between the three of them, her hands folded in her lap. She looked like she was on trial. "I should've recognized that clearly, he's been struggling. He told me last week he thought someone was following him. Just paranoid, you know."

My stomach did a quick flip.

"He seemed to be feeling better, but then yesterday he tells me he's breaking up with Amanda because he's not wanting to be tied down. Said he's trying to make moves with his music, that he might be going to Nashville. I was surprised about Amanda, such a nice girl, and I argued with him about it, not seeing this shakeup for what it is, which is a distress signal."

"Oh, my," said Momma, and placed her hand on Dee's shoulder. "What can we do?"

"I don't know," she said. "Figure he's embarrassed. He'll rally for the wedding, though. He wouldn't abandon Sonny."

I was sweating bullets under the black cape. I could say something about his birth family search, about Cody even, but stopped—Dee only needed to know where Clint was and if he was okay. I didn't see how hurting her feelings would help now. It occurred to me that Clint telling her he'd leave Texas wasn't exactly the erratic behavior she seemed to think it was, given he'd told me as much on the day he'd hired me. It sounded like what Clint had done was what Momma had been trying to say about me and Nikki. You hurt people to make yourself hurt less, to get out with less remorse. All this talk of Clint's depression made me wonder now if Cody had suffered, too. Depression ran in families—what if Lorena simply didn't want to see that Cody had the disease? The spark in the back of my mind, the needling, livid voice telling me the suicide designation wasn't right—was that a false flag?

"We understand, Dee," said Sherrilyn, genuine sympathy in her voice this time. "No need to worry just yet, hon."

She misted my head with hair spray. The beachy waves she'd created were now lacquered into place, and the baby hairs matted to my forehead pulled against my skin when I smiled at her in the mirror. Though flammable, my hair did look great. "Lots of volume," I said. "Thank—"

"Hey, y'all, I just got this from Sonny," Nikki interrupted, hurrying over to stand behind my chair. "Apparently Clint texted him a few minutes ago."

"Thank you, Jesus," Dee whispered.

Nikki's raised her chin in Dee's direction. "Yeah, well, apparently Mr. Big Time told Sonny he's not going to make it. That he has a chance to write with some producer in Nashville this weekend and that he has to go. That's all he said—not even that he's sorry!"

"Is Sonny real upset?" Momma asked, squeezing Nikki's shoulder.

"'Course he is. This is a real dick move," Nikki said, and immediately put her hand to her mouth. "I'm sorry, Mrs. Marshall. I didn't mean that—"

"It's alright, honey. Lord, these boys. Y'all excuse me," Dee said, looking at her feet as she scrambled down from the salon chair. "I'll be out here, Momma, I need to make a call," she hollered at Sonny's grandma, who was still sitting toward the back.

"I didn't mean to offend her, but come on," Nikki said after the door shut.

"Clint's not well," Momma said. "Apparently he's been struggling with his depression."

"Sonny's feelings matter, too!"

I watched Dee through the window. She hid under the awning of the laundromat next door, pressed the phone to her ear, and I felt a surge of gratitude on Clint's behalf. I shouldn't pretend to know the deal with Lorena, but I did know Clint was likely lucky to have gained a parent in Dee. What made Clint's and Cody's paths so different at the end of the day, if not partly for the difference between their mothers? Of the world they came up in? I got out of the chair and went outside. The call either ended quickly, or he—Clint or Sonny, I assumed—didn't answer.

"I'm sorry," I said, sidling up to her. "This has to be extra stressful for you being in the middle."

"I heard what you do," she said. Her face looked drawn, tired in the off-color light of the yellow awning. "Sonny told us. Now, Clint would see me coming a mile away and get mad if I were to go after him, but maybe you could do it quietly for me. I know he'll call once he gets back from his trip, but Lord help me, what if he doesn't?"

Not coming clean now was actually making me sick—my mouth tasted sour, the mimosa rising in my throat—and I swallowed hard.

"I can pay you for your time. I'm just a mom, you know, I'll always be a little worried about him, no matter how big he gets," she said, and her eyes turned glassy with tears. But there was also a steeliness to her gaze, the way she held mine. She loved Clint, no matter how badly he'd messed up, hurt her feelings, or embarrassed her, and I wondered if he knew that. Really knew that.

"Don't worry about money," I said. "I'll talk to him."

"Between you and me, Annie, I understand Clint's decision and would do the same. Big opportunities don't come around twice. You have to take what's yours. I always told him, no one's going to help you if you don't help yourself."

I opened my mouth, caught off guard by her comment. Bit my tongue to stop myself from saying anything tacky, or that I thought it sounded selfish. If I'd have done what Clint did, my mother would've lit into me. Thinking so made me feel like a scold. Kind of like Aunt Jewel any time we ate out. She'd get worked up over kids at other tables ripping the menus without recrimination, or coloring on the walls, then point out the parents exhibiting a variety of dipshit behaviors, like being rude to the waiter. She liked to say it's a hard thing to escape your raising, and I couldn't help but agree with her.

Chapter Thirteen

A front blew in right as we were leaving the salon, a stroke of good luck. Not too humid, only the memory of the earlier, wilting heat left lingering in the stillness, in the crunch of dead grass under high heels. Time had gone so slowly until that moment, when everything seemed to speed up, when the ceremony was really happening and there was no going back. The wedding went too quickly for how long we'd been waiting it seemed, and when it was over, a moonless night shrouding the pavilion, I felt stunned. I tried to forget all that was happening in time and space outside my universe of friends, family, and the twinkly-lit rodeo fairgrounds wrapped in pretty paper streamers. But the lines had blurred. Cody and his death weren't so removed from the flushed cheeks, the laughter, a night so full of life. It wasn't only his connection to Clint—whose absence felt like a presence in itself—but the ways the past kept overlapping.

The robbery twenty-six years ago was another presence in the room. At the reception, Dee clocked Leroy, recognizing him as the sheriff who'd saved her life that fateful day. I saw them talking at the buffet, and idled in front of tinfoil trays of brisket and vats of cole slaw to eavesdrop. Notes of admiration and thanks from her, bashful platitudes from him. No mention of the outlaw Ronnie Mott or of Clint's blood relation. Dee sat alone at her table after their brief conversation, her mind clearly elsewhere. She sat with her lips pursed through the speeches, until it was time to dance with Sonny, and even then, she seemed self-conscious, hyperaware of how people were watching.

For the past year—being home, working this job—I'd been trying to hold the love and the grief I felt over people and ghosts equally and at once, not pretending that one cancels out the other. It was hard. Drink-induced or not, for a moment I was able to get down to the layer underneath the love and the grief, to the place that's simply being. The place that's sitting under the pavilion waiting for the fan to complete its rotation, tasting a brown sugar scrim left on my lips after the last bite of cake, to Leroy sitting at the table telling me and Wyatt a story about how the river used to freeze over thick enough that he could walk across water. Listening so intently I felt the fragile blue wonder under my own feet, could picture the faintest crack in its mirrorlike surface.

Early Sunday morning, our doorbell rang. I woke from an open-mouthed, flatline sleep and stared at my phone—it wasn't even nine yet. Peeking through the curtains, I saw a Garnett County Sheriff's Department vehicle parked in the driveway and my heartbeat kicked up. Hands skating over the carpet, I grabbed my bridesmaid dress from where I'd flung it off last night and pulled it over my head. Shook Wyatt's arm to wake him, but he groaned and rolled onto his stomach. The doorbell rang again, and I hurried into the hall.

I opened the door wide, blinking in the bright sun. Sheriff Garcia looked like he'd been pulled out of Mass, wearing dress pants instead of his usual jeans, no cowboy hat. Standing slightly to the side of him was a second, younger man wearing a black windbreaker. I guessed he was also a cop by his neutral but tense facial expressions, eyes roving side to side. Sheriff Garcia and my family went far back, him being Leroy's successor, and we'd worked together on two recent cases. I knew him to be loud and blustery, prone to good-old-boy asides, and worried why his face was this somber. He must've come to deliver bad news—an accident, I worried—and tears rose quickly in my eyes. But Garcia shook his head. "Oh, no, hon, everyone's okay. We're coming by on account of you. Mr. Howland here's an agent with the DEA."

I'd been so scared I hadn't noticed that the man's jacket said as much, that his ball cap also had the agency's logo above the bill.

"Trent Howland," the man said, extending his hand. His grip was flimsy, the kind Dad would've corrected me on as a kid. He didn't seem to want to be on my doorstep this early, either.

I led them inside. Garcia looked toward the couch and I nodded, motioning them to sit. Manners and such, I figured I should offer them something to drink, but all we had in the fridge was milk and a single beer. I looked toward the kitchen. "Water?"

They declined, and I sank into the recliner opposite them. Given our relationship, Garcia should've called me before showing up like this. This felt weirdly confrontational. And I felt uneasy with them seeing me un-showered, in last night's wrinkled dress and no bra, with mascara and black liner smudged under my eyes. I looked—and probably smelled—like a racoon who'd rolled in a puddle of vodka.

Garcia frowned. "Name Eli Wallace ring a bell?"

I couldn't tell if he was being sarcastic. The wave of nausea I'd been fighting since they got here rose in my throat. "I saw him the other day. Not sure he saw me."

"I meant to come warn you he's back in town," Garcia said, and I stopped myself from making a snarky comment about a handy new invention called the cell phone. Hell, there's even text. My head throbbed. I hated myself when I drank too much—not so dissimilar from the self-loathing I felt when I let myself feel scared. When I let myself into the back room in my mind where such thoughts might paralyze me. Last spring, Eli Wallace had escaped prosecution despite a major raid on his place that turned up weapons and counterfeit opioids. Hearing rumors that I was responsible for the tip-off, he'd threatened to teach me a lesson, bragging about it to his cellmate while he was in county lockup. And yet, he'd left town not long after he was released. I honestly wasn't sure what to think after I'd seen him at the pool hall. Maybe I'd let myself relax too much these past two weeks when I hadn't seen more signs of him.

"Where was this sighting?" the agent asked me.

"Cowboys, out near the county line."

"Here's the deal," he said, his eyes darting over my shoulder. Wyatt had started making noises from the back of the house, and he lowered his voice a notch. "My unit is building up a case against Wallace. He's been on my radar for a while now, but recently we traced back lethal doses of fentanyl to pills he distributed. One of the deceased was fifteen, another, thirteen. It's my understanding from the sheriff here that you witnessed his counterfeit opioid production?"

"Yes," I said, looking at Garcia. "Like I told the sheriff, I saw what I believed to be a pill press on the property. I saw cash, drugs, handguns stored in an old woodstove. I also witnessed a violent assault on another man that day."

Garcia cleared his throat. "Would you be willing to testify down the line?"

"You'd be doing the right thing," the agent said quickly, slightly bumping Garcia's knee with his. I figured I didn't have a choice if subpoenaed, but Garcia must've thought differently or was worried. Eli Wallace was from a long line of semi-organized criminals, and I'd be on the family's shit list for the rest of my natural life if I testified against one of their own. Eli's grandfather, famous for selling moonshine and smuggling speed up from Mexico back in the seventies, was currently serving two consecutive life sentences for murdering a cop. Eli's dad, Doug Wallace, was less known, but still dirty. His liquor store on the county line was a front for the family's illegal activities, if I had to guess. Eli had most recently done time—manslaughter—after killing someone in a bar fight.

"Eli Wallace was responsible for the arson a few weeks ago," the agent said. "The fire that killed a man in his trailer. The victim had owed the Wallaces money and there was some petty double-crossing going on. He's a threat to society and we need to get him off the streets."

I could still smell the smoke, feel the sting of it in my eyes. The flume stark black against the soft, sunset-faded sky. Last spring, the stash house had also been half-burnt to the ground. An old house in the middle of nowhere coated in ash. "Why haven't you arrested him, then?" I asked.

"Because he didn't actually set the fire himself, another

man did. We caught this kid with the same accelerant, have footage of him, even a witness," Garcia said. "It was a sloppy hit, but a hit. This young man is a known soldier for Wallace. We arrested him, charged him with homicide last night."

Wyatt poked his head out of the bedroom. I shook my head and he nodded, closing the door softly. His curly hair was standing on end and his hazel eyes warm, sleepy-looking—I would've given anything to be back there with him. I felt like I was the one in trouble somehow. The agent speaking to me like I was dense, for one. Like all I needed to cooperate was to hear talk of "threats to society" and "the streets," maybe throw in a toy badge. I wanted Eli Wallace to pay for the poison he'd let leach into our town. For ordering another man's death, if that was true. Hell, what if he was connected with Cody? With his death? But I also wished I could skip back in time, squeeze my eyes shut and it be yesterday, or earlier, before I ever saw his bony face in the neon light of the pool hall. I felt a surge of adrenaline along with this fear. Felt like when I was a kid jumping in the river even though I'd heard thunder, then paddling, panting with fear when lightning inevitably streaked the sky. Was the rush, this chance to do the right thing, worth the risk? I tugged the silky hem of my dress down toward my knees, meeting the agent's gaze.

"I'm prepared to help you, sir, but honestly, I'm afraid of the potential for retribution," I said.

"Atta girl. Excellent," he said, smile forming on his thin lips. "And no, I'm not so sure you'd have to worry. The Wallace family isn't as, ah, organized as they used to be. You're honestly more in danger the longer Eli himself is walking free," he said, looking at a spot on the wall just over my head—not willing to lie to my face, apparently.

"You just said that he ordered a man be burnt alive."

Garcia's face was impassive now, but his eyes flicked over to mine, betraying his anxiety. "We'll bring Wallace in," he said, letting go a tight sigh. "It's really a matter of if they'll be able to build a big enough case to keep him locked up. You're clearly a part of this already, Annie, whether you want to be or not."

"I'll do whatever you need me to," I said. "But let me know what's going on—I don't want to be blindsided again."

The agent's smile tightened. "Fair enough."

"Communication goes both ways," Garcia said, studying me a moment. "Now, what I really want to know is why on earth Mary-Pat had me pull that license plate for you—"

"That's right," I said quickly, remembering the truck from Cody's apartment complex. The same black F-150 I thought I'd recognized from the VFW. I scooted forward on the cushion. "Well, whose is it?"

"I think you're in more hot water than you realize," he said, lines creasing his forehead. "Shoot, girl, that truck is registered to Eli Wallace."

Chapter Fourteen

After Garcia's SUV pulled out, slow-rolling down the dirt road like they were afraid of a little dust, I got in the shower. Tried washing away the stickiness, but couldn't seem to get clean. The night I'd seen Eli Wallace at his stash house, he'd assaulted a man with the butt of his pistol, a skull-cracking whip upside the head that'd left the man bleeding and concussed. Nearly killed him. Wasn't the first time I'd witnessed violence up close, but it was the first time I'd seen that kind of coldness. Eli hadn't flinched, not once. He seemed to me the kind of person who sees others as falling into one of two categories, useful or inconvenient—I already knew which column I landed in. I dressed in jeans and a plain black shirt, no makeup. I'd shampooed twice to rid my hair of back-combed tangles and perfumey spray. Wyatt was at the kitchen table waiting for me with more coffee.

"Don't understand why they think what you saw at the stash house will make a case now when it didn't seem to matter before," he said, rubbing his temples. "Damn, I don't know what I was thinking last night."

"Wasn't much thinking going on," I said, and seeing the aspirin was already out on the table, shook two loose from the bottle. "And no, I don't think they think my testimony alone would be enough to charge anyone. Might help corroborate their case, but actually, I'm pretty sure that DEA guy wants to use me as live bait."

"What?"

"Why else come to my house to introduce himself? And not exactly inconspicuously with that jacket and hat on when it's like ninety out," I said. "He's fishing. Thinks someone might tell Eli I'm talking with the DEA, get him mad enough that he'll take a swipe at me himself."

Wyatt's eyes were glassy and bloodshot. I could tell he was frightened.

"Maybe I'm not bait, but I do think their plan is to kick up a hornet's nest," I said, grabbing my bag and my keys from where I'd dumped them on a chair last night. Now that I knew it was his truck I'd seen at the complex, at the VFW, I was sure Eli had already tried threatening me once. The matchbook with the *X* under the flap—fire was Eli's calling card, wasn't it? I felt for it along the inner lining of my purse, wishing I'd never touched it in the first place. And seeing his truck at Cody's place meant what exactly? I wasn't sure if it had been there when I first arrived, or only later, while I was being interviewed. "When I explained to Garcia about Cody, he agreed I should tell the sheriff over in Price. I'm going to see if I can talk to her now."

"You need to sit down and eat something before you take off. I'll make us a quick plate of toast," Wyatt said. "I'm worried about you, Annie. You get all weird and mean when I say so, but I am."

Why couldn't he just say that then—that he worried?

Wyatt loved me, that was all. I loved him, too, but it bothered me how he never knew how to express his frustration
about being on the outside of things. At least that's what I
thought it was. I talked to him about work, but he wasn't
actively part of my cases—and whether that was to keep him
safe, my pride, or the little voice inside that kept part of me
for me, I wanted it to stay that way. He was right, though, I
did get defensive, hated being patronized. "I shouldn't take
my stress out on you," I said. "I'm sorry."

"It's okay," he said, rubbing his temples again. There was
something else he wanted to say, but he'd changed his mind.

"I think we both have low blood sugar."

He nodded and went to the fridge. I stared at the mess on
the table. Last night I'd been awake for an hour or so around
two with the unfocused anxiety of the drunk and the chronically sleepless, thinking—out of all the things I had to worry
about—how I still needed to find that photograph of my great-
great-grandmother and frame it for Leroy. Couldn't go back
to bed until I'd dug out Mamaw's Avon kit from the closet,
the box where she'd stored her photos and letters. I'd left it
sitting out on a pile of junk mail and Wyatt's school papers. I
slid a finger under the lid of the box now and it sprung open,
contents packed tight. Toward the bottom the pictures were
older, and below that were a few folded magazines, and *The
Garnett Signal* issue spotlighting my graduation. I came to
a small, black-and-white photo dated March 1953, its edges
curled and yellowed. A hunched, sharp-boned woman sitting
on the steps of a house, the view behind her of the escarpment. It was her—Sarah Anne, out on the place.

Sarah Anne had died in the mid-fifties, so this must've
been taken not long before. Her long white braid had made a
crown around her head, loose strands flew wildly in the wind

and across her mouth, the look on her deeply-lined face one of surprise. She wore a checkered housedress, white sneakers, and tube socks that sagged around her ankles. The other photo—the one with her hat and silver star—was the famous one I'd been wanting. I didn't see it here now, and part of me wondered if the picture I'd been dreaming of was really her.

After breakfast, I drove to Price County. Pressed the pedal down hard when I hit open highway, anticipation propelling me westward. When Sheriff Krause heard what I had to say, she'd be as certain Cody didn't commit suicide. The station was located in the town of Price, a squat, colorless brick building that loomed at the narrowing of a dead-end street. The area surrounding was mostly oil fields and wide swaths of ranchland. Only an hour or so outside Garnett, but it seemed so much drier here, more struck by the harsh drought. The trees looked ashen, shrunken in comparison. The wind stilled, only rust-colored pumpjacks left nodding on the horizon.

I got out of the bullet and walked toward the station. The front that had blown in teased rain, and the outside air was dog breath. I felt disoriented again, not in the hungover kind of way. Like how I'd felt yesterday when we were driving over to the rodeo fairgrounds—that time was on fast-forward—but now, this sense that events were happening beyond my control made my heartbeat skittery.

"I'm Annie McIntyre, here to see Sheriff Krause," I said to the young woman at the front desk, shivering at the blast of polar air-conditioning. "She needed me to give a witness statement, and I hoped I might have a word." The station was laid out like Garnett County's, with a big center room half-filled with cheap, office supply desks and cubicle dividers, a hallway toward the back leading to the closed-door rooms. The jail cell was in a separate building behind this one. It smelled like the communal coffeepot was low and starting to burn to the bottom.

The receptionist smiled nervously, glancing over her shoulder as if to locate the source of my concern. "Sign in here, and I'll go see if she's available," she said, taking her mug with her. Toward the back of the empty station stood two deputies, one of whom had been on the scene Friday night. I nodded my head in acknowledgment, but he didn't seem to recognize me. I only caught snippets of the conversation, the upcoming football season and coded bits of police-talk.

Sheriff Krause came out into the hallway and waved me back. Smiling now, her shoulders had relaxed. "You're lucky you caught me, Annie. I don't normally come in on Sunday, but I have a luncheon at the Baptist church in an hour and needed to pick up my presentation. I'll get you the statement form and you can fill it out in here."

Mugs stained with brown rings and lipstick marks had been left on every available surface in her office. Lean Cuisine boxes sat stacked in the trash can and their cheesy cardboard smell hung in the air. A matted hairbrush and a crusty, capless bottle of lotion had been left on the desk. All of this at odds with her appearance, a pressed, navy suit in a flattering cut, her hair in the same sleek bun as it had been on Friday night. She cleared her throat in a slightly embarrassed way, shuffling back behind the desk. "Grab a seat, if you can find it."

"Thanks," I said, taking the chair opposite hers, careful not to crush her dry-cleaning bag. "I know you told me to come by Monday, but I needed to sooner, now that I'm not so sure that Cody Mott died by suicide."

Her eyebrows shot up. "Well, Annie, that's not the medical

examiner's determination and I'm inclined to agree with the expert on this."

"Let me explain. You see, a man was arrested over in Garnett for setting fire to a man's trailer, burning him to death. This man, he works for a drug dealer named Eli Wallace. I'm sure you've heard that name," I said, and when she didn't react, I found myself talking faster. "The night I met Cody, we went to a bar, he saw Wallace there, and said in not so many words he was afraid of him. Then, the next day, I see Cody at a concert, and I also spot Eli's truck. The night he died, right as I was leaving the apartments, I saw the truck again. So, I'm thinking, what if Cody was a target like the man in the trailer? When I saw Cody's body, I noticed one of his boots had been loose, like maybe someone had dragged him, and—"

"I didn't see that."

"Okay," I said, wondering why she'd cut me off. Maybe she thought I was criticizing her—and I wasn't—but I needed to say my piece. "Well, Cody's mother said she didn't believe the note was real when I spoke with her. Said it wasn't his voice. Was adamant about that, really. I think all of this merits an investigation, if you're not already thinking the same thing."

She pressed her lips into a tight line. "You're doing a lot of speculating here. I understand it, of course. No one wants to get this kind of news. Loved ones never want to believe it, don't want to wonder why they missed all the signs. They don't want to feel"—she sighed and hung her head—"guilty."

"I'm not Cody's family, or even his friend," I said. "I think I'm being fairly objective here."

"Are you, though? I don't mean to embarrass you, but I'd assumed you two might've, ah, hooked up."

"No, I was seeing him in relation to a case."

"You regularly go back to a person's apartment with them

after the bar, or on Friday night all gussied up like I saw you? Talk with his mother the next morning?" She leaned back in her chair, satisfied she seemed to have caught me out. "I'll take all of this into advisement, but to tell you the truth, Annie, once the manner of death's been ruled it'll take mountains of evidence to move it in a different direction. I'm just not seeing that kind of evidence."

I felt like she'd snapped my skin with a rubber band.

"It's time to give his family some peace. Now, here's the state-ment form," she said, handing a piece of paper across the desk. "More of a formality, but write everything down, take your time, and then sign it of course. You can do it out there and leave the form with Misty. Start at the beginning when you ar-rived at the apartment and go till the moment when you called 911. Make sense?"

I gritted my teeth, nodded to stop myself from saying some-thing I'd regret.

"Good. I'd better get." She stood to let me out. "A Girl Scout troop invited me for a career day thing. Never liked public speaking. Comes with the territory, though."

"Best of luck," I said, not hiding my sarcasm, but she brushed past it, propping the door open with her high-heeled boot. Even if she didn't buy my credibility—I was still too shocked to be embarrassed she'd thought we were hooking up—why was she so set against examining what was going on in Cody's life? Regardless of what I'd told her, seemed to me she ought to do an investigation into *any* unattended death. Maybe my judgment of Sheriff Krause was clouded by what Mary-Pat had said about her, but this whole thing smelled like bullshit. I watched her lock the office, humming a little to herself, and couldn't imagine the two of them as a couple—too similar. The one ex of Mary-Pat's I'd known back when I was a kid was a woman named Lynn. Mary-Pat's opposite, personality-wise, Lynn had been soft-spoken and unguarded. Mary-Pat was, in a word, bracing. Like seeing a streak of blue in an otherwise colorless, cloud-dense sky. Sheriff Krause also struck me as bold, but she wasn't true. Not quite as self-assured as Mary-Pat or as prudent, she seemed harsh in the way self-interest might sharpen a person's edges.

"If you need to talk to someone about what you've experienced, Annie, there's no shame in it," she said, turning to me. "That was a grisly sight whether you cared for Cody or not. Call me later and I'll have Misty find you the number for someone."

She waved goodbye, left, and I did as I was told with the form. Sat in a plastic, hard-backed chair in the lobby and hammered out a statement. Left it with the receptionist like it was a pop quiz I already knew I'd failed.

Standing outside on the sidewalk a moment to collect myself, the heat seeped back into my pores. Cicadas had already started their desperate shrieks, a last stand. You couldn't feel it, but you could sense the ending up ahead. It was hotter now than it would ever be the rest of the year. I knew this more than I felt it—the light was thinner. I could walk away and forget about Cody. This was the point where I could still do that. I used to wish for moments like this, ripe with expectancy—I'd read way too many detective novels and paperback westerns as a kid, wanting to imagine my life as shaped by tests of wits and will. I'd believed in all the shine put on Sarah Anne, on Mary-Pat and Leroy, and wanted for myself this deep, private knowledge.

That morning, I'd lingered at the kitchen table with Wyatt for a few minutes, Sarah Anne's photograph still in my hand. Tate had rubbed against my legs, so I got up and fed him, had started to leave when Wyatt pulled me to him.

"Maybe you're right," I said, face pressed against his chest. "I should lie low. What if the threat extends to you, or my parents, or—"

And he'd squeezed tighter, heart beating hard into my ear. "I know you better than that, though. You're not the kind of person who backs down."

Chapter Fifteen

I want to say that I felt I owed it to Cody to find out the truth.
To his mother, Lorena, or to his brother, Clint. But honestly,
driving over to Shady Grove Place was for them and me both
at this point. Madder than a hornet after leaving the station,
I sped up onto the highway overpass, even the road noise hol-
lower, freer, and around me the world opened up. Sunlight cut
the clouds, blue strips of sky like ink bled onto a white page.
Forever-long stretches of interstate and the apartment complex
off to the side of it. The building seemed so small from up here
with the big sky pressing down. Too small, too insignificant to
be the last place on earth a man drew breath. Tatters of yellow
tape were left on the railing in front of Cody's, like manage-
ment couldn't be bothered to untie the tape and had ripped it
instead.

I got out and weighed which door to knock on first, settling on the unit directly above Cody's.

"Coming," called a scratchy voice straining to be heard over
the television. I waited, wondering why the complex was this
quiet. The wind kicked up, and a dust devil spun up in the dirt

lot beside the fence, its chain links studded with trash. When the person still hadn't opened the door, I walked a bit around the building. Roughly half the units were unoccupied—not just awaiting new leases, but straight-up abandoned looking. I hurried back when a woman's head poked out of the door I'd knocked on. Her white hair—what was left of it—was tied back with an elastic, pink patches of scalp showing through.

"Sorry to trouble you, ma'am, but I was wondering if I could talk to you about Friday night. I'm a friend of the family," I said, letting that last bit hang in the air, adding a downward glance at the stairs.

"I was just telling my sister what happened." Her knuckles whitened around the handle of her walker.

"I was wondering if you could tell me if you'd noticed anything out of the ordinary with Cody that day or recently? Anyone coming or going to his place? It's been quite a shock, and his mom, she wants to know what all was going on, what might've set him off—it's just so hard to understand."

She nodded furiously as I was speaking, lips parting, waiting for a chance to chime in on the matter. "Oh, I gotcha. My older brother, see, he took his life, gosh, nearly twenty years ago. Broke mine and my parents' hearts so I understand."

I felt bad that I'd assumed she wanted to gossip. "I'm sorry to hear that, ma'am."

"I didn't really know the young man downstairs. He was pretty quiet. You can hear just about anything through these thin floors, but he didn't bother me any. We talked a few times, like this time he come up to ask if he could borrow a baking dish. Friday, though." She whistled through her teeth and steadied herself, wetting her lips. "I was watching my stories and I heard a pop! Didn't realize what it was."

"Oh, no. That's awful," I said, prodding her.

"Thought it was the television at first. One of those cops shows I wasn't really paying attention to. Then, I look at the screen and it's on a commercial. *Pop* and I hear a big, heavy thump. I was going to walk out and take a look over the balcony here, but this leg was acting up and I couldn't quite make it. Besides, it's not unusual for kids to shoot off firecrackers in that empty lot—"

"Wait, sorry—you heard multiple gunshots?"

"Thought so."

"You're sure about that?"

She shrugged. "Least I think I did. But that wouldn't make much sense. Like I said, I was watching the television."

I rubbed the chills that had broken out on my arms. If she was right and there had been two gunshots, that likely refuted the suicide theory. I could see a worn brown recliner through her open door, a remote control and a candy dish on a TV tray next to it. Seated there, she would have a clear view from her window out onto the parking lot. "And when you looked up, you didn't see anything through the window?"

"I keep those blinds closed. Glare's too bad, and anyhow, I don't want people peeking in here. There's vagrants that come around looking for things to steal. That's what happens when a place sits empty too long."

"Is something happening with the building?"

"It sold to a developer and they're fixing to tear it down, replace it with condos for the people working at that new hospital down the interstate. I'm waiting out my lease and for my senior housing to come through. Got a spot opening up at the Villages."

"Do you happen to know a man named Eli Wallace? Big, fit guy with dark hair?"

She shrugged.

"I believe he was here on Friday—or maybe just someone hanging around here, uh"—I lowered my voice—"dealing drugs? Or acting suspicious?"

"Shoot, I tell you what, right next door," she leaned out farther, pointing. "Now that boy was trouble from the get-go. Glad him and his mother are gone. I don't know where either of them is living now."

"This boy, he was a drug dealer?" I said, watching her closely.

"Think so. Might've been he comes back here squatting. Know he's into drugs, seen him hanging around a few times. They do that, you know, hang around the empty buildings. He has problems," she said, tapping her head. "Bless his heart, he didn't stand much of a chance."

"How many of your neighbors are still here?"

"There's the woman with all the kids down yonder, in the opposite building. A few others. I hardly know anyone now. I'll be glad to get outta here. Now, you said you're a friend of the man's family? You going to take his stuff out? I ask 'cause there was this one time he borrowed a dish. Not like I minded so much, but it was a good Pyrex. Think you could bring it to me?"

"Uh, sure," I said, and took a step back. "One last thing— you said you were watching television when you heard the gun, but do you remember which show or what time it was?"

"It was early, before they called the numbers on the news," she said, her voice detaching. "After the talk shows, think a rerun of NCIS, so maybe three or four. Now, you'll bring me that dish?"

I nodded and thanked her for her time, and when she closed the door, I felt both wrung out and tense. To only be remembered for a once-borrowed baking dish made me sadder than it should have. If this woman was right about hearing the shots, their timing, and I'd gotten here a little after eight, that would've been plenty of time for someone to clean up and scribble a fake note. Two gunshots? Possible that the gun had misfired or he hadn't completed his mission with the first bullet. There hadn't been two wounds, not that I'd seen—I recalled the image, batting it away quickly—but, honestly, it would've been impossible for me to tell that. Maybe there had been a struggle, though. Maybe Cody had gotten a shot in at his killer, explaining the residue on his hands.

The wind gusted and a door down the walkway creaked. I came closer—this was the unit that the woman had said the boy drug dealer and his mother lived in—and found the lock was busted. The lights were off inside, even the sockets empty, the place stripped down to the beige carpet. There were signs of squatters—beer cans, a used needle that had rolled into the dirt-stained hollow where a fridge used to be. I walked through the bathroom and bedrooms, and seeing no personal items, hurried outside feeling woozy from the ammonia smell of urine on the floor. The woman had said there was another neighbor in the second building, but when I knocked on their door, no one answered.

The leftover strip of yellow police tape fluttered in my periphery. I was avoiding what I knew was wrong but had to do. I trekked across the parking lot toward Cody's, remembering again that I hadn't seen his car parked here that night. Someone had to have dropped Cody off then, or maybe he'd let someone borrow his car. Either way, it meant that Cody had to have been with another person.

The weathered, rust-red door to his unit was closed tight. A giant NO TRESPASSING sign taped over the peephole gave me pause, but not too much—I tried the knob anyway. Locked. The window looked more promising—old, loosely fitted.

I popped the screen off and leaned it carefully against the limestone siding. The window opened with a suctioned jolt when I pushed, like tilting the lid on a boiling pot. I shimmied it up, sweaty palms fogging the glass. I climbed inside, my feet landing on the couch cushion. Closing the window, I perched on the arm of the couch for a moment. Listened for anyone outside or in, knowing breaking into this apartment was probably too ghoulish even for drug-addled squatters.

I hadn't really taken a close look at the coffee table when I'd come inside on Friday night, but I remembered it had looked sticky, with layers of rings on its black surface, as it did now. Lorena must not have been in here yet. Nothing was packed up, and even the television was left on—not paused anymore, but on a grayed out No Signal screen. The black plastic bag and brown paper sleeve on the coffee table had been there that night, I thought. Coke, a lighter, a pack of Marlboros. Full ashtray. Strange this area was left a mess while the rest of the place was clean. I pulled a pen out of my purse and used it to open the shopping bag wider, thinking there might be a receipt, but it was empty.

I hadn't checked the bathroom on Friday. I flipped the overhead light on with the sleeve of my T-shirt and startled when a rattling old exhaust fan clicked on with it. The sink, floors, and toilet were spotless. It reminded me of how the kitchen had been, with that faint smell of Clorox and rubber. The trash bags had been emptied in the kitchen, and in here, too, the liner was gone from the can, which struck me as odd. I pulled back the shower curtain and found the tub to be stained from age, not grime.

A dark spot showed on the shaggy, pale blue rug. I bent lower and saw several darker, brownish-red flecks and a heavier, rounded drop. Blood. There was no way for me to tell how old it was, or know if it was from shaving or whatever, but I had a sinking feeling in my stomach as I went down the hallway toward the bedroom with my head down, bracing myself for a trail to the larger, deeper stain I knew lay beyond the door. The path between bedroom and bathroom looked clean to me, so maybe the blood on the shag rug had been old, then.

Pushing the door, my legs wobbled as I stepped carefully over the area where Cody's body had been slumped. The empty bottle of Jameson was still on the dresser. The bed, upon closer inspection, looked puckered and creased, like someone had been sitting on the blue plaid covers and shifting their weight around. On the nightstand was a metal desk lamp and a single ballpoint pen, a freebie from a local insurance agent. No books. I did remember seeing a folded sheet of yellow paper on the nightstand last time, similar to what Lorena produced on Saturday at her house—I knew now that had been his note, the one she swore was a fake. I opened the nightstand and dresser drawers with my sleeve. Nothing but his clothes, a glass pipe and flecks of ash, buttons, loose change, a Bible with an uncracked spine, and a mostly full box of condoms. There was no notepad, no paper anywhere. Where, then, had the sheet come from?

I walked the room, looking closely at everything and didn't see any evidence of another blood spill, or a mark where a second bullet would have nicked the wall, the floor, or any furniture. Lastly, I checked the area where I'd found Cody. It made me sick knowing that Lorena would likely have to clean this up herself. The blood had sprayed far and wide, and matter was now hardened to the carpet. I supposed that if someone else had been shot in the near vicinity of Cody there'd be no way for the naked eye to distinguish between the two people's fluids. I scanned the wall, the floor, and again, saw no other bullet marks.

Maybe the woman upstairs was mistaken. I left the bedroom and did a similar sweep of the entire apartment, found nothing. The television blared between the thin floors. I went to the kitchen cabinet to grab the Pyrex, searched around until I saw the yellow-brown dish, its bottom clouded with grease. There weren't more than ten dishes total in the entire kitchen. A few ceramic bowls and two mismatched plates, a saucepot, and a nice cast-iron skillet that had been ruined. I wasn't much of a cook and even I knew you were supposed to season those things—this one had been washed, scrubbed with a copper sponge, rust coloring the edges. I tucked the Pyrex under my arm, turned to leave, and paused; in the sink was the single glass I remembered seeing Friday, but hidden behind the Dawn and paper towels was one I hadn't noticed then—a second highball, one left sticky with the remnants of whiskey.

Chapter Sixteen

Leroy nodded as I talked, and leaned forward in his lawn chair, but didn't go the distance of reaching into the cooler by his feet. A red Coleman that was akin to a wallet or a purse, an accessory he rarely left home without. Especially to go to my parents' house where they didn't stock beer. My dad didn't mind people drinking around him—didn't have much of a choice in this family—but Momma had asked us to stop bringing alcohol inside the house. So, Leroy and I sat outside.

"Bet they're close to getting the spread out on the table," I said.

"That'd be mighty fine if you could fix me a plate, bring it out here to me. Mighty fine if I could stay put here where I'm comfortable."

"Suit yourself," I said, not wanting to argue. "I'll go in and check in a minute." I'd spent the afternoon knocking on the remaining doors of Shady Grove Place, but had learned nothing from the two people who actually answered. Hadn't eaten since that slice of Wyatt's toast, so around five, I answered Momma's text. There was leftover barbeque from last night and she and Sherrilyn needed to make room in the fridge. When I pulled up to the house, half of my extended family also had answered the call of duty, like a reception redo minus the couple. The beer I'd swiped from the cooler fizzed on my tongue. My hangover was finally gone. "I just can't figure out why the sheriff doesn't care. Maybe something to do with a heavy hand from the new owner of the property? Doesn't want a murder spoiling the investment? They're razing the apartments and putting in condos to be close to the new hospital. Think there's going to be an H-E-B in that shopping center."

"What, now? Shoot, I always thought there was more cows than people in Price County. Oil fields must be booming. But I don't know, darlin'," Leroy said, though I could tell the idea amused him. "I can see why she doesn't want to stir trouble, either way. Sometimes the right answer is the obvious one. Occam's razor. The things you noticed—two glasses instead of one, the neighbor's account, the paper—"

"The boot like he'd been dragged. His car being gone; don't forget that. Or hell, his mother not buying the note."

"Right," he said, fiddling with the bottle cap. "But you need proof. Solid proof of foul play."

"I know," I said, jaw tightening.

Leroy took a long pull from his beer, then rubbed his chin. "The truck you saw at the complex and the VFW is Eli Wallace's, then. You said Wallace is connected to the Mott boy—how?"

"Yes. I don't know how just yet, only that Cody said he knew him."

He ran his thumb along the brim of his Stetson, lowering it over his brow. "Wallace ought to go down, one way or another. Doesn't sound like Garcia or this DEA fellow actually have anything solid to tie him to the arson hit. What a sad shame. You'd surely have less to worry about if he was off the street."

I nodded. Was I too eager to tie Eli Wallace to Cody? Was I blinded by self-interest? Maybe. But I couldn't believe that all the pieces—edges shorn and rough, but loosely, gradually coming together in my mind—were a coincidence. Cody had seemed to draw ire when he was alive, based on what little time I'd spent with him, and had a host of personal demons. There was also his family to consider. "Learning about his brother, Clint, and his search for their parents might've set him off," I said. "God, you should've seen his face that night at the VFW. Hell, maybe Cody was already depressed and the news I gave him compounded it."

He shrugged. "Ought to speak with Clint, sounds like. How's he feel being kin to that mean bastard Ronnie Mott?"

"He shut me out a bit, so I don't really know," I said. A silence hung between us, the cicadas ripping into it. "I saw you speaking with his and Sonny's mom, Dee, at the wedding."

Leroy nodded. "I didn't recognize her at first. Been a long time since that holdup. Reckon she'd have never laid eyes on Ronnie Mott with him being the driver, still, that's an odd thing her son being a blood relative."

"Clint broke up with his girlfriend and blew off the wedding."

"I heard," he said. That Clint might've pulled a literal-not-emotional trigger on Cody hadn't escaped me, but the thought disturbed me enough I hadn't wanted to give it more oxygen. Couldn't quite rule it out, even though I'd seen Clint had posted about his Nashville gig on Instagram, sharing the details with his hundreds of thousands of followers, so it seemed legit. A selfie in the car, a black-and-white filter—you know, serious—aviator shades, a cowboy hat, a hint of a smile. *Headed to the opportunity of a lifetime. Going to play and write with one of my heroes, the legendary Tom Carpenter at his studio in Nashville. Opportunity don't knock twice, y'all. More soon. Peace, C.*

Besides considering him a jerk now, his post was so corny I'd wanted to throw my phone across the room when I'd read it. Had been muttering "Peace, C," to myself all day. A flash of irritation shot down my spine just thinking about it, and deeper, like all that had happened between him and his family was my fault. Leroy hadn't given me an "I told you so," about getting tangled with the Motts, but maybe he should have. The beer sweated in my hand, and I ran my finger over the scar that bisected my palm. I'd learned since becoming an investigator that there was no such thing as total control. The truth was out there, and it wasn't entirely up to me. What the truth produced—how it whittled people down, revealed their messy bloodred heart—that wasn't mine. A terrifying yet freeing thought, if only I could hold onto it.

"Old man, let this girl off the clock. She needs to eat," my dad hollered through the screen door, startling me. "Sweetheart, your momma's asking if you can come help her make iced tea for everybody."

Leroy frowned. "Son, how're you feeling today?"

"Doing just fine, sir." Dad pitched his torso forward but his feet stayed planted, like he'd wanted to come out and sit with us but had changed his mind. He looked at the grass, scratching the gray stubble on his chin. "Can't complain."

"Always glad to hear it," Leroy said, nodding once before going back to his beer. A small effort was better than none, I supposed. Leroy cut his eyes over to Dad, briefly sizing him up. Probably noticed how much weight he'd lost, that he'd gotten his color back. Dad was now driving to the chiropractor and massage therapist in Colburn every week, making an effort to stretch and exercise, and he'd even taken up doing a yoga and meditation video every morning, or so Momma said. And, keeping his boundaries.

He followed me inside the house, lingering in the open doorframe.

"Close that, William, you're letting all the bought air out," Momma said to him, then smiled at me. "Dang it, we didn't know *everyone* was coming. Your daddy made potato salad and had to go out and buy extra groceries"—she looked back at him—"you remembered pickle chips, didn't you?"

He shuffled over to the cabinet to retrieve them—another change, he wore these orthopedic slides everywhere—and I stood there stunned. Despite Momma having a full-time job as a bank teller, Dad, for the most part, left housework to her. I was too whipped to muster any kind of smart-assed comment. And, it was nice to see him helping out.

Dad looked over his shoulder at me. "Where's Wyatt?"

"Grades are due," I said. Wyatt was starting his second year of grad school at State this fall, and was teaching in the summer session.

Dad popped open the pickle jar. "Y'all get that leak under the sink fixed?"

"Sort of," I said. "Landlord told me to tape it."

"Wyatt couldn't fix it?"

I gritted my teeth—wasn't just that he casually assumed we split chores the way he and Momma did, it was that he acted ticked off when we didn't. "It's fine, Daddy."

"Okay, then." He handed me the pickle jar and joined the others in the living room. He really was getting better at not taking the bait.

Momma put her hand on her hip. "Nikki never called your aunt to let her know they got in okay."

"Well, she only texted me because I texted her first," I said. "It is their honeymoon." Truthfully, I'd wanted to reach Sonny through her. Ask him if he and Clint had talked any more since Saturday. She'd blown past the request, telling me how fancy it was at the Gulf resort and how she'd gotten a daquiri with a tiny umbrella. I took the hint and didn't press, though I'd have to try again soon.

"I've already got it steeping, just do the sugar and the ice," Momma said, and motioned toward a pot with a tangle of Lipton bags hanging over the side. I got down the big pitcher and the ice trays from the freezer. Through the door to the dining room, I heard Aunt Jewel scolding her poodle for chewing a hot spot on his tail, followed by Uncle Curtis showing my dad a video from last night on his phone at full volume. Momma looked at me. "You never stop."

"Stop what?"

"Worrying over your chicks! Just 'cause Nikki's a married woman now doesn't mean she doesn't have to talk to her mother. God, I keep thinking about Dee Marshall. How embarrassing."

The sugar scoop in my hand was sticky. Last I'd seen Dee, she was leaving early. "It's sad Clint's acted this way."

"Guess I've just been emotional, seeing our girl get married. It sunk in last night that you two are grown. One day," she said, sighing. "One day when you have a baby, Annie, you'll understand that it's like your mind splits in two. Two-track mind forever. You don't ever stop being my baby."

She folded me into a hug and I was surprised at my eyes watering a bit. Being seen, loved, I suppose. And also, the thought that Cody had been a baby once. Maybe it was Lorena's face flashing through my mind now, her eyes puffy and red—I had to pull back, look away from Momma. "So, did you talk to Dee last night?"

"Not much, poor thing. You know she and I used to be friends, back when you and Sonny were little? Don't know why we fell out of touch. Guess because they lived in Parr City. That extra drive time makes so much difference."

"No, I didn't know you were friends. I'd actually never talked to her before this weekend," I said, thinking a moment. "You worked at the Parr City bank branch before Garnett— that's where you met Dee?"

"That's right," Momma said. "Her and Luanne Davies— you remember her?"

I nodded, thinking of her current gym buddy, former bank coworker. She was also the second teller who'd been held up the day of the robbery. The one who'd been shot and had lived.

Sherrilyn shoved through the kitchen door. "Let's eat already! Good God, I drank like I was one of you kids last night, Annie. You talk to that cousin of yours?"

I nodded, poured tea over the ice in the pitcher. There was something satisfying about the cracking sound, the burst of steam. "Said they're having a great time and that she misses you."

"Paper plates and napkins and we're all set. I'm not doing any dishes tonight," Momma said. "You left the cake over at your house, didn't you, sister?"

"Yes, and the topper."

Momma had been adamant about wrapping up a piece of cake for Nikki and Sonny and hiding it in their freezer. Leroy hadn't known about the tradition of couples eating wedding cake on their anniversary and had eaten my parents' leftovers while they were gone on their honeymoon. He'd thought they wrapped it up special just for him. "The extra napkins are in your room, Annie, up in the closet."

I fast-walked down the hallway, avoiding being sucked into a wager with Aunt Jewel over who'd win whatever game show she had on mute. My old bedroom was mostly preserved in its original state. Same decorations and furniture shuffled around to make room for storage containers and a giant doghouse in the shape of an igloo—a Dogloo—that our dogs had never actually slept in because they slept inside under my parents' bed. Bulletin boards leaned up against the closet door, rainbow pushpins securing prom portraits and random images I'd cut out of magazines. My white carnation homecoming mums were yellowy now and brittle, the puff-paint-and-glitter-decorated ribbons dusty, trailing across the blue carpet. I sat on the floor and put my chin in my hands. Closed my eyes and took a breath before getting up on tiptoe to retrieve the napkins. My hand brushed against a shoebox on the shelf. I pulled it down with the napkins excitedly, thinking it was photos. Maybe that picture of Sarah Anne was in here, I thought, but was wrong—it was only old pictures of me.

Chapter Seventeen

I woke the next morning early, right as the sun filtered through the pink curtains over the big window by our bed. I loved that room. There was a softness, a warmth to it that allowed me to relax my mind. I'd had a dream I couldn't remember now, but I reached for my journal, scribbled one word, *family*. After coffee, I still agreed with my half-awake instinct. Cody and Clint had an older sister I still needed to look up. I showered, had one of Wyatt's smoothies, then ran a search on my laptop. Christa Mott—married name Christa Roberts—appeared to be living in San Angelo. Maybe she'd spoken to Cody recently and could give insight, or maybe Clint had tried contacting her—either way, it seemed like a good box to check.

I decided to make a day trip, and got out of the house around nine. The drive up that way wasn't bad, a few hours, and I decided to make use of the time by calling Clint's ex-girlfriend. She answered on the first ring, her voice lighter than the last time we'd talked.

"How's it going at your parents', Amanda? You said you were staying with them a few days?"

"Uh, it's okay," she said, laughing a little. "So, I saw on Nikki's Insta that Clint wasn't in any wedding pics. Did he seriously not go?"

"Nope. I'm guessing you saw his post? About Nashville?"

"Told you he was a turd."

I smiled. The sun was cooking me through the windshield, but it was a beautiful morning, the sky clearer and the blue darker, stratospheric-like. "Seems you're doing okay, at least."

"I feel sorry for Sonny. And I also feel a little relieved I'm not the only one who's hurting, which I know sounds terrible—"

"No, trust me, I get it," I said. But Clint still hadn't had a chance to defend, or at least explain, himself yet. I paused for a second, sanding the gossip-tone out of my voice. "Before you left his place on Friday, was he saying anything about what he was up to? Like, was he still planning on the rehearsal or do you think he'd already heard about the gig?"

"He did seem to be packing, and I remember him hanging up with his agent. I thought he'd just not unpacked after their bachelor trip, but the bags must've been him getting ready to go. He kind of laid it on me right when I got in," she said, her voice quivering. "The talk about his birth family and the breakup, I mean."

"Remind me, this was at what time exactly?"

"I remember I'd texted my sister that I'd gotten in at around four. He and I talked for a while, lost track of time—he wasn't thinking about the rehearsal, and neither was I. Poor Sonny. Are they, like, still worried about him or are they angry?"

If she was telling the truth, the timing of their breakup gave Clint something like an alibi. The neighbor at his apartment complex had said she heard shots from Cody's place at around the same time that Amanda said they were together. "Both, I think."

She was quiet for a moment, long enough that I thought the call had dropped. "People forget that to be adopted you have to have lost something first. They think, oh yay, adopted! There's the happy ending! But there's no happy ending without a doomed beginning and bad-luck middle."

"Have you found your birth family?" When she let out a long sigh, I could almost see her face. Her eastern European bone structure had made all her features come to a point; even her lips, as puffed with fillers as they were, had an archness to them.

"I haven't been able to, no. It's hard. It's like there's this ghost of me, this other person I keep worrying about? I feel hard for that little girl. I want her back, and yet, I also kind of hate her. There's a hole in Clint's heart like there is in mine, I think—I don't know if anyone who's not an adoptee can really get that."

"Thank you, Amanda," I said. "I'll try to."

I arrived at Christa Roberts's, née Mott's, house in San Angelo around midday. I stepped out of the bullet and my legs were like Jell-O, my ears muffled as though I'd hurtled into town through that stratosphere-like sky over the plains. She and her family lived in a small subdivision adjacent to a golf course and country club with a pool. Newly paved asphalt was soft underfoot, and hot tar chemicals carried on a mild, dry wind. The house was on a cul-de-sac, one of those tract homes that are set super close together and are secretly huge. A popular girl from my high school who'd married an older man with money lived in one like this. She'd posted on Facebook about them building their dream house according to the dream house blueprint, that they'd gotten to choose the countertops, tile backsplash, and had added in a custom outdoor fireplace—which, she noted, cost extra. The Roberts's house looked identical to those pictures, down to the big garage, gray stucco, and oversized stone arch entryway, the branch-like saplings staked into bright green sod.

No cars in the driveway and all the blinds were closed. They might not be home and I might have time for lunch, I thought. Maybe I could walk along the river to kill time, come back in the evening. I liked San Angelo, though I couldn't exactly tell you what was so special. The downtown had an Old West feel to it, murals of cattle drives and horses painted on the sides of yellow and redbrick buildings. It didn't take much for me to feel content, to walk a bit and live inside my head—a certain color, half a song's chorus. I rang the Roberts's bell for good measure and was surprised—and briefly disappointed—when I detected movement behind the frosted glass panel.

The woman who answered looked a little like Clint, and exactly like Cody down to the watery blue eyes and long face. Her blond blowout was on its last legs, a trace of dry shampoo on her hairline, yesterday's eyeliner darkening her lower lids.

"Christa, my name is Annie McIntyre. I'm a private investigator. I wanted to talk with you about your brother."

She opened the door wider. "Are you with the police?"

"I'm here on my own. See, I met Cody a few weeks ago when I was visiting your mother. I was hired by someone looking for their birth family."

"You must mean Clint. My God." Her voice was nasally, like she was congested from crying. "Well, the kids are at camp for another hour—I don't really want them, um, involved—just come inside, I guess," she said, leading me into the vaulted foyer. "Know that I'll have to go soon, though."

"That's fine."

She was tall like her mother, maybe five nine, also rail thin. She wore a dressy, sheer pink blouse with ruffled sleeves over old Soffe shorts, as though she'd gone out and might go out again after putting her jeans back on. As I drew closer to her, I smelled alcohol and wondered if she simply hadn't finished getting dressed in the first place. I, too, had the surreal feeling of being buzzed; something about the closed blinds and recessed lighting on dimmers gave the house weird, TV-marathon, no-real-sense-of-time vibes. Plastic toys were scattered across the beautiful wood panel floors. She offered me a seat on a plush, slate-gray couch, dark enough to conceal a crusty stain I didn't notice until my hand brushed it.

"Thank you for talking. I know this must be hard."

"I want to talk," she said, taking the love seat opposite me. She snatched up a giant, pastel-pink Stanley tumbler, ice clanking against the metal sides. Smelled like vodka and lemonade. "I don't really have anyone to talk to about Cody. Don't keep up with any of our childhood friends, and my mom and I aren't close. Haven't talked to Daddy in, God, seven years? Not since my oldest was born. We're not having a service"—her voice wobbled—"so, yeah."

"I'm really sorry."

"I do care. I do, even if it doesn't seem like it," she said, taking a deep breath. She'd made all the noises like she was about to cry, but her eyes were dry. Maybe she protested too much, more likely it was just complicated. I looked at my hands in my lap, letting her compose herself. "It's just that my husband and I agreed a long time ago that our kids wouldn't have to worry about our crazy families. The dysfunction. He's been really understanding of my pain and all, but it's like, are we supposed to carry on like my brother hasn't just fucking died? I don't know what to do, so I can't do anything. I'm know I'm not making any sense—"

"No, I understand. Is your husband at work now?"

She clutched her tumbler tighter, clicking the lid back and forth. "Yeah, he's an engineer at one of the big wind farms here. You see all those windmills coming in?"

The white turbines had looked to me like a cavalry cresting the hill; something about the sheer number of them marching into my field of vision was not altogether friendly. Rows and rows of tall towers, big blades arcing, waving like arms. The sight was both beautiful and strange. I wished for a gust of that famous West Texas wind—the smell in the house, underneath vanilla candles and fabric softener, was stale, garlicky, like dirty dishes and reheated leftovers. I nodded. "I take it his job is what brought y'all out here? You like it? Know it's hard to meet people in a new place."

"I like our life. I have friends—I mean, I talk to the other moms at drop-off and sports stuff," she said. "But yeah, not, like, a big group of besties or whatever. I'm too busy."

No one she thought wouldn't judge her, it sounded like. She caught me glancing at her tumbler and blushed. "Girl, you want a drink? I don't normally drink during the middle of the day—"

"I'd say it's understandable," I said, nodding.

"Yeah, my mind's not right," she said, and went to the kitchen, coming back with a spoon, a bottle of vodka, and a packet of Crystal Light. She dumped the contents into a glass filled with ice and a splash of water and stirred. A smile dimpled her cheek for a split second. "I call this Mommy's juice box. Now, are you from Branch Creek? Swear I've met you before."

"Garnett," I said. "But maybe we've run into each other."

"Oh, we played y'all all the time. I played softball in high school. Then again, you're probably younger than me." Christa watched me for a moment, her shoulders inching down from her ears as she drained Mommy's juice box. "This sounds terrible, and I was really shocked when I found out Cody died, but it also felt like a long time coming."

I nodded, trying not to look taken aback by her comment, such a harsh thing to say out loud. She sounded disappointed in him—mad over something, or a lifetime of things. "Had he attempted suicide before?" I asked.

She shook her head. "It's hard to explain."

"Had you and Cody been in touch recently? Did he tell you anything about your other brother, Clint, being back in the picture?"

"The last conversation we had, if you'd call it a conversation. He texted two weeks ago saying that he wanted to talk, but I was busy that morning, so I waited to call him until after everyone was in bed. Normal, right? But he was so pissed that I hadn't replied right away and we mostly bickered. Cody has abandonment issues. Shit, so do I, but you know, I understand when someone can't talk right this instant!"

Maybe she thought he was going to ask her for something—and probably not for the first time, I figured, watching her twist the rock on her finger.

"Cody told me he'd found out Clint was living in Garnett. Wanted me to come down in the next few months, see if we could maybe look him up together, but I said no." She sighed, drumming her nails against the side of the tumbler. "What Cody didn't understand was that doors close for a reason, and once they're back open, it's really hard to shut them again. Sure, this guy is our relative, but he's a total stranger now.

What would we do, invite him to Christmas? Plus, I didn't want to go down there and feel like shit because I didn't visit Lorena. Better to keep it clean. I wish Cody could've understood that—or hell, given it a try himself. Maybe he'd still be here," she said, and this time, tears, the real deal, dribbled from her eyes.

I sat quietly for a moment. "Your mom must have felt similarly. She wouldn't talk to me about Clint when I approached her."

She stopped drumming her nails. "Wait, Lorena is not Clint's mom."

"What? Cody said—"

"Cody told you she was? Oh God," she said, chewing her lower lip. "Shit, he was so little, I guess he didn't know? Or he didn't remember. I was only seven. But it was pretty obvious, even though they lied to us about it—I mean, Lorena wasn't even pregnant! What, he thought the stork dropped a baby?"

"Whose baby is he, then?"

She shrugged dramatically. "Clint was Daddy's, I knew that. Lorena took him in when he got arrested and then pretended that he was hers. No idea what happened to his real mom or who she was. Lorena loved Daddy like a kicked dog who keeps coming back for more."

I opened and closed my mouth, not quite sure what to say. I'd had a gut-level sense that there was something strange about Lorena's reaction to the mention of Clint, but I'd chalked it up to shame, to pushing away the ache of losing a child. It was one thing—an easier thing—to lie about a child's paternity. How had this lie been played off in the eyes of the state? Maybe if Clint's mother had given birth outside the hospital, hadn't gotten prenatal care, it would be possible to falsify her identity. But why? There was something deeply wrong here, and at the very least, I'd given Clint faulty information. "So, your mom literally took some other woman's baby?"

"Insane, I know," she said, thinking. "In my family, you keep it in the family. Like, if Lorena ever found out who called CPS on us, there'd be hell to pay. I always thought it was the old woman across the street, but who knows. We were living outside normal society for a long time. It took being in foster care for me to realize just how abnormal my life was—foster care! Like, I hadn't gone to school for more than a week or two? And I was seven? Goddamn, my therapist struck gold with me."

I shivered, watching her closely. "Your dad's way of life must have necessitated all the isolation? I'm sorry, that's really unfair."

"Yeah, and because we were siloed off, he could do whatever he pleased. For all I know, I have bunches of half siblings out there. He ran around on Lorena all the time. Charismatic, total sociopath. I'm sure you've heard all about his crimes. His 'infamy,'" she said with air quotes, snort-laughing. "Damn. Try being a Mott in Price County and see if you don't wind up hating yourself, too."

We were burning on a short fuse. I nodded calmly and took a slow sip of my drink, wincing at the taste. "Christa, I know you think I can't possibly understand, but my family is complicated in a way, too—my granddad has a reputation that precedes him. Not in the same way as your dad's, he's not incarcerated, but I know what it's like for people to already have formed an opinion of you."

She looked off, not really paying attention. Part of being a blank slate, a listener—people rarely returned the gesture. She wiped her eyes with the back of her hand. "I just don't want anything to do with Clint. Whatever his name is now."

"It sounds like Cody felt differently. And, I think there were lots of things going on in his life, maybe even involving Clint, that complicate the suicide theory."

"Theory? What, you don't think he killed himself?"

"I don't know, but I have reason to doubt the police's assessment," I said, and looked hard at her. "Anything you can think of—someone your brother complained about, arguments he had, people hanging around his place, stuff like that—anything might help."

"Honestly, when I heard Cody was dead and before I knew how, my first thought was he'd crossed someone again," Christa said, locking eyes with mine. "That he'd gotten into trouble."

"Who do—"

"You need to talk to my dad is who," she said.

Chapter Eighteen

We moved onto the patio so she could smoke. Come to find they'd also installed the fancy outdoor fireplace. Unlike Clint's ex, Christa had the markings of a smoker, and one trying to quit. Her whole body relaxed as soon as she took a drag, pure relief. She looked my way, blowing smoke out the side of her mouth. Her lipstick had rubbed off, leaving a dry, pink stain. "Cody and my dad didn't get along, but I don't think he'd ever hurt him. Not intentionally, it's just . . ." She trailed off, staring at the lit end of her cigarette.

"Your dad's in prison," I said. "What could he have to do with Cody?"

"I saw on his girlfriend's Facebook page something about him being 'released from his shackles soon,'" she said, and her body tensed again. "She's one of those nuts, writes letters to guys in prison she's never met. Can't believe it's been twenty-something years, end of his sentence, but I guess it has been. Anyway, what I'm saying is there's a lot of people who hate his guts. Even guys Daddy ran with in the past, old friends that might want to show him who's boss these days. That's a crazy long shot, but if I know my dad, he's probably trying to get back in the game, so to speak. Could be posing a threat to someone."

"Like who?"

"Heard Dalton's been out—Dalton's one of his ex-best guys—since a year or two ago. I could see him running something. There was a lot of drama from around that time. And man, those old-timers? Fuckin' ruthless."

I considered that for a moment. Maybe Cody talked with his dad before he died. Had a change of heart after learning about Clint, after thinking long and hard about severed family. He'd reached out to Christa, hadn't he? It wasn't just old-timers I was worried about in relation to Ronnie Mott, though. As far as I knew, someone much younger was the big name in Price County. "Do you know Eli Wallace?" I asked.

She sat straighter. "Our families go way, way back."

"Oh," I said, remembering that Cody had told it differently. Maybe I'd misread him, but he'd definitely made it seem like he and Eli got into it that one time he'd gone to work for him, not like an ongoing relationship.

Christa stared out onto the fresh sod in the backyard, rolled out like felt. I wanted to dig my toes in that grass. A bright green expanse punctuated with sprinkler heads and soccer balls, a wooden swing set. "Eli and Cody were in trouble together a lot, even as kids. Got caught with matches in the school bathroom in kindergarten." She laughed, shook her head. "When we got put in the foster system, we lost touch with Eli's people, but when Lorena got us back it was like no time had passed with those two. Though by then they were teenagers and the trouble was real. Drugs, fights, firecrackers, shooting guns into the air like morons."

My face tingled at the mention of matches. "Was Cody a firebug?"

She shook her head in a bouncy way that made me think she was completely plastered. Another juice box had been poured. "No, that was Eli's thing. But he led Cody around by the nose. It's always been hard for my brother, being Ronnie Mott's son and not being, um, what's the word?"

"An alpha male?"

"Yeah, that's it. That macho bullshit was so toxic. Our dad wasn't around, of course, but none of the other men in the family stepped up for Cody. Eli's dad, who was close friends with ours, was unofficially supposed to fill that father role for us. But it was complicated, and like, I think there was some bad blood there, given Eli's uncle Dalton was part of the big robbery that got them all arrested," she said, looking at me a little too long, and my face heated up. In hindsight, I shouldn't have mentioned my grandfather, though I didn't think she'd connected the dots yet. She shivered and looked away. "Lotta jealousy, too. The rumor was that my dad had hid money someplace and he was keeping it a secret from his crew. Now if that were true, I sure as hell never saw any of it. But Eli's dad would come around and like, spy on Lorena to see how much money she was spending, then take Cody out in the backyard with Eli, 'to throw the ball around'," she said, making air quotes, "but it was just an excuse to kick the crap out of Cody, knowing he wouldn't dare complain. And I mean really whoop his butt—like bruised ribs and a bloody nose."

My stomach tightened. I'd met Doug Wallace on a case last spring, and the man had genuinely frightened me, too. He was the type to let his body language do the talking and was big—maybe six five, arms like wood posts—and mean as a snake. I shivered and set my diet vodka concoction on the ground, not pretending to drink it anymore. "Is it possible that Clint coming out of the woodwork set the Wallaces off?"

She gave a loose shrug of her shoulders, swaying a bit. "I don't know what Cody was into these days, but if it was drug-related, the Wallaces are probably connected somehow. And yeah, if Clint stuck his nose in something he shouldn't, I honestly don't know what those guys would do to him—Cody included."

"Y'all didn't keep in touch with your dad. Was that because you didn't want anything to do with him, or—?"

"Daddy would've liked to have a relationship, I think. He used to write us. But at this point, the disconnect is mutual. I assume he's heard about Cody, but I don't know. If you're wondering if he'd talk to Clint, maybe, maybe not—but I can tell you that Ronnie Mott's always loved an audience," she said, and paused to take a drag, catching a glimpse of her phone in her lap. Her face stiffened. "It's nearly two, my God. I've got to go pick up my kids in fifteen minutes. And James is almost home—shit, why is he off this early in the day?"

"You okay to drive?"

She waved a hand in front of my face and answered an incoming call. "Hi, honey, yep, hold on, there's a salesperson at the door," she said, muting the call and beaming me with a red-eyed stare. "You need to get out of here. Walk around that side and go out the gate. Just hurry up and go."

"Alright, alright," I said, startled by the abrupt turn. I fumbled in my purse for two business cards and a pen. Had her scribble her phone number on one, and left the other under the pack of cigarettes, hoping she didn't trash it. I walked

around the side of the house as she'd instructed, barely dodg-
ing her husband, who cruised his big truck into the driveway
right as I unlatched the gate. I slunk along the hedges as he
idled and the garage door opened, making a break for it when
he pulled in beside her SUV. When I reached the bullet, I
texted Christa to ask that we meet up. Maybe this evening, I
suggested, someplace far away from home.

I waited a couple of hours for a reply that never came. I did
enjoy a good lunch at a Mexican restaurant, steak fajitas forti-
fying me for the long drive home. The only thing more awkward than ordering a giant, sizzling fajita plate that everyone
in the restaurant turns to look at is ordering one meant for two
people and proceeding to eat it all by yourself. I'd planned on
taking leftovers home to Wyatt but was starving, the fruity
drink I got to go along with the meal sloshing around my
stomach along with my twisting nerves.

I left the city, headed southeast, wind turbines in my rearview waving me on and on. Eli Wallace. I'd had time to think
at lunch and all I'd come up with in terms of a plan was that
drawing him out needed to be circuitous. And I would draw
him out—I wasn't going to sit and wait. The more I thought
about my talk with the DEA agent and Garcia, the more
alone I felt. A shiny bit of tackle on the end of a line over deep
water—a dummy, a fake. No, I would be the one who set the
trap. And whatever I did, I'd be the one to protect myself
and my family. The bullet swayed and I gripped the wheel.
The wind had kicked up grit, the force of it head-on offering
a good deal of resistance. I pressed the pedal down harder.
Kept thinking about the picture I'd seen of Ronnie Mott, the

charmer, the alpha dog, more like Eli than his own two sons. The legend in absentia, still fearsome. I'd do well to figure out who had a bone to pick with him.

I drove straight to the office. Brewed a pot of coffee and went to work finding anything I could about the robbery, to get a fuller picture of the Motts and the Wallaces, the heist that sent the men to prison. The county library system and our local historical society had recently teamed up to digitize issues of *The Garnett Signal* dating back to the 1920s. I'd used a microfilm reader before—I'd had a work-study job at my college's library—but was grateful to not have to now. Issues from that summer were online and I clicked through page by page. Some of the scans were crooked, blurry, but I lost myself for some time, reading all of the articles and poring over the ads, the businesses and restaurants from my early childhood long gone away.

There were numerous articles about the robbery, and they often quoted Leroy. I had to smile a few times—could hear him say one phrase in particular he offered a lot when asked for a statement: *figure we'll do our job if you leave us to it.* He'd always taken the work seriously, not himself, but it was clear that the reporter wanted to make the overarching story—across a series of pieces he'd written—be about the police's heroic efforts. Like those news segments they caption now with "How about something good!" or "Everyday heroes!" You could sense an invisible hand cupping the reader's chin, aiming to draw back viewers who complain about only hearing bad news. But what is news, if not a disruption of the status quo? Another, bigger part of the story, as bad as it made my grandfather's department look, was that Ronnie Mott had been a literal outlaw. He'd run like a bat out of hell and wasn't found for months—and then, only because he'd gotten pulled over in a little speed trap up in the Panhandle. While he hadn't gotten any money out of the bank, he'd had a true shot at freedom.

The man he'd done the heist with, Dalton, had been shot to wound by Leroy and Mary-Pat that day—had Ronnie heard gunfire ring out inside the bank and still hit the pedal? Dalton was Eli Wallace's uncle by marriage, I learned through another search, and his aunt the owner of a pool hall on the county line—Cowboys. The trial back then had been messy, full of backstabbing testimony, each man angling for a better deal. No surprise, then, the festering resentment among their families. And how, then, to root out a new motive for a crime among a group of hardened felons who, as Christa had said, kept family business in the family?

I paced at the window for a few moments. The late sun made the street outside wavy with heat shimmer. Watching employees from the courthouse and the handful of offices on the square walk to their cars to head home for the evening made me feel odd and uneasy, like I'd been left behind. I sat back down at the computer to keep reading. Fully down the rabbit hole, I was clicking through the pages, into August now, when a story, barely a story it was so brief, caught my attention.

A woman who'd been living with her boyfriend in Garnett had gone missing. The story gave a basic physical description and asked that if anyone had any information to call the sheriff's department. Faye Flores—where had I heard that name? I stared at the screen, the fuzzy black-and-white senior-year portrait of a young woman with swooping bangs and a wide smile colorizing, sharpening in my mind. The old woman I'd talked to who lived on the same street as the Motts—*that* Mrs. Flores. This was her daughter. Her Faye. I opened a new tab, ran a wider search, and the results made my stomach drop.

Faye had not only died young, but had been murdered. Her bones were found a decade or so after she'd gone missing, in the vicinity of a motel where it's thought she had been soliciting men. She'd been a runaway, only seventeen. A serial murderer had later copped to her killing while on death row in Huntsville. There wasn't much more written on Faye Flores specifically, only a *Houston Chronicle* article from a bigger series done on the "Motel Stalker," in the wake of his execution several years ago. The article interviewed several of his victims' families, and Faye's mother had gone on a tear about the local law enforcement in her hometown being partly to blame for her daughter's death. That the sheriff in Garnett wrote her daughter off, and had her missing person case been taken seriously, she claimed, her daughter might still be alive.

That sheriff was Leroy McIntyre.

The article ran a truncated quote from Leroy, given over the phone, "I'm real sorry for the loss of Faye Flores, but we did all we could to find her after she run off."

The writer noted Leroy had been voted out of office and had taken an early retirement from law enforcement amidst rumors of improper behavior, letting that last detail fill in and explain the gaps in Faye Flores's case, all without making a direct accusation against him. No wonder Mrs. Flores had yelled at me; she'd realized I was Leroy's granddaughter.

Face hot, I clicked out of the tab. *The Garnett Signal* page with the big story about the robbery, Faye's missing person bulletin a tiny box buried beneath the fold, stared back at me. I'd be upset if she were kin to me. More than upset. It was clear to me, with the long-eyed view afforded by time, that her case probably was written off, at least in the public's mind. Leroy would never neglect a missing girl in his jurisdiction, but I could also see him and his tiny department being consumed by the robbery investigation and the search for Ronnie Mott, who was still at large. I leaned my head back. Something like sadness washed over me, but sharper, a pang deep in the center of my chest. I needed to make moves, confront the gnawing dread that Cody's death might be swept away like that young woman's murder. Misunderstood, forgotten to time.

Talking with Eli's dad, or anyone at the liquor store on the county line was a no-go. Maybe I could speak with the pool hall owner, his aunt, to get a better sense of things. Find out what Eli, or the old-timers, as Christa had called them, might be up to. Risky to stick my neck out like that, though. Maybe just nosing around the establishment—discreetly as possible— would yield information. The thought of going back to Cowboys made my heart race. The bartender there had seemed familiar with Cody. Or, if nothing else, sensitive, decent enough to take Cody's keys and ask me to drive him home when he could've just kicked him out on his ass—or, let him continue to get it whooped.

Combing Facebook and LinkedIn—you never know—for Cowboys employees was fruitless. I searched Craigslist on a whim and was rewarded: Cowboys was hiring a barback. I answered the ad, emailing under a fake name. Maybe I'd go to the interview, maybe I wouldn't—I was more interested to see who, if anyone, replied. If the bartender wrote, or Eli's aunt, I might find an in, get them to speak on the phone. It was nearly six now, happy hour, but a Monday. Too sparse to wander in and hide. And besides, I already knew just the person who'd give me direct intel on the events of that one fateful summer.

Chapter Nineteen

Leroy was cooking supper, uncharacteristically bright-eyed for the evening hour. Yodeling and lowing along to an Eddy Arnold record. And I do mean lowing—he was listening to *Cattle Call* on high volume.

Mary-Pat sat with her chin in her hand, staring at me from across the table. "I don't usually care for liver and onions, but suppose I don't have time to grab a bite otherwise."

Leroy set a spatula on the counter, dripping grease onto the linoleum. If my mamaw were here, she'd have fussed at him big-time. "It's good for you, Pat. Get your iron," he said, staring at the pan like it might run off, and wiped his hands on his Wranglers. Like Dad, I couldn't think of a time I'd seen Leroy in the kitchen doing much besides raid the fridge. After Mamaw died, he mostly ate at Mary-Pat's or threw together elevated convenience store fare—hot dogs with fancy mustard, canned sardines and crackers, burritos. Lest we think he'd put on airs he slopped a can of Ranch Style Beans into a pot on the other burner, not bothering to stir.

Liver wasn't high on my favorites list, either, but I shrugged at Mary-Pat, going to the fridge for a beer. I'd already filled the pair in on my findings, on the conversation with Christa. Being an investigator often meant operating alone, which I was fine with, but it was nice to have a sounding board. Working beside them wasn't really "beside"—oftentimes it meant following a half-step behind—or worse, stuck cooling in their long shadow. I could be overly dependent on their approval, but was grateful for a reality check most times. Today I'd been met with an atta-girl, and I'm embarrassed to say how much that lifted me and revved my heart.

"Why, thank you, little darlin'!" Leroy said, cracking the can I offered him. There was a window over the sink, the sill crowded with the old glass bottles Mamaw liked to decorate. She'd painted them with bluebonnets and pink roses, white curlicues. The stereo beside the stove had also been there forever, and grease coated the dial. The sweet mellowness to Eddy Arnold's voice didn't match the song that'd been stuck in my head. Didn't match the biblical foreboding, the steady drumbeat pulse of a Marty Robbins number. You knew how a gunfighter ballad ended—a showdown, a public hanging, the speaker crying out to you from beyond the grave. His was more rootless, a campfire song, and I felt carried along on the warm yet lonely sound, smiled watching Leroy watch the stove, him mouthing the words. Lyrics about a yearning to wander, being next of kin to the wayward wind. He motioned for me to get our plates down from the bright, yellow-painted cabinets.

I set the table, looking between him and Mary-Pat. "What do you know about guys Ronnie Mott crossed back in the day? Money that he might've kept from his crew, from the Wallaces, specifically."

Mary-Pat harrumphed. "Why would someone go after money—if there is money—now, all these years later?"

"I don't know exactly, but maybe there's a tie to Ronnie's upcoming release. Like, what if Cody was caught in the crossfire between Ronnie and an enemy of his? Just seems like there might be something there, and it's what his daughter guessed at."

She nodded. "Money is hearsay, though. Guys like Ronnie Mott make themselves sound bigger and tougher than they actually are. Helps keep ahold on their turf—"

"You have to admit, nearly getting away with over two hundred and fifty K is pretty badass. It's no wonder people still talk about it," I said.

"Badass?" Mary-Pat's head swiveled between me and Leroy. "A teller just doing her job, minding her own business, your friend's mother—that's who they held up, Annie. And her manager, a mother herself, that was the woman they shot that day. That's whose lives were nearly lost. It's not badass what Ronnie did, it was risky and cowardly at the same time."

"I didn't mean I thought they were admirable, Jesus," I said, startled by her red face. "I just meant bank robberies are a bit of a David and Goliath story, you know? Like people might say, 'Well, the bank's insured and the robbers nearly outwitted the system' kind of thing. Also, they aren't small-time idiots. None of them. They're dangerous, those old guys hate Ronnie, and have a history of being violent with Cody."

"True enough," she said, her voice still tight.

Leroy was quiet a moment, thinking. "Pat, I wouldn't be so sure money or goods are not hidden somewhere. Remember, now, there was all kinds of jewelry, gold, and other items taken from a department store break-in and some home invasions not long before the bank hit. Was never recovered. No one officially tied him or his crew to it, but that was the word."

He brought the skillet to the table, plopped the meat onto

our plates, and the two of them launched into eating without preamble. The mealy, soft-cooked liver was breaded in corn-meal, the taste coppery, gamey. Hot and bloody. The taste was too much like the smell inside Cody's apartment, enough to bring the image of him back full force. I held the paper towel to my mouth.

"Shoot, I know it's not as good as your grandmother's."

"No, it's fine," I said, reaching for the bowl of sliced canta-loupe he'd set out. "I mean, it's good. Thank you."

"Naw, it's only serviceable," he said, pointing at the piece of melon I'd speared onto my fork. "But that there's a goodie. A Pecos melon."

He was right. The taste was extra rich and sweet—sunny, somehow, and earthy—and I forked more onto my plate, avoiding the liver. We ate quietly for a few moments, Leroy staring off. He nodded toward Mamaw's chair, the one clos-est to the wall phone. He wiped a sheen of perspiration from his brow. "When that robbery happened, it was this record-high summer—remember that, Pat? How hot it was?"

"Sure do."

Leroy looked at me. "Crime rate shoots up when it's hot. Gets people to fighting and not acting right and it was down-right nuts at the station—remember Garcia was on leave for some reason or another, Pat?—and then, darlin', your grand-mother fell and broke her arm on top of it all. I had to step up 'round the house, so she showed me how to make liver like this and fry a chicken. A strange time, and don't think I slept much."

"Yeah, I wonder if you could tell me about that summer," I said, and quieter, "I'm curious about another case, a young woman who went missing around then. Her name was Faye Flores."

Leroy stared at his plate and Mary-Pat stared at me, her ice-blue eyes piercing. After a long pull of his beer, he nodded. "We thought for the longest time she was running and wanted to stay gone. Her boyfriend worked in an auto shop in Parr City. They lived together after she'd run off from her mother's place in Branch Creek months before, to be with him. Wanted nothing to do with her family. Then—this is according to the neighbors—the hitting started. We figured she was between a rock and hard place, couldn't go back home but couldn't stay with him. Sounded like he'd isolated her from friends and such. So, that's why we think she ran. She ran and we couldn't find her. Never found her—it was some kid and his dog found her remains years later, way out in some little town in West Texas. Killed and left like trash—thinking about it makes me sick."

"That one haunted me for a long time," Mary-Pat said, pressing her hand to her chin. I could tell she wanted to say more, but stopped. The CD was skipping now, scratched. She got up to turn off the stereo and the quiet was deafening.

"I ask because I was reading about the robbery in the paper," I said. "I came across the missing person bulletin, and that led me to find a *Houston Chronicle* article—"

"Libel," Mary-Pat interrupted.

"Now, now, I don't care about that," Leroy said, meeting my gaze. "I do care that Faye's mother felt the way she did. Terrible."

Mary-Pat's cheeks were flushed again. "Her mother, the boyfriend—hell, no one—even reported Faye missing for three weeks. Three weeks! Her coworker at the Hastings up there in Parr City finally called around because she'd quit but never picked up her last paycheck. If her coworker hadn't done that, how much longer would it have been? The department did what we could, but it was easier to disappear back then. We're human beings, not superheroes."

I sucked in my cheek, not quite sure what to say. Mary-Pat was being too defensive—and none of us thought cops were superheroes. I did think people wanted to believe the wolf was kept at bay. That the law functioned as a kind of societal guardrail. Or, they didn't—hell, if you were brown-skinned, poor, or both, the law might be the wolf. Leroy had all but admitted Faye's case was waylaid due to external circumstances that summer—the robbery, the high crime rate, not enough deputies—and because Faye had no one advocating for her. I could see it happening to Cody in real-time. None of it was fair, and as I watched him sit with his beer and his supper, Mary-Pat crossing her arms over her broad chest as though *she* was the victim, I thought they should feel worse about the way those lost—Faye and whoever else—had slipped through their fingers.

"We had this theory at the time," Leroy said, a sigh rattling in his throat. "Aw, well, never mind. I don't want to get you more worked up, darlin', and—"

"What?"

"Faye Flores wasn't reported missing until mid-late July, if I remember correctly, but the last time anyone'd seen her was that June. Her family knew the Motts, and so I had to wonder, but it turned out to be nothing more than a coincidence. When it rains it pours," he said.

"Faye was a missing minor," I said. "She was still seventeen."

"No, eighteen," Mary-Pat said. "Just turned."

"Still, why wasn't the whole damn cavalry called in?"

"Afraid I don't have a better answer for you," he said, cutting his eyes away. On high speed, the fan sounded like it was about to detach from the ceiling, its whoosh-whoosh-click breaking our silence. The windows were closed, so the blades only churned skillet smoke around the room, the grease sticking to the curtains. What had been a gradual fade to dusk shifted fast, the light snuffed from the tiny kitchen.

Chapter Twenty

I left Leroy's house, drove the back way toward the county line, and stayed off the interstate. Took Ranch Road 30, which turned into Main Street in Parr City. There were oil fields and a new pipeline near the west of town, and the traffic and heavy equipment had banged up the roads—I bounced over a pothole, got stuck behind a truck hauling water. The light turned red at the intersection of Main and Guadalupe, and I rolled to a stop in clear view of the bank.

First Bank Garnett—Parr City Branch had been built in the sixties. The building sat low to the ground, square and flat-roofed, the stucco roughly textured and painted sage green. The front part was all windows. Big, mirrored glass windows that shone pink with the last strip of a sunset sky. Maybe it was in my mind, knowing what had happened here years ago, but all that glass made the bank seem too open, too vulnerable. In reality, the glass likely only made the inside bright, hot, and hard to cool, and it would've been impossible to see through the windows during the daytime due to the reflection. The light turned green and I hooked a left at the last second, pulling into the bank's empty lot.

I stepped out, exhaust from the water truck still hanging in the warm air. Heat rose from the cracked asphalt straight through the thin soles of my Chucks as if the ground was exhaling, trying to rid itself of a long day. I leaned against the hood, the engine ticking. Robbers had stood in this very spot. They'd gotten here at nearly nine, just moments before the bank opened. Dalton came in the side entrance using an employee's badge. I could now see the employee-designated parking spaces—it was Dee Marshall who'd had the gun at her back. Her badge. She wasn't the one shot, but had been forced to lie on the ground during the holdup. Sonny's mother years later adopting the getaway driver's son was another one of those things—a coincidence, yes, and part of living in a place where everyone's kin to someone—but also, you had to wonder if it was destiny that brought them close years later. Like Dee and Ronnie were living out their lives on cosmic tracks that kept merging and swerving over time.

I looked around, trying to orient myself where Ronnie would've been lying in wait that day. The getaway car had been parked at the top of Sampson Street before reversing all the way down it and peeling out on the farm-to-market road, avoiding the police cruisers that had quickly blocked off both entrances and exits to the bank, along with Main and Guadalupe.

I walked toward the edge of the lot and found Sampson Street was nothing more than an unpaved alley, and a one-way. A thick stand of cedar at the back of the parking lot still obscured the alley from the bank and the main roads. Not a great lookout spot, but good for hiding the vehicle. Me, I would've parked on Guadalupe, a straight shot toward the on-ramp to the interstate a short two blocks east. Here, in this narrow spot, you had a good chance of being trapped. I stood in the middle of the gravel alley. How would Ronnie have known what was happening inside without clear sight-lines, without a cell phone? Maybe he'd been sitting here blind while he waited for his partner to run and find him. But if that were the case, he'd been lucky leaving the scene when he did.

He needed a lookout.

Dust lifted as I walked, the alley clearly not well-traveled, and the dirt filling my nose was undercut by the rank smell of garbage. To my left was the back of a shopping center with rusted dumpsters and a concrete loading dock. I hopped over the weed-choked drainage ditch that separated the alley from the back of the shopping center, and that's when I saw it: the bank in perfect view. If Ronnie had been standing here—or better yet, on the loading dock—he could've watched the en-tire scene unfold. Like those fancy mirrored-glass windows, he would have had a perfect one-way view.

The loading dock was empty except for stray cardboard boxes that had blown out of the dumpster. I walked around the side of the building, unease growing in the pit of my stomach. A rat ran boldly out in front of me—her turf, not mine—and graffiti adorned the once-white façade, now a murky dishwa-ter color. The shopping center was all but abandoned. One store, a health food store of all things, was still open, as was a Goodwill. The anchor store, the one connected to the load-ing dock, had boards covering its windows. I pulled out my phone to try Google, when a waiflike man drifted out of the health food store. He lifted the kickstand on the door, ready-ing to lock up for the night.

"Hey," I said, jogging across the cracked parking lot toward him. "Do you know what this big store used to be?"

He was older, wearing a white linen tunic over faded jeans. Wind lifted his combed-over hair and puffed up his shirt, giving him a strangely ethereal look. "It's a Spirit Halloween for a few months a year now. But it used to be a bookstore and video rental chain, place you could buy CDs. Wish that were still the case."

"Really," I said, heart thumping in my neck. "Was this store a Hastings Entertainment?"

He laughed. "And here I thought you were probably too young to remember Hastings, Blockbuster, any of those type of places!"

"Thanks, but not quite," I said, stepping backward. Cutting across the alley back toward the bullet, I had the giddy feeling that I'd uncovered a clue. Mary-Pat said Faye Flores had worked at a Hastings in Parr City—what if she'd been some kind of accomplice to Ronnie? His lookout?

The rush of adrenaline dissipated as I walked the wide perimeter of the bank, its shadows blending into twilight. Leroy had figured the same thing, a possible connection between Faye and the Motts. He'd also come to the conclusion that it wasn't what had happened—why'd I think I could prove differently? I stopped midstride, realizing I was able to see through the glass windows of the bank. Security lights had flickered on, illuminating the interior and giving it the appearance of a stage set. The action running through my mind wasn't so unlike a film, the faces covered in bandit masks and pancake-makeup, heightened and distorted. Good guys and bad guys, damsels in distress, roles to fit. The robbery was one day, one act, and yet I couldn't help but see it as the whole of a thing. A moment—*the* moment—that collided lives, setting off car chases and gunshots, deaths and life sentences.

Nothing was ever as clear as it seemed. Not even with the benefit of hindsight, not after the curtain closed—there was no end of an act, not really.

Chapter Twenty-one

At the county line, driving along the beer-way toward the pool hall to see how crowded it was, I changed my mind and kept going. Crossed into Price County, into Branch Creek, into the little neighborhood behind the Methodist Church and around the back of the single-story houses, parking on the packed dirt lane. I walked the block toward the Mott house on the corner, which was lit up inside, and had a shiny Cadillac SUV parked in the driveway. The smaller Flores house across the way was dark but for the soft changing lights of a television coming through the open curtains. Mrs. Flores was outside on her porch again, no sign of the nurse. I could barely make out her shape from the darkness, but the moon was full, and there was a single lamp near a transformer at the end of the street casting a cold thin light. I couldn't see her expression quite yet.

"Who's out there?"

I came up her walkway lined with pretty desert plants and pinwheels, putting my hands out in front of me. "Ma'am, it's Annie McIntyre. I wanted to speak with you, though I understand if you don't want to talk to me."

She was quiet for a moment, and taking it as a no, I started to turn around.

"Wait," she said. "Come on up."

She motioned to a metal lawn chair beside her. I breathed in the heady scent of tobacco and the sprig of rosemary she'd plucked and rolled between her fingers, along with something sweeter, fruitier. Her steel-colored hair was unbraided, hanging down past her waist and damp from a shampoo—that scent. "It took me some time to put it all together," I said. "But I realized how you knew my last name. I wanted to let you know that I'm sorry about what happened to Faye."

"Why?" She let out a dry cough. "I don't blame you any more than I blamed those poor Mott kids for their dad being who he was. Powerful men are powerful pieces of shit, in my experience."

I bristled, a skeptical sound escaping my throat. I'd come here hoping she'd vent to me, that I'd gain insight, that I might offer secondhand remorse over the investigation. So, not sure what other reaction I'd been expecting, but calling Leroy a piece of shit still irked me. From what I understood, Mrs. Flores hadn't done much to help her daughter, either. "Why'd you yell at me the other day?" I asked.

"Seeing Lorena suffering brought back horrible memories. You can't comprehend the loss of a child, not unless it happens to you."

"I understand if you don't want to talk about her now," I said, watching her face, but her expression was unchanged. "But I've been wondering, what do you think actually happened to your daughter?"

She gripped the arms of her lawn chair to sit up straighter. "She'd had enough of her boyfriend and hit the road—but see, my theory is that he went after her. That's the part the sheriff, your grandfather, wouldn't hear. That her loser boy-friend caught up to her and killed her, and that if the police would've gotten to her first, or arrested him, she'd still be here." She looked off, her voice softening. "Not here, prob-ably. But alive. Someplace else but alive. Those cops tried to sell me some nonsense about it being a serial killer who met up with her at a motel—but how? No way!"

I opened and closed my mouth, letting the part about so-licitation hang between us. Didn't want to sound like every-one else—I'd hate that. No one would outright say hooking meant you deserved to be murdered, probably, but there were always the insidious implications. That wasn't what I believed. But sex work was how the killer had likely cornered her. Mrs. Flores thought it either untrue her daughter had done it, or more likely, that it spoiled the girl in all those framed pictures up on her mantel. Either way, denial. "He confessed, though, right?" I asked after a moment. "The serial killer?"

"That's another thing," she said. "He took it all back a few years later. And, if you'd done your homework, you'd know that when he confessed to it originally, when the detectives asked him details about where her body was and stuff like that, he got it wrong!"

I nodded, perched on the edge of my chair now, too. "That's interesting. No, I hadn't read that he recanted, or what he'd said in his original confession."

"Well, it's true."

If she was right, then who'd killed Faye? Thing was, even if it wasn't the "Motel Stalker," it could've been another like him. Violence had a way of arrowing toward a woman walk-ing the highway. I could assume Leroy had had good reason to believe it wasn't the boyfriend. I looked across the street. Lorena hadn't lived here until after the robbery, so that would have been long after Faye left home. But the house had been in the Mott family for years before then. "Did Faye ever hang around Ronnie Mott?" I asked, nodding my head in the direction of the house.

She pursed her lips.

"I wondered with your families being neighbors. You said he'd hung around his grandmother's place a lot."

"Faye was a lot younger than those kids. By the time she was a teenager, him and his brother had gone off and were adults," she said, then sighed. "Course, I caught him looking."

"She was beautiful."

Mrs. Flores looked down, her toes curling over the edge of her rubber slides. "I caught Ronnie up on my porch a couple times flirting, but after my husband had a little talk with him, he let her be. Faye was just a girl."

"You think they could've reconnected? After she left home?"

"No, and she did not run around with trash!"

She heaved herself up to standing. I offered my arm, which she refused, reaching for a cane laid over the bench. I'd crossed a line again; she was done with me. Across the street, a light flipped off inside Lorena's house, and the Cadillac that had been sitting in the driveway turned its headlights on and reversed out. "It's getting late," I said, fingering my keys. "Sorry to have bothered you."

"You're a private detective."

I paused.

"You do me a favor, and in return, I'll tell you something about Lorena Mott," she said, pointing across the street. A light had come on in another room, toward the back. Honestly, I didn't quite know what I was dealing with when it came to Lorena. Her daughter saying that she wasn't Clint's real mother echoed in my head. Mrs. Flores's eyes had darted toward the house when she'd said Faye hadn't ever gotten tangled up with Ronnie, as if she herself didn't believe the words coming out of her mouth.

"In return for this favor," she said, growing more animated, "I'll tell you whose car that was in her driveway and everyone she's been talking to. I don't know what you want with the Motts, but might could tell you things on the down low."

"I could probably find out myself, and besides, I don't barter."

"Girl, Lorena is never going to tell you nothing. You know that well as I do. Now, here's the favor: Faye's girlfriend," she said, angling in front of me with her cane. "I always thought there was something she wasn't telling. Faye didn't have a lot of friends I don't think, none she confided in—like if her boyfriend was abusive, or whatever else was happening—but maybe this woman she did. Get a message to her, tell her all Mary Flores wants to do is talk. Tell her I'm not mad, I just have some questions. Her name is Dee Marshall. Stays out in Parr City."

My heart pounded. Dee Marshall as in Sonny and Clint's mother?

"There's life to live and I get it. But that there's people out there doing what-all they want while my girl is dead still eats me right up—"

"Faye and Dee were friends from where?"

"I don't know, I tried talking with her myself and, well, it got complicated. She didn't want to speak with me, but this was a few years ago now. Just go find her and see if she'd talk—that's all I want." She took my hand and squeezed hard. "Please."

"Okay," I said, letting go of her hot, sandpapery grip. "I'll talk to her. And that person across the street, they—"

"I'll fill you in, promise!" she said quickly, and put her hand on my back, pushing me toward the edge of the porch. "You'll thank me later."

I took another look at Lorena's house, debating it. But Mrs. Flores was right. Fool me once, fool me twice—I didn't need to try for three with Lorena, not while her grief was still so fresh. And Dee? Small world getting too small. I walked back toward the bullet, the long day catching up with me, but on a second wind. I couldn't quite see how the past and the present might click or might rupture, but my frustration was tinged with something else—a knowledge, deep down, that I was getting closer.

Nearly home, I almost didn't see the car. Dark truck, lights off, parked halfway hidden in the trees. The neighbor's collie had started barking like nuts when I got out of the bullet. The dog knew me though she pretended otherwise whenever I pulled up, running along the fence line biting the air and giving a single, deep-throated bark to let me know who was boss. This was different—frantic bursts of yips and whines—she was scared. I spun around, thinking coyotes. As I squinted at the dark shape across the dirt road, an engine roared to life and the truck pulled out of the trees. Turned at the intersection up the road and was gone.

Wyatt's grad classes weren't over until nine, and he'd forgotten to leave the porch light on. I hurried up the driveway madder than scared, hand shaking as I held the phone flashlight out in front of me, keys tucked between my knuckles in the other. The property was fenced on all sides, but we needed the landlord to pony up for a gate. I peered around the house, checking the windows and screens. Nothing. Both doors sealed tight, locked. Head down as I crossed the front threshold, right as I was ready to exhale, I saw a burnt, shriveled match scraped on the concrete.

Hot wind gusted at my back. Smoke wafted the air. I turned, seeing an orange flame jump and lick the grass along the fence line. The driver must've thrown a second match when they sped off.

The hose was unwound, left in a tangle from when Wyatt had watered the plants that evening. I turned the spigot on at the side of the house and sprinted toward the fence. The neighbor's dog barked at the low flames, diving, nipping, and drew back with a yelp when sparks singed her fur. I whistled, tried calling her off as I aimed the hose, but she stayed, watching intently until I'd doused the fire. The grasses ceased glowing and popped once, sizzling with steam. It was suddenly quiet, quiet but for her fast breaths and the chugging of my heart. I dropped the hose and reached through the fence, rubbing the dog's long snout. Sank to my knees with her for a minute, maybe longer, before I reached for my phone to call the sheriff.

Garcia didn't answer, and the DEA agent's number was on a business card somewhere. I didn't want to call the emergency line—what could they do, now?

The difference between old me and new me was fear. Not that I didn't get as scared as I used to—might've been I felt more scared knowing the range of bad outcomes. But I trusted myself to stay solid in a way that comes from going through things instead of around them. Satisfied that the threat was gone, the dog ran back toward her owner's house, but me, I'd stay awake and keep watch. All night, however long it took to win the game of chicken Eli Wallace wanted us to play.

Chapter Twenty-two

The morning light looked dulled by the gray cloud cover. Another noncommittal sky, no rain, no thunder, only a thickness to the air. I checked the mirrors over and over as I drove. Sheriff Garcia had called back last night and offered to send a deputy out, but once I was talking, I felt less sure—I'd assumed it was Eli Wallace who'd thrown the matches. Garcia said the DEA agent was still in town, that he'd let him know what happened, and I didn't sleep much thinking he might check in. Wyatt came home and offered to keep watch for a few hours, but I couldn't relax. My fear felt weirdly like shame again. A lot like being the shy kid in class, something about sensing an audience. I needed to get out of my head and keep moving, but this morning felt like everything was taking two minutes too long, like everything was sticky—my skin, the steering wheel—that I was braking too hard, that I turned the bullet too jerkily.

I wanted to knock out the favor for Mrs. Flores first. She was right that I needed to know who Lorena Mott had been talking to since Cody's death. I was also curious to hear exactly how Dee Marshall knew her daughter, Faye. They'd have been near the same age—it was strange and it wasn't. Hell, what if Dee also knew the Motts? Before Clint's adoption, even? Uncomfortable territory for a variety of reasons, but chiefly, that I'd promised Clint that I wouldn't involve his mother. Murder investigation—off the record or not—trumped all, but still, you're only as good as your word in this business. I could make it seem like only Mrs. Flores had hired me. Dee worked as a salesperson at Roadrunner Ford in Colburn, near the university. State's stadium and the clock tower came into view, and I relaxed thinking about other, more normal people's lives running parallel to mine. I felt Wyatt close by.

No one approached me as I walked into the dealership. I didn't know whether to be offended or not. I clocked my faded jeans and once-white Chucks, knowing I looked like a student, but for all anyone knew I had a rich parent's checkbook. Nabbing a complimentary water and a granola bar from the showroom, I scanned the nameplates on the offices toward the back. Dee's was the first on my left, door cracked, and I knocked out of politeness.

"Morning, Annie," she said brightly, if not surprised. Her lipstick was red, but not too red, flattering her. It was hard not to appraise her in the way my aunt did—how the harsh light made her highlights look brassy, less blended. She looked more confident than she had at the wedding, and with her broad features, like what my aunt Jewel would've called a handsome woman. Maybe it was the blazer. "Didn't know you were in the market for a new ride! Has someone been out to show you around the lot?"

"I'm actually here to speak with you."

"Sit, sit," she said, brushing bagel crumbs off a silky blouse.

The office was mostly impersonal, with a fake plant in the corner, a dealership calendar on the wall. But on the desk, a framed picture of Clint and Sonny when they were eleven or twelve, sitting on a park bench in swim trunks, noses pink, skinny arms hooked over each other's shoulders. It wasn't an unusual thing for brothers, even close ones, to grow apart. But it nagged at me, the distance between them, even before the wedding fiasco. Was it simply diverging paths after eighteen—Sonny to Afghanistan, the tour that would wound him, Clint to college and rising stardom—or was it a specific moment, a falling-out that had changed things? Her eyes glided between me and the picture. "Good times, right there. Sonny has a summer birthday and we'd take the boys to Schlitterbahn every year. Make yourself comfortable, hon."

"Thanks," I said. "Actually, can I close this door?"

Her chin jutted out and she lengthened her neck—I couldn't tell if she was bucking me a little or not, but I felt the need to also straighten up. "What's this about?" she asked. "You talk to Clint yet? I haven't."

"No," I said, and closed the door anyway. "You know I'm a private investigator, and small world, a client of mine wants to speak with you. It's about a woman named Faye Fl—"

"Stop right there," she said, flapping her ballet flat hard against her heel. "Did Mary Flores send you?"

I nodded.

"She tried messaging me on Facebook and I had to block her. Annie, this woman, bless her heart and all, but she's been harassing me for decades. I actually took out a restraining order about fifteen years ago."

My stomach dropped. "Oh, my."

"She was stalking me here at the dealership. I was recently separated from my ex—he was a mechanic, so I know a thing about cars—but anyway, I really needed a job. It being a recession and all, I felt damn lucky to get this position and that woman nearly got me let go. Then she turned up at the boys' school, and that was the last straw. I'm surprised you didn't do your due diligence."

"Well"—I crossed my arms—"I think she only wants to speak with you about her daughter because she's heartbroken. But you're right. Clearly, I don't know everything."

She let out a tight sigh.

"You were friends with Faye, though?"

Her eyes darted to the opaque half-wall that separated us from the showroom, and her voice lowered. "We weren't friends, only acquaintances. It's a tragedy what happened to her, but Annie, this was nearly thirty years ago! Her mom thinks I have some deep dark secret I'm not sharing, but it's just not true. I barely knew the girl. Her boyfriend just worked in the same shop as my husband. Faye and her boyfriend seemed to be on the outs, you know, he'd said they were fighting—but I didn't know of any abuse."

It crossed my mind that Dee and her husband could've tried to protect the boyfriend, but maybe it wasn't anything so sinister. I pressed anyway. "Did you ever talk to the cops? Maybe there's something that in retrospect might mean something to them or to her mom. You don't think you'd ever be comfortable speaking with her? Even over the phone?" I felt torn, embarrassed that I'd been played, but also like I'd tugged on a loose thread. A little of what Mrs. Flores felt, just now—like Dee was giving me the brush-off. "If nothing else, it would be cathartic for her," I added. "Maybe you, too."

"They didn't interview me, 'cause like I said, we didn't really know her. Her boyfriend, he didn't stick around the shop, and I don't know whatever happened to him, either. I feel bad for this woman, I do, but I've been working on boundaries and I think this would really set me back."

Dee seemed to possess a real talent for turning the tables. Standing up for Clint's jerk-off move at the wedding, for instance. I took a breath, softening my voice. "Dee, you're a mom. I think it's mostly that she wants to feel closer to her daughter. You're maybe the only person alive she can think of anymore who knew her."

Dee hung her head, smiled a little when she looked up at me. "Well, Faye seemed like a pistol, you can tell her that. That kind of quippy sense of humor I never could pull off—smart girl. Heard her boyfriend was broken up when she left, but it also wasn't a shock to him. She was a wild one with—not to dance on her grave or nothing—a real mean streak, it sounded like. Intense, but a fair-weather person. Romantic or flaky, depending how you saw it. Again, not to be nasty, I just mean she seemed like the kind of person who'd take off to California with only the clothes on her back," she said, her own voice a little far-off. "Wasn't like it is now, with everyone on their phones. I was sad about what happened to her."

What happened to her? Something about the phrase, the passiveness of it made my throat close up. A man killed her—presumably a man—a person, an actor, not some mysterious force. "Do you think she could've left with anyone?"

Dee shrugged, but I sensed a tightness to her shoulders.

"Do you know if she was hanging around Ronnie Mott?" I asked, casually as I could muster. I was nearing the zone where this business with Faye connected with Clint's biological family and the robbery, and all that a coincidence or not, I felt I was on thin ice.

"Am I supposed to know who that is?"

"I don't know," I said, noting her face hadn't changed.

Maybe it was possible to adopt out of foster care with little to no knowledge of your child's birth family. Surely, she'd heard the name, if not at that point, then given his connection to the robbery. Maybe Ronnie Mott had sifted out of her mind, a detail lost to time. She wouldn't have seen his face that day, only in the media. We both startled when a paunchy, older man wearing a suit and bolo tie lumbered into the office without knocking.

"Dee, sweetheart, there's a couple in the lobby," he said, nodding at me. "Oops, sorry, see you're busy. Just that Jay's bustin' tail out there, and you told me you wanted a shot at the next commission—"

"No, we're done and I'll be right out," she said, cheesy smile plastered on her face. He gave a thumbs-up and left. "Sorry to cut this trip down memory lane short," she said to me.

"If you change your mind, you can always call me," I said, handing her my card, and my eyes landed on that framed photo again. "One last thing, I know you haven't caught up with Clint, but have you talked with Sonny?"

Her shoulders relaxed as she stood. "He's hurt, but he'll be okay. Sonny's happy and in love—what else can you ask for? I do hope the boys patch it up. Don't know for certain, but I think for all Clint's big success he might be jealous of Sonny. They've always been so competitive with each other. Thought they'd have grown out of it by now." She sighed for effect, her annoyance rising to the surface. She took my business card and dropped it on her desk—at least not in the can.

I drove straight back across the two counties, which took me over an hour. I felt light-headed, my lack of sleep catching up, and nervous to see Mrs. Flores. She unlocked the front door, hesitating behind the screen. Her face was stiff, her eyes half-open as if to guard against me leveling with her, braced for what news I might come bearing—like she'd never stopped reliving the moment the law had come here looking for the next of kin.

"You didn't tell me about a restraining order," I said, hedging a moment myself. "But I did speak with Dee, and she said there's nothing you don't already know. She said she didn't really know her, that her boyfriend was a mutual connection, is all."

"That can't be true. Faye's purse. When they found it with her remains there was a little notepad. A phone number was written inside the cover—Dee's number."

One person was lying, or, I supposed, Faye could've found the notebook in the auto shop, her boyfriend's apartment, or wherever. Still, strange. "I'm just telling you what Dee told me."

"What else did she say?"

"Honestly, not much. She said she'd heard it wasn't surprising she ran off, that Faye had wanted to get out of town—"

Mrs. Flores pushed open the screen door, stepped out onto the porch, and smacked me on the arm. "You think I'm crazy!"

Her nurse paused the television from inside the living room, hollering to ask if everything was okay. The slap hadn't hurt, but I was stung as though she'd belted me. "I'm sorry, but you're the one who put me in this position—I'm giving you what you asked for," I said, lowering my voice and nodding toward the house across the street. "A favor in return."

She gripped the metal porch railing, shooting daggers at me. "Harris Griggs."

"Who is he?"

"Ronnie's lawyer. Been hanging around that house all weekend," she said. "Ever since Cody died."

I nodded, tucking the information away for when I had

time to think. "Listen, ma'am. I don't think you're crazy, and I don't think there's been justice for Faye—nothing will ever be enough, probably. I can keep asking questions though, keep poking around if you'd like me to, no need to barter. See what it kicks up."

She seemed to consider my offer, then shook her head, pointedly turning her gaze away from me. I lingered on the porch step, and when she spoke, her voice warbled like she might cry. "I didn't want you to do anything but take me seriously," she said. "You couldn't even do that."

Her words hit like a second slap. All of the frustrations of the past few weeks rushed over me at once, brought to a head by being scolded when I was only trying to help—that was what I was doing here, wasn't it?

"I'm not going to forget about her," I said. "For the record, my grandfather hasn't, either."

Chapter Twenty-three

I stopped for chicken fingers and a cherry limeade at Sonic, not having eaten anything but that stale granola bar I'd pilfered from the dealership. There was no mark, no redness where Mrs. Flores had slapped me, but the imprint of her touch felt like fire. The cavernous anger she'd let rip had shocked me, though probably it shouldn't have. Didn't matter if it had been twenty-something years or twenty minutes, hers was a forever-type pain. The waitress brought my lunch and I kept the windows rolled down. Heat pulsed into the vehicle, no breeze to speak of—I kept thinking, weirdly, of this time my parents took me to Galveston, the first time I'd seen the ocean. A storm rolled in while we were playing on the beach, and it had hit me that the water was not tame, not containable. That it was ocean and it was wild—I'd known, of course, but I hadn't seen it, not believed until it was in front of me.

Thinking of Lorena, too, felt like watching a drowning woman. Ronnie's lawyer, Harris Griggs, was a fairly well-known criminal defense attorney. I didn't yet know what to make of him being at the house, but a likely scenario was that he was an intermediary, gathering information to pass along to Ronnie. I'd seen a picture of him, one of the media photos taken outside the courthouse during the trial. Wearing alligator boots, a very nineties-looking pleated suit and turquoise-studded bolo tie, he struck me as oddly flashy. Maybe he was simply close with the family and was offering condolences to Lorena. Hard to say—what I did know was that I couldn't shake my sense that what had happened to Cody contained echoes of that summer. Months before his baby brother was born, a couple of years before his family fully splintered.

My mind looped to Clint, and I found his Instagram page, wondering if he'd answer a DM. He'd posted a new video. Before he spoke, he narrowed the frame with his forefinger and thumb—a split second look of concentration, reminding you this was a production. I always had those break-the-fourth-wall moments when I watched reels or TikToks—be it a reaction to a pregnancy test, a song, show, or what have you—like, at the end of the day it's still a person alone in their room with their phone propped on the dresser, a friend acting as silent cameraman. Not real, even if the feeling is real. Again, Clint wore a hat. Aviator shades and a denim, pearl-snap shirt unbuttoned to reveal his vines tattoo and his pecs. "Big news, fam, big news," he said, laugh at the back of his throat. But his smile was tight. "Turns out I'm sticking around Nashville. Gonna cut a record here, for real real. Too soon to say much more, but this thing's gonna be big y'all—"

Mary-Pat called and I put her on speaker.

"Where are you?" she asked.

"Lunch," I said, hearing a ping from my inbox, too.

"No need to rush back or anything, but I found your guy from the DEA standing on the sidewalk outside the office. All suited up, thought he was here to bust you."

"You talk to him?" I asked, face growing hot, and opened my email.

"Said he was just checking in on you, then walked off," she said.

"Only took him, what fifteen hours? Jesus."

"You see anyone following you today?"

"No," I said, letting out a breath. "But thanks for the heads-up." Mission accomplished for that guy—if it was Eli Wallace who'd lit the fire last night, the plan to use me as bait was working. My heart thrummed in my neck as I stared at the screen. The email was a reply to the message I'd sent about the barback opening at Cowboys. Brief, unaddressed, and unsigned, said open interviews were tonight from six till nine. This combined with the DEA agent sniffing around felt like a mix between kismet and a reminder from the rational part of my brain that going by Cowboys was risky.

"Sure thing," Mary-Pat said a little breathlessly, her voice echoing like she was climbing the stairwell. "I'm fixing to make a deposit—you already filled out the slip, put your checks on my desk?"

"Yep," I said, jamming my trash into the greasy bag it came in. Her going to the bank had given me an idea about how I'd use the time between now and this evening.

"You okay?"

"Fine," I said, dropping the phone in the passenger seat after she disconnected. I took the highway east, back into Garnett County, headed to Parr City. Turned at the intersection of Main and Guadalupe and into the bank parking lot. The manager at the branch was Momma's friend, Luanne Davies. The same woman who'd been here at the time of the robbery, the one who'd been held up alongside Dee Marshall. Her being a first-person witness and all, I wanted to talk, hoped to catch her on lunch break. I glanced at the dash. Nearly two. I recognized her green sedan in the reserved space toward the rear of the building. I parked next to it, planning to go inside, and startled a bit when I looked over and found her sitting inside the car staring at me.

I came around to the driver's side and she turned the engine off and cracked her door. Swung her legs out and dabbed her mouth with a napkin. "Annie McIntyre, that you?"

"Hi, Mrs. Davies."

"I was bad and went to the drive-thru. Decided to eat in my car so I could listen to my audiobook and no one would bug me. How's your momma?"

"Good. I was hoping I might find you here," I said, leaning on the back door of the sedan. "Sorry you ended up getting bugged after all."

Her laugh was a high, tinkly sound. White-blond hair pulled back with a big, tortoiseshell plastic barrette, she fiddled where a few strands had come loose at her ears. The seam at the toe of her nude-colored panty hose had bunched and twisted out of her high-heeled shoe, which for some reason made my skin crawl. She stood up and hooked a leather purse over her shoulder. "Lord knows I don't mean you. Anyway, hon, I do actually have to go back in. Have a loan applicant coming by at two. What's going on? You thinking about buying that place with your boyfriend? Your momma told me it's getting serious."

"Oh, no," I said, though I smiled—Momma said that? It was honestly just nice to think of her talking about me. It'd been months of focusing on my cousin and her wedding from the women in my family, and maybe I'd felt a little sidelined. "Well, if we had the money to buy, who knows, but that's not why I'm here. I wanted to ask you about the robbery at this branch back in the nineties."

Her eyes got big. "Lower your voice, please," she said, closing her car door and locking it. "Can't go around during business hours talking about a holdup. Makes people nervous. What's it you want to know?"

"The shopping center across the alley—did you ever see anyone hanging around the back by the loading dock that day, or in the days before?"

She shook her head.

"Do you remember a woman named Faye Flores? Worked over in the video store?"

"No, sorry. That time in my life was really kind of a blur and I've tried to forget a lot of it. I'd just had my daughter—you remember Steph—my husband was working doubles and neither of us were sleeping. I'd gotten in extra early to let the other girl in, who was coming off maternity leave that day—I do sometimes think about that. Like, if she'd had her own key card, would I have been spared? She was normally here alone before we opened. Or what if they'd waited to put in the new security system even a couple weeks?" She rubbed goose bumps on her arms. "Dee, that was her name. We shared a sitter and I remember thinking at least our babies were looked after if we died. Strange the things you remember and don't," she said. "Sorry, Annie."

"No, it was a long time ago."

"Won't ever forget being in the safe room with a gun pointed at me. Felt like hours. I think about that, how when your grand-dad at the back of the ambulance told me it had been a long ten minutes in there, and I really thought we'd been in there hours. That and me punching the combination to the safe, my body shivering so bad, it was almost like a comedy skit"—she started shaking her arms wildly to demonstrate—"so shocked that I actually giggled. Wild what we do under duress. I don't remember what happened after I tripped the alarm. I blacked the gunshot out. Thank the lord it only grazed my arm. Bled a lot, but it didn't hit anything major."

"Did he ask Dee to try the safe?"

"Yes, but she honestly didn't know the combination. Could've given him the drawers, but not the big safe. If I hadn't happened to be there, he'd have probably killed her," she said, and started toward the building, her gaze lifting to the security cameras. "What's all this about, anyway?"

"Oh, my granddad. He's having me update his file keeping," I mumbled, realizing that it was true in some way—I was following the Leroy McIntyre method now, not knowing exactly where to aim my focus, cowboying it on instinct alone. Feeling it out, he liked to say. "Did you notice anything else out of the ordinary around then?" I added. "Or even in the weeks afterward?"

"Nope," she said, and looked at her wristwatch pointedly. "You work in a bank, you hear about holdups, you're trained for these scenarios, but it doesn't seem real to you. Not till it happens. He wore a mask like in the movies. A nightmare I hope I never relive."

"Thanks, Mrs. Davies," I said, stepping off the curb. "Appreciate you talking."

She waved goodbye, hurrying inside those shiny glass doors to meet her appointment.

Chapter Twenty-four

I woke on the couch near dusk. The disorientation I felt when I slept too long, when I realized the sun had departed and that the world had kept spinning without me morphed into one solid dread-knot. Last night's vigilance had caught up with me. Looking out the windows, checking the locks first, I hopped in the shower, my lips salty with sweat as the water ran down my face and our fan-less bathroom fogged with steam.

Getting dressed made me miss Nikki. We often took an evening nap before going out, back when we were nocturnal. We'd lean over the sink afterward and do our makeup, pregame with boxed wine, blast music on her phone while waiting for that text to come through like a dinner bell chime—here, possibilities served—the parties only beginning at eleven, twelve. Hitting Cowboys didn't exactly have me in party-mode, but there was something about my anticipation that felt familiar. We'd bet on who'd start what, who'd hook up with who—that was how it was now, me knowing shit would go down, only I'd managed to dissociate from the fact that I was most likely to be at the center of said throw-down. My neck was sweating and I gave up blow-drying my hair. I fed the cat, chugged a glass of water and half a beer, leaving before the knot had any chance at slowing me down.

The drive to Cowboys got me more twisted up. Glancing to my right, imagining Cody riding shotgun and telling me which way to turn. The gravel lot was crowded now with trucks and bikes. I parked the bullet at the far side, hoping I wouldn't get blocked in. It was so dark out; fields and a lot of nothing around on that dead-end road. Cowboys just about glowed in the contrast. A sickly-hued fluorescence bled out from the seams in the doors and the iron-barred windows. A transformer station in the empty lot behind the bar gave off a low, steady buzz, only adding to the sense I was headed straight toward a big bug zapper.

"Hey, girl," called a man's voice. Lilting, teasing.

I spun around, stepping off the shallow wooden porch. It was the bartender from the other day. He stood in the shadows off to the side of the building, waving me around back with him. I wiped my hands on my jeans, stealing a glace behind me as I followed. He stopped short of the kitchen entrance and a row of black trash cans. A backpack lay on the ground, along with a Coke and a pack of cigarettes. Either taking a break or his shift had ended. Above him, the bathroom window—I assumed based on the roar of a hand dryer—had been cracked, the light from inside shining onto his face. Younger than I remembered. "I was looking for you," I said. "Remember you behind the bar. I'm here for the job interview."

"Filled it and he's already running orders. You should've gotten here earlier—think a girl like you'd have been a better fit."

It was only eight, just after dark. I looked at the shanty-like building. The music (shitty, like some kind of country-rap remix) was loud, reverberating through the tin corrugated roof. I remembered Eli had gone through a door toward the back that day. "You sure we can't talk? Maybe sit in the office where it's quiet? I want to at least tell you my résumé—"

"Naw, come on." He smirked and glanced up at the window, making a point to lower his voice. "You heard about your boy Cody, yeah?"

"No," I said carefully. "What's up?"

"Offed himself," he said and mimed a trigger pull to the head, again with that teasing tone. But there was no mirth in it. His shoulders curled inward, and I thought his sarcasm was more of a leftover from adolescence, kind of like the acne scars. This way of looking at my forehead instead of my eyes, a habit meant to deflect since sincerity was akin to blood in the water. He looked like he lifted weights, wasn't bad looking— but there was a distinct uneasiness about him.

I stared back, my mouth hanging open in feigned surprise. One hand to my chest, the other grazed his bicep. "Can you believe that? Like, did you ever think *Cody* was suicidal? Jesus."

The corner of his mouth twitched. "Signing up for an ass-kicking on a regular basis aside, no. Goes to show you don't ever know what's really going on with someone, I guess."

"Can't help but think it's"—I shook my head, lips parting— "ugh, no, never mind."

"Honestly, yeah, if you're thinking what I'm thinking, it is suspicious," he said, eyes lighting up. If he was reluctant to share any theories at first, he was clearly finding some relief in airing them now. He let out a long sigh. "Man, he just wasn't the type. And I know the type. My brother-in-law, when he uh, died that way, he'd like, tried before—I'm putting my foot in my mouth, but what I mean to say is Cody didn't seem depressed. Not, like, clinically."

So, this guy and Cody were friends. He seemed mad, maybe scared, and I nodded along furiously. "God, you think someone . . . shot him?"

He looked behind him. "I'm not saying anything like that. Just surreal is what I'm saying. But I don't think you should go in there tonight. I don't know if you were dating him or what but—"

"No, it wasn't like that."

"Whatever. Point is, there's guys in there talking some shit about Cody. Must've really pissed someone off before he died. This fat-ass dude—I fuckin' hate this dude, but anyway—he actually bought a round and raised a toast."

"Seriously?"

"They're all in there laughing about it. Fuckin' weird."

"Who did this? What's his name?"

He stepped back. "Naw, I don't want anyone to start anything. But, I'm about to leave myself. Let me buy you a drink somewhere, or we can hang at my place, it's just up the road."

"No, I'm okay," I said, instinctively crossing my arms. I looked over my shoulder as two guys in leather biker gear ambled up the steps, chains jangling. "Do you know the owner of the bar well?"

He frowned.

"Or her nephew, Eli?"

"Don't mess with him," he said, cutting me off. He picked his backpack up off the ground, jammed the cigarettes and Coke in the front pocket and slung it over one shoulder, brushing past me like a sullen ninth grader. I kind of doubted he was that put off by my rejection, more that he was upset about Cody. I wasn't above laying it on thick, but I wasn't going to his apartment alone. Maybe if I'd massaged his invitation, convinced him to hang inside the pool hall with me, he'd have kept talking. Now I'd have to go in without an ally. I hung in the shadows as his headlights shrunk and pulled away, taking a slow, deep breath.

The door to the pool hall was sticky and swung back with unexpected force when I yanked the busted knob. I slid to the far corner of the bar and ordered a Shiner, and the bikers who'd come in before me nodded in my direction. I shrank a little more and took a few sips before finding an open spot along the wall, a clear view of the pool tables. Instead of all the people crowded inside masking the scent of unfinished plywood with their sweat and cologne, the heat amplified the smell of the wood, like the sweet, gluey boards had been sitting under a hot sun. There was a narrow shelf along the wall where people had deposited bags and well drinks emptied down to ice and shriveled limes, a few chairs leaned against it. I hid behind a group of guys waiting on a game and leaned my elbow on the shelf, pretending to look at my phone. The guy who'd toasted Cody's death was fairly easy to single out after a few minutes of listening. Thick-necked, with short, skinny limbs and a body that was all belly. His face was piggish, too—smushed and pink, beady eyes set deep—but he moved quickly around the pool table taking sharp, decisive shots. He wore a bright orange trucker cap perched on his head in a way that, for whatever reason—maybe in the way all places can feel like high school sometimes—told me he was the popular one in his group. The loudmouth, the clown.

"Eli's gonna call you," he said, leaning his belly over the felt. "I told him you were interested. Gotta be patient, bro."

The other guy—of similar size and thick-headedness—

held the pool stick tight like he might snap it. "Thought you said he was coming out."

"He might, is what I said. I don't know. I'm not his *girl-friend*," he said, and both men cut their eyes away from the table, sneering at a petite young woman leaning on the opposite wall. I must've been staring too hard at the men—I hadn't noticed that while they were watching her, she'd been watching me. I pretended to text again, but she walked across the room and sidled up to me.

"Waiting on someone?" she asked, her voice slurred.

"Ah, yeah. My boyfriend," I said, unnerved by how close she was. I could smell her whiskey breath, and her gummy, overly sweet perfume, which smelled almost exactly like the pink baby lotion I suddenly remembered my mom slathering me with when I was little. She wore a mesh top over a spaghetti-strapped camisole and pleather shorts. Jet-black hair, borderline goth makeup, and pale eyebrows. Really young, and trying really hard to look older. "Hate it when they keep you waiting," I added. "What're you gonna do?"

"I know you from somewhere," she said, leaning back for a better look. Unabashedly sizing me up and down the way super drunk girls do each other in the bathroom mirror, fumbling for the paper towels, gushing over an outfit that's wrinkled and wet with beer. Her smile slackened but her eyes stayed locked on my face.

"Just moved to Branch Creek! Working at the new hospital," I said, leaning now myself, drawing out my voice to sound drunker. "Seeing how I'm new here, you maybe know who could hook me up? Need to get my mind right."

"Oh, sure," she said, nodding. "My boyfriend can get you just about anything when he gets here."

My heart yo-yoed into my throat.

"Wait, I know where I know you from! You said you work at the hospital—you're the girl at the pharmacy!"

"Yeah," I said, deciding to play along. "Thought you looked familiar, too." Experience taught me that when someone's not playing with a full deck—whether heavily intoxicated or mentally unstable—it's better to not come crashing into their reality with yours.

"Well, I have weed, but what're you after? He doesn't deal anymore usually, but maybe you two could talk. It'd be good to have a friend at the hospital. Hell, if you could return the favor with some scrips?"

"I don't think that's how it works—"

She flapped her hand, wasn't listening. "He got into it with this family friend and then it didn't work out, and I told him, like, don't work with people it's too personal with. It's for the best this guy is out of the picture, but now, yeah, Eli has a lot going on to pick up the slack . . ." She trailed off, mumbling something I couldn't quite make out over the music. The pig-gish guy had won the game of pool and let out a whoop, steal-ing her attention.

I touched her arm to draw her back. "You mean Cody Mott?" I said, loud as I dared.

She turned her head sharply. "Yeah, you know Cody?"

My face felt clammy and tingly, my ears hot like I was about to be sick. Cody must have been working for Eli all along. Like his sister had said, ever the loyal, pitiful friend. *Out of the picture now*—was that a euphemism for suicide, or for murder? I looked back at her and shrugged, but knew my voice sounded strained. "Not really well or anything. What happened with him and your boyfriend?"

She fiddled with her lip ring for a moment, studying me. Her eyes were dilated, and I knew she was just high, but it looked like her soul had been sucked out. Eyes so wide open and vacant I thought I might see a tumbleweed blow across her pupils.

"Think I'm going to take off," I said, gripping my phone, balling my other fist to stop my hands from shaking too bad. Wasted or not, if I pressed her much more this girl was going to wise up.

"What?"

I held up my phone. "Getting late."

"You aren't waiting on your boyfriend?"

"Looks like you and me both got stood up," I said, and laughed, but shut my mouth when I saw I'd struck a raw nerve—when her cheeks colored and she gritted her teeth. The comments about her being his girlfriend from the guys at the table, her eagerness to assert her insider status to me, a total stranger—she was anxious about her standing with Eli, and here I'd made a dumb joke about it. I held out my phone and laughed again. "Oh, girl, I meant I did. Not you. My boyfriend just texted me he's not coming."

"Sucks," she said, sticking her chin out. "Mine'll be here any minute now. Why don't you just wait? You wanted to buy Molly—that's what you said, right?"

"Yeah, that's right. Sure, I'll be just a sec," I said, walking backward toward the bathroom. I had no intention of staying, but it would be weird if I ran out now. The door to the women's was heavy and propped halfway open with a cinder block. I'd hide for a few, let her get reabsorbed into the pool game. Hopefully before Eli arrived—I was willing to bet that he'd be later still, if he came at all. The concrete floors were painted blue, puddles of water, piss, or both in the low spots and around the toilet. The stall door creaked and I leaned against the graffitied wall, willing a few deep breaths to slow my heartbeat. It was stupid that I felt betrayed—I'd barely known Cody—but the realization that he was so two-faced when we'd talked about Eli felt like a kick in the stomach. I thought the fear he'd voiced to me in the car on the way to his apartment had been genuine, though.

The door to the bathroom shut with a heavy thud. The cinder block that had been propping it open scraped across the concrete, and then, a click. Whoever had come in turned the dead bolt, locking me inside with them. I closed the lid on the toilet seat and sat, inching backward.

"Get your ass out here."

I bent forward, and through the crack in the stall's frame saw Eli's girlfriend blocking the door. I held my breath, unsure if I could divert her, push past her fast enough to unlock it.

"Come out," she said, louder. "You've been screwing my man. Waiting for your boyfriend, my ass. Eli's *my* boyfriend and you're some piece of trash he doesn't even think about."

God, she must've thought when I said we'd been stood up I was serious—that I'd meant we were waiting on the same guy. I looked through the crack again, doubling back when she stuck her face up close to mine. She punched the door. I didn't think reasoning with her would work—she was rip-roaring drunk and mean, emboldened by no one else around to make fun of her. I considered crawling underneath the divider into the other stall, and then making a break for it, but a shadow had moved under the door.

"I'm not dating Eli," I said. "Come on, now—"

"You're a liar and a slut." Her fist was clenched in front of her, the other hand behind her back. In the smudged, water-stained mirror, I could see a blade glinted in her hand.

A crunch of gravel, a car horn—the bathroom window was

open, no screen. Too high up off the ground to climb out of though, even if I stood on the toilet seat. Balanced on the sink I might reach the sill. Hoist myself up and go from there. But how to get past her? I didn't want to wait her out—what if she brought in whoever was standing guard on the other side of the door?

I faked a sob. "Fine! I didn't know about you either, okay? He told me we were exclusive and I believed him!"

She flew at the stall, but I opened the door first. Slammed it hard against her face so she fell backward. She hit her head pretty hard on the concrete floor, lying motionless for a second before rolling over and holding her nose. The knife had fallen not far from her, and I kicked it back behind me. Shaking, I stepped over her and hopped onto the porcelain sink. The window was even higher than I'd realized. I took a deep breath and reached for the ledge. Pulled myself and shimmied so half my body was hanging outside the building. It was too narrow for me to put my feet on the sill. One more thrust forward and I dropped onto the ground face-first.

I'd landed hard on my shoulder, but stood. Felt in my pocket for my phone and keys, cursing myself for leaving the bullet parked at the edge of the lot—

"Hey!" She'd come out the front already, followed close behind by the piggish guy in the trucker cap. "Me and my brother's gonna kick your ass," she yelled, muffled by the wad of paper towel held to her nose.

They blocked my path to the parking lot. I'd have to take my chances and hit the open field behind the transformer station. I sprinted, the crunch of gravel and whoosh of blood in my ears drowning out the sound of them coming after me—I had to spin my head around, once, twice to see exactly how close behind. The piggish guy was sucking wind, but the girl was fast. My legs ached and my lungs had started to burn, but I kept going, hoping that the darkness outside the reach of the parking lot lamps would hide me. I cut through the field and the grass whisked against my jeans and itched under my shirt, the weeds nearly chest high. There was a stand of mesquite up ahead, and I ran low to the ground, partially obscured by the grass and a low hill, then crouched to catch my breath. Motionless now—afraid to breathe too loud—the heat flushed my skin, and sweat ran down my arms as I counted the minutes. They'd either tired out or had given up. I waited a while longer for my heart to not feel squeezed tight, and wearing the night like a second skin, walked toward the highway.

Chapter Twenty-five

I called Wyatt to come pick me up. There was a Valero off the feeder road a half mile from the pool hall. Prowling the convenience store's narrow, color-saturated aisles, I felt strangely guilty. The thought of me dating Eli or Cody, I guess. How I'd fixated on them, stalked them—Clint, too—wasn't so unlike a one-sided crush. Especially in comparison to everyone else, who all seemed content to let the dead lie. It irritated me that in the course of my investigation, the only way most people had conceived of me in relation to these men was as girlfriend. Hookup. Not being taken seriously worked to my advantage some days, let me slide under the radar, but other times it felt like being stuck behind a plate glass window screaming while no one could hear me.

The store was empty except for the cashier, and the country music piped in over the speakers sounded tinny and hollow. Every step I took made a squeak; the station was fairly new, the floor tiles shiny and polished. Smelled like bleach cleaner and wax except when you passed the rotating dogs. My phone buzzed. It was Nikki and she wanted to FaceTime.

I answered and drew the phone back; the unflattering angle under my chin caught me off guard every time.

"Hey," she said. Her face was flushed from the shower, hair wet, and she wore an old Garnett High cheer shirt over boxer shorts. She sat cross-legged on one of the hotel beds. Sonny was asleep, shirtless and face down on top of the other bed's rumpled, tropical flower–patterned comforter. He had a shiny keloid scar across his back from where he'd been injured on his last tour, and a skin graft from shoulder to collarbone that he often covered with high-necked shirts. He'd been discharged a little over a year ago, and was going to start college at State this fall, something tech related. She motioned in his direction. "They have these margaritas that are like, evil—I swear, they don't taste like anything but juice but they really mess you up. I think they're like straight alcohol, like a Long Island Iced Tea but a margarita . . ."

On the outer edges herself, she'd be passed out like him if not for the way tequila made her more up than down. "Sounds like you're having a good time," I said, tilting the syllable into a question.

"You know how day drinking does me."

"Does me, too. Can be like Sunday morning on Saturday night," I said, feeling that same strange mix of exhausted and hyper, and a little blue. It was only ten thirty, I noticed now, though it seemed like it should be two in the morning. "Is everything okay?"

"Yeah."

Had her eyes welled? The video kept freezing, blurring her. She blinked for a few seconds.

"I'm just tired is all," she said. "I know we came here to have fun, but I'm kind of overwhelmed. Like I'm supposed to be happy and in love and all the normal things but I'm too distracted or something. And Sonny, he's being really weird. I tried to ask him what was wrong and he said I was imagining things."

"He does that. Deflect, I mean," I said carefully. I liked Sonny, and besides, if I egged her on too much, she'd just feel uncomfortable around me later when things went back to normal. This sounded to me like a mood swing more than a serious problem. "The wedding was fun but it was also kind of stressful, Nik. You need a break. Can't you just read by the pool tomorrow?"

"We're going out on a boat." She sighed, but smiled, too. "Just us. I'm a little freaked out he doesn't know how to drive it well enough."

"You don't have to do anything that makes you uncomfortable."

"God, Mom, I know. But, yeah, if I don't come back, you know who to blame." She laughed a little. "Anyway, I wanted to say sorry. I know I snapped at you a few times on Saturday."

Not just Saturday, I thought. "I'm sorry, too. Let's forget it," I said, desperation creeping into my voice. I knew Momma was right, that we'd find our way back to each other. Would be like no time had passed once she settled into being Nikki, just Nikki, not one half of a couple. But the waiting was leaving me blue, too. Bluer than I wanted to acknowledge. And something else—a voice in the back of my mind saying all wasn't right. That it wasn't only a mood swing and Nikki wasn't telling me everything that was bothering her.

"I'm thankful for you and I mean it, Annie," she said, folding her knees up and tucking them under her T-shirt. "That business with Clint made me think how not everyone's lucky enough to have someone to stand beside them. Someone who'll always be there for you."

"You'd do the same," I said, and out of the corner of my eye spotted the cashier bend over the counter to see what I was doing (leaning against a flimsy chip rack) and I stood up straighter.

"There's no loitering," he said meanly.

"Wait just a second, Nik—"

"Where are you, anyway? I thought you'd be home."

I grabbed a bag of Fritos and an Arizona iced tea out of the cooler and waved them in the cashier's direction. "I'm fixing to buy something, hold on."

"Why are you at a gas station in the middle of the night?"

"It's a long story. But hey, I was wondering, has Clint talked to Sonny again?"

"No. I tried asking him about it and Sonny was like, no way am I talking to Clint again, and actually blocked him after that. You know Sonny. You know he's not the type to hold a grudge, so it's serious."

I did know Sonny. Enough to think he was solid. He loved my cousin, for one, and tended toward generous with people. Laughed at bad jokes, was the first one to get on the dance floor and draw you out. But being a good time was a mask as much as being strong and silent were—the rare occasion I'd seen him too drunk, there'd been that other side of him. The one I'd glimpsed at Clint's show. He could be too direct. Blunt not for the sake of honesty, not in the way being kind doesn't always mean nice, but to excise parts of himself. He wanted you to feel the way he did, which was that he'd gotten an unfair shake. Maybe being injured in Afghanistan did that to him, or maybe the dissonance between him and his brother, his friends, and the way the last few years had changed them. Nikki was right that Sonny didn't let petty crap drag him down, but he sure as hell kept a tally of the big stuff.

"Clint pissing him off is probably why he's been acting weird," I said. "Hey, did Sonny mention anything Clint might've said about his adoption? Remember how that came up the night of y'all's party?"

"Uh, no, don't think so."

"Okay," I said, slowly walking toward the front of the store. The cashier drummed his fingers on the counter, but I stopped midstride, remembering something. "So, what was going on with you guys that one night—at Clint's show?"

"Oh, I forgot about that," she said, pausing a second too long to be believable. "Gosh, Sonny thought Clint was hitting on me, but he totally wasn't. He was talking to me like a brother-in-law would, kind of close is all. Put his hand on my back," she said. The fact that she'd deny it made me believe her more—Nikki loved when guys hit on her and made no secret about it, even to Sonny. Or maybe she'd flirted first and was ashamed, otherwise she'd have been itching to tell me. I remembered how my heart pounded when he looked at me from up onstage—I could understand it if she'd felt a sliver of attraction toward him, too.

"So, they fought about it?" I asked.

"It was awkward for—" Nikki said, the video freezing on her midsentence.

"You still there?" I reached the counter and laid my goods down, smiling at the cashier. "Sorry, sir, hold on—hey, Nik, if you can hear me, call me later, okay? And be careful tomorrow," I said. As I pulled out my wallet, the cashier rang everything up, getting out a black plastic bag and one of those paper drink sleeves that I associated with flaunting open container laws.

"No need for a bag, thanks." I pointed to the door. "I have a ride coming, mind if I wait a little longer here?"

He shrugged and took the tea and chips out of the bag, opening his mouth to say something, when headlights shone through the glass. Wyatt pulled into a spot right in front of the store, his face through the windshield lit by the blue-white sign.

"Never mind," I said. "Have a good night."

Outside of the sterile air-conditioning, heat draped me like a well-loved blanket, complete with a collection of smells I knew but couldn't immediately name—August smells, like hay, and dirt, and sun-warm, stagnant water. I looked around me once, twice, making sure no one from Cowboys had belatedly followed through the field or had gone driving looking for me. The station was empty except for a long-haul trucker parked at the far end of the pavement, headlights off. Wyatt leaned across the console and opened the door.

"Thanks for coming," I said, dusting my jeans off before climbing inside. The seat belt rubbed against the raspberry on my upper arm, my shoulder sore where I'd landed. I hissed with a sharp intake of breath, keeping my other hand between the belt and my raw, stippled skin. Wyatt leaned over to kiss me, also to remove a dead leaf from my hair. No wonder the cashier hadn't wanted me loitering. "You haven't noticed anything at the house, have you?" I asked.

"No."

"I'm sorry," I said. Closing my eyes for a moment, I listened to Wyatt's sounds: his steady breathing, a history podcast he'd been listening to turned down low. Books and papers spilled from a canvas tote on the floorboard brushed against my ankle. I squeezed his arm. "How was class?"

"'How was class?'"

I laughed.

"Come on," he said, his voice teasing, but tight. I proceeded to tell him about the pool hall, that Cody had in fact been working for Eli Wallace. I also told him about what Nikki had said over FaceTime about Clint and Sonny. I didn't really know what to think about their relationship, or how it might relate to this case, but there was an itch there. Conversations with Dee, Mrs. Flores, and the branch manager echoed in my mind, the summer of the robbery drumming in the background like a sad-sounding ballad. I told Wyatt about Clint's Instagram video, too, and that he'd decided to move to Nashville, and he refrained from any commentary. Think he was afraid of me shutting him out if he said too much, though once or twice I noticed he gripped the wheel hard, squelching the rubber.

When I was quiet, the truck rolling onto our street, he said, "You think Clint shaves his chest?"

"Don't shave your chest."

"You girls like to drool over him and his chest."

"It's also the guitar."

"He dedicates another song to you it'll be his last."

I knew he was mostly messing with me. And that he knew me being with someone else—hot musician or no—wasn't real. Still, there was the idea. I was glad that in the dark he couldn't see my blush.

He gave me the side-eye, quiet for a moment. "I think Sonny's lying about something."

"I think so, too."

"Well, maybe not lying, but I think more went down between him and Clint than he's letting on. Before the ceremony when we were all hanging out, Sonny took this shot of expensive whiskey. Someone said that Clint had bought the bottle and he nearly spat it out, like a lunatic. He looked at me and said, 'Clint's mad that I tried to warn him. He can't ever accept that I might be right for once.'"

"Warn him about what?"

"I don't know. He shut it down after that. Said he didn't want anyone talking about Clint anymore, that there was 'no room for sad shit on a day like today,' and beat his chest and found a flask. You know Sonny."

You know Sonny.

I climbed out of the truck and used the flashlight from the glove box to check the yard, the porch, the trees beyond the fence. Neighbor's dog was asleep. Wyatt found me in the dark, wrapping his arm around my waist. We walked toward the house, safe, and I felt a quick flutter in my chest. That was the other constant in my life: anxiety. I couldn't ever just be. I didn't know what was beyond that night and its shadows, the quiet. Even the most solid ground could give way if you weren't careful—hell, even if you were, a world might bottom out. No telling. I hung back to look at my phone, saw Nikki had texted to tell me good night. By the time Wyatt had opened the door the flutter was gone, my pulse a rock-steady hammer.

Chapter Twenty-six

The pool hall was deserted when Wyatt dropped me off the next morning. He and I had stayed up late talking, made queso in the microwave, and split a beer, and after he saw me pull out onto the highway, he turned the truck back toward home and back toward our bed. It was six. I'd long given up on sleep myself. Had tossed, worried about my cousin. Not like I even wanted to sleep, given the nightmare I'd just had about Cody. The hot and coppery smell like raw meat. An old quilt draped over the couch, television paused, that sticky coffee table with a half-drunk bottle of Coke. The moment of perfect stillness before, before, before—how that moment, thirty seconds, tops, played in my mind on constant loop. I don't know what I believe about dreams and signs and the like, but I think there's something to be said for intuition, because I woke from this dream about standing still, stuck in Cody's living room, and that's when it hit me: the coffee table had had a bag on it. Black plastic, Coke bottle sweating and sticking to the plastic, and next to it, a crumpled, brown paper sleeve.

Likely, he'd been to a package store or gas station. Based on the bottle's condensation, it couldn't have been long before he was shot. Feeling juiced again behind the wheel of the bullet, the steering wheel cool in my hands, I drove the short distance from the pool hall to the Valero. Just beyond the interstate overpass from Cody's apartment, it was the closest convenience store by far. I walked inside and found that the cashier I'd spoken with last night had been replaced by a cheerful, round-faced woman with a gelled-up perm.

"Morning," she said, ringing up a customer ahead of me. "Be right with you."

"Thanks," I said, deciding to hit the coffee station in the meantime. The store was busy now. Old men in the booths watching the cars go by, paper coffee cups clutched between weathered hands. Tired travelers fueling up and soldiering on with their donut holes and chewy, heat-lamped sandwiches. I waited several endless moments for the cashier to be free of any other customers before heading to the counter.

"That'll do it?"

"Yes, ma'am," I said, handing her cash. "Hey, do you know who was working here on Friday afternoon or midday?"

"Friday, let me think," she said, and counted back the pennies. Matter-of-fact and nonchalant, as if people came in to inquire about the employee schedule all the time. Who knows, maybe they did. She shook her bangs out of her eyes and looked up at me. "That was yours truly. Got here at noon and stayed till eight."

I pulled out my phone to show her a picture of Cody. "Do you remember this man coming in to buy a Coke and cigarettes by chance?"

Her face scrunched up, relaxed. "Oh, sure! That's Smiley."

"Smiley?"

"Oh, yeah, he comes in all the time. Such a sweetie, always smiles at me—don't know his real name, 'course," she said, laughing. "Remember he came in and got his soda and his Marlboros on Friday, like usual. Probably two or three o' clock, know it was after lunch. We talked about the Mega Millions and he bought a lotto ticket. Said he'd gotten good news and was feeling lucky. So, I said, how about I join you in that mansion, and he bought me one, too. Said let's double our luck. Funny guy."

"Was he by himself?"

"Yeah," she said, frowning in concentration. "Well, maybe not. Usually, he walks over. Told me he lives over yonder, those apartments? I remember he got into a truck that took off. Green Tacoma, one of the old ones. I remember because like I said, he usually walks in here carrying on about how hot it is."

My heart pounded. Clint drove a used Tacoma. I remembered he had the small green truck parked outside his house the night of the party. Not the most uncommon vehicle, but that would be a hell of a coincidence. And that video he'd posted, the picture. Was he running away from something, not toward it? Had he had an argument with Cody—or had he witnessed his death? Worse? I swallowed hard. "You notice anything else about Cody or who was driving the truck? Anything unusual?"

She shook her head, bangs stuck to her forehead again. "Something the matter?"

"Cody, he—I'm sorry to tell you this, but he's been killed." It was the first time I'd said it aloud with such assertiveness, my chest expanding as the words escaped. There were other, more tangible reasons for me to believe he'd been murdered at this point, but it was that silly little lotto ticket that burned me up. Knowing Cody had planned on hearing the numbers called on Saturday night. That he'd been happy, looking forward to a stroke of good luck—I balled my hands into fists. There was a line forming behind me now. I fished out one of my business cards and slid it across the counter toward the woman. "If you think of anything he might've said or that you saw, please call me."

She covered her mouth, a squeak escaping. I hated that I'd broken this news to her and she had to keep trucking behind the counter. You never realize how attached you get to the people you encounter in customer service. You don't get that the forty-plus hours you spend in the company of strangers makes them no longer strangers to you, not until one of them leaves. It was that way for me at the café. The singsong chime over the door always echoing a good-bye. "Thank you," I called over my shoulder, and she nodded once, her face pale in the harsh fluorescence.

I drove to Clint's place in Garnett, mashing the pedal down. His street was quiet. Last week of summer vacation, still too early for people to be up and leaving for work. Not really sure what I was looking for yet, I pulled up to the curb and got out. Steam rose from the dewy grass under the big sycamore, and sun through its branches painted the world a green-hued gold. The house looked lush, charming, homey in this light—twinkle bulbs were still strung around the porch railing, same spot where we'd listened to him play guitar. Trash cans were now wheeled to the curb. The front door was locked, lights off inside, and there was no sign of the Tacoma, but I walked around to the back and found the gate unlocked. In the backyard, a second, stronger sense of déjà vu—looking over my shoulder, unease building in the pit of my stomach when I'd smelled smoke that evening, seen it billowing from the southwest. No smoke now, only ashes in a coffee can on the back steps full of cigarette butts and spliffs, a chalky heap in the charcoal grill. The screened-in back porch was the same as it had been, cluttered with bike tires and boxes. A sudden breeze coursed through the yard, and the door flapped open.

I hopped up the steps. The back door was locked, but I could see in through the kitchen window, which offered a clear view of half the house. It was a mess in there: dishes left in the sink, trash, and the kitchen can was left lidless and bagless, and a pile of clothes draped over the back of the couch. On the table, his laptop. Their dad had owned this house, I remembered, so maybe he was just going to park his stuff here until he found a place in Nashville. Still, this was not exactly the kind of scene you'd expect from someone who was planning on a move, or even a short trip. The hair stood up on the back of my neck when I saw his guitar case was left in the middle of the floor.

The garage, too small to be called a garage really, was closed with a chain and dead bolt. Pacing the driveway, I realized something: no one else had their trash cans pulled to the curb. Collection day had been on Thursdays when I lived with Nikki in her house, which was also within the city limits. The schedule on this street was the probably the same as hers. I'd assumed a neighbor had rolled Clint's trash can down, but if that were the case, why a day early? And the can wouldn't have been left out since last Thursday—this was a nice street, the kind where a neighbor would've kindly moved it back. Plus, according to Amanda, and possibly that Valero cashier, Clint had still been in town on Friday afternoon. It made more sense that Clint had moved the can down to the curb himself before leaving, but based on the state of the house, it seemed surprising he'd had the foresight to do so. That is, unless there was something he wanted to be sure disappeared.

I rolled the can inside the fence, and the rush of hot, foul air when I lifted the lid gagged me. There were two bags to sort through. I held my breath as I untied one and more air escaped. Mostly food waste and coffee grounds. Normal stuff, the only papers a Bass Pro Shops catalogue and a credit card offer. I opened the second bag, knotted multiple times so I had to rip it. Clothes, like a donation bag. Upon closer inspection, most looked unfit to be donated—worn out or too intimate, like holey socks and pit-stained undershirts. The clothes smelled like they'd been washed recently; nonetheless, touching someone's old boxer briefs turns the stomach. Nearing the bottom of the bag and feeling more than a little insane, my fingers grazed something slightly damp. A reddish-brown bath towel, taken too soon from the dryer based on the laundered but soured stink. I held it up to the light. The towel was actually white, though. Or it had been before it was soaked through with blood.

Chapter Twenty-seven

I put the clothes back in the trash bag, placing the blood-stained towel on top and tying it shut. I hid the bag under a bench on the porch so it wouldn't be further disturbed—what if the towel was evidence? I rolled the trash cans back and paced the driveway. If Clint was really in Nashville, I didn't exactly know how to corner him. I wasn't the law, and I didn't see anyone rushing to my aid, not while Cody's death was still ruled a suicide. Clint was free. Able to toss old bloody towels and leave his home a wreck, drive wherever the hell he wanted. No dice there, not enough proof. The house's shadows grew narrower, sharper as the sun rose, and the air compressor hummed dully, so ordinary as to be unsettling. It struck me that it wasn't even that hot out yet. The thermostat must have been set low—one more signal that Clint had either left in a mad rush or that he was returning. Getting inside the house wouldn't be so hard, assuming he didn't have an alarm system. The shed, however, was padlocked.

"Morning," called a woman's voice, light and almost breathless. Maybe in her late forties, in swishy shorts and running shoes, she stretched her calves on the curb. Hands on her hips—possibly out of recrimination, definitely because she was airing out her underarms. "I saw that car and I was like, who's this? You cut your hair!"

Maybe she thought I was Amanda? We didn't look much alike, but we both had brownish auburn hair—mine a few inches shorter—and were twenty-something, thin. I decided to play along, smiling and waving. "Yep, just checking on things while Clint's out of town!"

She gave a thumbs-up, poking at a Fitbit on her wrist before she went along her way, which unfortunately was only to the next house. I scrambled into Clint's backyard, and right as I was about to step onto the screened porch, I heard a door—shit, she'd gone into her backyard, too. She rolled out a yoga mat onto the grass. It would be obvious I was waiting her out if this went on much longer, and there wasn't anything for me to pretend to check on—the two potted plants on the steps were already brown and shriveled, no pets. And how long before she peered closer, before she realized I wasn't Amanda, or whoever she thought I was? I couldn't risk breaking and entering now. I'd come back later, approach on foot.

Slinking back to the bullet, I debated my next move. Leroy always said that when you feel scattered, stop the chase and route to the beginning. Make a timeline. What I knew of Clint's whereabouts prior to Friday were sketchy: two weeks of unaccounted time between the VFW show and the rehearsal dinner, the same day he was likely at the Valero with Cody around two, the same day he'd broken up with his girl-friend. And according to her, they'd broken up here at his house around four. Clint didn't have a job, so what had he done all the rest of the day? He'd said he planned to chill since his tour had officially ended—which meant what? Sleeping late, smoking weed? Writing, maybe. And, of course, spending time with his friends and family.

At this point, bringing in Dee was inevitable. I also needed to reach out to Sonny today, but based on my conversations with Nikki and Wyatt, getting Sonny to talk about Clint would be like pulling teeth. Clint was going through something like a quarter-life crisis, considering his dreams, his identity. Presumably he'd wrestled with the results of my investigation, had done his own research into the report—and at some point, he'd attempted contact with the Motts. But when? Amanda had said he'd been upset that Lorena had turned him away. Had he similarly reached out to Ronnie? I'd never heard back about being added to any prison visitor list, no calls or letters from him in return. The lawyer who'd been at Lorena's house was likely Ronnie's proxy. If nothing else, close enough to provide some insight. I turned the engine, glancing at the dash. It was about nine now, time for businesses to be opening up.

I drove to the address I found on Google for Griggs Attorney at Law, which was on Main Street in Parr City. The office was in a shared building with a seasonal tax preparer, a dry-cleaner, and a dentist, but its entrance was cut off from the others, a private door at the back of a low-slung, sprawling complex that looked like a limestone 1970s ranch house. The dark-tinted door was locked, but a light emanated from inside. I rang the bell, waiting long enough to wonder if he opened up late or by appointment only, when the latch turned.

"Help you, miss?"

Harris Griggs looked older than the picture on his website, maybe in his mid-seventies, with thick gray hair. He was wearing a plain white Oxford shirt and blue slacks, scuffed loafers, and none of the flash I'd seen in the courtroom photos.

I wondered why he hadn't yet retired, and as if reading my mind, he gave a tired shrug of his shoulders. "I'm not really taking on new clients at this point, but I can refer you to a colleague—"

"Mr. Griggs, I'm a private detective and I'm here to speak with you about a client of yours. May I come in?"

His bushy eyebrows raised. "Heard of attorney-client privilege?"

"Yes," I said, inching forward. "But it's actually more about a family member of your client, and I think he might be in trouble."

He rubbed the back of his neck for a moment before he opened the door wider, standing aside for me to enter. The reception area had a glass-topped coffee table and two green plush chairs, a Thomas Kinkade–like nature painting hanging crooked on the wall, and a dying rubber plant in the corner. He led me toward an inner office where there was a drafting table covered in manila file folders and banker boxes. Guess I expected fancier, like a mahogany rolltop and leather chairs. Plain, half-emptied bookcases and metal filing cabinets lined the walls. "Moving?" I asked, pointing at a roll of packing tape.

"To a home office. Like I said, I'm only working with a few existing clients these days. My wife and I want to do some traveling, so I'm unofficially-officially retired," he said with a fake chuckle, like he'd be trying the line out at dinner parties.

"I'm here about Ronnie Mott."

He turned his head sharply. "Oh—no, I'm afraid I can't help you, then." He'd been bent over the desk like he was going to sit, but straightened his back, glancing toward the outer door.

"You didn't let me explain," I said, and took the chair opposite his desk. "I know you know about his son, Cody."

216

He let out a sigh.

"I don't think it was a suicide."

The old man frowned, and just when I thought he was going to ask me to leave, he plunked into his chair. Curious, or resigned to my presence. "So, Lorena hired you to look into Cody's death?"

"No, but although she won't hardly speak to me, I know she feels the same. We met several weeks ago, when I approached her about a case I was working. Ronnie Mott's biological son—"

"Clint Marshall, that's it! I know who you are now," he said, his blue eyes flashing. "You're the McIntyre girl, the one who wrote to Ronnie in prison."

"I did," I said, waiting for him to say something about me being related to Leroy, but he only stared at me. "I wanted to know if you'd talked with Ronnie about Clint, which sounds like yes—and I wanted to know if they ever reconnected."

"I don't know," he said. "I haven't spoken with Clint since last week."

My heart pounded—he'd talked to him. "Well, me neither, and I need to find him. I think he might either be in danger or was involved in Cody's death."

"Hell of a story," he said, his voice conveying no emotion. His face, however, was slightly flushed, his hairline damp. "Annie, right? Now, what proof do you have about any of this?"

I nodded, pressing my hands together under the desk. "Can't share that with you now, but I think it'd be in your best interest to tell me what you and Clint discussed. Doesn't Ronnie want to know exactly what happened? To both of his sons? I could be of help here, if you'd let me."

"We're not going to pay you."

"I didn't ask you to."

Griggs smirked. "Maybe you're right. Ronnie did tell me he was adding you to his list."

"List?"

"Of approved visitors. I think his unit block has visitation on Saturday. Usually takes time to get on the list, but the warden will be sympathetic and get you in quick, given the circumstances," he said, watching me a moment before shrugging in a tired, screw-it-then way. "I called Clint after Ronnie asked me to. He got your letter and decided to make some last grasp at fatherhood to the boy. Had me contact Clint and deliver him a key to a PO box—and before you ask, no, I don't know what was being sent to the address, only that it was sensitive material."

"Okay, so, what did Clint say?"

"He seemed interested and said that he'd wait for further instructions. This was Wednesday last. But thing is, Ronnie tells me that Clint didn't answer his call. Said he called him twice and that he never responded. Now, you're right, Ronnie wants to know what's going on here—and yes, he's wondering if this has anything to do with his other son, Cody."

"How did he take the suicide news?"

He shook his head. "Ronnie's in the dark. Full of sad, sour regrets. He's understandably, for lack of better term, losing his shit."

I thought about that for a moment. "What do you *think* Ronnie wanted to tell Clint? The sensitive material?"

"Ronnie has pancreatic cancer," he said, and his eyes drew down. The reticence bordering on exasperation I'd detected earlier seemingly evaporated, his voice softening. "It's stage four. Terminal, so he's not going to outlive his sentence anymore. If I had to guess, his contact with Clint is about a, uh, retirement fund turned inheritance, if you catch my drift. Think when you made contact with that letter, old Ronnie took it as a sign."

My heart pounded in my chest. Griggs must mean the hidden money everyone had been nosing around the Motts for after Ronnie went to prison. If so, this meant the loot wasn't only the stuff of legends. It was real. "How much money?"

"I don't know, and even if I did, I'm not at liberty to say."

Griggs was getting cagier. I chewed my lip for a second, widening my eyes. "So, Ronnie never tried making contact with Clint before? Even with someone like you, an expert who could help him make discreet contact?"

Luckily, he puffed up a bit. "Not that I know of, no. He did have me look him up several years ago—gosh, must've been seven or eight years ago now—when Clint turned eighteen. The terms of the adoption had stipulated no contact, but Ronnie thought since Clint was technically an adult, he might be able to initiate a relationship with his son. Then he changed his mind and turned it into a fact-finding mission only. He really just wanted to know that his son was in a good place"—he shrugged—"but I've always kept tabs on Clint. Saw to it he was in a good home situation, just like he'd asked. Oddest payoff I'd ever finagled."

"Do you know who Clint's biological mother is?"

"Thought you'd met Lorena."

"Yes, but I was recently told otherwise. I was told that he's actually someone else's."

Griggs narrowed his eyes, a smile forming for the briefest moment. "I don't know who would tell you otherwise"—he made air quotes, giving a quick eye roll—"but Lorena is the mother of Ronnie's children. Did she always act like a mother? Now that's a different, longer story."

I nodded, watching him. I didn't see what reason the sister would've had to lie, but if some other woman was in fact Clint's mother, why cover it up? It really didn't make much sense.

"Now, Cody," he said, and frowned. "You know, I always looked down on the fact that Ronnie never made any efforts with him. But Cody was an adult, nearly thirty years old himself. He could have reached out to his dad, right? I think—not saying this is correct—but I think that Ronnie saw his relationship with his oldest son as spoiled and not worth the effort. And then, here comes your letter about Clint. Here comes another fresh shot at being Mr. Dad. A way to clear his conscience."

"Clear his conscience about something other than being a deadbeat?"

Griggs shook his head sadly, raising his hands up in a defenseless motion. "I don't know how I can really help you much more—"

"I saw your car at Lorena's, Mr. Griggs."

He opened his mouth to say something then stopped, calmly folding his hands on the desk. "Listen, I don't know Cody well enough to have an opinion about his mental state. But I can tell you that if anyone in that family knew what inheritance was coming to Clint from Ronnie, there'd be hell to pay. Lorena and those kids were hungry and at the mercy of others for years. Could there have been fighting? Sure. Could Cody have gotten caught in the crossfire? Certainly, he could have."

I studied the old man for a moment. His face was placid, but his shoulder blades were taut, his knees bouncing under the desk. How would anyone know about Clint's inheritance if Griggs himself hadn't told them? Maybe Griggs had a soft spot for Lorena, telling her Ronnie's plan out of loyalty, vengeance, or some combination of the two. I aimed for a neutral tone to match his, but could barely control the frustration bubbling up in me now. Griggs might think he was better than Ronnie Mott, but I was beginning to think he was just as petty. "Any idea who might've found out about the inheritance, then?"

"No."

"What about the Wallaces?"

His blue eyes went dark, all pupil. Like when a rabbit gets cornered by a dog. "Lord, you're dragging in those Wallace cretins? Wash your hands of this. Surely there's other work you can be doing. Heck, I know of a colleague who could use a part-time investigator. We were just talking about it the other day."

"Thanks for the concern, but I'm already in deep, and so are you, for that matter." I looked around the room pointedly, nodding at his packing materials. "If you've known about this money all along—"

"I don't know anything." He got up from the desk and crossed his arms. "We're about done?"

"But you do, sir," I said, more confrontational than pleading—I hoped—standing to meet his gaze and hold it. For all I knew, Griggs was packing up his office to skip town. He'd have no reason to tell me as much, but I sensed that provoking him was the best way to get him to speak. Multiple times now he'd taken the bait. He seemed to me like the kind of person who took genuine interest in people and their dramas—that even when it didn't serve him, he stuck his nose in. A pot-stirrer and he couldn't help it. "Come on," I added. "Did you take the cash?"

His face turned so red it was almost purple. "You're kidding.

Christ, for one thing, I don't know where it is. God's honest truth. Could I have copied the PO box key? Sure. But I wouldn't, because looking over my shoulder for the rest of my life isn't worth it. I've represented criminals—not all, but let's be honest, most were criminals—my entire career. I know what carrying around that kind of burden does to a person. Nope, not worth it to me. You should ask yourself if finding out what happened between those guys and their dad is worth it to you. That's all I'm saying."

"Why would that make *me* feel guilty?" I asked, unable to resist the bait now myself. "You and I both know that something is not right here—with the suicide, with Clint being MIA—so, why would some clarity here not be worth it, whether to me or to the police?"

"Because sometimes it's best to let the past stay past," he said, staring back hard. "I think you'll find, Ms. McIntyre, it was you who started this whole thing. You and your goddamned letter."

Chapter Twenty-eight

The post office in Parr City was only a short walk from Griggs's office on Main, so I didn't bother moving the bullet. I knew no postal worker would be remotely willing to open someone else's PO box for me, but wondered if they might ID Clint. I went inside, questioning the man behind the counter to no avail. I kind of knew this wasn't the move—Ronnie wouldn't have sent sensitive information here. Not right in Wallace territory, not on a busy street in full view of anyone who'd seen Clint leaving Griggs's office.

Maybe Garnett, though. I drove back toward the courthouse square, relief washing over me as I passed the city limits sign. I took a deep breath and clicked my blinker, pulling into the tiny parking lot of the town post office. The postmaster, Alma, greeted me with a single-finger salute. She had her glasses on a beaded chain that considerably brightened the blue uniform shirt. She was good friends with Leroy, knew where I worked, so I didn't bother with a preamble. Went up to her counter and held out a picture of Clint. "Hey, Ms. Alma, have you seen this man in here recently?"

She slid the glasses onto the bridge of her nose, taking my phone and zooming in with her bent, arthritic fingers. "Sure have," she said, and her gaze cut over toward the wall of metal PO boxes. "Why?"

"He's possibly in danger," I said. "I'm trying to trace his steps over the last two weeks. Remember when it was that he came in?"

She bent below the counter and rummaged around for a moment, returning with a desk calendar. Took her time reading her handwritten notes, licking her finger as she turned each page. Her index landed on a date and she tapped it twice, making a satisfied hum. "Thursday last. Yep. Had to go get a filling over lunch and was in a hurry to get. Remember I was right about to drop the gate when he rambles in here with another young man. Reckon they were brothers or cousins, definitely kin to each other."

I scrolled through my camera roll. "This him?"

She zoomed in again, nodding as she squinted. "Sure is."

"If you can recall anything else, maybe what they were talking about or—"

"I'm not a dang spy, Annie. I was minding my own business as I always do, here to accept a parcel or to help if they needed it. That's all," she said, straightening her back. Alma took pride in her work—that was at the root of her slowness, her stubbornness—and I didn't want her to regret her candor with me. I thanked her and turned to leave. My phone was still unlocked in my hand, the screenshot I'd taken of Cody's Facebook profile zoomed in, and it took me a second to remember I'd heard a new text come in while she was holding it. Mary-Pat had asked if I wanted lunch. Was it already lunchtime? Ms. Alma cleared her throat and started rolling down the metal gate.

* * *

Cody knew about the inheritance. I tried imagining what it would be like to know your father reserved all his affection for a son he'd never met. How I'd feel if he cut me out of money, money I could really use. I'd be wounded, envious—if not completely furious. And if it were me, I wouldn't be able to look my brother Clint in the eye, not for a long, long time.

Mary-Pat had parked her vintage Silverado in front of our office, striding across the square to meet me in front of the café. She had a long, loping gait and carried herself like she always knew where she was headed. Her confidence was something I'd worked toward cultivating, but it was also inherent to her—though I knew she'd once been a rookie like me, Leroy's deputy, I couldn't imagine her as anything but cool. Hand on her hip, she stood blocking my path. "Come on, Stomper, let's get us a seat. I'm hungry."

"Just needed to think a minute," I said, reaching for the door. When we were in the office together, Mary-Pat liked complaining that she could hear me pace clear across the building. But I had to walk the miles or drive them when I was working out a problem. The problem now was practical, of course—I needed to figure out what exactly had happened to Cody, find solid proof of foul play—but what weighed on me was emotional. I didn't want to believe Clint might've harmed him, but it had to have gone down one of two ways: either they were arguing over the inheritance money and Cody was shot by Clint, or the brothers were working out a plan to retrieve the money and a third person intercepted, killing Cody and sending Clint on the run. Either way, no separating the crime from Clint in my mind, not anymore. I'd gotten too attached. It wasn't just the situation that saddened me, but what could've been. His posts about Nashville and the outpouring from his fans, his performance at the VFW and all that hard, shiny talent, a voice that sounded like cut glass—what a shameful waste.

Mary-Pat sat in the window booth. "Done thinking?"

"Been a workout," I said, opening the plastic-sheeted menu just to do something with my hands. I already knew what I'd order.

"When we talked, I noticed you skimmed a bit over the part where you went to that seedy old pool hall last night. You find out anything useful? Or just stick your neck out like I've warned you not to?"

My jaw tensed. "Like I said, I found out that Cody and Eli Wallace were working together at the time of his death. Also, that no one is exactly mourning his departure. I don't know why you always feel the need to scold me."

Dot, our waitress, came and took our orders—migas for me and a steak finger basket for her, old reliables—and Mary-Pat sipped her ice water for a moment. "Sometimes I worry you know just enough about things to be dangerous."

"Pot, meet kettle."

"You're worked up about the Flores case and yours, I know—"

"You don't think you and my granddad could've done more?"

She shook her head. "We did our best at the time. What I don't know is why you're going around madder than a wet hen lately."

My neck felt hot, remembering how I'd left Leroy's house, giving them the silent treatment after we'd talked about Faye. "If you think I'm so reckless, why'd you make me a partner?"

"Meant to tell you, I promoted myself to senior partner."

Dot wordlessly deposited our lunch onto the table, pretending to not see me hold out my water glass. I didn't have the energy to flag her down as she gripped the pitcher and hustled her wide behind back to the register. Couldn't trust myself to not say something tacky, and this wasn't about Dot—I didn't even really think it was about Mary-Pat. I felt like a teenager, full of steam. But honestly, when I was a teenager, I hadn't rebelled against my dad's opinions or been smart with Momma. I always thought the kids who'd hated their parents were just afraid of seeing so much of themselves in them. Resented what was coming. I didn't resent being kin to anyone because I'd always been a little gone. Kid everyone took pride in and did their best to shove along away from here. Not so unlike Clint, in that regard. Homesickness was literal when I went off to college—I'd felt thinned out, wrung dry—and now that I was back, it was the stickiness of love. It was looking in the mirror or avoiding it, and deeper, my fear that love might go away if I let myself get too comfortable. If I let them see I hadn't made good on it all.

We tucked into our plates, eating like we were starving. She probably had also burnt her mouth, and looked up at me with her eyes a little watery. "You know, one of your best qualities actually is your nerviness. Good investigators question everything, even themselves, it's true—not saying you should question me, of course." There was a laugh at the back of her throat, but I didn't think she was altogether kidding. "Lean into doubt, just don't forget you have to trust people sometimes, too."

Mary-Pat paid the bill, her being senior partner and all. I had the idea of going to Walmart and buying my own bolt cutters, but figured my parents weren't at home to ask questions if I wanted to borrow theirs. My plan was to loop back to Clint's house and break in, and I needed cutters if I was going to get past the padlock on his garage. My parents were sharing a car after my dad's had bit the dust, a dented blue sedan that was gone from the driveway when I pulled up in the bullet, and I breathed a sigh of relief.

Momma's head poked through the curtains. Surprised, I stood in the driveway for a second. Maybe she didn't want to talk, either—she opened the door in pajamas, blond hair standing on end, exposing her dark roots. "What's the matter, sweet pea?"

"Nothing, just borrowing a tool from Daddy. There's a leak under our sink," I said, at least only half a lie. "Are you sick?"

"Had a migraine sneak up on me and I called out." She folded me into a hug as I came up onto the porch. "Want some lunch?"

"Sorry I woke you up. You should keep resting," I said, following her inside the dark house. She had the air cranked higher than normal and I shivered. "I already ate, but I can fix you something."

"Well, I do feel a bit woozy, and a bite sounds good. You sure, doll? Is your sink leaking real bad? Your landlady ought to fix that."

"I don't mind—no, it's not that bad, got a bucket underneath." I dug around in the fridge for sandwich fixings and she perched on a barstool. I opened a Country Crock container that was actually full of my dad's potato salad and tried to remember when he'd made it; I don't think my family has ever parted with a scrap of leftovers. Rewashed Ziploc bags lined the dish rack like beached jellyfish. We drank from old jars and our change and loose buttons were kept in those weird Danish cookie tins. "Thought I'd make you a grilled cheese but I don't see any butter. Maybe some of this pimento cheese? Ham?"

"Too rich. Think there's turkey in the drawer," she said, rubbing her temples. "That and a little of that light mayo will be fine. Just a swipe and one of those good tomatoes sliced. Have you had any luck talking to Clint Marshall?"

I looked down at the cutting board. "Not yet."

"I called Dee yesterday, poor thing. Been thinking about her since the wedding. Anyhow, that Clint sounds like a selfish brat. I was going to tell you that if you or your cousin or Sonny talk to him, tell him to make it right with Dee. She's there all alone in that house."

"When y'all worked together, were people still talking about the big robbery?" While I knew Momma wasn't part of the holdup at that branch, that she hadn't even worked there at the time, her employment there had started not long after.

"Yep, I'd just interviewed when it happened. Your daddy didn't want me to work there, which was just silly. He's always been so protective," she said, pressing her hand to her jaw after she took a bite as though the chewing made it hurt. "I was glad to transfer to Garnett later that year, though. Parr City branch was a viper's nest, everybody talking behind each other's backs. The police were still investigating some. They even questioned me, but I obviously couldn't tell them anything. There was even a nasty rumor going on about Dee. You've met her—your aunt doesn't like her, but she's fine—and even she was mixed up in the drama. They thought it could've been an inside job."

The hair lifted on my arms. "You didn't think that, not even back then?"

"Dee? Good lord, no way she'd be able to pull something like that off." Momma shook her head, winced. "I eventually asked your granddad after some time had passed, and he was a little more forthcoming. Said they never could connect Dee, or Luanne Davies, or anyone who worked at the branch. He'd monitored them closely for a long time and found there was no payoff. And besides, bless her heart, Dee couldn't fight her way out of a wet paper bag. I worry a little about your cousin and Sonny's future offspring and their math homework. Your grandmother was always telling me and your aunt, you plant a pea, you get a pea—"

"Oh, but Sonny's so nice," I said and laughed, but distractedly—an itch in the back of my mind. Sonny was a goofball, but he definitely wasn't stupid, and I didn't think Dee was, either, for that matter.

"Annie, you're a devil like me," Momma said, and pushed her plate away. "Oh boy, here I thought I needed some food in my stomach and it's just stuck in my throat."

"I could make some coffee, maybe the caffeine would help?"

"I'm fine," she said a little breathlessly, standing and pulling me to her. "Might rest my eyes again, though."

My stomach twisted. Momma rarely got sick, and even when she did, she usually took pride in soldiering on without complaint. Liked teasing my dad that he acted as if he were dying when he caught even a mild cold. My dad took up space with his back pain in a way that the women in my family weren't allowed to—or chose not to, I wasn't always sure. There was never anything so pounced upon in this family as having a whiff of self-importance. Fewer worse insults for a woman than to be parading herself around. Maybe part of why I wanted, so badly, to be the hero of this story and why I was so afraid of it. I hugged my mother back and brushed my lips against her cheek. Whispered that I loved her, softly enough I wasn't sure that she'd heard me.

Chapter Twenty-nine

"Lovely" comes to mind. That's the best word to describe the Marshall place. The property must've flooded pretty badly backing up to the creek like it did, but the garden looked green and lush, and the yard had tall water oaks and pecan trees throwing prime shade toward the house. The wooden bungalow had been built around the turn of the twentieth century. It was painted a cool creamy white with pink trim, and had a tin roof and wavy, leaded glass windows. Reminded me of what I thought an English cottage might look like. I wished we were meeting for tea.

Before knocking, I poked around and didn't see signs of Clint or his truck. Only Dee's Explorer sat in the driveway. It was two, but when I'd called her at the dealership, they said she'd taken a half day. She came to the door in shorts and an over-sized Cabela's T-shirt. Maybe one of the boys' or their dad's? Clint's warning about Dee's tenderness and fear of abandonment struck me again—if he was so worried about protecting her feelings, how could he up and leave? Dee was swallowed by the clothes. "Annie, please tell me this isn't what I think it is."

"Hi, Mrs. Marshall," I said, hating that my voice shook—I could tell by the crease in her brow that I was making her nervous, too. "We left on a bad note last time, talking about Faye Flores, and I'm sorry. But I need to talk with you about Clint now. Have you spoken with him?"

"You were just doing your job, hon. And no, I haven't heard from him. Come on, sit," she said, motioning me inside. Her flip-flops made a sticky sound against her feet. The hallway was shadowy, air a little damp, and she led me to a big kitchen table covered with mailers from all the grocery stores. She must be one of those extreme coupon cutters. Had to admire the effort. I couldn't bring myself to spend the time, though I could've used a few extra dollars. Her curly bob bounced around when she plopped into the velvet-cushioned chair. There were two brand-new tablets still in their boxes on the table like no big deal. Maybe she'd actually won one of those crazy contests? She caught me staring. "I hadn't gotten any shipping updates on this new iPad I ordered, so I told them I never got it and they shipped a new one. But the first one was just mixed up in the mail, came the next day, and now I've got me two," she said, doing her one-sided shoulder shrug. "Want to buy one? I can cut you a deal."

"You're not going to return it?"

"Those big companies don't need the money. That's pennies to them."

I nodded politely. Wasn't like I disagreed about the money, more that it was, well, a little like stealing.

"Oh, pish, you're a Goody-Two-shoes." She looked down at the pinking shears she'd been using to clip the newspaper and ran her finger over the blade. "Anyway, this long of a silent treatment is unusual even for Clint. Maybe he's mad at me for something. He'd be mortified to know this, but I do have social media. Don't post or anything, just use them to keep up with his music stuff. He made this video I saw."

"I saw it, too," I said. "You think he's in Nashville, then?"

"That's what he said. Figure he'll come by and see me when he needs my help moving or renting out their dad's place. That's my lot in life, being the one you call when you need something," she said. Her laugh was half-hearted, pained. I could see why my mom had reached out to her. The woman wore loneliness like a thick perfume. "But is that why you're here? What's wrong?"

"A few weeks ago, Clint hired me to find his birth parents. He asked me to keep it between us, but I wanted to bring you in now because I worry that he's gotten mixed up with them in a bad way. Do you know who they are?"

Her face blanched. "We heard tell of the situation when our lawyer and us were working with the court, but I don't know specifics. It's why I never wanted to discuss them with Clint," she said. "I have to tell you, I'm a little upset by this, Annie. He's a big boy now and I would've been frank with him if he'd have actually asked me. Why did you not say so before?"

Based on the way her voice was shaking, she was more than a little upset. I inched backward in my seat. "I don't know all of Clint's motivations, but I do know that he cared about sparing your feelings. He was worried about telling you because he loves you, Mrs. Marshall. He specifically told me that, and I—"

"Yeah, well, I had to work on him to get him there! Worked very hard with him at the beginning," she said. "Very hard to train him out of his behavioral issues and rehabilitate him."

She was making it sound like he was a dog who hadn't been housebroken.

"I just"—she rapped the table hard with her knuckle—"I

just worry it was all for what? If he was going to sink right back to such godawful roots."

I could hear my aunt Jewel's voice. *You pay for your raising,* she'd say. Dee's reaction now—her insinuation that Clint was a charity project—told me a lot about how he must have been treated. A lot about why he felt the need to walk on eggshells around her, and where exactly he'd learned to be so callous. He'd been stuck in this karmic loop for a while, if I had to guess. "Let's get back to where you think Clint is now," I said. "If you're certain he's okay in Nashville, or if you should report him as missing to the police. Or at least speak with the cops. I don't know how it would go over coming from me. I really think it would be better from you."

"I'd do anything to protect my boys. It's why I did what I did, rescuing Clint from that awful—squalid—group home he was in. They called it Sheltering Arms," she said, and let out a long sigh as if to calm herself. Looked at a spot on the wall and nodded, as if telling the story to someone other than me. "But those kids were all but fending for themselves. Wish I could've taken them all. There was a little girl a few years older than Clint, and the look on her face, lord. Like an adult's it was. Haunts me still. The social workers said if the child wasn't a baby the chance of them getting adopted was slim to none. Our lawyer filed with the court for Clint, who was nearly school age himself, and I never looked back. But that was a long time ago. He's grown. He's made his bed and he's going to have to lie in it."

"I hear you," I said. "But honestly, ma'am, we need to find him."

"Well, what kind of trouble are we talking?"

I hesitated for a moment. I hadn't really trusted her after our conversation about Faye Flores—and I still didn't have a good gut feeling. If I told her my theory about Cody's death and the inheritance from Ronnie Mott, would she be more interested in finding Clint or in finding the money? A cold assessment, and even colder, I wondered how much she might already know. Where had *she* been on Friday night before the rehearsal? Her upturned face, thin lips pursed white—a look of concern—barely masked a strange intensity. Like a cat narrowing in on a mouse in the grass, her muscles coiled tight.

"I worry he might've gotten into some of his bio brother's drug activities," I said. "There's been fighting between this brother and a local drug dealer. I worry Clint's running scared from these guys."

Her shoulders relaxed. "That sounds far-fetched to me. Clint's too focused on his music for that kind of nonsense. You saw his posts. And besides, if you're somehow right, why would I want to get him into more trouble by involving the cops? He'll sort it out. He's in real trouble, he'll ask for help. Trust me, my boys aren't shy about asking for what have you. Shoot, maybe it'll be a valuable lesson. Maybe Clint ought to learn that you are who you associate yourself with and—"

"Yes, I understand," I said, a quick pinch in my chest. Dee cared but she cared not all the way, which was somehow harsher, harder to swallow than even Lorena Mott's raw rejection had been. "If you hear from Clint, you have my phone number," I said, standing.

She let me out, mumbling a goodbye, her face pressed against the glass pane in the door as I went to the bullet. I drove down the road toward the bridge where there was a wide shoulder, idling. I pulled up the video Clint posted on Instagram—I'd never actually watched it to the end. The comments were full of congratulatory emojis and atta-boys, spammy requests for collaboration, and questions about when he'd drop the new single. I wondered again why the hat and glasses—like a disguise. Right at the end of the video, for two seconds, maybe less, his hand jerked and I caught a flash of landscape in the car window. I'd never been to Nashville, but wasn't it an urban area? I watched again, taking a screenshot. Clint looked someplace out in the country, though not in Garnett, either. The dirt was red. The earth flat as it was endless, small underneath the canopy of blue empty sky.

Chapter Thirty

I parked three streets away from Clint's and approached on foot. The bolt cutters were zipped inside a backpack and the straps stuck to my shoulders, my T-shirt damp with sweat. Not completely inconspicuous, but it was three thirty in the afternoon, and I was willing to bet his next-door neighbor had long gone about her day. Breaking in now versus at night seemed less obvious and less risky. It was 106 degrees out, according to my phone. Wasn't just uncomfortable when it was this hot—dehydration and heat stroke were real possibilities, death stalking anything arrogant enough to be out in this— and there was a ringing alarm inside of me, a sharp, primal fear jutting up against the slowed-down stickiness. Like when you feel yourself nodding off at the wheel and jerk awake.

The latch to the back gate jammed and I had to shake and bang it until it popped up. Relieved no one had come to see about the noise, I shut it and waited a second to be sure. I felt close enough to Clint now that I could smell his warm, pine-sap cologne, touch his tousled hair. There was the real possibility that he—or someone else—might return at any time, so

I needed to hurry. If there was a security system in the house I'd have to run, so I would start with his garage.

Dad's bolt cutters were an easy match for the rusted chain, and I broke two links with little force. A quick, satisfying snap and the chain piled onto the concrete like a decapitated snake. The wood was once barnyard red, now weather-faded to a dull reddish brown. The towel, damp, sour, that exact shade flashed across my mind, and my hands shook as I pulled the doors open. It was dark, and as I stepped over the threshold, breathing in the sweetish scent of sawdust and bottled pesticide, I put the bolt cutters out in front of me with one hand as if to shield me from a monster. Reached with my other hand until my fingers grazed a pull chain. Yellow light from a bare bulb cast across the space, larger than it looked from the outside.

Large enough to fit a vehicle.

Clint's green Tacoma sat parked in the middle of the garage, oil spotting the concrete underneath. I rushed to the driver's side window, stomach tightening as I peered inside. Clean. So clean, it seemed as though no one had driven it in ages—no cups, stains, nothing hanging from the mirror, no phone holder clipped to the dash, no random receipts. With the way the bulb-light angled in, I detected a residue and a swiping pattern on the hard surfaces. Rubbed with rags and solution. Using the hem of my T-shirt, I tried the doors and they were locked. The bed of the truck was empty, also spotless.

What if Clint had never left town? But the video. I knew he was at least alive—or was yesterday, when he'd posted it. Maybe he'd simply taken a different car out of town Friday night. Hell, maybe he'd taken a Greyhound. There could be something wrong with the Tacoma, which was at least ten years old. That, or he was afraid of someone recognizing it.

Cody's vehicle was still not accounted for, I remembered. Also, Clint's mother worked at a dealership—had any cars disappeared off the lot? That seemed like a long shot, though, like he'd easily get caught, and something Dee might've mentioned. Could be Clint wasn't alone. Maybe he'd left town with someone else behind the wheel.

I walked outside and closed the garage, staring down the white bungalow. The sweat that had soaked my shirt made me cold like I'd broken a fever. I hopped onto the screened porch, then used the handle of the bolt cutters to break the glass panel on the back door. I listened for one moment, two, and not hearing any alarm, I reached carefully, slowly around the broken glass and unlocked the dead bolt.

The memory of walking into Cody's apartment came rushing back. The before and the after. I smelled the air, but there was nothing now—no smell of death. No blood drip on the floor, the sink, any of the cabinets. Just a messy house, the only rotten scent from overripe bananas left on the counter. Checking the bedroom and bathroom, it looked like he'd packed in a hurry. Contents of the medicine cabinet were strewn about the sink—curled tube of whitening toothpaste, a straight razor, and his cologne, which I could see now was desert cedar, burnt sugar, and anise—and the toilet seat was left up, a shower mat wadded in the corner. The bedroom was just as chaotic. Jeans and vintage western shirts left hanging out of a duffel bag. His guitar was on the bed, the velvet-lined case left open in the living room. I riffled a bit and didn't come up with anything unusual. I thought that Clint—accompanied by Cody, I knew now—would've probably kept the letter Ronnie had mailed to the PO box, so I combed through any papers, but found nothing of the sort.

His laptop was sitting slightly ajar. A slender orange Moleskine peeked out from underneath. I hesitated before opening the notebook, why, I don't know. I'd broken into the man's house, his garage, dug through his underwear and his trash, and yet it was looking at his journal that gave me pause. Maybe because I kept one, or that I knew he was a writer, I felt Clint's presence over my shoulder so strongly. If I caught who killed Cody and framed it as a suicide, then invading Clint's inner thoughts was a line I'd cross a hundred times. Still.

Only a quarter of the pages had been scribbled on, and he liked to fill a page completely, adding curlicues to the margins, etching with pencil so his words looked silhouetted. Lyrics. Scratch-outs and question marks, underlines and stars. The first few pages were slightly different versions of a song about a guy who needs a cold beer, his ex-girl showing up to the same honky-tonk as him, "slipping into the neon lights like a tight-fitting dress," flirting with somebody new. Would sound alright played with a fast tempo and live in a loud bar, a good dancing number, but it was the kind of familiar, throw-one-back-with-the-boys anthem that was also kind of forgettable. Not a bad thing, but Clint struck me as the type who called himself a songwriter in a sense meant to convey that he wrote poetry. Sonny had said Clint referred to himself as "the artist," after all. It was clear the notebook was meant for writing more than it was a place to keep reminders or dates—probably used his phone for stuff like that—but I kept reading. The last page was a new song, this one more of a ballad. More personal than the first, apparently, a man whose father was "like Jesse James, not a thief but a bold robber, running away with Momma's heart."

The refrain was the song's speaker, the son, "running into blue as fast as an old pony or bottle of whiskey might take me away and out of my head. I'm not a bad man but I'm half my old man, I'm running into the blue beyond—"

He'd abandoned the work. The rest was blank. I closed the cover and pressed the pages tight between my fingers, as if by some transformative property Clint's heart poured out might beat back into mine. Might tell me where that blue beyond really was—I wanted to believe it was Tennessee. Wanted to believe he was halfway to a colder beer, far away from what ailed him, from this little town where everyone knew everyone. Maybe Clint hadn't been hurt, ripped up by the roots and left to die someplace, because that's what the state of this house really said to me. I couldn't see how he'd have left without his truck, but more than that, I knew he wouldn't have left his heart on the page and not taken the page along with him.

I opened his laptop, a little Toshiba covered in bumper stickers, the charger wrapped with tape. I ran my index finger over the track pad and the screen lit up, no password needed. Clicked through his files and found mostly college essays and scanned venue contracts. Also, a folder of photos that he must've taken over a decade ago with a digital camera, pictures of him and his friends going on a school field trip to the Alamo. I recognized Sonny immediately. He'd been a big kid, too, taller than the other boys and athletic-looking. Even more of a towhead back then. He and Clint had their arms over each other's shoulders in one, a giggly-looking girl giving them bunny ears that they'd barely seemed to notice. Sonny loved Clint, didn't he? Had he really blocked his number, like Nikki said? The rest of the folder was more of the same, and I clicked open the web browser next.

Mostly booking stuff in his email, and a lot from Ancestry .com about "census clues," aiming to get him on a subscription.

Nothing from Sonny. I searched "Cody," "Mott," "Ronnie," and even "Harris Griggs," and found nothing. He and Amanda had emailed most recently a couple months ago. A thread of potential rentals, all in Lubbock. The listings had all been sent by her, his replies brief and noncommittal, straight-up negative as she sent the next batches, and then, kindlier, "Thanks for this, taking a look. Love you, babe," after she'd gone quiet for a few days. The separate accountings of their relationship hadn't quite jibed when I'd spoken with them, either, and not just in an imbalance of affections way. I'd taken her word for all of what had happened between them. I did remember Dee saying Clint had told her he was going to break up with Amanda, corroborating her story to a degree, but I felt strongly there was something missing.

Clint's search history said he'd last used the laptop—or the internet on his laptop, anyway—on Thursday night, near midnight, and the most recent page visited was a Wikipedia entry for the town of Buell, Texas. He'd looked twice, and ten times done a Google map search for a specific address, also in Buell—Buell was up near the Panhandle, wasn't it?

I jumped when I heard a slapping noise outside, almost like a screen door hitting the frame. A woman's voice, humming. My eyes landed on the broken glass scattered on the kitchen floor—any closer, she'd know there'd been a break-in. I took a picture of the laptop screen, closed it, then ducked under the window. I didn't see anyone in the backyard, but still heard the humming. A flash of bright pink caught my eye—the neighbor hoisting a kiddie pool out of her garden shed onto the grass. Wearing a bikini top and rolled-up shorts, now unwinding the garden hose. The pool filled and she untied the top so she could lay on her stomach, looking over into Clint's yard a few times as she did, and I wondered if no tan lines was for her benefit or his. I reached for my backpack and stayed low as I made my way toward the front of the house. Left out a window that would stay unlocked if I needed to come back. I fast-walked to the bullet, and luckily, remained unaccosted. Sitting in the car felt like closing myself inside an oven, and I cranked the air while I looked at my phone.

1257 Thorne Rd, Buell, TX

The address was on the outskirts of the tiny town, farther south of the Panhandle than I'd thought, and near the Caprock, maybe an hour or so outside Lubbock. A big lot that backed up to Highway 84 and a place called the Ranch Hotel. Photos on Google Earth were of a dirt lane, the barbed wire fence at the start of a driveway. If there was a house on the property it was obscured by trees. I dragged the icon over to the highway. To the strip of outside-access-only rooms of the motel, stucco siding the same color as the red dirt. Like a locker combination clicking, the recognition was quiet as a whisper, more felt than heard. Small satisfaction quickly turned to dread as I realized how I knew the town and this motel. It was the place where Faye Flores's bones had been found.

Chapter Thirty-one

I sloughed off the backpack onto the floor of our office, the
bolt cutters landing with a thud. Leroy had apparently re-
claimed the catbird seat, leaving his reading glasses and an
empty beer can resting on top of my files. I hadn't seen them
leave when I was parking the bullet, but the scent of his Old
Spice and Mary-Pat's starchy detergent hung in the air. I sat
behind his and my desk and plucked at my shirt. The windows looked out onto the square and were original to the
hundred-year-old building, tall and beautiful, but no shades
fitted them properly and the temperature inside the office
nearly matched the outside.

My hunch was that the address Clint had searched was
related to the contents of Ronnie's letter. That this property
was where he'd hidden the alleged inheritance. If that was the
case, Faye's bones being discovered so close by, and her disappearance at the time of the robbery couldn't be coincidences.
Mrs. Flores was probably right—partly, anyhow. Ronnie
must've taken Faye. I moved Leroy's glasses and the beer can
aside, opening my laptop. Pulled up the Buell address and

wrote down all the addresses surrounding it. The motel was near a major intersection of the state highways, a turnoff for truckers to hook back up to the interstate. On the satellite images and street views, the properties around the motel were mostly farmland, cotton and peanuts for acres and acres.

My stomach clenched as I remembered the flash of sky and earth at the end of Clint's Instagram video. Didn't look like Nashville, but a whole lot like West Texas. I dragged the cursor to the streets that ran parallel to the highway on either side. They, too, were sparsely populated roads, only a handful of mailboxes and gates, one derelict trailer. After that, I looked up all of the addresses in a database of public records that the county had moved online. The property Clint had searched in particular was a big, fifty-acre tract that stretched from the street all the way back to the motel, the property line jutting right up against the edge of the motel parking lot. The land was currently owned by someone named Fred Hull, last sold in 1983. When I searched Fred Hull, I found one man who was also from Price County. My jaw dropped when I found a Facebook photo of him—in it, a young Fred Hull was pictured with another young man, both wearing Branch Creek letterman jackets. The post was shared by Hull's sister, a kind of memorial about the anniversary of a car crash that killed their friend Robert and left Fred disabled.

Robert Mott—as in Ronnie's late brother.

Fred Hull's last known address was in South Dakota, in an assisted living facility. I debated calling the facility and seeing if he might speak to me, but I didn't necessarily want the interference—

"Little darlin'?" Leroy's singsong voice echoed in the stairwell, followed by Mary-Pat's boots. He patted his chest when he reached the door, clean out of breath. I stood to pull out a chair, but he waved me off. "Pat's filled me in on what's happened with Griggs and the letter from Ronnie Mott," he said. "That you're thinking Clint came into a windfall and the deceased, the brother, knew?"

I nodded, still a bit stunned from my research.

Mary-Pat walked around Leroy and sat on the edge of her desk. "Got a bead on him yet?"

"Yes and no," I said, blinking back green spots forming in my vision. I'd been staring at the screen too hard, reading for over an hour. Leroy coughed into his fist, finally accepting the chair, and my face flushed as he sat facing me at the desk like I'd usurped his throne. "I think I might know where Clint either was or will be headed. He searched on his laptop repeatedly for an address up north in Buell. I have to wonder if that was what was in the letter Ronnie Mott mailed him—"

"Buell?" Leroy sat up straighter. "Little town up near Spur?"

"Yes. A property that backs up to the Ranch Motel," I said, and softer, "I think you know it. It's where Faye Flores's bones were found back in 2005."

Leroy swiveled to look at Mary-Pat, but she was pacing now. He turned back to me, not quite meeting my eye. "You're sure?"

"Yes, I just checked. That property must've been Ronnie's hideout, right? And I don't know how well you followed Faye's case after you retired, but her mother says that the accused killer recanted, for what that's worth. There was not enough evidence to ever charge him, besides."

"I know," said Leroy, his voice strained. "I never stopped following her case, and I know."

"The property is owned by a friend of Ronnie's family," I said, and Mary-Pat stopped pacing. "This guy named Hull owns the land, has for decades. He was close with Ronnie's late brother, Robert. They were in a car accident in the early nineties in which Robert died and Hull was disabled after-ward. He lives out of state."

Leroy let out a low whistle, shaking his head.

"It can't be a coincidence," I said. "Maybe if the address were around here or in Price County, but all the way up there? Too random."

"I agree," Mary-Pat said.

"Who knows what all Ronnie might've hidden around the property," I said. "Maybe he was telling Clint to—"

Mary-Pat cleared her throat. "Yes. Find the money, his inheritance the lawyer mentioned. Yeah, you'd better go up there."

"Yeah," I said, irritated that she'd cut me off—I was going to say the same thing, if she'd have let me—and gave her the stink eye as she measured out coffee grounds from her giant tub of Maxwell House. I was still a bit stung from our lunch conversation. Normally, Mary-Pat got my goat and I took it in stride, took it for the affectionate ribbing it was meant to be. This was different. I'd felt real animosity between us ear-lier, and I knew it had to do with me questioning her and Leroy's work. I took no satisfaction in being right now. That Faye's case had been mishandled, and what had happened to Cody was an echo of that summer years ago. I simply wanted to scream. I wanted to jab my finger and say *look, here.* And I wanted, more than anything, to know if this ended at that address in Buell. I envisioned the pieces assembling before me and had to stop myself, tell myself to breathe, to think. If I went up to Buell, what was I even going to find? It had been not quite a week since Cody died, plenty of time for Clint or whoever else knew about the inheritance to hit West Texas, get the money, and run. What if I'd missed the window?

"Putting your big expense to good use," Mary-Pat said to

me, and pushed the button on the new coffee maker. She dug around the top drawer of her desk and pulled out her new, fancy night-vision binoculars—much more expensive than a Mr. Coffee, I felt like pointing out. "Sounds like we've got a long evening ahead of us."

"Us?"

Leroy nodded. "Pat, you can watch Clint's house in case he or someone else comes back. You and me, darlin', we can head on up to Buell. Hell of a way to spend my eighty-fifth. Shoot, guess I'll never retire."

Today was Leroy's birthday. I'd completely forgotten. That must be why he and Mary-Pat had been hanging out together, why he'd left a beer can up here. He'd have been alone otherwise. Leroy wasn't so childish as to care about cake and candles, a birthday card. But I cared. Pictured him alone on his porch all morning, waiting on me to arrive—usually, I came over first thing the morning of his birthday with a box of kolaches and took him to see the ponies across the river, maybe go fishing. My stomach twisted. I was worried and I loved him and I felt this was all tangled up with the shine coming off in some ways. Missing his birthday now felt like recrimination on my part, but I really had just forgotten. "I'm sorry I didn't think to at least call," I said. "Been a little preoccupied as you know. You're sure you're up to this drive? It'll take like six or seven hours to get there."

"Had a few birthdays in my time. Many less eventful than this, so don't make a big deal about it, darlin'. I'm fine for a trip and I think you'll need the backup." He smiled weakly. Despite his protests, he looked a little put-off. "Now, what's Clint drive? I don't think the sheriff would put out a BOLO for his vehicle, but maybe if we were to frame it as he was missing and in danger. Pat?"

"I can ask Garcia."

My palms started sweating. "That's the other thing. His truck was inside his garage all cleaned out. He either found another way out of town or he's not alone."

"First things first," Mary-Pat said, ice-blue eyes zeroing in on me. "You checked on your Pontiac lately?"

"No." I stood and went to the window, scanning the courthouse square, the short line of cars idling at the intersection in what passed for rush-hour traffic. The bullet was where I'd left it, parked on the side of the vaquero statue, which threw about an inch of shade—you took what you could get—and didn't see anything amiss. "What's wrong?"

"The Wallaces. I worry they've got eyes on you again, Annie. Your door's been keyed, and we found these strewn about the hood, some more under the tires," she said, reaching into her back pocket and handing me a fistful of matches.

Chapter Thirty-two

Taking Leroy's busted vehicle instead of mine was not the way I wanted to begin a mission. I'm superstitious like that. Why I called my Pontiac the silver bullet in the first place—for protection. Hindsight, as they say, but I didn't know what was coming, all I knew was that we didn't want Eli—or whoever was working for him—following us to Buell. The fact that I'd been up since dawn didn't sink in until I'd settled behind the wheel. Warm drowsiness hit me right when the sun sank below the horizon and the long line of highway dimmed in the purple dusk. I've never liked driving at night, the vastness overwhelming to me in a way an infinite blue never was. It could be so dark out here. Each dashed line was a sliver of broken rope I'd have to inch along. I keep an overnight bag in the bullet, so all I'd had to do was fling that into the truck bed, and now, every time I braked it slid and thudded against the wheel well. Leroy had brought his Coleman along with a road map—his 1980-something truck didn't have any cable to plug in my phone. He had, however, installed a new stereo system a decade or so ago, and was enjoying flipping through the CD booklet he kept under the bench seat.

"Need to eat a bite, don't we?" he said, looking up.

My stomach had been growling for a few miles. Heat and adrenaline staved off an appetite only until it got to be too inconvenient, of course. "There won't be any place to stop for a bit."

"Up yonder there's a pretty good spot. You have to get off the highway, but you need the fuel, darlin'. Then I was thinking we could stop out at Luckenbach—it's right near there, wouldn't be much of a detour."

"You seriously want to go sightseeing?"

"I've got to have me a beer and it'll be more scenic than any rest area. Besides, it's hallowed ground. We need us a shot of good luck, I reckon."

"After it gets dark you can just drink one in the truck," I said. "Doubt we'll get pulled over, even with your expired tags."

"It's not very far," he said, and selected his CDs: The eponymous *Ol' Waylon*, and after that, *Red Headed Stranger*. Outlaw songs. "We won't be able to do much when we get in tonight, besides. Long as we're there by dawn."

He cranked the volume, skipping to the Luckenbach track. I normally would be a go for this type of detour, but with sunset thinning and darkness chasing, stopping felt wrong. Going to a place like Luckenbach on a weeknight struck me as arriving to a party just as everyone else was leaving it, but I couldn't drive straight through without a break. And it was his birthday, after all.

"Okay, whatever," I said finally, and he pointed me to turn off at the next highway intersection. We were in the Hill Country now, past the stretch of highway known as the Devil's Backbone for how the road curved and dropped off steeply, and driving it felt like an initiation of sorts, barrier one. The restaurant he had in mind was a burger joint outside Fredericksburg. Looked like they were about to close up for the night, but when we poked ours heads in the door, the waitress offered to let us sit inside, saying they didn't close until ten. The smell of charcoal and grilled onions intensified as we walked past the kitchen, making my mouth water. White walls and countertops had faded to a soft yellow, the floors scuffed but clean. There were only two other cars in the parking lot, and I chose us a booth by the window so I could keep an eye on the truck. I sipped a Dr Pepper while we waited for our food, fiddling with the straw wrapper.

Leroy had been quiet. Sat tapping the toe of his boot against the table leg. "I know you're disappointed in me. About the Flores case."

"No, I'm not," I said, unable to look directly at him.

"I know you are and it's alright. I ought to tell you, though, there's a difference between believing a thing is true and proving it. Proof might take twenty-odd years to come out. You being so young and all, that's hard to think about."

"Do you think Ronnie Mott killed Faye?"

"I don't know," he said. "I'd thought there might've been a connection between her disappearance and the robbery. Timing was a hell of a coincidence, but no proof."

"You thought Faye's boyfriend killed her?"

"I didn't think anyone had killed her, not until they found her bones years later. I really thought she'd run away and was living her life someplace else. Really did," he said, his voice uncharacteristically sharp. "Where they found Faye, it was out of my jurisdiction—hell, I wasn't even a lawman anymore. Then they said she was a victim of that famous serial killer stalker, and Faye's mother, she went ballistic. Rightly so. I might've figured Faye's boyfriend had caught up to her, or that the serial killer theory was only a theory, but I had no reason to doubt the new investigators."

I shook my head, not quite sure what to say.

"Folks think the man with the silver star is a hero—"

"No, I—"

He put his hand out to shush me. "Yes, darlin', a lot of folks do. Deep down, people want to believe help's coming. I think you and me, we're the same in many ways. You have ideas you like to sit with."

Throat tight, I only nodded.

"You want to be the hero. Then folks deal with you and you're just this regular old dope. They realize you're less there to save the day than you are to just make sure the day don't get worse. Law and order's not the same as justice—I wished I'd have been able to do more *just* work. Why I started the firm with Pat instead of retiring. But sometimes, damn it, you keep adding up your efforts and it never equals much of anything. You have to stop picturing yourself on the white horse. Be a mule. An old mule keeps plowing. Second chances don't often come along, but when they do—like tonight—you take them."

"But," I said, so much landing on that one little word—I rarely contradicted Leroy, never to his face, and my cheeks flushed. "Actually, no, I think second chances come along plenty. More like no one wants to acknowledge something is a second chance, because then they'd be admitting they were wrong the first time."

"Well, you've got the mule in you yet."

"Stop calling me an ass."

He laughed a little.

"I'm not disappointed in you," I said after a moment, the

knot in my stomach hardening at the half-truth. "I'm just frustrated—with everything."

The waitress brought our food to the table, depositing the baskets without commentary, either sensing tension or regretting letting us in the restaurant so late. Leroy was quiet again, a dark look clouding his face as he ate. The bell chimed and a man came in, startling me—in my seat facing the parking lot, I could see everyone who drove up, and he'd appeared out of nowhere. He wore sunglasses despite it being dark, and despite the heat, thick camo pants and a hooded sweatshirt. He reached in his back pocket, revealing a sidearm in a holster around his waist. Not unusual in these parts, but something about how he paced instead of sitting, the way he kept the glasses on, and the growing sense he was watching us made the hair on my neck stand up.

"Don't look now," I said.

Of course, that was the first thing Leroy did.

"He seem familiar to you?"

"No, but get to be my age and everyone starts to remind you of someone," Leroy said, turning back to me. "You?"

"Not really."

"Will keep an eye out." Leroy took my last onion ring and spun it around on his index finger. "I'm thinking a little dessert might be good."

I felt my phone vibrate against my thigh. Pulled it out of my purse but kept it below the table. A local area code, not a number I'd saved but one I recognized: Dee Marshall. I was still uneasy about how I'd left things with her, and for whatever reason—guilt over the way I felt like I'd messed up by involving her, perhaps—I didn't want Leroy to hear the call. "Going to the restroom," I said. "Watch the truck."

"Get me a dipped cone while you're up. Birthday treats."

I nodded and strode off. Turned the knob to the single-stall restroom, latching it and leaning against the door. As I was debating whether or not to call Dee back, a text came through: *More I think about it, what you did connecting Clint and his bio family is irresponsible. I'm really thinking I ought to see how to get your license revoked!!!*

Ms. Marshall, I began to type, *I'm sorry for how you feel,* then on second thought, I deleted the last part. Typed simply, *I'm sorry.* As I was thinking about what else to say, if anything, the three dots appeared and disappeared a few times.

Get him to call me and I will leave you alone

Fine, I lied, erased the apology, and hit send. I wasn't sorry. Leroy himself had just said that mistakes in our line of work were inevitable, that your efforts might not produce. But what if your efforts weren't so much ineffectual as wrong? Dee wasn't the first to accuse me of fault—I'd written Ronnie Mott in prison, as his lawyer had reminded me of earlier. Surely, I hadn't invented all this suffering or had altered what was already true.

But I'd tripped the wire.

There was a loud bang on the door, like someone had hit it with the flat of their hand. "Be out in just a minute," I said, and they banged harder. When I pushed it open, expecting a child to be there fidgeting, it made me irrationally furious to see the waitress and her scrubbed-red hand raised.

"Dang it, you didn't flush, did you? Commode's broke."

"You scared me."

"Scary is when that thing backs up," she said, and made an exploding motion with her hands. "Forgot to tape the sign."

"I'll get out of your way, then," I said, feeling all my nerves and all my irritations tingling under my fingernails.

Leroy was at the counter talking to the man who'd been

staring at me. As I made my way toward them, the man turned to leave and was gone. Leroy handed me a mountainous swirl of vanilla soft serve with a chocolate shell. "Don't know him. Wanted to be sure after his eyes followed you to the restroom."

"Didn't you see he had a gun?"

"Better to tackle a situation head-on. He's just a long-haul trucker who's got a big rig parked out back. Strung out is all, got the stares."

I nodded, a long sigh escaping. The cone dripped onto my hand. Snap of chocolate and the faint, light-as-Cool-Whip vanilla that reminded me of hitting the Dairy Queen drive-thru as a kid. Momma used to take me there to reward or placate, which felt a bit like what Leroy was doing now. We ate as we walked toward his old blue truck. The night was alive with bullfrogs and cicadas, the air thick and humid.

He finished his cone and hoisted himself into the truck cab. I reached my arms down to my toes to stretch before doing the same, but stopped—the side mirror was bent. I scanned the parking lot, dim in the orange glow of a single sodium lamp. No one, but I got in the truck and reversed quickly. I drove down the highway, picking up speed as miles separated us from the restaurant.

"Turnoff to Luckenbach's right up ahead," Leroy said.

"You need your beer right now?"

"Shoot, guess I can have me one at the service station," he said, wagging his finger at the dashboard. "Reckon it's time to fill up."

The tank was down to a quarter. "Swore it was full when we took off," I said, questioning again the decision to drive when I was this tired.

"That gauge is funny, meant to tell you. Don't worry, there's more in the tank than it shows. Pat filled me up after she got the oil changed last month and I haven't driven since. Better to keep it near full though, before we get too far out in the country."

The turnoff was up ahead, and before I could change my mind, I took it. Too sensitive, I've never been able to let the people I love feel an unevenness from me for long. I sensed Leroy's mood darkening again. And yet, I couldn't say how I felt—tell him I was scared. Another roadside attraction put off the inevitable, I knew. A beer at the bar distanced me from that dead-empty field behind the motel, part hidden treasure site, part cold, barren graveyard.

LET'S GO TO LUCKENBACH, TEXAS, WHERE EVERYBODY'S SOMEBODY! read a sign posted along a road petering out to raked gravel. A wooden stage on a wide, open field. I parked near lights around a stand of gnarled, arthritic-looking oaks and got out. Leroy was still in the truck, so I came around to the passenger-side door to get him his cane, thinking he was tired. He frowned, waving me off, and I went on ahead. I'd give him a moment. Maybe he wanted to reminiscence, not so unlike him. He'd play Waylon and Willie a lot when he was in a mood. Talk about coming here for the live music many summers ago, in such detail I'd almost forgotten the memory wasn't mine.

The dance hall was closed now and there'd be no show tonight, but a rust-roofed general store/post office/bar looked open. A handful of people milled around outside the building. Inside, TEXAS EXES bumper stickers, postcards, jars of salsa and pickled okra, beer koozies, and souvenir shot glasses stocked the ceiling-high shelves. I ducked past a couple ceremoniously drinking Lone Stars and taking selfies. A stuffed armadillo sat by the register, and because I was too tired and this was somehow not what I'd expected, my chest felt tight and I had to walk out. I breathed in deep the humid night air, but there was still that antsy feeling under my skin. Sturdy cedar picnic tables spread across the front of the lawn, empty. A game of horseshoes had been abandoned in some sand. I cut the corner around the building and found Leroy was still in the truck with his seat belt on, drinking one of his own beers from the Coleman. It was too dusky to read his expression, and the signs in the store window bathed him in barfly pink and blue. That kind of light hung years on his face.

Chapter Thirty-three

The silence between us wasn't unpleasant, but it wasn't an easy silence, either. On the road out from Luckenbach, Leroy cracked open another beer, his eyes on me, but I didn't comment. Stuck behind a horse trailer, I gripped the steering wheel and pushed hard on the pedal to pass on the left. Nothing happened. I stepped harder and the engine sputtered.

"And we're out," Leroy said, right as we began coasting. "Shoot."

I pounded the wheel with the palm of my hand. Let the truck roll as far as possible then eased onto the narrow shoulder. "I thought you said we had more in the tank. You really need to get this looked at. There a gas can in the back?"

"Yep, and I believe the next service station is right that-away," he said, pointing to the highway winding and pitching uphill in the headlights. "I'll stay here and keep watch over the vehicle."

Squeezing my eyes shut for one second, two, I got out of the truck. Took my phone out and paced until I had a couple bars. Leroy was right, there was a Texaco about a quarter of a mile down the road near the city limits of some little town. The tailgate swung down with a screech and heavy thud—the latch, also busted—and I sweated as I climbed under the camper shell to retrieve the can. Out of the bed I felt an unexpected breeze, God or whoever was in charge throwing a bone. I tipped my head back, breathing in the smell of hot exhaust and tar, and far off, smoke. The subtle whiff of ash and tinder, even the hint of it made the hairs lift on my neck.

"I'll be back," I said, shivering as I looked out onto the darkness. This felt overly risky, but what choice did we have? It would be a long wait for a tow—expensive, too. The station was just close enough. I took the flashlight from the glove box. Didn't want to kill my phone battery, and the Maglite was heavy, a potential weapon. I waved at Leroy as I came around the front of the pickup. "Turn your cell on."

He leaned against the hood. "Careful, now."

Cans, tire treads, smears of fur and red innards littered the gravel. Each car that passed left me swaying in its wake—crazy how much faster sixty looks when you're on the outside of it—and headlights blinded me. A trucker honked and hollered at me from his cab. I quickened my pace and the can bumped against my thigh. Faye had been hitchhiking, they'd said—but no, she must have ridden out with Ronnie, flying down this same highway. Whether against her will or not, I didn't know. Sweat beaded on my forehead. Maybe because I could hear the cars coming for miles, a low, threatening hum, I felt again like I was being followed. The rushing in my ears growing louder, louder, I braced for impact as each vehicle passed. Seeing the Texaco sign in the near distance, I hooked right into a field and cut across. Snakes, trash, coyotes—all more appealing than turning into roadkill.

The station sharpened into clear view. It was old and looked empty, the parking lot weed-choked and riddled with hunks of broken asphalt. I worried for a moment that it had closed— there were yellow plastic bags tied over all of the pump handles except one—but a light was on inside the convenience store, and I could see what I assumed to be an employee's sedan parked beside a blue dumpster toward the back. I tucked the Maglite under my armpit and put my card in the reader, punched in my zip code, and started filling the can. The pump must've been low, the hose stopping then sputtering back to life a few times.

A big black F-350, too shiny to be anything but brand-new, with custom, big rim tires, swerved off the highway and barreled toward the pumps, breaking the relative quiet. "Come on," I whispered, watching the meter creep up.

Three quarters of a gallon now.

The truck circled the pumps once, twice, three times. Gun rack in the rear window. No one else had come into the parking lot, and when I looked again at the convenience store, I saw that the sign had been flipped to CLOSED, the lights turned off. The employee's sedan was pulling around the back.

One and a half gallons.

The driver of the truck idled inches from me. The engine blew hot at my back and I was pinned nearly to the grille guard. What if this was the truck that had been in front of my house that night? Eli or one of his guys—what if they'd followed me to Leroy's place, seen us switch vehicles? The can held five gallons, but I couldn't carry that much anyway. At two, I let go of the pump. He—I assumed it was a him—

revved the engine. The cab was higher than my head, the window tint probably a shade darker than legal. Hands shaking, I screwed the cap on, cussing when I spilled a bit on my jeans, but before I could move out of the way, he sped around me and jetted onto the highway.

I fast-walked down the road, which was downhill coming back. Went straight to fill the tank. But I opened the metal flap and the gas cap was gone. Had it been that way our entire trip? Leroy was being awfully quiet—I looked in the window and he wasn't there, and neither were the keys.

"Granddad?"

I called his cell phone and it rang out from the glove box. The land on either side of the highway was steep, thick with cedar. Maybe he'd climbed up the hill, to be out of the trees so he might finish his beer under the stars. It was a full moon, not so dark, and that seemed like something he might do. Still, chills broke out on my arms, and my legs felt like jelly as I waded into the tall grass. There was a lot of cacti and a limestone boulder at the crest of the hill, but beyond it, the land plateaued. I walked through the trees, and underneath the canopy it was chillier, a pocket of air that had remained untouched by the sun that day.

"Howdy ho, little darlin'," Leroy said, and as I'd suspected, was seated on a big rock drinking his beer.

"I worried when I didn't see you."

"That gauge is broken, but I do believe this was no accident. You saw the cap is gone? Reckon someone siphoned fuel off of us. Whether to steal or to stop us, I don't know."

"We both got distracted at the restaurant. That's all I can think of as far as opportunities for someone to have messed with the truck." I climbed the rock and looked out in the direction he was facing. In the dimness you could still make out the highway below, a black, unfurled ribbon winding and twisting, the Texaco lights down by the intersection. Turn around, you could also see the truck. He'd found an eagle's nest. "You were up here watching me the whole time?"

"Not the whole time. I was—pardon me—going to relieve myself, when I see someone pull up right behind the truck. Poke my head out from the bushes and walk back, guy sees me and peels out—"

"Was it a big black Ford? Gun rack and tinted windows?"

"Yep. I tried to read the plates but they were going too fast."

"The same truck came up on me at the gas station. Here I thought we were the ones doing the chasing—someone doesn't want us getting up to Buell. It's not the same truck as the one I saw at Cody's apartment, not the one Garcia identified as Eli Wallace's," I said, thinking aloud. I'd been assuming that it was Eli who'd set the grass fire, the one who'd left matches and keyed the bullet. But how did I really know that? There were others I'd personally angered—Mrs. Flores, Dee Marshall—others who would've been keen to chase down the inheritance money, including Lorena Mott or the lawyer. Then again, Eli—or someone in his crew—could also simply have taken a different vehicle for this mission, or bought a new truck. Down along the highway it was empty, only the echo of cars driving over the hill sounding like a low growl.

"We'll keep our eyes open. Change the route if need be."

I offered my hand as he slid down the rock after me, his boots slipping a little, and we found our way back to the truck in the light of the moon. We stopped back at the Texaco, filled the tank all the way, not speaking until we'd put a few miles between us and the station. It was after ten, and most of the vehicles we passed now were eighteen-wheelers, if we passed anyone at all. I felt past the point of exhaustion. Wired, afloat on a second wind—I got both looser and more focused the farther we drove.

"When Faye's bones were discovered, who was it that found them?" I asked, turning down the volume on Leroy's *Country Classics* CD.

"New owners of the motel. They were expanding the parking lot and had cleared out the back section of overgrowth. Family who owned it had kids, and it was a boy and his dog that come across a skull while playing back there. When the law located the rest of Faye's remains, they found a soiled nightdress along with some personal items. Even found her wallet."

Mrs. Flores had said she'd had a notepad in her purse, the one with Dee's number. I wondered what else was recovered in her belongings. "I know you weren't a part of the investigation at that point—do you think we ought to speak with the local law enforcement about any of this?"

"The sheriff up there, he's not the sharpest knife. Political, gossipy fellow. Better to fill him in when we have something to fill him in on. If we go in there middle of the night saying we have suspicions about the Mott family and their hidden monies, that we think there's a murderer or two on the loose, they'd laugh us off."

I turned the rearview mirror up slightly. High beams in the reflection blinded me. I eased into the other lane so the driver could pass, but the driver drifted right when I did, slowing so they stayed behind me.

"Maybe the sheriff would be right to," he said.

"You don't actually think that, else you wouldn't be here," I said, hands tightening around the wheel. "I've been thinking about what you said at the restaurant, and it's not nothing—

trying to find out what really happened, I mean. We're getting somewhere, even if it's not exactly closer and this is a dead-end. I'm in it for the long haul."

He was quiet, but I sensed a shift in his energy as he leaned forward, pulling out the belt as he straightened his back. Real or imagined, I felt us realigned. Like taking an outstretched hand. I'd meant what I said, too. Cody, Faye—they were more to him and me than ghosts, not two filaments lifted in the wind. *Solid proof.* That's all we needed to get the law reinvested in Cody's death, but I wouldn't stop there. The car—a truck, given the height of their headlights—now hugged my bumper. I accelerated, but they also gunned it. Leroy spun around in his seat.

My eyes swept across the road for a turnoff. I veered toward the shoulder, but before I was all the way over, the truck clipped my bumper. "Shit—"

Propelled forward by a second hit, I stepped down hard, the speedometer dancing around eighty, ninety. I stole a glance in the mirror and saw the truck still gaining. I couldn't tell if it was the same truck as we'd seen earlier, but was pretty sure. The heavy metal grille guard now seemed less defensive, more like a battering ram. The steering wheel rattled in my hands, the engine whining—this little old pickup was not in any condition to win, whether it be in a chase or in a collision.

"I don't know what to do!"

"There's a highway turnoff a few miles up ahead if I remember correctly. Maybe five minutes," he said. "Focus on steering, and I'll keep an eye on the back."

"My phone fell onto the floorboard when they hit us," I said. "Probably under the seat. Call 911."

Just as the engine kicked into gear, the truck hit again. *Snap, jerk* like the crack of a bullwhip.

The impact sent us skidding across the highway. I over-corrected and lost control. We spun out—I don't know how many times, it happened so fast—ending up across the yellow line, headlights pointed into opposing traffic. Miraculously upright. I gunned it and swung the wheel wide, crossing the median and turning us back in our original direction. The impact must have derailed the other truck, too, or they'd kept going straight, because I didn't see it in my rearview as I picked up speed.

"Hit my damn face," Leroy said. He had a bloody nose, was pressing his sleeve to his face. He caught my eye and shook his head. "Just drive."

I focused on the farthest point my headlights touched. Yellow specks grew larger in the mirror, the truck materializing out of the darkness, gaining on us again. A car passed going the opposite direction and I laid on the horn—but what could they do to help me now? To my right, a green road sign flashed past.

"There's the turnoff," Leroy said. "The highway splits and you'll have to pick a lane. Take the wrong one, take the road that runs toward 35."

"Okay," I said. "Here goes."

I let my foot off the pedal ever so slightly. As the truck shortened the distance between us, I kept straight ahead to stay on Highway 84, and at the last second, veered sharply to the right. We bumped over the graded divider onto a two-lane ranch road that cut toward I-35. The truck kept sailing down 84, zooming up ahead and to my left as we drifted east.

"Shoot. Here's hoping," Leroy said.

I let out a long breath, too shaken to speak. "I know we need to check the damage," I said after a moment, clearing my throat. "But I don't want to stop till we're certain they're gone."

"No way to be certain," he said. "And they'll probably be back if they were able to find us this far out in the first place."

Chapter Thirty-four

Leroy let me sleep until dawn, when he banged on the door to our adjoining rooms. Single-lane back roads and uneven blacktops had added time, and we'd rolled into Buell around two in the morning. I hadn't slipped under the motel bed's covers so much as collapsed. Sank into a vivid dream where I was thrashing, screaming with no sound coming out, and waking felt like filling my lungs after being underwater. I bolted upright and rolled off the bed, went and splashed my face in the bathroom. Our destination turned out to be sixty-five a night, the kind of place where they have dark towels to hide—what, I didn't want to think about. Or think too hard about why my arms itched. I put my boots on, stepped outside, and listened for the door's automatic lock after I closed it. Card readers appeared to be one of the only updates to the motel made in this century. The neon sign had looked original to the sixties-style building. Whether to be clever or save cost, there was no space and no second *h* between the words, so it appeared as *RANCHOTEL*. Rank hotel indeed, its orange stucco walls were webbed with cracks, the sidewalk glittered with broken glass, and a funky, sour smell emanated from the laundry room.

Leroy leaned against the rail in a fresh shirt. His face looked bruised, but I didn't think his nose was broken. The woman in the office had pitied him and his bloodied nose last night, enough to give us our pick of rooms. From here on the corner landing, we could see the property that backed up to the motel and the dirt road snaking around behind it. I'd also discovered that if I popped out the window on the shower wall and stood in the tub, I had a decent view of the side lot.

"Don't know about you, but I feel better now," he said, though he walked stiffly down the stairs, slowly enough that I paused midway to not get so far ahead. "Morning has that effect."

It was barely light out, the sky blush pink and faintly purple. The metal railing under my hand was cold and damp with dew. No one else at the motel seemed to be stirring yet, and we cut through the parking lot and made it behind the building with no encounters. No sign of the truck from last night, only Leroy's blue Ford with a curled-in bumper and cracked camper shell to remind me of the chase. The sunlight emboldened me now, too—as we neared the field, I felt my stride lengthen and my head clear.

Leroy paused at the end of the motel's asphalt lot. There was a strip of grass separating it from an overgrown field, with red clay soil showing through the weeds. In the distance there was a thick stand of mesquite and a taller tangle of brush. The dirt road made a border beyond that. He pointed to the shallow ditch behind the motel dumpster. "This is where they found Faye's bones, I believe. And that right yonder is the property you believe Clint was, or is, headed to."

"I'll walk up the road and start searching at the entrance,

if you want to start here. That way we'll meet somewhere in the middle," I said, tramping into the field before I realized I didn't quite know what I was looking for. Wasn't like we had a map. Obvious disturbances in the property, I supposed—holes dug, tire tracks, recent trash.

"Do a slow, wide sweep," Leroy called after me, making a horizontal motion with his finger.

The dirt road off the highway was rutted on the shoulder, the center relatively smooth. Well-traveled, then. There were visible tire tracks, but I didn't think it had rained recently, or that the tracks were from any single vehicle—the red clay was packed hard in the ruts, and dust had layered over them. Cicadas, cowbirds, and a dove cooing along on a telephone line, the chorus nearly obscured the highway noise. A mailbox was at the top of a long gravel driveway that ended at a cluster of trees. The image I'd seen on Google Earth was actually from better times—the brush was even higher now—but as I walked down the gravel, I spied wooden slats through the overgrowth, a spindly small oak and a pecan choked out by the switchgrass and mesquite. A house with tan-painted siding that was peeling and rotting. Closer, I heard branches snapping, rustling. I paused, heart thundering in my ears until I saw a pack of feral cats prowling under the shack, darting under a gap where cinder blocks raised it up off the ground.

The rickety porch looked like it might not hold my weight, and I stepped carefully, testing each board. I could see the motel from here, and beyond it, the highway. Leroy's gray Stetson bobbed in the distance as he walked the fallow field. The windows were intact and coated in tinfoil, but the front door was gone altogether.

Inside, the air was dank and cool. An old brass bedframe

sat in the center of the room—it really was a one-room shack. My eyes adjusted and my stomach dropped. Knowledge, deep down, that something bad had happened here, like an ache in my bones. Death had stricken whoever had laid in that bed, nothing left of a mattress but its coils. Faye in her taffeta prom dress, smiling down from her mother's mantel—I couldn't reconcile her fairy-tale image with such decay. Other than a bed, there was no furniture, only a stove, sink, a toilet, and a standing tub. The wooden floors were coated in a thick layer of dust, no footprints, only a smattering of pawprints. One of the walls had been graffitied with indecipherable tags, and there were some beer cans, but the labels were old. A dead rat lay curled in the dry toilet bowl. I backed out onto the porch again, fighting the strong desire to run.

Nothing indicated anyone had come here in a long time. Maybe we'd beaten Clint or whoever had this address. Of course, the property was quite large—Leroy and I could rip apart the shack looking for the supposed inheritance, but who even knew? Fifty acres to hide the money, money that could be buried, hidden under a rock, down the well—it could be anywhere. I was willing to bet there'd been something like a map in that letter Ronnie mailed Clint. I left the shack and walked the land in a horizontal pattern, following Leroy's instructions. When we met near the middle, he hadn't seen anything, either, and it was clear that the exercise had tired him.

"Let's hit the Ranch and ask a few questions," he said, and we tramped back to the motel. A cleaning woman dressed in jeans and a hot-pink T-shirt took out her earbuds when I blocked the path of her cart.

I held out a picture of Clint. "Have you seen this man?"

She shrugged, moving a bleached section of hair off her

shoulder. "But you know, there's a whole lot of people coming and going come off the highway. Maybe I could keep an eye out, know what I mean?"

Leroy rolled his eyes, but I figured you never know. He was already halfway to the front office after I thanked the woman and offered her a cash tip. She tucked it in her apron pocket, laughing when I turned my back.

"The clerk working last night hadn't seen him," Leroy said when I caught up. "But there'll be someone new in there now."

The counter was chipped and blackened around the edges, and the young man behind it was a red-faced teenager busy picking at the breakout on his chin. He looked related to the owners based on the family photograph hung on the wall. I wondered if he'd been the same little boy who'd found Faye's bones. I wanted to ask but bit my tongue, knowing that it was better that we kept a low profile. A wire-frame shelf of dusty brochures for area attractions—a one-room school-house museum, a Mexican restaurant, an Assemblies of God church—was the only other adornment in the office. The boy stopped picking his face and frowned. "Wi-Fi password is on the router in your room."

"No, son, but thank you," Leroy said, his voice warbly. "We're wondering if you've seen her brother, my grandson. Darlin', hand me that picture of your brother."

I held out my phone, not wanting the pimple popper to touch it. "His name's Clint Marshall. He might've been here under a different name, though."

"We're worried sick," Leroy said, letting out a sigh that ended in a wheeze. He was laying it on thick, but I didn't think he had to act too hard. His hand on his cane was white-knuckled, and my chest panged. "Our boy's off his medicine. He might be in trouble, son."

"No, sir, I'm awful sorry," the kid said. He looked to me guileless, but I studied him a moment. He probably knew not to give out this kind of information.

"You're sure?" I asked. "It's important he get his pills."

"No, I don't recognize him. I can look in our system for a Clint, though," he said, and typed, waiting for it to load. "Ah, nope."

"That's alright," Leroy said. "Reckon he might be coming through, though. Tell you what, son, go ahead and book us for another night. We'll make it a regular stakeout."

After we'd split a bag of Doritos from the vending machine, Leroy pulled a chair out from his room and parked it at the end of the walkway outside our doors. No one seemed to mind that he'd scooted the Coleman out and was drinking a beer, his boots propped on the lid, binoculars in his lap. So much for the low profile. But unless Clint—or whoever might have intercepted that letter—was coming up the stairs, they wouldn't get a good glimpse of us before we saw them first. I rotated between the landing and the bathroom window where I'd planted a chair in the tub.

At about three o'clock my eyes were so tired they started to cross. I went down to the ice machine and back to wake myself up, and Leroy stopped me before I went back to my tub post. "Go on and get some sleep. I can see the dirt road well enough from here. Then, tomorrow, I'll rest up while you take watch. I can be bright-eyed for Saturday," he said.

"Saturday?"

"Visitor's day at the prison. When you'll meet old Ronnie Mott. Bingley's, what, an hour and a half from here?"

My stomach did a quick flip—it wasn't that I'd forgotten

about visiting Ronnie in prison, more that time had gotten bendy. It felt like both an eternity and no time at all since I'd written to the man. "I can't leave you here alone without a vehicle, though. You don't think you should come with me?"

"No, no," he said, crushing his beer can. The sun had moved nearly into his eyes, and he pulled his Stetson lower. "As much as I'd like to grill Ronnie myself, warden wouldn't let me in. Besides, I'd better keep on this here. If there's any action, you'd be back soon enough. Worst case, I've got the sheriff's number and my own protection," he said, opening the Coleman. He lifted out a couple of beer cans, revealing his pistol. Despite growing up in a house with firearms—and around people who knew how to handle them—I chose not to carry. Never forgot the advice Leroy once gave, that if you held a gun, you ought to be prepared to use it. Knowing a pistol was within his reach made my stomach twist again, and I felt better when he rearranged his beers and propped his boot on the closed lid.

"You do think someone is coming to that address, don't you?"

"Only one way to find out," he said, chuckling. "Darlin', a stakeout takes patience. A couple days is nothing."

Nothing—I didn't buy that. I felt like the noose was tightening the longer we sat here at this rank motel. Invisible threats around every corner and whistling through every crack, like a wind at my back laced with smoke, something fierce.

Chapter Thirty-five

The visiting room at the federal prison camp at Bingley was whitewashed and bright, the hard plastic benches nailed to the linoleum a retro, school cafeteria shade of green. The room also had the stale, cup-of-noodle-soup smell of a school cafeteria, and a familiar, anxious energy, but it took no more than two seconds to remember that this place was far from anything I knew. A guard eyed me warily as I waited alone at a table. I observed the other visitors for cues and any unspoken dos and don'ts, feeling that at any moment the jig would be up and the guard would escort me out.

Ronnie's lawyer was right that the warden had gone soft, given the diagnosis, and had allowed him new visitors. I'd driven to the facility at noon, arriving in time for his cell block's scheduled visitation period. Friday had been quiet at the motel, no sign of anyone coming to the abandoned property, no sign of anyone tailing us, and this visit now felt like the conclusion to a strange detour. We must've missed our window. Hell, maybe I was wrong about the address. The closer I got to meeting Ronnie though, the more my energy revived. He hadn't felt real to me—a mirage on the horizon, a riding-into-sunset outlaw—but when I arrived, it sank in that he had in fact been caught. That he was a man and nothing more. After waiting at an intake area for forty-five minutes, then being searched and questioned, I was granted two hours to begin the minute he sat down.

When everyone turned their heads sharply, I knew it was Ronnie who'd entered the room. I'd have been unable to recognize him for how different he looked from his photographs; the tuft of hair on his head was now yellow-white, and his beige jumpsuit hung off him, skin stretched tight over his bones. He probably weighed just shy of a hundred pounds. He'd never been a tall man, but he appeared to have shrunken down to the size of a child. And yet, there was something fierce about his eyes. Darkest of browns, they had a lightless quality to them. Black holes sucking in everything and revealing nothing. That his cheeks were sunken—both from weight loss and toothlessness—made his eyes protrude, like a seer foretelling death.

"Look here, girl," he said, his tongue making a sticky sound as though his mouth were dry. "You gonna tell me the fuck happened to my kid?"

"Nice to meet you, too," I said, and held up a Ziploc bag of quarters. "That's what I'm trying to figure out. Refreshments?"

He looked at my chest—covered in a loose, zip-up hoodie despite the heat—and I scooted back uncomfortably and curled my shoulders. "Get me two Cokes," he said, sticking out his lower lip almost defiantly. "And a Snickers."

"Done," I said, feeling those black eye holes bore into me as I walked to the vending machine. Making my purchases, I took a deep breath. In a weird way, I wanted to bet that Ronnie was a lot like his lawyer—the kind of guy who'd gladly dish it up if he thought you might dish it back. I didn't want my visit to end prematurely by me going at him too hard, but I also didn't want him to think I was an easy mark for bullshit. He reminded me of a shark with those eyes. Like in those nature videos how you could barely detect the whites of an animal's eyes as they roved past the cage—I didn't want to leave a drop of blood in the water. But I also needed him to open up. I brought back the candy bar and three sodas, which seemed to work in my favor. He ripped into the Snickers and leaned back, devouring half the bar before swishing the Coke around his mouth and swallowing loudly.

"Used to worry my sweet tooth'd give me the sugar diabetes. Don't care now. Sugar's all I can really taste."

"I needed a pick-me-up, too," I said, fake-smiling back. My Dr Pepper wasn't cold, the carbonation rough on my tongue. "Mr. Mott, I—"

"Ronnie, doll. Call me Ronnie."

"Ronnie, I don't know how much you know about me." I paused, wondering if he'd ask about Leroy. "I talked to your attorney, Mr. Griggs, about the letter you mailed to Clint in response to mine. I also met your son Cody through this investigation. I'm sorry for your loss. If you're thinking what I'm thinking, that it wasn't a suicide, with your help I might be able to get some answers."

"Yeah, Cody ain't killed himself. Telling you, no son of mine would be such a coward to take the easy way out, no matter what stupid shit he got himself into. Wouldn't go hurting his mother, a good Christian woman. Cody was all but dead to me a long time ago, but he's still kin. A Mott. If you know who done it, you better go on and tell me. I've got a few favors to call in yet."

I leveled my gaze at him. *Dead to me. Coward.* I wouldn't

pretend to know what happened between him and his kids, but at the end of the day, Ronnie was the parent. I knew I was lucky mine had never let me doubt the unconditionality of their love, but moments like this still staggered me. "I'm pretty sure Cody got in the middle of whatever was in the letter you mailed Clint," I said.

He smacked the table, making the guard's head turn. "I loved Cody. I did love him. But my inheritance is meant for Clint and no one else."

"What kind of inheritance? And what about your daughter, Christa? Or their mother, Lorena?"

He waved me off as though the mere suggestion was foolish.

"What exactly did you write to Clint?"

A big, screw-you shrug.

"Tell me this," I said, forging ahead with the theory I'd been holding tight in my fist all this time. "Is Faye Flores Clint's real mother?"

Ronnie lowered his head, quiet for a few moments. I'd done the math the day that I saw Faye's picture in the paper, when I realized she'd grown up across the street from Ronnie. Clint was born in December of the year she'd gone missing. Even still it seemed far-fetched, but the man hadn't denied it yet.

Finally, in a near-whisper he said, "Faye was my girl, yes."

Spoken softly enough I had to lean forward, and as soon as I did, I felt a physical, swift kick of revulsion.

His girl.

She was in fact a teenager at the time, him a forty-year-old man. He smiled sadly, or fondly, like you might recall a friend. This close to him, it hit me that his smell was of near-death. I'd been with my grandmother in hospice and this was a smell I didn't realize I'd stored away until now. Bodily, like bedsheets. Like breathing in the air of a sealed-off room, a sad, sour-breathed ache from the lungs. Ronnie hung his head, the ridges of his spine protruding up to his nearly na-ked skull. I couldn't yet tell if this sadness was over what he'd done to others or what others had done to him. Both, maybe. But what was Ronnie doing now that he knew he was about to leave this Earth? Had he been content to leave this shame—the death of a woman he'd loved, the mother of his child—buried in the red dirt?

"Did you kill her?" I asked.

He raised his eyes up to mine, and with a sick certainty, I knew.

"No!" he said, rapping the table with his bony knuckle. "You kidding me, I loved that little gal! Might've been the only one who ever done anything for her. Her parents had kicked her out and she was seeing some loser till I came along. In the end, even I couldn't save her, though." He shook his head, still eyeing me. "I'll tell you what happened, if you promise me that you'll tell it to Clint, verbatim. If you tell him what happened to his beautiful momma."

I nodded, unable to control my knees shaking under the ta-ble. Ronnie's fingers twitched, rubbing chocolate between his thumb and index finger. He smiled, seeming satisfied that he'd regained favor with me, his audience. The desire to perform, to convince himself he was the smartest person in the room was apparently winning in a battle with his self-preservation. Or maybe it simply didn't matter to him anymore.

"Saddest day of my life was realizing I'd fallen in love with a woman who wasn't my wife."

"How'd you break that to Lorena?" I said, trying not to sound sarcastic. Love—when he'd said "love," my mind didn't go to him mooning over Faye, but to her mother. Mrs. Flores in that little house with her shrine on the mantel.

"Lorena, yeee-ikes. Have to say, in the end, my brother, my buddies, they were right about her—they always said she and I weren't a good fit, personality-wise." He waved his craggy hand as if to shush me. "Now, now, I can tell you're probably too young. You don't know what it is to be in this kind of a scenario. Just because you get older don't mean you get wiser. Don't mean you don't get puppy love. I knew Faye since she was a kid. And then, boy did she grow up. Really blossomed. How was I supposed to not see that? To not love her for how well we knew each other? We were going to start fresh. Blow that crap town and run. Hell no, I didn't kill her. Faye died giving birth to Clint."

When I didn't say anything, he hammered his point home. "She gave everything for that boy."

"How—"

"It happened too quick, the labor did. I thought she was fine. So fast—it was like one minute I was holding my son, this tiny baby, and then she's real quiet all of a sudden. I get the baby put down and she's passed out, bleeding to death. Hemorrhaging they call it. By the time I got my wits about me it was too late," he said, his voice barely scratching above a whisper now. "I'd planned on a nurse I knew lived in Buell being there for the birth, but Clint was weeks early. Had to do it myself in the house, all alone."

"Not at the hospital because you were in hiding," I said, letting the accusation hang in the air. "After the robbery?"

"Yeah, well." His black eyes narrowed. "Not my fault nature is cruel."

"Had Faye helped you pull the getaway off?"

He smiled; the three teeth left in his head were stained with chocolate. "Guess it's no secret then, that. Faye was a good scout."

"And when you dumped her body—"

"Watch it now," he said, spit gathering. "I already told you to watch your mouth once, little girl. I gave her a proper goodbye and saw to it that her baby was cared for by a Christian family. I did that because I loved her. And lord, she would've loved that baby. It's only right that he gets what was half hers and mine. Really, everything I ever did was for my children—and let me tell you, at this point in my life, Christa is not my daughter. She gave up on me, just like Cody, so what's mine will be Clint's. Whoever tries getting in the middle of that will have hell to pay."

"Did Cody get in the middle of it?"

He stared at me.

"Would you ever hurt your own child?"

"Tell you what, smart mouth, I've changed my mind. Keep out of my family's business and maybe I'll pretend like I don't know where you live and who your people are, Miss Annie McIntyre. I make myself clear?"

"Crystal," I said, making eye contact with the guard.

No one besides Ronnie would ever really know what happened. Maybe he was telling the truth, or maybe Faye died by his hands, a fight between two lovers who couldn't keep hidden forever—he'd been at fault either way. He'd left her like trash in an unmarked grave, in a tangle of mesquite and dry switchgrass. I believed I'd gotten an approximation of the truth from him, but couldn't know for certain, and this physically pained me. What I did believe was that Faye was Clint's real mother. The tuning fork in my chest had been humming from the moment I'd seen her photograph on Mrs. Flores's shelf. Clint had her nose, her thick eyelashes, and heavy lower lip. He was hers, and if she had been his, if Faye had lived, what would their lives be? Impossible to know, but easy to imagine. A countdown to death or capture had been set into motion the moment Faye got into Ronnie's getaway car. The road out of town had to end somewhere, and wherever he had promised her—Mexico, Bahamas—was never going to materialize.

I pulled up to the highway intersection outside the prison, right as a railroad crossing arm lowered. No cars sat behind me and yet I had the feeling of being watched. Kept checking my mirrors for the black truck. I needed to get back to Leroy—*hurry, hurry, hurry* on repeat in my mind, all my nerve endings firing right under my nails, my skin—and yet, I had the strong desire to drive south and see Cody's mother, Lorena. The longer I had to reflect on what Ronnie had said, the more layers of disgust kept peeling back. Ronnie hadn't cared about Lorena's broken heart or Cody dying except as it related to his own legacy. The man was about to die and all he cared about was whether or not a bunch of shitty people in Price County were still afraid of him. Lorena at least cared about Cody for Cody.

Lorena. They were right about her.

I often riffed off my intuition—I'd never been trained any other way, not by Leroy. Was my nature and it was his. *They were right about her.* The train lumbered down the tracks, blocking my field of vision. Stuck there behind the wheel of a car, that one sentence kept ringing in my ears. There had been an echo, somewhere—

I called Nikki, stomach churning when she didn't answer. I'd texted her while on the stakeout yesterday and she'd never responded—weird, but not so weird. I'd chalked it up to this being the last days of their honeymoon, but there was that tiny voice in my head, my heart. My hands felt clammy now, the phone slipping in my hand as I dialed Sonny next—he was my intended target, but I had thought him less likely to answer. Again, I was sent to voicemail.

I pulled up Clint's ex Amanda's Instagram page. She and Sonny didn't follow each other, and weren't Facebook official, either. Sonny was Clint's brother—wasn't that a little strange that he and Amanda weren't "friends" online? They both had active accounts. Maybe not, but in retrospect, all the strained smiles, the stiff, sideways hugs with little to no eye contact, how they'd ignored each other at the VFW that night, all made me think Amanda and Sonny didn't like each other. I wanted to know if that's what Sonny had been referring to when he talked to Wyatt the day of the wedding—that he'd been right about her, *Amanda*. When the last railcar lurched around the curve, the flat field of cotton beyond the tracks widening like an open window, I was overcome with an urge to yank the brake. I wanted one minute longer. I had to turn the car one way or another, and I'd better choose wisely.

Chapter Thirty-six

"Haven't seen a thing," Leroy said. Wind whipping over the balcony muffled his voice. "Young guy pulled up earlier, looked like could be him but wasn't. Been watching the dirt road and not a single car's gone down it. Reckon that's all I've got now," he added.

When I'd called to check in, tell him about my talk with Ronnie, he'd answered the way he usually did, which was to not—he picked up the phone and waited for me to speak first. I don't know if that was a cop thing or a Leroy thing. Likely the latter. He let information sit before speculating, enough time to regulate his own emotions, square them off and keep them sealed. When I told him about Faye, he went so quiet I thought he'd hung up on me.

"You haven't had a break or eaten anything all day," I said, my own stomach making threatening sounds. "Are you okay there alone for a bit longer?"

"Made me a quick run to the office for a donut. I'm alright. Do what you need to do and get back here soon's you can. I want to walk the property. See a few things for myself again"—he paused—"now that we know this was indeed the hideaway."

"I'll hurry," I said, and disconnected. There was a McDonald's at the next intersection and I pulled in, needing to use the Wi-Fi. I ordered a cheeseburger—day three without a vegetable, I actually could've gone for one of Wyatt's smoothies—and chose a seat by the window, my back to the wall. Waiting for my meal, I texted Wyatt back to let him know I was okay. We had a deal that I check in every twenty-four hours. I told him I loved him, debating whether or not to say more. He'd asked me where I was, but I chose not to tell him, deciding the less he knew, the safer we'd all be. I didn't know who to trust, and worried he'd inadvertently tip my hand to someone with less-than-stellar intentions.

My location wasn't so far from where Amanda lived in Lubbock. I'd quickly located her address, but decided to keep digging, see what else I might dredge up before confronting her. According to my search results, she'd graduated from a private Christian academy thirteen years ago. This gave me pause—she'd said something about her and Clint being in school at the same time, but according to this she was in fact five years older than him, over thirty. Not everyone went to college right after they graduated high school, of course, but it was a bigger gap than I'd expected.

Her dad was an accountant, her mother a homemaker. I jotted down their address, too, then started scrolling through a general web search. There was a news story at the bottom of the fourth page of results—results that were mostly in reference to her dad's accounting firm, blog posts from their church, obit for a grandparent—and I clicked on it when I recognized a kid that looked like Amanda in a video freeze frame. She looked about thirteen. Skinny, black bangs stuck to an oily, broad forehead, her long nose and angular cheek-bones prominent in a way that was still more ugly duckling than top model. I stuck in my headphones and pressed play. It was a segment called "Wednesday's Child," where the local news showcased foster children up for adoption in hopes it would spur interest from would-be parents. I'd seen the segments before on our local news, always a little unnerved by them. If the end result was a kid getting out of the system and into a permanent home, great, but every time I saw one, I'd wanted to yell at the screen that the kids were real people. People, not puppies.

The news anchor said that a former "Wednesday's Child" feature, Tiffany—clearly a younger Amanda—had been adopted along with a four-year-old little girl named Sondra who wasn't her biological relative, but a much younger child Tiffany had taken under her wing at their group home. The social workers and their prospective parents had agreed the girls needn't be separated, and the happy ending was cause for celebration. A photo of Tiffany and Sondra's new parents came on the screen next. Todd and Jenny Lambeth were smiling wide, both blond and good-looking and in love, the portrait taken on the day of their wedding. The next photo was of the whole big bunch at Christmas—now a family of seven—all in matching shades of cream and evergreen, sweaters on the boys and dresses for the girls, boots for all. Two were twins, the couple's biological kids, and the others were also white and blond but with slightly different features, similar-looking enough to make one guess. Dark-haired, teenage Amanda towered over the other children with a sullen expression. I clicked through to the embedded link in the text, to the original "Wednesday's Child" segment featuring just Amanda/Tiffany.

She was younger in this clip, maybe ten. Her voice baby-like when she said, "I want someone to play with me, read me a story every night, and tuck me in," pleading eyes watering behind smudgy pink-framed glasses. Lip trembling as someone off-screen caught her attention, coaching her perhaps, telling her to wrap it up, and her tiny body nearly collapsed in on itself. My heart sank—no child should have to ask for love— and my mind whiplashed to Cody again, to his dad Ronnie's callousness. The voice-over said that Tiffany was great with younger children, that she would thrive in a home that had clear boundaries and set routines, with a family who was familiar with caring for kids who've experienced trauma.

I wondered why she'd lied to me—or, had she lied?

Clint told me she'd been adopted from Romania, not her. What was the point of making up a story about a foreign orphanage, other than making her seem more exotic? If nothing else, it obscured the past, which I could assume from her televised backstory, her words to me about a hole in her heart, might be worth running from. Before leaving the McDonald's, I checked her social media again. She hadn't posted recently except once on Instagram. A black-and-white, airbrushed selfie, taken in a public restroom mirror, doing that thing where you lengthen your neck and tilt your chin, her mouth a pretty pout. The caption was cryptic, an unattributed quote corny enough to make me unsure if she'd actually just written it herself: *"Life's a journey. You got to take the road where it leads, curves and all."* #keepmoving #travel #adventure

Was she running along with Clint? Why post about it, though?

I jammed my laptop in my backpack, hurrying out of the restaurant. My phone buzzed with a text right as I settled in behind the wheel of the pickup. It was Wyatt again. *Seriously, where are you? A cop was at the house earlier looking for you.*

My pulse thumped. That goddamn DEA guy. *What for?* I asked.

Don't know. Just said to reach out. 830-555-0104.

OK, I replied, and put the phone down, deciding to shelve this for later—the last thing I needed was the DEA agent using me to provoke the Wallace crew. Didn't need Eli following me if he wasn't already. I checked my mirrors, praying I didn't spot that black F-350.

It took me thirty minutes to get to Amanda's apartment, which was actually a two-story carriage house at the back of a larger property. When I was sure no one was home in the big house, I walked up the driveway to Amanda's door. Her car wasn't here—no cars were—the blinds drawn, and the door locked. I rang the bell, watching for any movement, listening for sounds coming from inside. Maybe I could check in with her parents, who lived not far from here. She'd said she'd stay with them when she got back to Lubbock on Saturday, though who knew if that was true. What I did know for certain was that she'd stayed at a La Quinta down in Garnett on the night Cody was killed, the night Clint didn't show at the rehearsal. All because he'd broken up with her. It was more than plausible that she was too tired to make the long drive home, but even then, she had seemed a little weird. I walked around the apartment's exterior, giving the place a good once-over before I got back in Leroy's truck.

The Lambeth family lived in a bland and tidy house near the university, a single-story, redbrick ranch. I knocked on the front door and waited, the hot, high wind ruffling my hair and kicking up a dust devil in the yard. I rapped on the door one more time, and finally, a young blond woman answered. Nineteen, maybe twenty, wearing an oversized sorority T-shirt over Nike running shorts.

"Is Amanda home?"

She frowned. "Amanda doesn't live here anymore."

"Sondra?" I asked, recognizing something of the toddler from the "Wednesday's Child" segment in her upturned nose and blue-gray eyes.

"I'm Leighton." She folded her arms, fiddling with the scrunchie on her wrist. "Um, how do you know that name?"

"Sorry, Leighton. Amanda told me about you—you know, about how close y'all were since being adopted." I was kicking myself for not having prepared a better story. "She and I are good friends from school. We were supposed to hang out yesterday, and I thought it was weird when I didn't hear from her. Do you know where she is?"

She ran her tongue over her bleached teeth, recognition flickering in her eyes. "I'll be right back, Dad," she called over her shoulder, then closed the door. "Seriously, I don't know where Amanda is. Who are you really? This is something to do with her mother, isn't it?"

"No," I said. "But maybe? I don't know. I'm just a friend who's worried about her."

"Right, sorry," she said, exhaling loudly as if to calm herself. "It's just whenever we talked about Sheltering Arms, she said her mom's people would come back around one day and we'd better watch out. Thought of it since you mentioned my old name."

"Sheltering Arms?"

Her eyebrows knit together. "I haven't talked to Amanda all that much lately, but she's never mentioned a friend from school I don't know. What was your name again?"

"Oh, it's Ashley," I said.

She shook her head, her face reddening. "I don't know who you really are, if you're one of her old family members looking for money or what, but you need to leave us alone. I'm about to call my dad and—"

"No, no need for that," I said, stepping backward off the porch step. She closed the door behind her, locking it.

I walked back to the truck. Sheltering Arms must've been the name of her and her sister's group home. I buckled in and did a quick search on my phone, thumb hovering over the screen when I realized where I'd heard that name: Clint's mom, Dee. She'd said Sheltering Arms was where she'd met him for the first time. Online images were grainy, taken from the street and posted on Google. There were even customer reviews (two stars), as if it were a restaurant and not a place where kids had been assigned by the state. There was a weathered wooden playground visible from a side yard, sun-faded plastic toys and a sandbox in the grass out front, a chain-link fence. What really gave me pause was the corral to the far side of the big property, far out in the country. Inside the fence stood two alpacas with matted fur, and a sad, dirty-looking pony standing inside a smaller pen.

Clint's childhood memory—I could still hear him telling it to me at the café, see the smile flit across his face. God, how long ago that seemed. Holding out a sugar cube, it tickling when the animal nuzzled the flat of his palm, the smell of hay, manure, and hot breath snorted from the animals as they pushed their heads through the fence. It had to be the same Sheltering Arms. Had Clint and Amanda known each other as children? Had they lived here together?

I looked up, detecting movement from the house. Amanda's sister had come back out onto the front steps and was holding up her phone. Must've been taking a picture. She appeared to be texting now, her eyes darting up at me every few seconds. I'd bet anything she was talking to Amanda, and the last thing I wanted to do was to send her running if she wasn't already gone.

Maybe she and Clint hadn't broken up. I wished I'd have asked her sister about it, though it didn't sound like I'd have gotten a straight answer. The pair could have some kind of Bonnie and Clyde act going, killing Cody when he'd gotten in the middle of their plans to take the inheritance and run. There were holes in this theory, though. Why wait to hit the property in Buell for one thing, why pretend to break up at all, another—but I didn't know where else to go now. I turned the engine on and drove back toward the highway, back toward the Ranch Hotel. The sun had dipped below the flat line of earth, light fading when my phone buzzed in my lap.

"Where are you?" Leroy asked.

"About twenty minutes away."

He sighed, cussing under his breath. "Car has been driving up and down the dirt road. Maybe they're turned around, or maybe they're not—I'm gonna get a closer look, see if they turn in. If it's nothing, I'll be back by the time you're back."

"Wait for me—"

I realized he'd hung up. I called him back, then tried again. When he didn't answer a third time, I stamped my foot on the pedal, arrowing toward Buell, unable to slow the sudden gallop in my heart.

Chapter Thirty-seven

Blue thickened to black, the risen moon casting a faint white glow over the cotton fields rushing past my window, the rows and rows of still-green plants. The Ranch appeared like an oasis in the middle of all that nothing, a speck of neon on the empty horizon. A desert mirage, like the closer I got, the more it inched away. The parking lot was fuller than it was when I'd left it, maybe with weekend travelers. I pulled into a spot nearest our rooms and ran up the stairs with the key card in hand. Leroy was not inside, and his perch along the walkway had been abandoned, his Coleman wheeled inside the door. Knot in my throat, I opened the lid. His pistol was gone. I grabbed a flashlight from my bag, made sure I had my phone, and walked out of the room again, headed toward the abandoned property.

I was just under the awning of the first floor, not really paying attention, just thinking *go, hurry,* and was nearly to the dumpsters when a hand closed around my arm. I dropped the Maglite, the metal pinging. Yanked backward, I instinctively made my body heavy, letting my feet drag the concrete as I was pulled toward the dank corridor behind the ice machine. I swung wildly with my free arm, landing a blow to whoever held me, my fist meeting a man's tight, muscled abdomen. The man spun me around, and gripping my shoulders, slammed me against the door of a supply closet. I was too shocked to really take in the face underneath the hat or what was happening. He shoved me inside the closet, still gripping me, and for a brief second, I recognized the maid from earlier standing in the shadows.

"Help, please!"

She acted like she didn't hear me. Shuffled through the closet door with her head down, squeezing past us. The man closed the door behind him and flipped the overhead light.

Eli Wallace stood in front of me. He reached into his waistband, then aimed a gun at my chest.

Strange, but what stopped time was not the weapon; what took me by surprise was his face. For all the imagining I'd done, I'd never seen him up close. I'd known it was him, but didn't, couldn't quite believe this was happening. He had thick, dark brown hair cropped short, buzzed on the sides. His features were chiseled, and I could see now his prominent chin had a deep, uneven cleft. He had dark blue eyes—unsettled, with large pupils.

He barked out a laugh. Dimples appearing in his rough, unshaven cheek was somehow more off-putting than if he'd frowned. His breathing was ragged, his face gleaming with sweat. Nervous. Like he'd also been building up this moment in his mind, not quite knowing what to do now that he had me here pinned. The closet was narrow, lined with metal shelving, the air heavy with cigarette smoke, bleach, and the cherry-scented soap they put in the rooms. There was a loose pile of ash and a lighter on the shelf, like he'd been waiting here for me for some time. I felt like I was going to vomit.

But if he was going to shoot me, he most likely would've already done it—or at least dragged me someplace more private. No, he wanted to talk.

"Where's my grandfather? Did you hurt him?"

He shook his head like I was a moron, leaning against the door and lowering the gun ever so slightly. "Oh my God." He laughed again. "So that's who you were in the shitty truck with? What the fuck are you doing out here anyway?"

We stared at each other for a moment. We'd never met, but it felt like we'd just picked up where we'd left off. It felt natural to me, too, this thing between us. I'd been thinking of him for months. Months, I'd been looking over my shoulder, a tension that had grown so familiar I barely noticed it anymore. He seemed genuinely curious as to what I was doing here—bemused, even—still grinning. Maybe he didn't know about the Mott money. Or if he did know, he had an excellent poker face.

He low-whistled. "You and pops did give a good chase. Took me a hot minute and pulling a few strings to find you again."

"I don't know what you're thinking," I said. "Messing with me like this is stupid."

"You're not a cop, but I can see that you're just as full of crap," he said, and raised the gun. "Actually, you're even dirtier than the one I've got. You had something to do with what happened to my boy Cody. That's why I'm up here in bumfuck nowhere—but what the hell about you? You were there that night he died, and what, not a week or two after I seen you two at Cowboys? You think you're above it all, but girl, there's hell to pay for anyone who touches my crew."

My mouth opened and closed before I could think what to say. Number one, which cop was feeding him information? Or was he bluffing? And here I thought he and Cody were adversaries all this time—

"Cody was like a kid brother to me," he said. "It's my damn fault he's dead, him being associated with me."

My hands shook. "Did Cody ever drive your truck?"

"So, what if he did?"

I shrugged, though the pieces were clicking into place. His truck, and not Cody's sedan, had been at the apartment complex—not because he was stalking Cody, but because Cody'd driven it there himself. Eli's face reddened. "You bitch. You went after him to get to me, didn't you? Killed him when he didn't help you? I know you and that DEA asshole are trying to nail me."

"Jesus, no," I said. A bead of sweat rolled down my back, both out of fear and a palpable—if short-lived—relief: I was almost certain Eli didn't know anything about Cody meeting up with Clint, or about any inheritance money hidden on the property. I looked at the gun and took a deep breath to steady myself. "You even hear yourself, Eli? How crazy that sounds? You're acting paranoid. It's sad what happened to Cody, but it's not anyone's fault."

"Yeah, okay. But it can't be a coincidence him talking to you, some goddamned informant. I think you must've got in his head, pushed him over the edge to do it—put him in a hard place whether to rat on me and he couldn't handle the pressure. I don't know. You've got a vendetta or some shit on me and I want to set the record straight now. Let you know you can't mess with me and my people."

"No, I don't," I said, eyeing the gun again. "And I haven't told the DEA anything they don't already know."

"What do they know?" He leveled his gun higher, aiming between my eyes.

"A lot. They know the guy who set the house fire was linked to you. They know you sold pills laced with fentanyl to those kids who OD'd. They know it all"—I paused, swallowing hard—"but they don't have any proof. They're scrambling."

"They don't have proof 'cause I'm innocent," he said, some of the tension drained from his voice. He tucked the gun in his waistband. Patted his shirt pocket for the cigarettes. "Hey, toss me that lighter."

A smoke? Shit, how long was he planning to keep me here? I picked the yellow Bic lighter up off the shelf, but held it, watching his hand graze his waistband. "Listen, I'll leave you alone if you leave me alone," I said, squeezing the plastic into my palm. For however crooked Eli Wallace was—for how much I hated his guts—I felt the tiniest crack webbing around the edges of my disdain. He loved Cody—wasn't just in the way he was acting protective of his crew, the macho bullshit, but for how his voice wobbled when he'd said his name. *Like a brother to me.* If things were different, this might've been a fragile thing shared—how I wanted to zero in on the one other person that I was sure felt the way I felt. Tell him I believed him. But I couldn't.

"They would've arrested you if they had anything but theories, right? They're going to keep an eye on you, though, so why give them more reason? Why complicate things? You know there'd be absolute hell to pay if something bad happened to me, the daughter of a law enforcement family."

"Insurance policy. I know you saw me with product at the house a few months ago, and I know you'd scurry up to the witness stand given the chance," he said, smiling again. He pulled the gun, pointed. "That's why I've been warning you. I don't know why you didn't listen. You're right that there's no need for this to get messy, for now. But I'm watching you, girl. I'm *always* watching."

Two long strides and he was leaning against me, pushing me to the wall. He smelled like cigarettes and something else I couldn't place—sweetly rotten, like bruised fruit. He wet his lips, tilting his head down like he was fixing to bite or kiss me. Standing so close to me I couldn't see the gun, only feel it pressed into my soft stomach. He held himself against me like that for thirty seconds, maybe less, but it felt like years that I couldn't breathe. Couldn't think, only hope that he was all bluster. Wonder whether I should step on his insole and make a run for it because I'd rather die fighting than whatever he had in mind before shooting me, when finally, he palmed the shelf and pushed himself back.

He walked out, turned the light off, and closed the door.

I sank to the ground. My hand closed around his goddamn lighter, the one I'd uselessly dropped. I took out my phone. Nothing from Leroy. Maybe he was hiding and couldn't answer a call, so I sent a text. *Where are you? Just text you're OK. I'll come find you.* I waited a second, then typed again. *Wallace is here, I'm calling the police.* Paused just as I'd dialed 911, my thumb hovering over the green button. What if this was a test? What if Eli had Leroy restrained somewhere and was waiting for those sirens? Waiting to see if I'd rat again— would he hurt Leroy to teach me a lesson?

Staring at my phone, I remembered Wyatt's text from earlier about the cop that had come looking for me. I opened it again. Was this the DEA agent's cell? I pressed the highlighted number, thinking he might be able to help—discreetly—if I explained the situation. The line went straight to voicemail.

"You've reached Kate Krause at the Price County Sheriff's Department . . ."

Why was *she* at my house?

Mind racing, I hung up before the beep. I knew, deep down, that I needed to get to Leroy faster than any outside help was coming. And I remembered why I'd been running down the hall in the first place—the car that had been driving down the dirt road toward the abandoned property. I stepped out of the closet, holding my breath as the door squeaked open, and was met only with the steady hum of the ice machine. Dazed, I blinked hard a few times, looked out on the parking lot, and didn't see Eli or his truck. I ran toward the dumpsters out back, and saw a spark cut through the thick black dark. Far away over the empty field, nothing more than a pale-yellow glint, a light flashing on and off in the one-room shack.

Chapter Thirty-eight

I bent low and ran. The field between the motel and the shack seemed bigger, more overgrown in the dark as tall weeds whisked over my jeans. My phone vibrated. I stopped to reach for it, praying it was Leroy, but it was Sonny calling me back. My questions about his and Clint's fight would have to wait. I silenced it along with the nagging voice wondering where my cousin was—why hadn't Nikki called me herself? It had been hours now—and kept going. Closer to the shack, I saw through the tangle of trees and heavy brush the dark, beat-up sedan Leroy had described from earlier parked haphazardly at the top of the driveway. It was black as pitch and the windows were tinted so I couldn't see inside, but could hear that the engine had been cut. The light I'd seen was coming from inside the shack, and I crept toward it. At the edge of the rickety porch, I sank down onto my knees and heard shuffling inside, cabinet doors being opened and closed. I scooted on my knees around the corner so my head was at the level of the top step.

Amanda strode across the single room. Her profile was

to me, her face in deep concentration. A battery-powered camping lantern in her hand. I shrunk back as she set it on the ground and the light bled onto me. She was wearing all black, a pair of yoga pants and a T-shirt, running shoes, and her auburn ponytail was looped through a Red Raiders ball cap. She really must think of herself as some kind of modern-day Bonnie—but where was her Clyde? Where was Clint? I swiveled my head around, but the field was quiet save for the singing cicadas. And, shit, where was Leroy? Maybe he could see me and not the other way around, keeping watch from a hiding spot in the thicket of mesquite.

God, what if he was inside the shack?

Amanda hunched, looking down at her phone. The screen was bright, tinting her face with a bluish glow, but I was too far away to see what she was looking at. She started typing, and believing she was sufficiently distracted, I crawled up the porch steps, moving out of the doorframe to just below the window. I stuck a finger around the broken pane, feeling where the tinfoil met the wood groove, slowly peeling—

Rotted wood beneath my foot splintered and snapped. My ankle twisted as the board cracked and I bit back a yelp, spinning around and pressing my shoulder to the side of the house.

It was too late. Amanda rushed out of the open door, and for the second time in one night I had a handgun leveled at my chest.

This time, I wasn't so sure I'd talk my way out of a bullet.

"Amanda, thank God," I said, trying to ignore the throbbing in my ankle and think. "I was so worried about you! Are you okay? Did Clint hurt you?"

Her expression turned from open-mouthed surprise to smug grin. "Don't waste your breath, Annie."

"Please, Amanda." I threw up a prayer, hoping Leroy was out in the field or that he'd gone to call for help. If nothing else, that she didn't know he was around—that she hadn't cornered him, or worse. "Please put the gun down."

"I didn't think I could do it. I'd only shot a gun once and I forgot how hard it was to like, physically handle it," she said, her voice quivering. She sounded scared, talking to herself more than she was me.

"When you shot Cody, were you alone, or—"

She interrupted me with a choking noise that sounded like no, but I couldn't be certain. Unclenched one hand from the gun and wiped her eye, smearing her mascara. "Clint told him about the money from his dad. So fucking stupid. We didn't even know how much money it was going to be, and here he was ready to split it how many ways? He even wanted to go talk to the sister! He wouldn't listen to the truth. Those two never gave a rat's ass about him—like, why didn't they come looking for *him* if they cared so much? Why'd Clint have to be the one to find them in the first place?"

"You were right, Cody was a prick," I said, hoping that me aligning with her on something would soften her stance. "Christa is awful, too."

"I know, right? So, we're at Cody's apartment, like, strategizing for god's sake, and I just did what needed to be done. What ruined it was Clint started fucking crying after I'd done it. Crying! He was going to call the police! I had to stop him."

My heart was going so fast I felt dizzy. "Wait, so did you shoot Cody *and* Clint—to shut him up?"

"I'm training to be a nurse. I know what I'm doing, goddamn it," she said. Sensing my shock perhaps, she lifted out of her reverie and narrowed her eyes. "And damn it, I've got to do you, too, now."

"No, wait. I get it," I said. "You have to look out for yourself. No one else is going to do it for you. Just, Amanda, please, before you shoot me, you need to indulge me a minute—please?"

She nodded once, working her jaw back and forth like she might grind out a molar.

"How'd y'all meet?"

"What?"

"You and Clint."

"Met at one of his shows."

"No, don't lie," I said, trying a different, more confrontational tack. I needed to shift control somehow. "I know about Sheltering Arms, Tiffany."

She stared for a moment then tittered. "Wow, you really are the girl detective. Well, um, we were there living together. He was too little to remember me, I guess. But how could I forget him? He was beautiful, even as a kid. Those eyes. It's no wonder he turned out to be a lead singer. He was always special."

"Where is Clint now? Is he dead?"

Her eyes darted over my shoulder, toward the driveway, then back. "The social workers, the staff, they all knew who Clint's daddy was. They called him 'son of a wanted man.' Talked about how his dad was this badass bank robber who hid treasure out in the desert over the border in Mexico. Little did we all know the money was under everyone's nose, right here in West Texas. I knew he was the same Clint from the minute I saw him at that show—hell of a coincidence, but it changed everything. Me hooking up with him, it really wasn't even about the money—honestly, I thought that was a made-up story. God, I spent so much time trying to forget about my shitty past, all that pain, knew I needed to move on. Date someone else or be honest with him. But I fell in love—like, real bad love, the kind that makes you fucking

303

crazy"—she waved the gun over her head—"and by then it was too late to tell him the truth. That it was me, Tiffany. I bought him that DNA kit on a whim, and look what happened. Goes to show you can't escape your past."

I squinted through the dark at the car way off at the top of the long driveway, making a point of craning my neck. "Why did you wait a week to come out here?" I asked, stalling. She looked where I was looking, long enough for me to reach my back pocket. "You don't know where the money actually is, do you? You never got the other part of Ronnie's instructions."

"I know it's here somewhere," she said, her chin tilted defiantly.

"Well, I know exactly where it is," I said, heart thumping in my neck as I came closer to her. "But you have to put that gun down, else I can't help you."

"Back up," she said, her hands gripping the gun tighter. "I have all night to look, especially now that I won't have your nosy ass following me—"

I flicked Eli's lighter open and lunged. Held tight and swiped at her long ponytail, her shirt. She screamed as I shoved her down, flailing wildly. She slapped at the flames with one hand then the other, dropping the gun. I rolled after it and reached my hand around the warm metal right as she kicked me in the kidneys. Wincing, I curled into a fetal position to protect my grip on the weapon. Held tighter as she kicked me again. I gritted my teeth, took a deep, steadying breath and rolled onto my knees, aiming the gun back on her. The fire to her shirt was not quite put out, and a flame licked up her torso. She didn't even register the gun. Yanked the shirt over her head and yelped. Her ponytail wasn't on fire anymore but had melted at the tips, stuck to her welted neck.

She stood shivering in her sports bra. It began and it ended with her—all of it had. I aimed the gun in her direction, though I could tell she'd lost some of the fight in her. She wrapped her arms around her bare middle and bawled. My ankle was throbbing, my back still stinging from her kicks, and I had to resist the urge to slap her. I wanted to believe she'd gotten in over her head—that killing Cody wasn't pre-meditated. What I couldn't stand was that she didn't see him as a real person, that he was nothing more to her than a road-block.

"Cody wasn't so unlike you," I said. "In and out of foster care. His family was a dysfunctional mess. He kept getting pulled back into the past like it was quicksand—you know about that, don't you? Cody also wanted to live a good life, like you. But the difference is that he wasn't bitter. He had every right to be bitter and pissed off and he wasn't—"

"Oh, Christ, save me the sermon! I've had enough in my life of people like you, who think you're so great. On your high fucking horses."

"Get up," I said, raising my voice when she didn't move. "Get on your feet and tell me where my grandfather is."

"How the hell would I know where your grandfather is? The fucking home?"

"We'll do this the hard way," I said, and led her inside the shack. The temperature dropped once we crossed the thresh-old, the air smelling of stagnant water and rust. I scanned the single room and saw no sign of Leroy or of any kind of strug-gle. The sense that something bad had happened here was so strong; I pictured Faye and her wailing newborn sprawled across the bedframe, life and death, all of it, right here. A cord dangled from the blinds on one of the windows, and I bound Amanda's wrists with it, praying she didn't fight me. I still had the gun in one hand, and it was heavy—too heavy for me to really hold one-handed. She whimpered, crying softly as I ordered her to sit on the bedframe while I bound her ankles. Singed hair filled my nostrils as I secured her legs with the T-shirt she'd ripped off.

I backed slowly out the door, gun still pointed in her direction, but Amanda was out of it, staring blankly at the floor. I walked around the outside of the shack with the weapon raised. Seeing no one, I took my phone out with my free hand. Hadn't yet dialed 911 before I heard the wail of sirens in the distance, and not before I came around the side of the porch and saw two figures limping up the gravel road toward the shack. Leroy was a pace behind Clint, shiny pistol aimed at the younger man's back.

Chapter Thirty-nine

"Clint and I got in a nasty fight at my bachelor party," Sonny said, sighing into the phone.

The static I was hearing wasn't static—it was the ocean. He and Nikki had decided to stay one more night on the Gulf.

"I told him Mom was going to cut him off when he told her about Nashville. Knew I'd be right about her. Hot and cold, just who she is. Get on her bad side, she won't throw you a bone. I didn't tell him he shouldn't move to Nashville, though. I said he should choose, and if he went, he'd have to get a real job until he made it big—if he made it big."

I nodded as if he could see me, couldn't quite speak. I'd called back before I thought better of it, wanting so badly to hear a familiar voice. I'd needed to make sure Nikki was okay.

"That pissed Clint off good, even though I was right," Sonny said, hurt in his voice. "That and me talking crap about our mom. They've always been more alike than me and her. Don't blame him on that one."

It had only been a couple of hours since I'd confronted

Amanda. We were still waiting outside the shack for further instructions from law enforcement. The county sheriff interviewed Clint, a foil blanket wrapped around his shoulders glinting in the blue and red lights. He seemed to be making a point of not looking at the squad car where Amanda was restrained. Both would be brought to the station shortly, and Leroy was giving his statement to a deputy now that I'd finished giving mine. My head felt like it was stuffed with cotton. "I'll tell you more later, Sonny, but let's just say your brother thought he'd worked out a new source of income. He's physically fine, though, I believe."

"Annie, wait," he said. "I'll say this now while Nikki's not here. She ran back to the room to go to the bathroom again—"

"She just gets nervous before trips, like even the night before. She doesn't actually have a bladder the size of a peanut, she—"

"Oh, I know." He laughed a little. "Just, I wanted to ask you something. You have to share her with me, okay? This talk about Clint choosing makes me think I don't ever want Nikki to feel like it's me and our family versus you and yours. Know what I mean? Guess what I'm trying to say is we love you. Both of us do."

"Of course," I said, but the hair on the back of my neck stood up. Sonny didn't sound drunk and this was weirdly effusive, even for him. "I mean, I love y'all too—"

"Hold on, she's back here now," he said, then said something muffled to Nikki that sounded like *come on, tell her.*

"Annie?" Nikki's voice was high and shaky as she took the phone.

"Hey," I said. "I worried about you when you didn't call or text."

"I know, I'm sorry. Nothing's wrong, it's just I've got big news I wanted to tell you in person and I didn't think I could lie to you," she said, a little breathlessly. "I took a pregnancy test yesterday. I thought I was really late or maybe skipped a month because I was on that crazy diet for the wedding. I got super sick on that dumb boat and decided to see," she said, letting out something between a hoot and a sigh.

"Are you happy?"

"Jesus, yes! What kind of question is that?"

I didn't know why I said that out loud. All honest like it was just me and her, not on speaker with Sonny. I did wish she'd have waited to tell me. Not here. Not while my brain was scrambled, my pulse still racing. Ever since she'd gotten engaged, I'd been thinking we'd go back to our old ways. That Nikki would be the old Nikki after she'd stretched her wings for a time. That wouldn't be the case, but it was fine. Even if I couldn't have articulated it then, I knew I'd figure new ways for us to be close. My cousin and I were more solid than blood, bigger than the stories we told. Love was like a prism that shone or looked flat at different angles, one I'd need to tilt every so often to catch the light.

"Well, shit. Congratulations," I said, and laughed—like, really laughed. The kind that comes when you're giddy. "I'm happy, too, Nik, I mean it. Let's celebrate when y'all get home."

Leroy came up beside me as we said goodbye, the phone hot against my ear. He laid his hand on my shoulder, steadying himself. "Clint's not in great shape, I think they're going to hospitalize him instead of taking him to the station. This wasn't never going to end well—don't know what this woman was thinking keeping him held hostage. Though, sounds like he did have a touch of the Stockholm syndrome. Did I tell you when I found him in the backseat of that car, he didn't want me to untie him at first?"

"Amanda was telling the truth, then," I said. "She murdered Cody so she and Clint could run off together with the money, it'd be just the two of them."

"He doesn't know exactly where it is, either," Leroy said. "The goods, that is."

"I'm sure the law will tear this place up until they find it."

"And they ought to," Leroy said, his voice hardening. "Ronnie stole from hardworking people. Not just cash, but jewelry, family heirlooms. He broke in, beat an old woman, I—" He pursed his lips for a moment. "That man is a poison. It never gets easier to accept things like this. I'm sorry to tell you that."

"Ronnie's lost anyone who's ever come close. He'll die knowing that," I said, though not quite sure I believed it. Ronnie Mott had seemed to be missing that core piece. The click inside that makes you want for another. I wanted to hug my grandfather, or rather, for him to hug me back. I looped my arm through his and leaned against him, listening for his slow steady breaths.

A deputy escorted Clint into the back of an ambulance, and not long after, the squad car holding Amanda pulled out onto the dark country road. Leroy was right, this was a hard lesson to accept. All your efforts might lead up to a big moment of justice served, or they might not. Maybe you'd get someplace decent, a place between victory and defeat. Like here, like tonight. Justice would be served for Cody, but not quite for Faye. You might live your life in pursuit of the truth, nose in the dirt, and if the pursuit was all it was, the pursuit would be honorable; I still believed that. And despite feeling that so much of my life was an echo—that my spirit favored Leroy's, I looked the perfect image of my mother, was willful as Dad—today was mine and I'd plan on tomorrow, too, if I could only keep moving. Back down in Garnett, I'd have a task, and knowing this relieved me from the feeling of grasping at an unraveling thread.

A few days later, I drove out to the Marshall property. I'd heard Clint was freed, no charges brought against him, that Amanda had confessed to everything. The creek wasn't running anymore, but the air here was cooler. The hiss and trill of cicadas rang out, mourning doves cooing. Dee Marshall didn't see me coming, though I could see her. She sat folding laundry on the couch in her living room, the window blinds left open. When she registered that she wasn't alone, her face fell; she heard the doorbell and squeezed her eyes tight, seeming to wince with effort as she rose and came to the door. "I don't have anything to tell you that you don't already know," she said, cutting off my greeting. "I haven't been to see my son yet."

"You knew about the new security badges, right?"

She opened the door a little wider, though her face was pinched with fear. On the verge of slamming it, if not for her slight curiosity. I held up a photocopy of a *Garnett Signal* news story, offering it to her. The one where Diedre Marshall, the bank teller who'd been held up, was interviewed. Dee took the paper from my hand, not reading it, only clutching it to her chest.

"When the robber fired the gun at the other teller, were

you surprised?" I asked. "Scared he might've killed her? Or was that always part of the plan?"

She stared back impassively, slightly twitching her shoulder.

"My grandfather had suspected an inside job, but he couldn't prove it. No one had told you about the new security system that had been installed while you were on maternity leave. He'd thought at the time your plan—if it was in fact a setup—might've been foiled by that misstep with the new badges, but in reality, that was always part of the plan. You needed the other woman to let you in and also to let the robbers into the big safe. What he didn't realize was you and her also shared a sitter. That you'd heard her mention the new badges, maybe seen it on her keys? You knew she'd be there early that morning to give you yours and let you into the building."

"No, that's not true."

"See, my granddad also didn't know that you knew Faye Flores. That Faye had asked you about the routine."

"You sound insane," she said, sweat gleaming on her forehead.

"What's insane is that you knew, all this time, not only who Clint's birth mother was, but what had really happened to her and you never did a thing," I said, my throat tight. *Insane?* I squeezed my fists and took a breath. I had built this moment up in my head; I thought that given the chance to say what I wanted to say, I'd be clear-eyed, confident—not a hot, prickling fire under my skin. I hated how my voice strained. How all these feelings rose swiftly to the surface and I had to tamp them down. "There was the remarkable coincidence of Clint's biological father being part of the robbery you were held up in, but Jesus, it was actually what Ronnie's lawyer

Griggs had said—that was what tipped me off to your role in the end. That his lawyer had seen to the fact that Clint was in good hands. That was the proof my granddad had been missing: proof of a payoff. The payment was Clint."

Her lips parted but no words came. When she spoke, her voice barely scratched above a whisper. "There was no monetary compensation for taking Clint, but I apparently could've gotten a good chunk if I'd asked. I didn't know there was money hidden out there, I really didn't. I thought there was no reward for what I'd done after the robbery went sideways. Felt like fitting punishment. I would've taken it to my grave. It was never like that—no, I didn't adopt Clint later on for any reason other than I cared. I cared about what happened to Faye's baby. When Griggs told me that baby was alive, that she had actually delivered him, that he was in the system, all the while my husband and I couldn't . . ." She trailed off, tears leaking down her face. "We wanted to give our son a brother. And it did turn out to be the greatest gift."

I looked down for a moment as she collected herself. "Right. So, Faye masterminded the robbery?"

"A lot of it, yeah, I think so," she said, and shook her head as if in awe, a burst of surprised laughter cutting through her tears. "Lord, she was bold enough. Ruthless, really. I had to admire it in her. Like I told you, my ex-husband worked with her boyfriend at the time. Same auto shop. Faye and I got close almost immediately—I don't think she had a lot of friends at that point, the kind of girl who burns bridges and doesn't look back. She wasn't like any of my other girlfriends, and I think that was part of what attracted me. She came to see me when Sonny was first born. I didn't have any other help and was lonely, paranoid, sleepless. Faye confided in me about how awful her boyfriend was to her. Told me about this other guy she had on the side, Ronnie. She said he was her real love and the baby's daddy. I don't know how, but she really got under my skin. I was angry then, too, I think. Hell, I was nineteen and bored out of my mind. I didn't want to get married, I—"

She let out another big, heaving sob. Cried with no attempt to hide her face or stop the onslaught, looking at me in the angry, unfiltered way a kid throwing a tantrum might. Like I had better fix this. It wasn't just that forcefulness that unsettled me—it was that she'd let me see her. Really see her. Apparent remorse didn't move me like I thought it might, and yet, I made myself look at her and not away.

"Thank you for being honest, for whatever it's worth now," I said, once she seemed to have run out of steam. "I did share this theory about Faye with the Garnett County sheriff and D.A. yesterday. I don't know if they'll open a new investigation or not. There's a decent chance they won't, but it's not up to me."

Her dark eyes welled again, and I put my hand out to stop her.

"You participated in something that caused irreparable harm the minute you told her your routine, and I have to tell the truth," I said, watching her face change. Her shoulders loosened, and I realized she was relieved. The truth had been burdening her all these years.

"I'm a mother, I'm a good person, I—I'm just so sorry."

I bit the inside of my cheek and turned to leave. Clouds drifted in the late afternoon breeze, casting large shadows on the grass. The bullet was parked at the edge of their driveway, next to Clint's truck, which had apparently been released from evidence. I supposed that Dee was the official owner—I knew from Sonny that Clint was back at their dad's old place, not staying here with her.

"Annie, wait," she called after me. "Do the boys know?"

"No," I said as I turned around, one hand on the door. "And I'm done getting in the middle of it."

Chapter Forty

That turned out to be a lie. One I regretted a few days later as Clint finally told me his story. I'd offered him a ride to Price County knowing Dee still had his truck, and partly to hear the tale firsthand.

And it was that—a story, one I wanted to believe but was unsure of. Perhaps I resented him. Clint was out here living his life. Even if he didn't actually commit a crime, he'd intended on acting the part of some self-righteous bandit. The money Ronnie had offered was never his to give. Clint was selfish, and I couldn't be so two-faced as to act like I didn't care, no more than I could act like the gruesome details of Cody's death wouldn't be burned into my skull forever.

"She hit him with cast iron," he said, swallowing hard. "Whacked him with this big black skillet. We'd been drinking at his apartment, and he and I killed a bottle. I wasn't even thinking about the wedding rehearsal at that point, sadly. Amanda was drinking, too, but not like us. Cody and I were riled up, thinking how amazing it was, like all along, not even an hour away lives my brother. Incredible. That and the money—we assumed it was a lot—and that we were all of us going to score big-time. Hell, maybe we'd go up and get our sister in on it, too. We're drinking hard and I have to piss, so I'm in the bathroom when I hear this grunting sound. A big *thwack*! I stumbled out, my head's already spinning, and there Amanda is holding that skillet and standing over him on the floor in the bedroom. Cody's face is, uh, God"—he made a choking sound—"it was really bad. She had to have hit him twice, maybe more, but still I'm thinking self-defense? Like maybe he was so drunk he put his hands on her? I tell her we need to call an ambulance, and that's the last thing I remember."

"You were unconscious after she hit you?"

"Out cold," he said, his voice growing louder, his breaths coming fast. "I woke up I don't know how much later. The light had changed, so I thought it must've been the evening. My head is pounding so hard I can't hardly think or see. Noticed she'd wrapped a wet towel around my head. Then I realized it's not water, but that I'm bleeding. She'd zip-tied my hands behind my back and had me on the ground. Took my phone. I roll and I see Cody not a few feet away. She'd, oh, God—"

"Used his gun to make it look like he shot himself?"

"Yeah."

I felt like I was going to be sick again. "So, hold on. The two of you weren't ever going to break up?"

"No," he said. "But I thought that at one point—she and I had been fighting and I said some stuff. But then I thought, maybe we could make it work. What the hell. She and I could start fresh with the money, move to Nashville. Try Mexico for a year or something, me get a gig at a resort and us kick back. I don't know—Amanda probably sensed we weren't clicking. I don't know if she really held me hostage because she loved me, or because she thought I'd cut her out. All the time she had me hostage she'd go on about us together, that three was a crowd and she had to do Cody. But she probably wanted the money for herself and just needed me alive to help her find it. You don't hold a butcher's knife at someone's back if you love them."

"Typically, no."

"Yeah—" He smiled faintly, his breath catching. "She led me out of Cody's apartment with that knife after I came to. Told me she'd kill me if I made a sound, then drove us back to my place in the truck. My neighbor saw us together—I should've taken my chances and yelled for help, but I was still seeing double, way too out of it. We go inside and Amanda gets my gun, makes me curl up in the trunk of her car. I went in and out of consciousness for who knows how long. The heat, that probably was what nearly killed me more than the head wound. She only let me out when we were on the road to her place in Lubbock."

"So, that's why the whole story about the breakup and why she spent the night. Someone had already seen her down here in Garnett?"

"I guess," he said. "She obviously lost her fucking mind. She doctored me up and posted pics, then made me record a video so no one would think I was missing. All week she was glued to my phone, waiting for Ronnie to call. I should've known better than to tell her about the property where the money was. I did burn the letter after I read it, like he in-structed, thank God. Otherwise, she'd have known that when I said Ronnie would get in touch with the exact location, he wasn't going to call my cell phone. Obviously, right? How would the man have my damn number? He said he'd call a pay phone by the motel at a specific time. She didn't know that, and we missed him. Probably the only thing that kept me alive."

"She eventually got desperate enough to drive out to the property and take her chances."

"Yeah," he said. "And if y'all hadn't come, chances are I'd be gone."

Gone. Layers upon layers settled into that void. Hard to grasp all of what might've been. We drove in silence for a few miles. The land flattened out, dried to a crisp shade of yellow. Along the horizon, pump jacks nodded steadily and lazily, like a line of black ants crawling to their queen. The highway—the beer-way along the county line—was wavy with heat shimmer. I took the turn toward Branch Creek, toward the Mott place and the Flores house, palms sweating as though I'd be the one meeting my grandmother for the first time, not Clint. I didn't know if he'd heard the news yesterday evening. Ronnie had died a prisoner, succumbed to his cancer. I opened my mouth to say something now, darting my eyes over to him in the passenger seat, and saw that he'd been crying.

When was it no longer my place? Maybe it had never been. Clint ought to speak with his kin about such matters going forth. I was glad that Clint was alive, and I was glad that Mrs. Flores would catch a glimpse of her daughter again, in him. Satisfied that in one way, I'd delivered. When Clint had hired me, I thought that this was what he'd been after—a reunion, an opening of possibilities, healing the primal wound and whatever that entailed. I hadn't bargained for the fact that an opening wasn't only forward motion. It was a redoubling of the past, and yet never again being able to go back to that one, perfect moment of before: the last time you could imagine yourself a prince, not the son of a wanted man.

When I got home that evening, the hay-like smell of dry grass and cedar met me at the door. I shook out the rubber pasture boots I'd left on the porch, checking for scorpions, then braved our overgrown yard. Tate followed, rubbing against my calves until I petted him. I needed to wind down, and the sky was so big and so clear. An early risen moon in the paling blue gave me a feeling of no importance—not in a bad way or a good way, just that it made me more serene in the vast of night, in the dark that was coming on quick. Mrs. Flores had been sitting outside like this when we'd pulled up—like me, with her head always tilted back. She'd assembled sandwich cookies on a TV tray and brought out a pitcher of lemonade for him. Like he was a little boy, not a man. Before I left, I'd felt this part of my brain click on, the part of me that had been worrying over Nikki's baby. Talk about the vastness— that was what was next, a brand-new person with a whole life ahead of them. Suddenly, I knew that I'd do anything for that baby.

Wyatt came out and handed me a beer, and I stuck the cold longneck to my cheek.

"Your case is closed," he said. "How're you feeling?"

"Good," I said, but knew even then that traces would linger in my head and my heart for some time, contrails painted on a clear and cloudless sky.

"Clint's still going to Nashville?" Wyatt asked, popping out the legs on our camping chairs and brushing them off.

"That's what he says."

I felt for Clint, I did, and I hoped that he made it big as a singer. But that vague, best-of-luck feeling was about where the goodwill ended. The more I thought about him, the more uneasy I became. Songs written about a half-brother and beautiful mother, both died young—I loved a romantic, blue-note ballad of the hurting kind, but worried whether he'd do them right. Be true. I felt something like stinginess when it came to all his second chances. Though I knew myself to be a believer in redemption, it was hard to overlook the universe's uneven distribution of such favors. It didn't help that Eli Wallace was out free. He'd left me alone in the days since our encounter, but every so often I detected woodsmoke. Real or imagined, like coming home from a campfire and smelling it in my hair and the fibers of my clothes, and for days on end.

Hopefully, I wouldn't feel this way for long. I was cooperating with the DEA again, but this time, the investigation had teeth. I'd told the agent I suspected Sheriff Krause was feeding Eli information, that she was the dirty cop he'd mentioned while cornering me at the motel. Probably why she'd been at my house that day, and earlier, why she'd written off a potential hit on one of Eli's crew as a suicide. Eli most likely wanted her to let him deal with Cody's death personally. Alternatively, she, like me, might've thought Eli had killed Cody and was granting him a reprieve. This all felt like a long shot as I was telling it to the agent, but it turned out others in Krause's department had long suspected she was tangled up. The agent had a sting in place already, and that was the real, secret reason he'd been up here from San Antonio. Last I heard, he was securing a warrant to tap her phone, thinking it would lead to an arrest for both. These things take time, he'd said, and to rest assured the trap was set.

I believed him, but it was hard to relax. To wait. Wyatt

rubbed my shoulder, and I took a long pull from the bottle, feeling my limbs loosen as warmth spread from the center out. We watched Tate, fierce hunter that he was, chase a butterfly.

I put my arm around Wyatt's neck. "Did I tell you about my gift?"

"Aw, shit—your granddad's birthday party is tomorrow, isn't it? I forgot I was going to go get him some nice whiskey. Think he'd like that?"

Still guilty over forgetting his milestone birthday, I'd convinced my family to throw him a belated celebration. "'Course he'll like it. The party's not till seven, you'll have plenty of time. One sec," I said, setting my beer down on the concrete. Dashed inside the back door, grabbing the bag I'd left on the kitchen table, and showed Wyatt the professionally-framed and matted photograph. "It's him when he was a little boy. Him and my great-great grandmother, Sarah Anne, on her pony Riot."

"Wow," he said, leaning close enough to brush my cheek with his. Close like this, I could feel his face break into a smile.

"Mary-Pat knew where to find it, of course. It was stuffed up in the closet at the office."

"You look like her."

"Maybe," I said, though I could see it. Her eyes in the picture were crinkled, her face animated by the whipping wind and bright sun. Leroy looked thrilled the way any kid would be on horseback and in a pair of kickass boots, but something else—content, I thought. The way he leaned back against her, held safe in her arms—that was more than anyone could ask for when they felt scared, when they felt lonesomeness stretch like a shadow over the valley. "Mary-Pat said he doesn't know about the party. Don't know how anyone in my family has managed to keep it a secret this long. Guess we have his anti-social nature to thank."

Wyatt laughed. "Well, it's good to know there can still be some surprises."

Acknowledgments

I'd like to thank my wonderful agent, Sharon Pelletier, for being a great champion of this book, and my wonderful editor, Hannah O'Grady, for taking my writing to the next level. Thank you to Kayla Janas, Sara Eslami, Madeline Alsup, and all of the talented people at Minotaur Books/St. Martin's Press who work brilliantly and diligently to shepherd books into the world.

Thank you to my friends and family: I'm forever grateful for the wealth of love and support I have in my life. Special thanks to Lauren Hughes for dropping everything to read the manuscript when I needed fresh eyes; my trusted early reader, my sister Olivia Tanner, for always being willing to bounce around ideas, and for babysitting; my mom, Donna Tanner, for reading, for lifting us up—caring for my baby, caring for me—for being the source of light in any room; my dad, Joe Tanner, to whom the book is dedicated, for his unwavering enthusiasm and the inspiration to dream big; my husband, Dane Allen, for being a steadfast and caring partner; and our daughter, Rosalie, for already loving stories.